Offspring

Offspring

a novel by

MICHAEL QUADLAND

RED HEN PRESS | Pasadena, CA

Offspring
Copyright © 2012 by Michael Quadland
All rights reserved

Book layout and design by Andrew Mendez

Library of Congress Cataloging-in-Publication Data

Quadland, Michael C.
  Offspring : a novel / by Michael Quadland.—1st ed.
    p. cm.
  ISBN 978-1-59709-502-0 (alk. paper)
  1. Families—Fiction. I. Title.
  PS3617.U354O34 2012
  813'.6—dc23
                          2011040907

The Los Angeles County Arts Commission, the National Endowment for the Arts, and the Los Angeles Department of Cultural Affairs partially support Red Hen Press.

First Edition

Published by Red Hen Press
Pasadena, CA
www.redhen.org

All living things contain a measure of madness that moves them in strange, sometimes inexplicable ways.
—Yann Martel, *Life of Pi*

For Rod

Offspring

1

HANK MAKES A DONATION

I lie under a stack of blankets. Day-old briefs hug my thighs. My fist makes a miniature vibrating tent of the knobby wool. I should get a life!

I'm due at the New York Hospital Fertility Clinic in half an hour. My Raleigh three-speed stands ready to hustle me to Sixty-Eighth Street and York Avenue, about as far across town as you can get from this one-room walkup at the corner of Fifty-Seventh and Tenth. Yes, I donate my semen. Though it isn't exactly a donation. I get paid thirty bucks a shot, so to speak. I need the money and childless couples need . . . well, me. A pretty straightforward transaction, you might say, with the added satisfaction of helping somebody out in a cosmic sort of way. Though I have a bad feeling about it sometimes, like this morning, the vague sense that I'm doing something wrong, and one day it'll all catch up with me.

Maybe it's the idea of charging for something that should be the natural outcome of a good time, even love. Or maybe it's the thought of a bunch of kids running around with dark wavy hair and eyes that sometimes read gray, sometimes green, like mine. What if two of them met some day and fell in love, not knowing they're half-brother and sister? Or what if I saw one of my obvious offspring on the street twenty years from now? I'd have this weird feeling, and he—or she—would look through me like I wasn't even there.

I think about these things.

My clock radio buzzes to life with the news that Nixon and Brezhnev are meeting in Moscow to discuss nuclear disarmament, which they've been sparring about for weeks now. And OPEC is ending the oil embargo it put in place after the Yom Kippur War. Maybe now my landlord will consider filling the tank and cranking up the heat.

The inch of snow that accumulated on the window sill overnight is already dotted with soot. A truck downshifts on Tenth Avenue, five dingy floors below. I imagine the smell of its pluming exhaust, half noxious-half enticing, like cheap perfume. In the three years I've lived here, I've learned to tell the time of day by the traffic sounds. The morning rush hour starts at six with the belching semis and switches to honking taxis an hour and a half later. That continues until about nine-fifteen, or maybe later. Depends. Tuesdays in winter, like this one, are quiet. And cold. I take a guess—7:25—and lean over to my Big Ben windup, which serves as backup for the radio, it's metallic tick hardly even noticeable anymore. I'm shy three minutes. Can't quibble with that.

I adjust the radio's Formica case to line up with the Big Ben which evenly straddles a crack in the floor. A sense of order can get you through sometimes.

I pick up where I left off with the pumping, working at what should be fun. The cracked ceiling overhead, a parchment map of water stains from the roof, sparks thoughts of traveling ancient roads to some remote village, a place I would call home, a concept I find elusive. Fact is, this dump feels more like home than Vermont ever did. I like New York. So why would I think about leaving? Because I can, I guess. Because there's not that much holding me here, because restless is my middle name.

Home, a fifth floor walkup, basically a tenement. The hot water's as iffy as the heat. Druggies use the dim area under the first-floor stairway to consummate their deals. So does the occasional prostitute. Glad somebody's consummating something around here.

I peak under the blankets. You can't really blame my dick for feeling put upon.

Three years ago, fresh off the bus from debriefing at Fort Bragg, North Carolina, I took this place so I could live alone, a priority after a year-long stint in Vietnam, where you're never out of sight of somebody, friend or foe, twenty-four/seven. Since I was a kid, I'd heard stories about New York City. My mom had lived here when she was in her twenties. That was 1954, when New York was as upbeat as the two-way traffic on Fifth Avenue and the pennant-winning Brooklyn Dodgers. She had landed a secretarial job, met my father, had me and gotten divorced, all in the space of two years. Ended up outside Bennington, Vermont, with a couple of hundred bucks and a cache of thwarted dreams. I sometimes wonder if I'm headed in that direction, myself. Of course, you have to have dreams before they can be thwarted.

These thoughts are not doing much for the task at hand, so to speak.

Plenty of nights, I drifted into sleep listening to stories of skyscraper canyons and psychedelic streets, of a place called Times Square, where the lights never dimmed, where theaters lined up one after the other like used cars—take your pick. Since she was a girl, my mom had dreamed of being an actress, but the dad I never met got in the way of all that. Men got in the way of lots of things, according to her, though I can't really see her letting that happen. Still, the idea of disillusionment probably settled into my heavy-eyed half-sleep and made me cautious of ever giving my own ambition free range. But the thought of living in New York City stuck with me and when I left North Carolina, this is where I headed.

The first thing I noticed, stepping out of the Port Authority bus terminal onto Eighth Avenue, was the tantalizing scent of exhaust, sweat and fast food, all jumbled together and spilling onto the street like an overflowing trash can. For a couple of weeks, I just wandered, rubber-necked, ate hot dogs and apples from street vendors and took it all in. Then I found this walkup advertised in the *Village Voice*. I was fine with the seedy neighborhood, the stink of piss in the alley, the occasional early-morning fight outside the bar on the first floor—the 'top Light,' once the 'Stop Light', before its neon S burned out. I was in Manhattan, which was one very long way from Southeast Asia and as unlike Vermont as pineapples are snowplows.

I take up the pumping. The radio announcer reports the date, Friday, February 4, 1974, and the temperature in Central Park, thirty-four degrees. I figure my room is maybe ten degrees warmer. Less cold. I blow on my fingers and wrap them back around. Cold must be a natural form of birth control. Turn down the heat in suburbia—end of population crisis, oil shortage, beleaguered moms, frazzled dads.

Twenty-three minutes to delivery time. I'll be late if I don't get something going here pretty soon.

Those first weeks, I pulled scraps of the previous tenant's underwear out of gaps around the window and attached weather-stripping to the dry-rotted casing. Washing the glass with a wet sock, I leaned out over the city, fired up by its big dirty anonymity. "Hey!" I yelled to nobody in particular, "It's me, Hank Preston. I made it!"

For most of that first month, I stripped wallpaper, yanked up layers of cracked linoleum and painted the walls and woodwork and floors all an optimistic white. I adopted an easy chair from the street and a baggage cart on iron wheels which, with the addition of a futon, made a sofa bed I can push around with my foot, following the light from the window. I made the place mine, though everything had somebody else's imprint on it. So much the better. I like a sense of history. I keep the place neat as a military barracks. The easiest thing about boot camp for me was keeping my gear in perfect order. Growing up in Vermont, the more chaotic things got—and they got pretty crazy sometimes—the neater my room became. In three years here, I've nearly filled one wall with used books, sorted alphabetically by author, and a collection of playbills sorted by date of performance.

I inherited this love of theater, of course, from my mom, who used to drag me to summer stock performances around New England, way back when I had to strain to see over the seatback in front of me. My particular fascination with plays, to this day, is a little weird. Instead of hanging on the action or looking for hidden meaning in the dialogue, my heart's in my throat thinking how brave the actors are to put themselves out there like they do. I pretty much always fall in love with the ingénue, though she, of course, only has eyes for her leading man with the great voice and the perfect hair.

Maybe it's the thought of the ingénue, but with a couple of quick strokes, my hard-on rises, finally, like an Atlas missile and I have a liftoff. I fumble with the little vial the clinic provides for transport, as a paltry stream of cum worth the price of a week's groceries dribbles over my thumb and forms a viscous puddle on my belly. I scoop up all I can and jam on the lid. Vial-ent sex!

My feet hit the icy floor. I pull on my jeans and reach for a flannel shirt and two sweaters, all lodged inside each other like firemen's garb. I tie my spit-polished boots and stuff the vial into my shirt pocket, where it'll stay warm against my chest. Parka zipped, knitted cap pulled down around my ears, I shoulder my bike, step into the hallway and double-lock the door. I take the four flights to the street two steps at a time. Nothing I hate more than being late.

Fifty-Seventh Street lags with cross-town traffic, the night's precipitation ground into a thick gray ooze that clogs my tire treads. I ease into a lane of yellow cabs, the occasional paneled truck, a stretch limo. A damp wind whips off the Hudson providing a much-appreciated eastward shove at my back. I turn north on Eighth Avenue to Columbus Circle and into Central Park, where a morning haze shimmers in skeletal trees. My frosty brake rubbers whine. I imagine myself a dad carrying his kid, a tiny warm package wrapped in Eskimo blankets, home to his mom, a former Miss Alaska with a white-as-snow smile and ebony hair. She has a hot walrus stew on the fire and can't wait to climb naked under a bear skin with the man of her dreams.

Of course, I'll never see the potential kid I'm carrying against my chest. Or the mom, either.

I take the Seventy-Second Street exit from Central Park and pedal my butt to the East Side. It's six minutes after eight as I pull up to a Gothic stone building at the east end of Sixty-Eighth Street. Damn! The first time in three years I'm late.

Every Manhattan neighborhood has its own particular character, I've noticed. Here, it's the sense of distinction that emanates from the giant hospital buildings, majestic yet austere in the gray morning light. The sidewalks are cleaner than where I live, which isn't saying a whole lot. This is a real neighborhood, not a tasteless collection of tenements and warehouses that have nothing to do with each other, despite their proximity. The dampness off the East River carries the vague scent of coffee, absurdly homey.

I shoulder my bike and pull open the building's heavy bronze door, my legs wobbly as rubber. Warm yellow light spills from the resting elevator to my right. The marble stairway looms to my left. Dr. McAvery, the clinic director, told me to always take the stairs, no matter what, never the elevator. But he's probably never had to haul a bike up four flights, his fingers and toes half-frozen, running late. I look from the elevator to the stairway, elevator-stairway, warm-cold, light-dark, like I'm taking in the tennis at Forest Hills.

I duck into the elevator and press five, noticing a warm wetness against my chest. I run my fingers up under my sweater. The vial is turned on its side and leaking into my shirt pocket. As I right it, a woman's leather-gloved hand interrupts the door's closing. She hustles inside, glances from my face to where my arm juts under my sweater, and presses five, though its indicator is already lit. She turns her back to me. I take in her auburn hair, her fresh citrus fragrance, the tension in her body, visible even under the mink coat, which I can't help wishing were wool. I've always believed those scurrying little mortals should be allowed to keep their own coats. Obviously this woman doesn't, which might be fine if I didn't strongly suspect, if I weren't somehow completely convinced and therefore panicked to realize, that she is to be the recipient of my sperm. That is, if it hasn't all leaked onto my chest by now.

Heat rises to my face. I look down at my faded jeans, my boots soaked with slush. Clearly I belong on the stairs. At least there's no mirrored wall to reflect our images to each other, though I know hers pretty well already—the heavy eye liner, the lipstick-lined pucker, the forced calm. Has she sensed who I am? Will she tell Dr. McAvery she met a waif in the elevator who smelled of semen and a shortage of showers? I glance at the floor numbers advancing overhead, feeling guilty, and, I have to admit, curious.

Neither of us risks another glance. My bike tire drips. The mink glistens in the overhead light. I imagine touching the short hairs at the nape of her neck, so vulnerable and sweet. Should I tell her I know who she is and suggest that it's not too late for one of us to turn back, that we don't have to plague ourselves with the "birth parent" image already fixed in our brains? But I say nothing, of course.

The elevator slows to five. The door slides open and she darts to the right. I step into the hallway behind her, my bike pressing into my shoulder. Her legs are muscular, athletic. Her heels click the terrazzo floor like a tap dancer's. Her lemony fragrance lingers. I lower my bike and recheck the vial. As she pulls open the clinic door, her eyes dart back to me. She grins and—I will wonder, later, if I made this up—winks. The corners of my mouth twitch into the beginning of a grin as she disappears inside.

Feeling weirdly bereft, I make my way to the clinic's rear entrance. Now I really get why McAvery insisted on the stairs. He knew how strange it would be for a donor to run into the mother of his potential offspring, to picture her stomach swelling to the size of a basketball, to imagine the sweet little shared likeness evolving from this cold morning moment. And what about her, seeing the dad who's not really the dad but just a stand-in for the dad she wishes was able to make her a mom? Yeah, McAvery had his reasons all right.

He's waiting for me at the back entrance, dispenses with his usual friendly greeting and ignores my apology, as much of a rebuke for my tardiness as the old man can muster. "There might be a problem," I say, reaching under my sweater for the vial. "I think it leaked." I hold up my sweater for him to see.

He glances at the wet spot, then takes the little canister and holds it up to the light. "It'll do," he says, handing me three tens.

"You sure?" I ask him.

McAvery raises an eyebrow in my direction as he slips the vial into the pocket of his long white coat.

I picture the semen dripping from my semi-stiff dick half an hour ago, the frigid cross-town ride, the demeaning glance of the woman in the elevator, and this crazy longing comes up in me. I want McAvery to hug me. I want him to say I'm doing a decent thing, that I shouldn't always be worrying about everything the way I do.

"Is there anything else?" he asks me.

I blink into the florescent light and shake my head.

"I'll be in touch, then," he says, turning back into the clinic and closing the door behind him.

I remove my handkerchief from my back pocket and wipe down my bike, recalling the tour of the clinic McAvery gave me during my interview three years ago. I noticed a bulletin board by the front desk, pinned with baby photographs—the clinic's proud successes. "We should move along," he said. But I lingered there, taking in that array of cherub faces, homely little angels with drunken eyes, trapezoidal heads and wacky hair. "Donors come and go, Hank," he said, chuckling and leading me away.

Very funny.

What if this donation business is just some sort of hedge against the worry that I might never have a family of my own? Pathetic as it sounds, the only girlfriend I ever had was in tenth grade, and she only lasted two months. I couldn't even maintain her interest long enough to bring her to my birthday party, the Tuesday before Thanksgiving. The guy my mother was seeing at the time was there, along with a couple of his drinking buddies and a woman whose breath smelled like dated hamburger. I was always uneasy about inviting my friends to our house, few as they were, so the celebration wouldn't have had much to do with me anyway. Still, I remember sitting in my mother's lounger by the night-blackened picture window and thinking about the girl who'd somehow singled me out that fall. What had she found desirable in me? And what had I done to change her mind? That week, she had steered around me at school like I had BO or wicked acne, or something worse I hadn't even considered.

My birthday cake had been lifted out of its windowed box and set on the counter. While my mother searched for candles she swore she remembered seeing in a drawer, the woman with the meat breath stole a swipe of icing off the side of the cake. She looked across the room divider at me and shrugged as she sucked her finger. For some reason, this had made me miss my no-longer girlfriend all the more.

I hoist my bike to my shoulder now and take the four flights down to the front door. Maybe the mink-clad redhead will make a good mother. Who knows about these things?

2

KAREN AND (LLOYD)

Early one morning—that is, before ten—I stare at my television screen. A warehouse fire rages out of control somewhere in Queens. Rainbow tongues of flame lick at a brick wall as smoke roils and billows. Swaying arches of water, delicate as orchid stems, divide the crisp morning sky. Life-quashing destruction, as beautiful and thrilling as it is terrifying.

I stand and switch off the TV. The picture shrivels to a static dot. I sigh and climb back into bed.

Sometimes I wonder why I sigh so much. Being thirty-eight? Something to groan about for a moderately successful Broadway actress juggling a demanding career and a bundle of nerves. Or could it be the previous news story—the abduction of Patty Hearst by a bearded bunch calling themselves the Symbionese Liberation Army, who resemble no army I've ever seen. They want four million dollars ransom from the Hearst parents, banking, so to speak, on their love for their pretty young offspring. Money to buy food for the poor, they claim. Four million? That's a lot of French fries!

Lloyd, my wildly successful husband, moves about the kitchen at the far end of our SoHo loft. I hear him set a bowl on the gleaming countertop, the clink of a spoon, the sucking sound of the refrigerator as it seals itself closed. The loft takes up an entire floor of an old sewing machine factory at the corner of Broome and Prince Streets, nearly four thousand square feet of high-ceilinged, sun-drenched space. Fabulous!

After seven years of marriage, I know the precise progression of my husband's morning, even the inevitable splash of milk that I picture him sponging up, eliminating any suggestion of imperfection. He hasn't yet tucked in his white shirttails or looped his rep tie into a perfect Windsor. His luxuriant graying hair, worn longish—a man familiar with assets—gives off the fresh scent of Herbal Essence shampoo. He hums the final number from my performance last night at the Shubert.

I prop myself on pillows stacked against an elegantly carved, Tibetan headboard. I am both adored and bored by Lloyd. Isn't that always the way? Lying here, a generous dining area and living room away, I can appreciate how attractive he is, even at forty-eight—his tall, athletic frame, his eyes the gray-green of worn currency, his level eyebrows confirming a lifetime of dependability.

He came backstage one evening, eight years ago, with one of the play's financial backers. I noticed immediately that Lloyd was more attractive than the usual VIP. He was neither shy nor overly admiring, which theater fans can sometimes be, crowded into those backstage carrels with a horde of half-naked actors darting about. I sat on a folding chair, unlacing a boot. When I reached out to shake his hand, he turned my palm up and kissed it. I had all I could do not to giggle. "You're so lovely," he whispered, as if this were an indisputable fact, like the closing price of some stock at the end of a day's trading. Looking so far up at Lloyd—he's well over six feet tall—had only enhanced what had seemed his natural, commanding presence.

"Can I do that for you?" he asked, crouching and taking hold of the laces, his elegant Chesterfield spreading across the scuffed floor. It occurred to me that Lloyd Tuckwell was just the sort of man my mother would approve of. How silly—What was I, thirty-one at the time?—to still be considering my mother's preferences! As far back as junior high, she had pointed out to me which boys she deemed to be marriage material. Predictably, they were from the best upstate New York families, the sons of doctors, car dealers, politicians, and replete with unrealized potential.

This Mr. Tuckwell seemed to have long-since realized his.

When I opened my mouth to thank him, I went suddenly mute, as if it had been my father's fingers unlacing my white baby shoes and I hadn't yet acquired words to express the complex of emotions such a simple act brought on.

An only child, I had endured my mother's ongoing negative commentary on my father, which had caused me to fear that one day I too would marry someone who would disappoint me. And, of course, true to form, my first lover had been the opposite of the young men my mother had singled out for me—a dancer, whose gorgeous body would give out in ten years time, leaving him bereft of possibilities. And ultimately, I had, in fact, been disappointed by him, though not for any material reason, and long before the ten years were up.

"How long have you been on the stage?" Lloyd asked me that first night, as he unlaced my boot.

"Twelve years," I replied.

"Impossible!"

"I had an early start," I said, enjoying the dissonance of flirting with someone who reminded me of my father but was actually the man my mother would have preferred. I sensed that this Mr. Lloyd Tuckwell was going to ask me out for a drink—champagne, no doubt.

"Could you join us for a drink?" he asked, as if on cue.

"No, I'm afraid I can't," I replied, suddenly aware that my being slightly out of reach would appeal to Mr. Lloyd Tuckwell, a man who was no doubt used to having his way, a man possibly even bored by all that ease of acquisition.

See how carried away I can get? God, I hate to think of life without fantasy. As you can see, mine can get pretty elaborate. Lloyd does seem quite real sometimes. I sigh again. My shrink, serving up heaping portions of rational suggestions at fifty bucks an hour, thinks I should be careful not to confuse imagination with reality. But I argue that if Lloyd exists in my mind, doesn't he possess a certain life, at least for me? I'm teasing, of course, and yet. . . . Acting is my truth, I tell him. Anything else is up for grabs. Such amusing skirmishes pass the hour.

If admissions weren't so laden with failure, I would own up to a certain loneliness. Still, I can't help but smile now, as I pull my chestnut hair—tinted to eliminate hints of gray—to the top of my head and lean into my very real foam pillows, purchased amid a crush of bargain-seekers at Macy's. It's a new day. A stripe of sunlight rests on the window sill. I'm working. I'm eating. My muscles are still taut. I should count my lucky stars, as Lloyd always does, enjoying a cast-iron complacency in which each person sees to his own particular cog, however major or minor, in the perpetually spinning wheel of life. Me? I worry about the environment, about starvation in Ethiopia, about a homeless man in the street. Though what to do about any of this baffles me. I look around my dingy, very real bedroom—lipstick-rimmed butts overflowing an ashtray, a peril of discarded shoes, the coat (a splayed, fury body reaching over a chair) I wore last week to my third semen insemination at the New York Hospital Fertility Clinic. I've wanted a baby for years. There'd been moments when this or that courtship seemed headed in the direction of offspring, but then they had evaporated like raindrops on a blistering Manhattan sidewalk.

I shake a Salem out of the pack by my bed, light up and inhale. I image Lloyd coming to my bedside and bending down to kiss me. But, in truth, I don't really want anyone kissing me right now. Only someone to want to kiss me. Actually, I long for that feeling I had last week on returning home after my insemination, hearing my apartment door click closed behind me, flipping on the light. Potential, it was, amid some sort of wavering agitation, akin to the way I felt as a girl when I entered my parents' empty house after school. A silent sense of possibility, and of abandon. That word—abandon—at once letting go and being left.

I sigh as sun kindles the Calder poster on the wall next to my bed, dazzling the liquid red, the resounding blue. Most mornings, I wake up famished at six and Osterize myself a breakfast of yogurt, banana, orange juice. But this morning, I'm slow as a slug. Too much thinking, not good. I swing my feet to the floor, an actress's feet, bruised from years of pounding a stage floor. I run my fingers down the muscular calves men admire from their orchestra seats. Men!

I stand, let my nightgown fall and step to my reflection in the mirror. My shoulders are broad. My breasts are no longer those of a twenty-year-old. In a leotard, they hardly exist. Well, better than some pendulous sacks to hoist around. My stomach is still flat. All that will change, of course, if we're successful at the clinic. My high school pregnancy, by that sweet young dancer twenty-odd years ago, hardly showed at all. He'd seemed so much older, my first love, sixteen to my fourteen, all optimism and charm, blithely self-centered, and quite potent evidently. If I'd only known then what I know now. What would I do differently? I'm not sure, actually. It's questions like this that confound me.

I remember so little about that pregnancy, as if it had never happened. Some other person, a child herself really. Though I do remember throwing a fit until they allowed me to hold my glistening and blotchy newborn son, even if only for a minute or two. And then the stab of separation. I remember that.

I dip and rise, swinging one leg out perpendicular to the line of my torso. Back, forward, back, forward. Yes, ironically enough, I carried two babies by the time I was twenty, the first whisked off to a Midwestern couple, the second aborted to the garbage bin.

I flip on the bathroom light, turn on the shower and step in, recalling that feeling of the syringe being inserted into my vagina last week, Dr. McAvery saying, "Slight sting here," preparing me. Slight sting? Years of frustration and regret? What does McAvery know about stings?

I let the water flow over me, relaxing my neck and shoulders. When it turns cool, as it does far too quickly in this old brownstone, crudely carved into floor-throughs, I turn it off and step onto the mat, burying my face in a towel. I sit on the edge of the tub and dry my legs, recalling that, in the midst of the insemination last week, I had felt a sudden extraordinary flood of warmth within me. I must have constricted physically, because the doctor said, "No, not yet. Just a little longer." That lovely sexual sensation had evaporated as quickly as it appeared, replaced by a flash of brilliant winter sky beyond the window. Shaken, I tried to focus on the combed furrows of the doctor's scalp, the room's pungent odor of disinfectant, the pressure in my abdomen. As the nurse patted my forehead with a cloth, one final image intruded, that of the young man with the disheveled hair and frosty cheeks, the man I'd encountered in the elevator on the way to my appointment. It occurred to me, lying there, waiting for McAvery to finish, that he was my semen donor. I felt quite certain. After all, the building had been nearly deserted at that early hour. Who else could he have been?

My handsome knight carrying a slush-spattered bicycle and a dose of semen. Innocent. Sweet. And sexy as James Dean.

I realize now, dropping the towel, that I dreamed of him last night. In the dream, McAvery's nurse is taking my baby from me, like when I was fifteen. But then, it's not McAvery's nurse, it's the handsome guy in the elevator, and he's handing the baby to me, not taking it away, his lovely face smiling down at me, that warm rush flooding my senses all over again.

At my dresser, I step into a leotard and a pair of black bell-bottoms. I pull a turtleneck over my head and twist my hair into a clip. What sort of young man donates his sperm? There'd been a clinic questionnaire about eye color, hair color, skin color, ideal height and weight. I suppose the kid in the elevator did somewhat resemble the qualities I had chosen, qualities that resemble Lloyd's, if truth be told.

I drape a scarf around my neck. What if we met again, my donor and me, and this whole odyssey of having a baby turned from a solo performance into a pas de deux? I fluff my hair. It's a ridiculous idea, and I hear my shrink say, "Don't go there."

And yet, stranger things have happened.

3

HANK DECIDES

We lived in a two bedroom ranch, stuck in a mud yard like a boot in a spring thaw. My mother bought the unfinished house from a couple who ran out of money, or love, or maybe just endurance. The sheetrock walls were taped but never sanded. Resigned plywood floors, once destined for wall-to-wall, were scuffed smooth in darkened paths to the kitchen and the bedrooms. Mt. Anthony got reflected in the bathroom mirror, the one cool thing.

A sullen man named Lick came around from time to time. Imagine a name like that? He arrived carrying a shoebox under his arm, drank a six-pack of Utica Club and stayed the night. In the morning, he left without breakfast, carrying that shoebox, presumably empty by then. Had the box been stuffed with marijuana? Some game? Cash? Of course, I never dared ask. My mother was adamant about her secrets. Also acting in plays, believe it or not. And, I suppose, in her way, Lick.

When sober, she could deliver a competent performance with the local stage company, channeling all the anger and frustration she held back in her real life. On the stage, crying or throwing a dish, or hugging a child for that matter, was scripted and therefore manageable. She used to plop me in an empty seat when I was barely big enough to see between people's shoulders. My mouth ajar, I would wonder, Is this who my mother is?

Most days, though, she coped in near silence. She was not a woman who worried her "issues" out loud, a practice that was beginning to take hold among the dropouts migrating to Bennington,Vermont in the late sixties. I wish I had a dollar for every hangover I nursed her through, every purple-lidded eye or puffed lip. She was peevish when she drank, and Lick, like the others before him, tired of that pretty fast. A tall and physically powerful woman, she didn't just take a slap and forget about it. She'd be on him, her thumbs bearing down on his Adam's apple, her knee slamming his groin. Two o'clock in the morning, startled awake by the racket of a revved engine pulling out of the driveway, I'd find her sitting at the kitchen table under the fake Tiffany shade, a boxer down for the count, mumbling something about what Lick had said, which always upset her more than being hit. I'd run a towel under the faucet and dab at her lip.

"He insulted me."

"What'd he say?"

"Not for you to hear. Not for anyone."

"Jesus Christ, Maggie." Since I can remember, I called my mother by her given name. No doubt I picked it up from one of her boyfriends, thinking I could grab her attention if I was more like him. "Why can't you just let it be?"

She looked at me as if I'd suggested she run for the State Legislature. "Don't you ever take an insult from anybody," she said, narrowing her one good eye. "Your self-respect is all you've got."

Years later, when I received my notice from the draft lottery that I had pulled number seventeen, a ticket to conscription if ever there was one, my thinking was colored by all that talk about behaving in a way that fit with your beliefs, about not doing anything shameful, about defending your pride. I was never sure exactly where she drew the line on these things, yet clearly she had her standards. I never knew her to lie, for example. And she always managed to find people who needed our limited funds more than we did, though exactly how she made that determination was never clear either. Our house was a local soup kitchen before any church got the idea.

I always hated fighting, probably because Maggie was such a scrapper. In grade school, I went out of my way to avoid the class bully. Even my collection of model airplanes had excluded fighter jets. The idea that I could be trained to fight, much less to kill, was not something I could visualize, even at eighteen, when draft notifications were going around like invitations to a game of Russian roulette.

Mine wasn't a moral stance. Senator Eugene McCarthy had come to our school and his speech had made sense, though I couldn't seem to figure out just where I stood on that war in Vietnam. One argument was that we were defending Democracy on the other side of the world, where communist dominoes were falling and stacking up like some sort of bulwark against freedom. Another, more readily comprehended, was that we were protecting our economic interests. How, exactly, was an aggressively unaware eighteen-year-old, living in a Republican state like Vermont, with a clan of make-love-not-war hippies moved in down the road, to decipher the truth? The body counts each night on the TV, like some gruesome scoreboard, faded from my consciousness the next day, too grisly to dwell on. Truth, it seemed, depended on who you listened to.

I went about the business of graduating from high school and entering the work force, like a spindly quarterback ducking his head and racing straight into the opposing line, knowing it's just a matter of time before he gets knocked flat. I took a job as groundskeeper at a new motel on Route 7. I'd always been a loner, so the idea of solo outdoor work had its appeal. I mowed lawns, tended begonias and geraniums, repaired fences, painted shutters. I sported a tee shirt tan, with sun-soaked face and neck and arms, pasty torso and legs. I took my breaks leaning against a tree, staring up at the granite Vermont hills, stalwart with grit. All the while that number seventeen ricocheting inside my head like a crow caw by a cliff.

College was not a serious consideration. I had little ambition, a dearth of successful men for models, and no money. The few friends I did have worked their family farms or in one of the mills or granite quarries around Bennington, waiting for their own numbers to come up. I had perfected a brand of contentment that required a high level of oblivion, maintaining an obsessive sense of order and control over the physical trivialities of my life, while most of my thoughts turned into mist and drifted off like dry ice vapors.

The man with the shoebox, Lick, stopped coming around the year I graduated from high school. My mom cut back on the beer. I seeded the mud bed out front and mowed it Friday evenings after work. I put in a vegetable garden out back, the rows as neat and straight as railroad ties. I bought a tired pickup and tinkered under the hood, sanded and primed the rocker panels smoother than new, still not able to fathom the idea of stepping into some new life on the other side of the world, wearing a uniform and carrying a rifle. Could I do that? The one conviction I'd held my whole life was that there was no way I could, or would, kill.

"I don't think I can do it, Maggie," I said one night, picking at a slice of meatloaf.

"Can't do what?"

"Kill somebody. I mean if I get called up. I don't think I can."

She took a pull on her coke and set it down next to the wet ring it had left on the Formica. I slid it into position.

"I wish you wouldn't do that," she said.

"Do what?"

"Always trying to make everything perfect. You'll drive yourself crazy, and me too." She elbowed the bottle out of position. "And they're not just somebody," she said. "They're communists."

"Somebody's brother, maybe. Some kid's dad."

"They say communists could take over that whole area."

"Since when do you care what 'they' say?"

She took a bite of her stewed corn. Rusty-looking grease accumulated on one side of her plate. I'd heard a lot about communists, yet I'd never seen any hard evidence of a threat. Our borders hadn't been invaded since the British left here two hundred years ago. We were the most powerful country on earth. What did we have to fear from a tiny little place like Vietnam? Of course, what did I know?

"I just picture myself looking through a set of cross hairs dividing some Oriental guy's face. I couldn't pull the trigger. I know I couldn't. Christ, I don't even hunt squirrels!"

Maggie took another sip of her coke as I imagined the resistance of the trigger against my finger, the kick to my shoulder, the flash of red. "Could you?" I asked her, pushing my plate away.

Since Lick left, my mother's eyes had softened into something approaching composure, with a dose of sadness underneath. Her jaw had slackened and her shoulders had settled. Yet I could see, deep down, she was as scared and confused about the draft as I was.

"I feel like I need to know why," I said. "I don't know why."

"Because you're told. Isn't that why men fight wars? Because some guy in charge tells them to?" A gust of wind twirled the exhaust fan over the stove. Maggie had given up on life's complexities, a worthwhile bargain, evidently, in exchange for some peace. But her ready rationalizations only confirmed my own emptiness. Why should I worry about fighting a war when I was dead already? Dead inside, I mean.

"I don't think I can kill anybody," I said, repeating the one thing I believed with some certainty.

"You would if you had to."

I picked up my plate and set it in the sink.

With my paychecks from the motel, I spruced up the house with some carpeting, a new divan, a hot water heater that took the worry out of a shower. I felt like the father I never knew. Weeks passed and I bided my time. I bargained. I'd forget about ever living in New York, I'd devote my life to helping people, I'd forget about girls, if only I didn't have to kill. Finally, exhausted with the whole idea, I put the war out of my mind, avoidance being the thing I was probably best at.

Then, one wintry Saturday afternoon, the order to report to Fort Dix spilled out of the mailbox. I dropped it on the kitchen table and went to my room, where I lay on my bed, imagining Maggie, in the months ahead, carrying firewood across the icy yard, shoveling the walkway, unable to raise the frozen garage door. Was I going then? Did picturing me not being here mean that I'd decided to fight?

I heard her setting supper dishes on the table in the other room. She'd have read the notice by now. More than anything, I wanted to be decisive when I went out to supper. Being clear seemed as important as whatever I elected to do. Until now, I'd never decided anything, never even questioned Maggie's dubious determinations. I needed to take a stand, finally. My life was at stake, and I'm not talking about taking a bullet in some jungle in Southeast Asia. I'm talking about the simple act of taking charge, of growing up, of being a man.

Maggie sat at the table. She hadn't set out silverware or napkins, as if she'd reached her limit after the plates and collapsed into her chair. She smoked a cigarette, her forehead glistening in the hollow light of the overhead lamp. I sat down opposite her. We both stared at the table, as if the answer was written there in the fake grain of the Formica. The time for my pronouncement passed. She seemed to regain her strength in the face of my continued wavering, crushed out her cigarette and pushed herself to her feet. She ladled brown portions of stew onto our plates, set down spoons, sliced bread and two cokes.

Three weeks passed that way. I exhausted myself at the motel during the day and went straight home at four-thirty. I hung my parka on the peg by the door, unlaced my boots and lay on the bed in my room, my ankles crossed, my fingers clenched behind my head. A stack of secondhand paperbacks lay unread on the floor. That hour before dinner was harder than shoveling a foot of wet snow off the motel walkways or trying to repair the plow attachment in ten-degree weather. Getting clear was just not something I could do, no matter what. I put aside my worries about Maggie. She'd manage, just as she always had. I could probably get my job at the motel back in a year. Or some other job. I'd be a survivor, like her. It was the killing I still couldn't get my thoughts around, taking that strong a stand. I had no convictions. How would I survive a war without convictions?

At five-thirty, another hour passed with no inkling of a resolution, I emerged from my room and joined Maggie in the kitchen, where we ate in silence. She probably had an opinion, but she wasn't saying, which I appreciated. My tentative thoughts could never have withstood hers. No doubt she knew that.

Finally, early on the morning I was scheduled to report to our local recruitment center, I found her sitting on the new divan, dressed in a plaid skirt and cable sweater, her long wool coat thrown over the arm. She'd set a small suitcase at her feet, its leather handle dried and worn. I suspected that it contained a change of clothes for me—a warm sweater, a flannel shirt, some underwear and jeans. The cluttered kitchen smelled of fresh corn muffins. Two had been set on a plate for me alongside a glass of orange juice. The rest, from the greased look of the paper bag, sat at her feet next to the valise. "There's coffee," she said.

I poured a cup and sat at the table. I bit into one of the muffins.

"I thought we'd take a ride," she said.

"Where to?"

"North. See where we end up."

Canada. She was forcing my hand. It was time.

We donned our coats and closed the door behind us, stepping into the brittle morning. I dusted new snow off the pickup, a dry cold withering my nostrils. The brilliance that often follows a snowfall loomed all around. I took the suitcase from Maggie and set it behind the seat. She moved slowly around the truck, propping her hand along the fender, the hood, the other fender, and pulled herself into the cab. She set the muffins and the map down next to her and pulled the door closed. I looked back at the house glowing orange in the rising sun, the tufts of confetti that dotted the roof, our one-way footprints on the new wooden steps. We'd never spoken of Canada as an option, though of course I'd been thinking about it, deciding yes, deciding no, picturing myself walking alone down a deserted street. Where would I live? Who would give a damn about me?

Obviously, Maggie had been thinking about Canada, too, and this Sunday morning drive was her offering. Not a decision. She would leave that to me. But an option as clear as the iridescent eddies of snowflakes swirling along the highway as we pulled onto Route 7 and headed north. Driving alongside those majestic Green Mountains I'd known and mostly ignored my whole life, I felt like I was going to split in half, one side veering off to the left of the highway, the other to the right. I imagined the truck swerving and Maggie bracing herself against the dashboard as we rolled over and over in the soft drifted snow. But, of course, breaking down was not in our repertoire, never had been. We were Vermonters, New Englanders, sturdy as posts, responsible to the point of. . . . Well, that was the question, wasn't it?

I gripped the wheel tighter and drove on.

We stopped in Brandon for hamburgers, which we played with a while and set aside. We walked the town's side streets to stretch our legs, and I suppose to delay the end of our journey. We ate her corn muffins and drove on. I couldn't remember ever having spent this much time with my mother, just the two of us, each other our only distraction. We spoke little. I stole glances in her direction, taking in her right-angle jaw line, the streaks of gray at her temples, the erect posture, the slight squint of her intelligent eyes, the resignation, the courage.

In Newport, at her direction, I turned right onto Route 105, and drove through East Berkshire and along the frozen Missisquoi River, which, she pointed out, extended north into Quebec. She directed me to pull over to the side of the road once again. I shut off the engine and we stared out my side window, the only sound the slight hiss of her breathing, the click of the engine cooling. The white expanse of the river stretched ahead and out of sight. Plum juice stained the sky's graying verge. It would be dark shortly.

"Pretty, isn't it?" Maggie said.

Desolate, I thought. Lifeless.

"A guy could walk that frozen river and make a new life," she said. "It wouldn't be that hard."

Yes, I supposed that was true, the walking part anyway. But making a new life? I'd never made an old life, any life. Where would I even start? I stared at the river a while longer before reaching for the ignition key. The pickup's engine roared with that familiar metallic odor of gasoline flooding the carburetor. I pulled back onto Route 105. As we entered a tiny town called Richford—Last Town in Vermont, the sign read—Maggie had me turn left at the single crossroad. A mile up the road, she told me to pull over again.

Lights burned in the windows of a farmhouse up a long driveway. A barn loomed alongside, lighted too. We could see the occasional head of a Holstein bob into view through one of the dim windows. Maggie reached back for the suitcase and set it on the seat between us. We stared at the black road ahead, glancing occasionally at the farmhouse.

"The owner will take you in 'til you decide," Maggie said.

Misery overtook me, as dark and forbidding as the night making its decisive descent around the pickup, and I was grateful, finally, to feel something. I had underestimated Maggie my whole life. I'd blamed and resented her for all sorts of things, some legitimate. What I wanted most, sitting there in the cold, shadowy truck, with its dim angles of light caressing Maggie's nose and cheeks and chin, was a way to leave her that would make her proud of me. We had never hugged or kissed, even when I was little. We had never said hello or goodbye because we had never really left each other. We were a pair, always had been. Eighteen years old and I had never left my mother.

I pulled on my gloves and reached for the valise. "Can I ask you something?" I said, gripping the handle.

She nodded, hands folded in her lap.

"Did my dad fight in World War II?"

She turned to me as if she were about to say something, but then pressed her lips back together. I knew so little about my father. If he had fought, maybe I could, drawing on some genetic potential I knew nothing about.

She shook her head.

I swung open my door, letting in a gust of powdery flakes. Before stepping out, I leaned over and kissed her dry cheek.

"You can always come back home," she said. "Whatever happens, we'll deal with it."

I stepped out and pushed the door closed. Maggie slid behind the wheel and rolled down the window. "Hank," she called, her breath a wispy veil hovering in my direction. "Break a leg." She smiled and I waved.

Packed snow crunched underfoot. Partly up the driveway, I turned and watched Maggie pull the pickup across the road and head back the way we'd come, glowing taillights dimming eventually in a low gust.

Beyond a fidgety line of fir trees, a black bowl of sky emanated an immense silence, restless with sprouting stars. Cold nipped at my ears and cheeks. Of all the things I might have felt just then, I had the faint stirring in me of some sort of faith in myself, the completely unexpected, budding conviction that I would survive whatever lay in store for me. I loved Maggie, but the only way I was ever going to figure out what strength I might possess was to be away from her. That time had arrived and, piggybacked on it, I made out an opportunity.

Cows bayed beyond the barn's night-blackened walls, studded with squares of yellow light. I pictured their heads bobbing impatiently for the evening's toss of grain. The warm odor of manure and fresh hay snuck from under the wide door. It seemed stupid to knock, so I slid the door open and stepped inside. A gray cat scurried to me and arched itself around my ankle. A man in overalls and flannel shirt, a peaked cap pulled low over his eyes, finished pouring milk into a can and walked over to me. As if he'd been expecting me, he took off his hat and reached out to shake my hand.

I spent three days with my mother's old boyfriend, Lick, helping with the milking and other chores. The first floor of the farmhouse, an old cape, had been gutted to make one big room—kitchen, dining and living. Evenings, we ate our meals near a woodstove stuck into an old hearth. I noticed a shoebox on the mantle like the one he used to carry into my mother's house years ago. It even had Size 11 printed on one end, like before. "What's in the box?" I asked him. Lick got up, took it down and opened it for me to see inside. Pine cones. He took a handful, opened the stove and tossed them inside. "Makes the room smell pretty," he said, grinning.

Other than brief exchanges like that, Lick and I spoke little. On the third morning, I got up before he did, dressed and tiptoed down the stairs. In the brisk dark, I pocketed some rolls and cheese, and let myself out of the house. Several miles walk along the river and I knew by the license plate of the occasional passing car that I was in Canada. I spent another day there, walking from one village to the next. That evening of my second day, I caught a bus to Montreal, and from there to New York City and finally to Fort Dix, in New Jersey, the first leg of the rest of my life.

KAREN GOES FOR IT

I descend the stairs to the street humming, a first for me at seven-thirty in the morning. "Imagination is silly, it goes around willy-nilly." Wasn't that Peggy Lee? Circa 1950? I make a mental note to check, knowing too well the fate of my mental notes.

Walking to Eighth Avenue, I pass a toothless woman with her hand out, a man with a Basset Hound, peeing against a trash can—the dog in this case. New York! To me, these are opening scenes, preludes to urban dramas in which anything can happen. Legends, myths, minor tales, they're all right here in front of us, all vivid and real, if we would only pause and pay attention. A suited man crying, a kid pinching a pear from a fruit cart, a sexy guy delivering his semen to a fertility clinic—stories in which, like it or not, our accidental presence casts us in a role. Add a little imagination and the possibilities emerge like a photo in an acid bath.

Shy away from your dramas and you miss your life.

Two weeks after encountering my donor in the elevator—yes, the more I thought about it, the more certain I became—I'm heading uptown to introduce myself to this Henry Preston. He doesn't know it yet, but he's about to play a part in my drama. Could be just a walk-on, but you never know. Since we met—okay, saw—each other, I haven't been able to flush him out of my mind. I mean— Come on!—his semen was about to be ejaculated—okay, injected—into me. This sort of thing doesn't happen every day. Wouldn't any woman be curious?

As luck would have it, at a follow-up appointment yesterday, I found myself alone in the examining room, waiting for Dr. McAvery. My file lay on the counter next to a pair of opaque rubber gloves and a gleaming set of forceps. The label read Tuckwell, Mrs. Lloyd. Sure enough, attached to the inside cover was the donor's profile. Henry Preston, 501 West Fifty-Seventh Street, Apartment 5S. Age 22, brown hair, green eyes, six feet two inches, 172 pounds. The Polaroid close-up didn't do him justice, his expression bemused, as if he'd been caught zipping up after performing his crucial function.

My taxi pulls to the curb in front of Preston's building. Jesus, it's a dump! I recheck the number over the door. What did I expect, the Sherry-Netherland? I pay the driver and mount the littered steps to the front door. Inside, Preston's name is taped over a dented mailbox. No buzzer. I kick aside a dated sports section of the *Daily News* and head for the stairs. Tortured strains of Roberta Flack singing "Killing Me Softly" sneak under a third-floor doorway. I considered calling ahead, but worried that my donor was the sort who sticks to the rules. He might even tell McAvery I called, and the good doctor would know I'd been snooping in my file. Besides, in person, I can win Henry Preston over. But for what purpose? I wonder, as I climb the last listing flight of stairs. My shrink, demonstrating an excellent grasp of the obvious, says I get ahead of myself.

The fifth floor hallway, lit by a single bare bulb, is a ruin of brown—the scarred wooden doors, the wrinkled linoleum, the dust bunnies in the corners. The odor of fried onions probably plays better in the evening. I fluff my hair, clear my voice and knock. Nothing. I should have gotten an earlier start. Or is the cosmos telling me this visit is not such a great idea? I knock again. Footsteps, a pause, and the handsome young donor opens the door the few inches allowed by a chain lock. His hair is disheveled, a look he seems to have perfected; his eyes sparkle as before, though slightly blunted with the coffee-starved look appropriate to the hour. Eyes the gray-green of the sea bending backward at the crest of a wave, as if it were having second thoughts about crashing over on itself. Spindrift I believe that spray is called. Where do I store such trivia? Boxers and a t-shirt, cute as a Calvin Klein ad. He blinks into the dim light of the hallway.

"Hi," I say, as cheery as I can muster at this hour. He blinks again and takes in the full length of me. I've worn my usual winter outfit—leather jacket, wool scarf, bell-bottoms, platform heels. "I'm Karen Tuckwell." I extend my hand toward the narrow opening. Henry Preston has elegant legs, moderately hairy, and shapely feet.

"What do you want?" he asks me, glancing over his shoulder into the bright apartment. I wonder if he has someone in there, a woman perhaps. "Give me a minute," he says and disappears, leaving the door ajar but still bound by the chain. All trust and etiquette, this one.

I glance back at the grim hallway. I suppose sperm donors, by definition, occupy the lower socio-economic echelons, like actors, but this place gives me the creeps. When Dr. McAvery advised me that they would be using fresh sperm, not frozen, for a better chance at success, he assured me that I would never know who my donor was, nor would he ever know me. Don't worry, he'd said, which I hadn't. What, exactly, had he feared, if we met? That we would end up putting him out of business?

My donor looks something like an actor I knew in summer stock a few years ago. Dan Bailey was his name. Yes, definitely, if Dan had lost the sideburns, which were never right for him. He dropped out of sight after our affair. Once, I thought I saw him working in a men's boutique downtown, but that may only have been my mind playing tricks. People take me for the worldly sort, a modern woman, but the truth is there haven't been that many men. I remember each one vividly, and mostly with regret.

Footsteps again and I put on my perky face as the donor releases the chain and opens the door. He's wearing jeans and a sweatshirt now, no shoes or socks. I was right—he has elegant feet, rare in a man. We stand just inside the door of his one-room studio, with its smell of sleep and limited resources. "Hank Preston," he says, offering his hand.

A sink and hot plate crowd the corner of the room, a once overstuffed chair cozies up to a wall of books at the far end. An oversized window affords a bohemian feel and a narrow glimpse of the gray, glimmering Hudson River to the west. I probably shouldn't have come.

"Have a seat," he says, pointing toward the chair by the window. "You want some coffee?"

"That would be lovely," I say.

I keep my jacket on—it's chilly, despite the cheerful glow from the window. At the bookcase, I run a finger along the spines of books, noticing that they're alphabetized by author. This man likes order. As I move back toward the window, he spoons Sanka into mugs and pours in boiling water. "Milk and sugar?" he asks, without looking at me.

"Black, thanks."

He hands me a steaming cup and I take the lumpy chair. He sits on the edge of his cot, not three feet away. I cross my legs, feeling suddenly shy. We sip our feeble brew.

"It's decaf," he says. "The real stuff makes me nervous."

I nod.

"How did you find me?" he asks.

I'd been excited about this meeting, but now—it never fails with me and men—something gives way inside me, leaving me weak as the coffee. "I guess I wanted to know more about you," I say. "I hadn't much wondered what the father of my child might be like. I mean if this whole thing works out. That was my third insemination, the day we met, so it's all a little uncertain. But then, when I saw you that morning . . . I've been . . . well, curious, I guess."

He stares into the reflecting ring of his coffee, blows steam away. Everything seems slowed down with this guy, a singer behind the beat. "What do you want to know?" he asks, glancing at me. His eyes are the color of the Bermuda Triangle, and no doubt similarly perilous. Wouldn't a sperm donor be a complicated person, almost by definition?

Outside, a ray of sun elbows its way through the haze and shimmers off that distant slice of the Hudson. A tanker, framed by sulking warehouses, enters and exits the narrow corridor, its solid bulk momentarily stealing the scene's radiance. I realize it's not answers to questions I want from Hank Preston. I can see already that he's one of those nice guys that inadvertently land in New York and don't last. Not cut out for it, not a mean bone in his lovely body. I want to watch him move, hear the timbre of his voice, consider the tension in his shoulders. That's how you get to know somebody. Not by what he says. "I'm not used to getting up this early," I say, apropos of nothing. "I didn't want to miss you."

He glances at his watch. "I do need to get going pretty soon."

"Where to?"

"I shelve books at The Strand bookstore, down on lower Broadway."

"You're kidding! I adore that place."

"You know the Strand?"

"I like to buy old scripts, original editions of the classics, Thornton Wilder, Noel Coward, Tennessee Williams." Hank stares at me a few seconds longer than seems necessary, that missed beat. "How long have you worked there?" I ask him.

"Three years, almost."

"Why have I not seen you?"

"You probably didn't notice the guy behind the book cart."

"I would have noticed you. Trust me. Do you mind?" I extract a pack of Salems from my jacket pocket and offer him one. He shakes his head. "Don't worry, if I find out I'm pregnant with our child, I won't come looking for you, if that's what you're thinking."

He flashes those Bermuda eyes again. "It's not my child you're having," he says. "What did you say your name was?"

"Karen. Karen Tuckwell."

I set a match to the end of my cigarette. There's no ashtray, so I pocket the cinder, still warm.

"It's your kid, yours and your husband's."

Since I can remember—at least since living in Manhattan—I've assessed people within minutes of meeting and then set about giving them what I sense they want, playing opposite them, so to speak. It's automatic, and smooth as a Shakespearean sonnet, until I get bored and resentful when the whole relationship inevitably becomes about them. My shrink says it's a bargain I strike in which I give up whatever I want for a sense of control over what happens. He asks me if it's worth it. I shrug. Is there another way?

"You talk," I say, feeling a little stung by Hank Preston's quick rejection of anything to do with this baby. "What's it like, working at the world's greatest bookstore? You must have to deal with a lot of people, and that's never easy. I prefer the stage—five feet up and eighteen feet back from the first row. Closer than that makes me nervous, if you know what I mean."

"You're an actress?"

I nod.

"That's cool." He sets his empty coffee mug on the floor, suddenly more attentive. A lot of men like actresses, or maybe it's that distance they like, hidden in their orchestra seats, watching the woman reveal herself, or so they think. "My mom was an actress." he says.

"Really? What's her name?"

"You wouldn't know her. She did local stuff, in Vermont."

"I've done summer stock in New Hampshire. Small world."

Hank Preston's smile is at least as disarming as his sea-green eyes and shapely feet. I wonder if all McAvery's donors are as attractive as this one.

"That must be such a kick," he says, "playing in front of an audience every night. The last thing I could ever do."

I know it's weird, but I feel all warm about this guy, like we're a couple of lovers before she's washed his underwear or smelled his morning breath. I sigh. He glances at his watch. "I'm keeping you, aren't I?"

"I do have to shower and get to the store."

The bicycle he had shouldered in the elevator leans against the wall by the door. "Do you ride to work?"

He nods as that dusty shimmer of sunlight corners the window frame and reaches like a magic wand to his left sideburn. Auburn strands flicker among the black. I watch this shaft of sun inch its lingering way across the glass, marveling at what specks we all are, whirling in perpetual, frivolous motion. Emboldened by the thought, I ask him, "So who *are* you?"

"I told you. . . ."

"I don't mean your job."

"That's a pretty big question then."

"Don't you think . . . I mean, the occasion calls for some pretty big questions, doesn't it?" I stand and walk to the sink, where I drop my palmed ashes into the trash.

Hank Preston stands too. "McAvery probably has good reasons for keeping his donors and recipients separate, don't you think?"

Some of the ashes missed the trash can and fluttered to the linoleum. Hank Preston tears off a paper towel and wipes them up. I'll bet he was a boy scout once, a sash full of badges across his chest. Again, I think I shouldn't have come. Whatever I had hoped would happen seems unlikely now. "Why do you do it?" I ask. "Donate, or whatever you call it?"

"Why do you want to get pregnant?"

A painful sensation stabs my chest. Why, indeed? It's such a simple question, and yet the correct response eludes me, or worse, might make me cry if I attempt it. I set my cup in the sink. "I got tired of writing checks to Save the Children," I say.

Hank Preston thinks about that for a minute. "Why are you here?" he asks again.

"We met."

"Does your husband know?" He sets his cup next to mine, runs water over them.

"How much does McAvery pay you?"

"Thirty bucks," he says.

Something tells me Hank Preston doesn't know a whole lot about women. He's as uneasy as I am, overly earnest, suave as Smokey the Bear. "You're not gay by any chance, are you?"

"Just because you're pretty and I'm not coming on to you, I'm gay?"

"Sorry!"

"I should never have taken the elevator that day."

"What seems like chaos can be part of a plan we know nothing about." This sounds like a line I read somewhere, though, actually, it's something I've thought a lot about lately. I take a final pull on my cigarette, dunk it in my cup and drop it in the trash. "You seem like a nice guy," I say, debating how much to tell Hank Preston. Some people clam up when they're nervous. I blab. "I was pregnant before," I say.

"What happened?"

"I was barely nineteen, a budding actress, single. Not a time to have a baby. The abortion was . . . not easy, you might say. I nearly died." There's nowhere to pace in this cramped space. I turn left and then right. "Why am I telling you all this? I don't even know you."

"Look, I think this whole thing is not cool. Meeting like this, when we. . . ."

"When we might be having a baby?"

"When you might be having a baby. You and. . . ."

"Right, my husband, Lloyd."

"So this is your replacement? For the baby you got rid of?"

I play with a loose thread on the hem of my jacket. "I want to hold my child," I murmur, "press her to me, protect her, make her feel safe." Some rush of feeling brims in my eyes. I hate internal surprises, little bolts from the blue, emotional pranks. "I don't want to be alone anymore," I say, turning back to Hank Preston. "Is that so bad?"

"What about Lloyd?"

"He makes me feel even more alone. He's so not there."

Hank seems to soften suddenly. "I know what you mean, I guess. Hell, I work in a bookstore, but I can't put more than three words together in a way that makes sense to anybody, including me."

"You're sweet." I rest my hand on his arm.

He pulls away and looks at his watch again. "I really need to get downtown."

My exit cue. "Maybe we can get together again sometime."

He offers his hand. "You take care, Karen," he says, holding the door for me. My platforms echo in the brown stairwell. I repeat his name in my head. Hank Preston. Hank Preston. Not that I'm about to forget it.

5

HANK AT THE STRAND

I wheel my overloaded book cart off the elevator, bowled over by the sudden swerve in my life, the surprise visit this morning by the recipient of my sperm, this Karen Tuckwell. She's not like anybody I've ever met before. Except maybe my mom, now that I think about it, in her younger days, anyway. She's out there in the same sort of way, saying what's on her mind even if it doesn't quite add up, saying more than anybody really needs to hear. But this Karen Tuckwell is too pretty, too New York, a little too much of everything in general. And me with a lifelong thing for an ingénue. Coincidences like this make me uneasy, like there's some grand scheme of things I don't know about, like I was absent the day life schedules got handed out.

Karen Tuckwell isn't exactly an ingénue, but she's got some sort of magic about her. Maybe she's what all actresses are like up close—brash, taken with themselves, pent up like a grenade. Probably they need that kind of personality to step in front of an audience and convince people they're somebody they're not. Like my mother. The only time she ever thrived was when she was somebody else. In the real world, she sputtered and died like an engine with a clogged fuel line. She panicked at food shopping, getting her old Ford serviced, anything where she had to be herself around people. She lost perspective. A request to move aside in the grocery aisle registered as hostile, same with another car passing us on the road. Yet, inside a theater, this paranoia evaporated like morning fog curling off the trees behind our house. For her, real was unreal, unreal real.

I wipe a heavy medieval music text with my sleeve and slide it onto a shelf. Lately, I've had my doubts about this whole donation business. I don't need the money the way I did when I first got to New York, with no job and no prospects. And now, three years later, after siring maybe twenty or thirty babies—an awesome thing to think about—I run into some sperm-less guy's wife in the elevator, and she makes an issue out of it. Pretty and forward as a Corvette, she tells me her life story, which I replay over and over, like a song you can't get out of your head. One time I break the rules, and look what happens.

I glance around the store, looking for some distraction, but it's always empty at this hour. Things will pick up about eleven. I lift another music tome off my cart, read the author's last name on the spine and search for its proper slot.

The Strand, at the corner of Broadway and East Twelfth Street, a couple of blocks south of Union Square, is a haven for book lovers from all over the city. The outsized storefront, with its block letters above the door, has faded to a grimy gray. Dusty windows don't reveal much of what goes on inside. Sidewalk bins, that same washed-out gray, display leftover paperbacks for fifty cents apiece. A good deal, if you're a reader, and the Strand's customers are serious readers.

A couple of weeks after stepping off the bus at Port Authority, the last stop on my twelve thousand mile trip home from Vietnam, I happened on this place, not knowing it was the venerable literary locale it's been for years. I walked everywhere then, my body repeating those daily marches from the other side of the world like an echo that wouldn't die. Up and down the island, east and west from river to river—Harlem, Washington Heights, Battery Park, Wall Street, Sutton Place, the derelict piers jutting into the Hudson River from the West Village, the bridge over to Roosevelt Island. I read day-old newspapers fished out of trashcans, sat in the park, took the time I needed to adjust to being in New York City rather than the jungles of Vietnam, to no longer being a soldier, to being free, to being lost.

In a TV store, I watched reports of an anti-war rally in Washington, D.C., in which government business was interrupted and over 12,000 protesters were arrested. It was a weird feeling, seeing how many of your own people hated what you'd done. Of course, we grunts had heard about the protests, and a lot of us felt similarly about the war, though we didn't talk much about it. The reality that you were risking your life for something that made no sense, or worse, for some immoral slaughter, wasn't something we dared confront, much less discuss. Seeing the extent of that protest on TV felt both alarming—the terrible, fruitless waste—and reassuring, that I'd been right about the war from day one. I should have stayed in Canada. I had made the wrong decision. These thoughts churn inside me still.

What if these sperm donations have some stupid connection to my time in Vietnam? What if I'm trying to "replace" some of the innocent kids who died over there? A really crazy thought, but there it is.

Maybe not so crazy. There I was, three years ago, transferring all those jungle marches to Manhattan. Walking, walking, walking, switching one hemisphere for another, substituting another conscription as meaningless as the last. Trying to rid my head of all I'd seen and done over there, insert my mom's bedtime stories, drench myself with her long-ago fascination with Broadway, Times Square, the New York Public Library, the Metropolitan Museum (free admission on Wednesdays), the Sheep's Meadow in Central Park, the Brooklyn Bridge, Wall Street, the Empire State Building. And, among all these destinations, I found the Strand, a place where you could warm up, sit on the floor, read, or just take in the quiet. One day, I asked the cashier if they needed any help. I'd do anything, I told her. She sent me upstairs to talk to the manager, one Joey Maxima. More about him later. And here I am, menially— yet to me, meaningfully and gratefully—employed. The way I see it, the Strand rescued me by giving me long days of finding the proper slot for a book, of repairing its binding, of dusting and sweeping up. The Strand saved my life. I know this for a fact.

The store's customers have a different way about them from most New Yorkers. For one thing, they aren't in a big rush. They browse, they're willing to overlook a few fingerprints or a coffee stain on a book jacket. In fact, it almost seems like they value a book more when it's scarred, as if the volume offers its own history of survival in addition to the wonders it contains inside. That may seem incidental, but you can miss a lot when things have to be perfect all the time. Trust me, I'm an authority on that subject, having kept everything neat as a needle my whole life. But, after some months at the Strand, I began to see that there was a certain kind of beauty in imperfection, a subtle artistry in nonchalance. The staff here would flip if they heard me say that, since I'm the one who's always lining up book spines and squaring off stacks. But I see it. I do. And I've been trying to make impulsiveness a little bigger part of my life lately, to let things take their own course for a change.

Has Karen Tuckwell appeared to test this new spontaneity? I wonder.

The Strand's interior is exactly what you'd expect—a no-nonsense devotion to the printed word. High ceilings accommodate towering islands of books under fluorescent lights. Rickety step ladders and cross-legged readers clutter the aisles. The place smells of parchment, storage and old print. A library, a warehouse, a museum, the Strand makes no attempt to display or attract, like an old lady who knows her charms are internal. Sales at the single cash register, stuffed into a corner like an afterthought, are the result of far more important processes of cataloguing and preservation, search and discovery.

At the rear of the store and up two cramped flights of stairs is Joey Maxima's office, the guy who keeps the whole place afloat, though he's only somewhere in his twenties. He won't reveal exactly where. Desks are set at working angles to each other. Heaps of books and files crowd the typewriters. Metal cabinets do double duty as a partition for his assistant, Celeste, who has been here almost as long as Joey. The mood is subdued, as if the staff, more interested in reading than profits, would rather be downstairs among the stacks, noses down into books.

After finishing up in Music, I roll my cart further down the aisle into Astronomy. The other shelf-stuffer tends to leave the heavy volumes for me, since I get a kick out of hefting a million words enclosed in a single binding, each one insignificant until it was weaved among the others into some unique pattern of meaning. I pick up a text entitled *Light Years Away* and thumb through maps of the heavens, with labels of constellations and distant galaxies, some familiar from lying awake on a grass mat next to my buddy, Ted, in Vietnam. All those nights under the stars of another hemisphere, stars over jungles and muddy rivers and peasant villages, stars over killing, stars over Ted's restless half-snore. Not trusting the night enough to do more than doze, I waited for the first light to clear those serene and menacing hills. Not that you could see your enemy any better in dazzling sunlight.

Joey appears at the end of the aisle. Like a lot of us here, he landed in Manhattan with no special skills and needed to eat. Now he's the head honcho. "Hello, Henry," he sings, squeezing past my cart, making a big deal out of compressing his gut though he's skinny as a periodical. He's the only person on two sides of the world who ever called me Henry.

"How's it going, man?"

"You know I hate being called that."

Joey's shoulder-length hair sports blond highlights, and he has a habit of tucking it behind his ear, where it never stays more than a couple minutes. His fingernails are filed and clear-polished, his pinkies in a constant state of elevation. He wears a single, gold earring and a scarf draped artfully around his shoulders, a man ahead of his time, to put it kindly. Obviously Joey didn't have to worry about the draft. The army isn't that eager to employ guys who act like girls. I try to imagine him carrying a forty-pound rucksack, his blond highlights dripping down his back. The funny thing is, Joey would probably have made it through. He's a whole lot tougher than he looks, and I've never seen him miss as a judge of character, an essential to survival when all you've got is a weird assortment of fellow grunts to count on. Joey senses the truth about a person right off, and if somebody's initial presentation doesn't add up, he doesn't give them the time of day. But when he sees potential, he will pull out all the stops to make things happen as he believes destiny dictates.

"Listen to this," I say, turning back to the book cradled in my arms. "'The Virgo Cluster has a hundred trillion suns.' Jesus, how many zeros is that, anyway?"

"A trillion? Are you sure?" Joey leans over the book.

"And get this—'its gravitational pull is sufficient to retard the expansion of our own local universe.'"

"Isn't that an oxymoron, local universe?" Joey looks up at me and flutters his eyelashes.

"This is science, not literature," I say, stepping back.

"How much more space do we need, anyway? In our universe, I mean."

"It all makes you feel kind of small, doesn't it?"

"Yet, we go on, don't we? Which right now means re-shelving that fascinating book." He checks his nails.

I shrug, close the text and slide it into its slot.

"Pay checks at five," Joey says. He grins. "Don't forget."

"Not likely," I tell him.

He stares at me, raises a pointy fingernail to his chin. Three plastic bracelets—orange, yellow and green—clink dully as they slide up his forearm. Joey seems to be ratcheting up the whole feminine look these days. "How about meeting for drinks later?" he asks me.

Joey and I talked a lot when I first got here, which is a long story, though not what you're probably thinking. We were buddies, best friends, until he got the crazy idea he was in love with me, and that put an end to everything. I have to admit I've missed seeing him. The thought of having a drink now, after nearly a year of avoiding each another, excites me in a way I wouldn't have expected. Sure, I've thought about being friends again, wished for it at times, but his suggesting it now catches me off guard. That's Joey—full of surprises. Still, I wonder if we're not better off keeping our distance. "I don't know," I say, my usual decisive self. "The smoke really gets to me in those places."

"Dinner, then?" There's some of the fearless Bette Davis in his tone, and in the raised eyebrows.

"What about next week?" I ask him, thinking I could use some time to prepare for something you can't really prepare for. In the last year, Joey has brought me coffee on occasion, an appeasement at first, and then a way of—I don't know—staying in touch, I guess. I always thank him, but never know where to direct my eyes when he stands there waiting for me to say who knows what. Dinner sounds hazardous.

"Friday, then, a week from this evening," Joey says, not pushing for tonight, as he might have once.

"Where?"

"Let me see to the details," he says, grinning again. He hooks his hair behind his ear and disappears at the end of the aisle, leaving the vague scent of perfume in his wake.

I decide not to worry about this upcoming dinner. Let it happen. All I have to do is show up, enjoy the food, say goodnight. Life isn't that hard, right?

In Biology, a book on Genetics catches my eye. I pull it and leaf through to Mendel's theory of inherited traits—a blue-eyed parent and a brown-eyed parent are three times more likely to produce a brown-eyed child than a blue. Dominant and recessive genes duking it out for dominance. I try to recall Karen Tuckwell's eye color, but I can only picture a rope of blue smoke curling from her lips into her nostrils as she inhaled, and that quick little skip of a woman in a hurry down the hallway, her glance back at me before she disappeared into the clinic's waiting room two weeks ago.

I'd been down to my last fifteen bucks when I called the New York Hospital Fertility Clinic. I'd seen their ad for donors in the hospital bulletin I picked up on one of my walks. The New York Hospital cafeteria, like the Strand, had become one of my stopping off points where I could get a cheap lunch and linger over a cup of coffee, taking in the invigorating urgency of a medical center—an orderly wheeling a gurney, a doctor's emergency page over the public address system, the wale of an ambulance arriving on First Avenue. I was put on hold, of course, when I called. Then, all of a sudden, I was talking to the director, himself.

"Are you a medical student, Hank?" Dr. McAvery asked me, vestiges of a brogue swelling his r's.

"No, sir."

"Well, we generally only use our own medical students as donors. That way, we assure a minimum level of intelligence."

Having known a medic in Vietnam, dumb as a spent shell, I wondered about that, though I kept my mouth shut. "I'm going to be finishing up my BA at City College," I told McAvery, which was my intent, eventually.

"Are you Jewish?" McAvery asked me.

I guessed that he was short on "gentile" sperm, though it had never occurred to me that the little marathon free-stylers were religious. "No, sir," I replied.

By afternoon, I was shaved and showered and in McAvery's office on East Sixty-Eighth Street. Under a starched white coat, McAvery wore a tweed vest and trousers and a plaid wool tie, probably his tartan from the old country. He held a clipboard in his lap and made entries in blank spaces as we spoke. He explained how they generally got better results with fresh semen rather than frozen, which meant that I would ejaculate at home into a little vial they provided and deliver it here by eight o'clock in the morning.

"Are you a morning person?" McAvery asked me, chuckling.

"No problem. Early to bed, early to rise, that's me."

"What color are your eyes, Henry?" he asked, leaning over to see for himself. He smelled of well-oiled leather.

"Blue, sometimes green, depends," I replied, covering my bases.

"Never brown, though," McAvery assured himself, leaning back. "Women want blue eyes and wavy hair like yours and good teeth."

I flashed a grin.

"I don't understand some of these women," he said. "Why do they marry these chubby bald guys if they want somebody like you to father their kids?"

"Love?"

McAvery studied me, biting his moustache with his lower teeth. "You've got a sense of humor," he said, making a note.

"Maybe they're just, you know, frustrated. And scared."

"You're a smart, too, Hank. They want brains, too. They want everything, these women." He glanced down at his questionnaire. "Relationship status?"

"On hold," I said.

McAvery chuckled. "We'll have to check your blood."

VD, I figured, which, for better or worse, was out of the question. I found the few Manhattan women I ever approached kind of strange. If you aren't well-situated in a law firm or some bank downtown, they lose interest before they reach their stop.

McAvery had asked everything in that interview but my sexual orientation. If my sperm could be Jewish, couldn't they be gay? I pictured the little squiggly guys pausing for some water ballet on their way to a date with an egg they'd just as soon skip. I would have answered "straight," though the more accurate and embarrassing answer would have been "unemployed."

As I close the biology text now, a chill goes through me, remembering McAvery's warning never to take the elevator. Karen Tuckwell. It must not be easy, having some stranger's sperm injected into you. And where was her husband? Shouldn't he have been there with her? And what was she doing coming to see me at eight o'clock in the morning?

The final stop on my tour of the office that day had been the waiting room, a large, bright space with high windows overlooking the corner of First Avenue and Sixty-Eighth Street. A receptionist made notes in a chart. Three men in business suits sat on metal chairs, hiding behind copies of *Newsweek* and the *Wall Street Journal*. Small-minded as it sounds, the sight of those guys with low sperm counts, men who were going to have to rely on me to impregnate their wives, made me feel a kind of potency that was rare for me. I had already created some reproductive ball field, there in McAvery's clinic, where I could be the relief pitcher called in from the sidelines to save the day.

I replace the text. My cart is empty now and I feel worn-out all of a sudden, though there are still hours to go before I can head across town on my bike to Tenth Avenue where I'll make a beeline north to Fifty-Seventh Street, pick up a couple of cans of tuna, some chips and a six-pack, and get back to my collection of O. Henry stories.

In the basement, loading more books onto my cart, I try to picture Karen's life in some fancy Eastside apartment or maybe a Westchester County dream house with a swimming pool and a good school nearby. And, of course, I try to picture the baby, only it's a five-or-six-year-old kid I see, running around the yard, a Golden Retriever yapping at his rear, his only worry that his dad might be late getting home from his office in the city.

Finally, five o'clock arrives and I wheel my cart to the elevator. As the door slides open, Joey appears, all smiles, with three or four envelopes in his hand. "You're rich," he says, handing me one.

Scrawled in a flourish on the back is the name of a restaurant—The Paris Commune—and an address on Bleecker Street, and next Friday's date, February 25, 1974, 7:00 pm.

Joey winks and minces down the aisle into Religion.

6

JOEY'S FIRST LOVE

The idea of meeting Henry for dinner next week has me skipping through Religion, skimming my fingers over the spines of who knows how many meditative and indecipherable tomes.

Henry Preston. Sounds like the name of a Royal Canadian Mounted Policeman, doesn't it? And he looks the part—square-jawed, square-shouldered, refreshingly square in every way. I vow, despite my tendency to make him fidget, to curb my penchant for excess at our first real rendezvous in almost a year. I will make the evening a success. I've missed him like a stool misses a leg.

When Henry arrived here at the Strand three years ago, I felt sorry for him. He seemed so lost and alone after his service in Vietnam. He never did open up about that awful war, not to the extent he needed to I don't think. Something happened to him over there, something to do with his friend who didn't make it back, a man named Ted. More than that, I can't say. It was the least I could do to give him a job. We owed so much to all those men who returned home forever scarred by that war. I assumed, after he got himself established in Manhattan, he'd move on to brighter prospects beyond the Strand. But, happily, he stayed on.

And then, to my surprise, I discovered that I enjoyed talking to him, enjoyed silently filling in the gaps in his halting speech, understanding somehow, without his actually having to say the words, just how disheartened he'd been by the war. But long before that, too. I identified a lot with some of the things he said, though it took me a while to realize this, since the details of our childhoods were very different. The essentials, though—feeling different, feeling left out and lost—were the same. Over time, I found comfort just being near Henry Preston, taking in his quiet demeanor, his scent of books and flannel and the oil he uses on his bicycle. He calmed me, slowed me down, made me notice and appreciate smaller things. Time, for example, though surely that is a very large thing, companionship, affection, hope. Come to think of it, these are all big things! Frog to prince, Henry went from a timid book schlepper to my Mounty. I should have been more wary of these schoolgirl feelings. Falling in love, after all, was something I had put on hold indefinitely. Or at least until I was the woman I am determined to be. But the evidence became overwhelming. Suddenly I was spending ages in front of the mirror, humming sappy tunes, longing to be touched. I realized at some point that I had installed innocent Henry into the space reserved for my fantasy life partner. Of course, he was nothing like the debonair man I'd always dreamed of. But that mattered about as much as a late notice on my credit card. He was the man I wanted, period, end of discussion.

It would be a struggle, of course, getting him to see me as the love of *his* life. But struggle is my middle name. I would make that happen too.

And, in fact, he did get beyond the surface confusion of Joey Maxima, and our relationship flourished when we got to know each other, sharing a closeness that few people ever attain. Henry, despite his inner complexity, has always viewed the world in pretty straight-forward terms, with an emphasis on straight! And yet, I know that my adorable and virginal Sgt. Preston has the potential to see beyond the normal bounds that limit us all. Time, time was all we needed.

The trick, at our upcoming dinner, will be to hold back and not scare him off this time, as I did a year ago with an unnecessary protestation of my feelings. And yet, I can already feel the tingling pleasure, the relief, of seeing him alone again after all this time. And I believe I detected, just now, some similar sort of anticipation in Henry. No woman will ever know him or understand him the way I do. What I find mysterious and unspoiled in Henry, she would likely consider boring or naïve. And she would miss his melancholy. Of course, that's easy to say, since there is no other woman, since Henry is so delightfully chaste.

What is love, anyway? Attempting to explain it seems to demean it somehow. Thank God there's something in this world we can't account for or control. Like the last person I fell in love with, who was also the first. Yes, love, no other word for it, though I was only a precocious thirteen at the time. No doubt we love more profoundly at that age than we do after caution and cynicism have creeped in.

First loves take us over and never entirely let us go.

On the opening day of eighth grade, my mother pulled her Lincoln Continental to the curb in front of Evanston Junior High. Ancient elms buttressed the deceptive calm of School Street. A whiff of autumn apprehension wafted through the car's open windows. I hated my outfit.

They were rich, my parents. No need went unmet that September of 1964, except my secret ones, those agonizing hourly needs of an adolescent would-be girl. My father was the kind of man who, had he been poor, would have installed a home-made manifold in the lawnmower to improve its efficiency. And he'd have expected me to join him in each greasy, odiferous moment. Instead, he had invented a tiny dehumidifier which fit perfectly into every United States tank and fighter plane and helicopter of World War II, and in every commercial jet rolling off the line at Boeing or Lockheed after that. He believed in money, status, and of course the mind-boggling value of tiny objects. In other words, he was oblivious to anything that mattered to me.

His marriage, like his factory, ran smoothly, with minimal and mostly delegated effort. There was only one blemish in the whole shiny surface of his life—me—and before that, the twelve-year absence of a better me—his own biological son. My parents had waited that long before deciding to accept a stand-in. That twelve-year strain of trying and failing to conceive might have brought them closer—their first and apparently only adversity—or it might have driven them silently apart. Who could tell? Most likely their barrenness was the essential hidden element that held them together while simultaneously cooling them toward each other, like those trusty little dehumidifiers that made the rest of their lives so enviable.

The grand piano in the living room was littered with black and white photographs in silver frames. Me in my long christening gown, my one legitimate opportunity to wear a dress. Me holding a cluster of balloons. Me standing next to a pony, eyes averted from the smelly beast. The three of us look stiff and artificial, like those cardboard figures of famous people you can get your picture taken with at carnivals, a convincing deception, from afar.

I used to stare at those photos, wondering where the truth lay. Truth, I was already learning, was not what you see; it's what you don't see. It's not what people say; it's what they don't say. Though as the three of us age over the years of these photos, the truth seems to emerge, despite our efforts to keep it at bay. I look increasingly as if I'm about to burst into tears. My father looks progressively apprehensive, as if he'd made an unsuitable investment that wasn't paying anticipated dividends. My mother looks ever more careworn.

Before she turned left, onto School Street, I thought about asking her to drop me at the corner, out of sight. But I didn't want her to think I was ashamed of her, because I wasn't. I loved my mother, though her taste in dresses ran to the matronly, as did her sense of interior decor. But these were the least of the things I couldn't tell her.

I rode in back like a little prince, one hand on the door handle, the other a brace to the front seat. Brilliant patches of sunlight slid across the car's gleaming hood, dazzled the windshield and passed overhead. I loved fine automobiles, even then—the flashy hood ornament, the whisper of the leather seats, the reassuring hum of the electric windows. Yet I told myself that money wasn't important. It was 1964 after all, and I was in sympathy with the negroes marching in Alabama and the hippies moving into Haight-Asbury in San Francisco. Dissonance was my closest friend.

"Bye, Mom," I said, leaning to kiss her powdered cheek. I grabbed the stitched leather handles of my monogrammed briefcase, a present from my father in honor of the first day of school. Inside were special slots for my slide rule and protractor—efficient, expensive, and as uncool as acne. The back doors of the Lincoln opened toward the front, suicide doors they were called, appropriately enough. I was prepared to run as soon as my feet hit the pavement. No, maybe not run. The peculiar gait I possessed was somewhere between a grandmother's late-to-church skip and the lurch of an adolescent in her first pair of heels. A brisk walk would do, past boy clicks and girl clicks to the side of the building, where I could disappear into its shadow and wait for the opening bell. In a rush of self-consciousness, I pushed the car's heavy door into a group of tight-sweatered, grade-repeating black girls from the south side of Evanston. One had dated a high school senior last year. Another wasn't at all modest about the baby she left at home with her grandmother. Together, they lowered the temperature of the entire area and sapped it of every last gasp of oxygen.

"Watch out, girlfriend!" the tall one yelled. I slammed the door shut and kept moving.

"It's only Josephine," the young mother added.

"Oh, her," said a third.

My pits dampened. Crossing the lawn, I pictured my mom—jaw set, shoulders braced—slipping the car into gear and gliding, mortified, away. She didn't deserve the letdown that was me. Worse, I imagined her telephoning my father at his office, her voice stiff with indignation. He'd mention boarding school again, to him a face-saving respite, to me a school day's tribulations stretched round the clock.

At seven-thirty that morning, I had procrastinated, attempting to calm my first-day-of-school jitters. T-shirts and jeans and corduroys spilled from open drawers like severed body parts. I believed that the right outfit, if I could only come up with it, would provide the armor I so desperately needed to face a new school year. But fitting-in clothes—khakis, button-down shirts, loafers—felt like quicksand engulfing me one taper and crease at a time. Standing in my underpants, I took in my reflection in the mirrored closet door. At thirteen, when boys jostled toward the exacting sort of manhood that would always elude me, my thighs were still skinny and hairless and left an ambivalent space where they met my torso. My chest and hips still refused to provide some swelling, rounding confirmation of what I so urgently felt—female.

People who think that dying is the worst thing, don't know a whole lot about living.

I pulled on a Rugby shirt—wide blue and yellow stripes, white collar. Rugby, a huddled bunch of sweaty, mud-spattered men grunting and pushing against each other. For what purpose? I tied a silk scarf around my neck, purloined from my mother's bureau, and let the ends cascade over my shoulder. The paisley pattern complemented the bold stripes, sort of. Maybe not. I discarded the jersey and pulled on a pink polo shirt that fell to mid-thigh. I turned left and right into the mirror. Yes, this was more like it. A pair of flip-flops would complete the look. But I'd never be allowed in school in this getup. I pulled off the shirt and scarf and kicked them into the closet where they landed atop a row of shoes. I have always loved footwear, arranging and rearranging rows of penny loafers, slippers and sneakers, a favorite pastime. A dusty, never-worn pair of hiking boots occupied the far corner; an outgrown pair of sandals with a slight heel was too prized to throw away. Whenever I was left alone in our sprawling house overlooking Lake Michigan, I snuck to my mother's dressing room, where I tried on my favorites—an esteemed pair of green alligator pumps, an open-toed crimson heel. In the shuttered darkness of her room, I was a young woman, not an effeminate freak whose only recourse was to hide, as if anybody could hide who they were.

After the third hurry-up call from my mother, I retrieved the Rugby shirt and pulled it on over a pair of khakis and ran downstairs.

Rounding the corner of the school building now, I expelled a sigh of relief, like the day they cancelled gym class due to fumes in the locker room, as if the locker room was ever anything but rank. I flattened myself against the brick wall, glancing up at the windows overhead, those ever-gaping merciless perches of the princes of meanness. The sun skulked behind a cloud. Soon, fat raindrops splatted the macadam. I let my back slide down the bricks. The blotched surface of my new briefcase seemed to symbolize my life—fine and yet unwanted, ruined by elements beyond anyone's control.

I began wiping away the drops with my sleeve when I noticed a pair of feet just visible behind the dumpster parked at the edge of the asphalt lot. Restless brown tie shoes, in need of polish, drooping athletic socks, once white. Who would ever wear such things? The weight they carried shifted nervously from one to the other. My impulse was to flee, just as the shoes made their way around the side of the dumpster, bringing their owner into view.

He was new at Evanston Junior High, and older, fifteen maybe. My heart warmed to the sight of someone who seemed as out of place as I felt. A lusterless belt buckle held up ill-fitting jeans, frayed at the knees; his wrinkled shirt struck me as a delightful vision of happenstance. Raindrops nestled in a mushroom of wooly curls. Spotty sideburns billowed from skin the exact color of his shoes.

He leaned against the dumpster, an affected nonchalance I recognized as my own, and pulled a pack of Winstons from his shirt pocket. He shook one loose and withdrew it with his lips. Some unprecedented exhilaration crowded out my usual wariness as this apparition raised the pack and pointed it at me. I shook my head.

His right hand hid in his jeans pocket. I imagined the warmth there, a bunch of pennies and the occasional nickel or dime nestled among tiny tufts of lint. He extracted a lighter and in one quick motion, brushed it against his thigh and set the flame to the end of the cigarette. I do love affectation! He drew in deeply and let out an airy plume that drifted alongside the dumpster, a hopeful striated cloud in a mottled sky. I made a mental note to take up smoking.

The school bell rang out. He took another drag, cupping the cigarette against the rain like a construction worker on a scaffold. He wiped his forehead with the back of his hand. Could he be more sensational?

I inched my way toward the corner of the building, unable to extract my gaze from those intense brown eyes. I was tempted to glance behind me, unable to believe that his attention was truly on me. The second bell rang out—two long blasts. My hand seemed to rise from my side of its own accord. He stood away from the dumpster, dropped his cigarette and stepped on it. I waved and ran round the side to the front steps.

For the rest of that week, I arrived early for school and walked straight to the rear of the building, where I took up my position against the school wall, waiting for the boy with the brown shoes. I didn't sleep well those nights, with long dark hours of trying to decipher the strange feelings gyrating inside my body—concentric rings of excitement, trepidation and dizzying anticipation. What had he wanted? Would he come again? I dared to believe that he wasn't planning to trick me, that we were somehow destined to relieve each other's dreadful aloneness.

Twice that week, we passed in the hallway, two thrilling flashes of linked eyes. Yet, he never showed up again at the dumpster. On Friday, it rained again. The wipers of my mother's Lincoln made psychedelic streaks of the taillights ahead of us. I brought along my new push-button umbrella. I was running late. Stylish outfits for inclement weather are a challenge. I had settled on a white shirt, tails-out over khakis, cuffs left unbuttoned to flap around my wrists. I kissed my mother goodbye and made my way across the lawn, dodging puddles. Stragglers hurried up the walk, hunched against the rain. Juggling briefcase and umbrella, I ran along the side wall and rounded the corner to the rear of the building, where I halted, in horror. The dumpster had disappeared. Raindrops obscured the parallel scars its iron wheels had left in the pavement. It had been hauled away, and with it my dreams of ever encountering the beautiful boy again.

The second bell rang out. I turned to leave and there he stood, not three feet away, this curious and remarkable fellow misfit with stubbled chin, a diamond of rain dripping from his ear and crinkles of apprehension widening heartrending eyes. "Whoa," he said, taking hold of my shoulders and steadying me. His damp brown skin glowed in shiny perfection.

"Who are you?" was all I could think to say, a good question, as it would turn out.

The dimple in his cheek deepened with his smile. He let go of my shoulders. "Jarmon," he said.

One hand gripping the wet handles of my absurdly elegant briefcase, the other my unfurled umbrella, I thought, Take me with you.

"I ain't gonna hurt you," he said.

Imagine the thrill—his first declaration the one I most needed to hear. I guessed that this strange boy, Jarmon, had known ridicule and probably other sorts of pain as well. The final insistent blasts of the school bell rang out and we ran together under the dripping eaves to the front door. Heaven!

All that September and well into October, I met Jarmon where the dumpster had once sat. I prevailed upon him not to smoke since it would mean a week's suspension if he was caught, and how then would we have our lovely morning rendezvous? Jarmon complied, providing me with a fledgling sense of power. Eventually, we began to meet in the afternoon, after school, under a giant copper beech tree in Crown Park, just off Main Street.

"Where do you live?" I asked him.

"South Evanston."

South Evanston was littered with decrepit, once grand Victorian houses that had been broken up into apartments. Mostly blacks lived there, a few Hispanics and Asians, people who mowed lawns and cleaned houses like my parents' on the opposite side of town.

"What does your dad do?" I asked him.

Jarmon grunted and looked at me as if this were an impertinent question, which of course it was. "What dad?" he said.

"You live with your mom, then?"

"She's dead."

It had been hard, those first weeks, to know what to talk about with Jarmon. The things kids usually discussed—dates, drama club, football games, school dances—were not in our repertoire, and what we really needed to tell each other, what neither of us had ever put into words, would be weeks in coming. We never expected to be invited to each other's homes. We never expected to go to a movie together. It had been clear from the beginning that our friendship would be secret, involving only one another, which for me, and probably for Jarmon, had been a relief and eventually a joy.

Being with a boy two years older than me was the one thing that seemed perfectly natural. I always felt, and very much acted, older than I was, one way of distancing myself from my adolescent tormentors, no doubt. My feigned maturity cast them as juveniles and therefore discountable. Jarmon and I, on the other hand, were peers, however weird we may have looked together.

On Saturdays, he rode his bike from the south side to meet me. I imagined this bicycle to be his one prized possession, its chrome gleaming, its three gears meshing in the faint odor of fresh lubricant. We walked everywhere, Jarmon steering the bike with one hand on the leather seat, turning it left or right with the deft tilt of his sleeveless, sinewy arm. Seething or simply laconic, he looked to me to fill the vivid space between us with stories about myself, which I became only too willing to do. I romanticized my future as a reckless, thrill-seeking individualist who would have little time for ordinary people like our classmates. I would design clothing or cars or buildings. I would travel the world as a special envoy to some distant and exotic somewhere. Jarmon never doubted the veracity of these fantasies, which caused me to believe in them myself, nor did he seem to place himself in them as my partner, my fellow traveler, my lover, as I secretly did.

"My parents took me to a shrink when I was five," I told him one afternoon in November, as we meandered along a path that bordered Lake Michigan. Jarmon, unfazed, steered his bicycle around a puddle. "My father discovered me cleaning my room in a housedress."

"He shoulda been happy you were doin' your chores," Jarmon said.

Simple wisdom, one of the things I loved about Jarmon. "The shrink let me play with all sorts of toys scattered around his office. I, of course, zeroed in on the doll house." My eyes darted to Jarmon, who grinned and flipped a toothpick across his ample lips. "The shrink wanted to know what the man and woman in the pretty little house were thinking. And the little boy, of course."

Jarmon flung his toothpick into the grass. I had treaded, quite deliberately, into the precarious terrain of my femininity. Not that Jarmon hadn't noticed, of course, but words had yet to be put to even the most obvious personal facts. The idea that I might be able to share this aspect of myself with someone filled me with excitement. Also dread.

"I remember wondering where the little girl of the family was, but I sensed that asking would mean I would have to spend even more time with this man." Unable to decipher how the laconic Jarmon was reacting, I decided to drop the story there and maybe pick it up later on. "We should go," I said, gesturing to the street that lead back to the center of Evanston.

"Wish I seen you all dressed up like that," Jarmon said.

I turned to him.

"I bet you was pretty."

A flood of warmth invaded my chest, some incipient thawing of my icy center. "You mean that? You're not making fun?"

He shook his head.

"You're the strangest, most wonderful person I ever met," I told him.

"You too," he said.

Jarmon ignited some new boldness in me, setting fire to the smoldering future I had always imagined when I finally met somebody like him. That's the thing about stories—you tell them often enough and they become real. "Do you want to kiss me?" I asked him.

Jarmon looked down at his bicycle, then back up at me. "Never kissed a boy before."

"I'm not so sure," I said, "that I'm a boy, I mean."

He nodded again.

I raised my face to him and closed my eyes. Seconds passed, whole minutes it seemed. Then there was the brush of his sweet dry lips against mine and that exquisite thawing inside me spread right and left and up and down until I thought I might collapse right there on that path by the lake.

"Think you might dress up like that for me sometime?" he whispered.

"Maybe," I said.

Jarmon and I saw each other every day during that winter of ninth grade, except Sundays when he accompanied his two aunts to church and had dinner with various family members he didn't seem to know very well. We were best friends, though that designation missed the mark entirely. Sometimes we kissed. Sometimes I cried at a perceived slight and he reached that sinewy arm around my shoulders, mumbling reassurances. What words could I have possibly come up with to describe the intensity of my feelings? I believed, even then, that an accurate verbal description offered mastery of a situation. But with Jarmon, all descriptors failed, and this only enhanced my view of our remarkable pairing.

We rarely fought. In fact, we had none of the steep ups and downs that seemed to plague the first loves of our "normal" fellow ninth graders. We took walks, rode Jarmon's bike and discussed the inevitability of our luminous futures. We were so steady, I began to wonder if something was missing. Did we not ask enough of each other? The point of being with Jarmon, it seemed, was simply that, to be together.

We were never at a loss for things to talk about. In February, the Beatles made their sensational appearance on the Ed Sullivan Show and Jarmon predicted that these four odd-looking English lads would change the entire face of rock-n-roll. In March, Jarmon told me about Malcolm X, how he'd been suspended from the Nation of Islam and was forming his own group of black nationalists. Jarmon believed that Malcolm, like the Beatles, was destined to make great changes in our country, maybe even the whole world. Finally, a black man had stepped forward who understood all that was wrong with society and how to fix it. I listened, not always following, but wanting to believe because Jarmon did. I feared that this most obvious difference between us had the potential to do us in, and the more I could learn about it, the better my defense. I would never be black, of course, but I could be a cool white person, like the ones who marched alongside Dr. King and his people in Alabama. I could understand the plight of a negro boy because my body had betrayed me too, its gender, not its color, but misery and shame hurt the same, whatever their source. Wasn't that our bond, that we were different and somehow the same—less in the eyes of the world, but astonishing to each other? Wasn't this differentness what had placed us there by the dumpster that first day of school? And wasn't our shared hope that we could prove everybody wrong?

Then, later that month, Kitty Genovese, a twenty-eight-year-old woman from Queens in New York City, was attacked. Thirty-eight of her neighbors watched and listened and didn't respond as she was stabbed to death right there in front of her home. Thirty-eight! Jarmon was outraged. Such a total lack of caring for your fellow man was beyond his comprehension. What sickness had invaded our country? What future did we have if we cared so little about one another? At one point, he even threw his bike to the ground and stomped off, leaving me to wonder, as I righted his single physical possession, at Jarmon's immeasurable pain and how I could possibly help.

That winter, it seemed, his whole being became the site of some exhausting struggle to make sense of a merciless world. He appeared actually to diminish in size from the heroic, Winston-smoking tough at the dumpster behind school to a lost and irate waif, gnashing away at his own overwhelming impotence, like a beaver caught in a trap. I was at a loss for what to do to help. I had only myself to offer him, and that I did, hoping to ease his sense of alienation as he had relieved mine that fall. But he hardly seemed to notice my devotion. It seemed I wasn't as important to him as he had become to me.

I had nobody, of course, with whom I could share my gradually increasing trepidation over Jarmon. That left my mother. One Friday afternoon in late April, I sat across from her at the kitchen table where she worked a crossword puzzle. A gentle spring breeze wafted the curtains, the hopeful fragrance of new life competing with the smolder of her cigarette.

"Outcast," she said, touching the pencil's eraser to her chin. "P blank blank i blank blank."

"Pariah."

She grinned and entered the letters, unaware of the irony in the question. "You're amazing," she said.

"I know."

"Plenty. P-R blank-blank-blank, S blank-blank-blank."

"I met someone," I said. Of course I had known Jarmon nearly eight months by then, but I needed to ease her into this discussion. She drew on her cigarette and set it at the edge of a crystal ashtray. "At school," I persevered. I had the urge to pick up her Pall Mall and take a drag, anything to shock her into some sort of response. I had tried a puff or two of Jarmon's Winston, but they'd only left me with a nasty taste and a headache. Could my remote mother help me decipher my own perilous puzzle? "Actually, behind school, near the loading platform," I said.

"The loading platform? What were you doing back there?"

"Talking to someone I like."

"That's nice. What's his name?"

His. Was my mother more intuitive than I had realized? I felt dizzy and glanced over at her puzzle to steady myself. "Profusion," I said. She looked at me quizzically. "Plenty in nine letters—profusion."

She studied the page. "My God, you're right!" she exclaimed, entering the letters.

"Jarmon. His name is Jarmon."

"What sort of name is that?" We locked eyes a few seconds longer than we had in the entire thirteen years I had known her. She knew just what sort of name Jarmon was and very likely suspected that Jarmon was far more than the casual friend I was describing. "Who are his people?"

"I don't think he has any people."

"What does his father do? Where does he live?"

"His father's dead."

"Oh, dear. How old is. . . ."

The princess phone rang out from its perch on the wall by the kitchen door. We both reached for it. She won. I could tell from her side of the conversation that it was my father on the line, with his nightly offer to pick up anything she needed on his way home from the office. The last time my mother had needed him to stop for something was six years ago—a jar of mustard—and he'd forgotten. Apparently she'd taken this oversight as part of a larger disregard, because since then, she hadn't, or wouldn't, ask anything of him. Still, daily at five o'clock, he called and inquired one more time.

She said goodbye and hung up the phone. "You must try not to annoy your father, Joey. He has a lot on his mind right now."

Annoy? What had I done? "Like what?"

"Oh, like that Barry Goldwater ruining Republican prospects. And Johnson's War on Poverty. Your father says we'll all be going to the poor house."

The things that upset my father were the very glimmers of hope Jarmon discerned on the political horizon. My mother moved to the cupboard over the sink and began to set out plates, forsaking the question of Jarmon's family lineage or anything else about him. "I think it's lovely you've found a friend," she said, putting a period after our little talk. "That's all we really need in this world, a good friend or two."

As far as I could tell, my mother lacked this essential ingredient. I wondered if, like me, she was some sort of misfit, though it wasn't obvious why she wouldn't fit in just fine with the wives of my father's business associates. I pitied her. She held back, for no apparent reason. And her isolation appeared so desolate, whereas mine, with Jarmon, was new and splendid and amazing.

The next day, I carried my briefcase to my rendezvous with Jarmon, emptied of notebooks and science texts and stuffed with a silk scarf of my mother's and a "gypsy" blouse with a scooped neckline. I even slid a stolen lipstick into the slide-rule slot.

We met, as usual, in Robert Crown Park at the foot of the giant copper beech tree that afforded a view of Dodge Avenue to the east and Main Street along the south side of the park. We liked to lean against the tree's massive trunk and take in the old man who read the *Evanston Gazette* every day on a nearby bench, the housewives and nannies pushing strollers, finicky leashed dogs sniffing the edged corners of nascent flower beds. Cheering Jarmon became an increasingly daunting task. I commented on people's fashion choices, taking encouragement from the occasional deepening of the dimple in his left cheek. "Check out the wrap on that one," I said, pointing to a woman's pink car coat, and "Fuuunky!" about an elaborately furled, orange hat with a cascade of green feathers oozing down the back.

Bored, we climbed onto Jarmon's bike, me on the seat, Jarmon pedaling through traffic lights and pedestrian crossings without so much as a pause to consider his right of way. This recklessness was new, one part thrilling, two parts chilling. His untucked shirt flapped; his lean back muscles rippled like the waves of Lake Michigan. He smelled of the park's rich April earth as he leaned into turns. I abandoned the impulse to right us, letting Jarmon take charge, and discovering that surrender could be exhilarating.

Six traffic lights and a couple of side-streets later, the sparkling surface of Lake Michigan came into view—smooth and flat, its subtle currents hardly visible from the street. Jarmon cut across a blotch of scrub grass by a service station and turned down a path through low brush, screeching the brakes as he angled around branches and rock outcroppings. Glarings of sun-dazzled lake flashed through low foliage, momentarily blinding us. When the path got too steep, we dismounted and hid the bike under a stand of budded burning bush. Jarmon took my hand in his rough palm as we ducked under a wild grapevine so thick it made hammocks between trees. Of course, I wouldn't have known a grapevine from a sunflower or a burning bush if Jarmon hadn't pointed them out.

Arriving at the shoreline, he threw himself onto a rock outcropping and patted a spot next to him. We sat, taking in gentle eddies around shoreline boulders and the trunks of trees clinging at impossible angles over the water. The eroding bank exposed great masses of intertwined root systems, down to the delicate hairs that held them in place and supplied them with their essential nutrients. Even these scruffy oaks obtained what they needed in order to survive, I mused. Of course, some didn't and fell away. But the ones remaining proclaimed that life was possible, even under the most adverse of circumstances.

"Ever wonder what it'd be like to walk straight out in the water and just keep on goin'?" Jarmon asked me. "Do you think you could keep from savin' yourself?"

"Personally, I prefer terra firma for a stroll." I said, squinting into the lake's blinding surface, unsettled by the question.

"So what's in here?" he asked me after a while, pointing to my briefcase. "Didn't drag your books all the way down here, did ya?"

My heart thumped with that familiar mix of excitement and dread Jarmon brought up in me. Would he understand that being female was as essential to me as the grasping roots of those oaks were to them? Would he laugh? I unclasped the briefcase and pulled out my mother's scarf. Its pattern of golden urns filled with ivy appeared just right in the dappled sunlight, or ludicrous, depending on your point of view I suppose. Jarmon eased the scarf from my hand and ran it back and forth over his arm, letting it slide along the smooth dark surface of his skin. He sniffed it. "Wow," he whispered, apparently engrossed in that flood of sensations. He lifted the scarf to his cheek, then to mine. "Sweet, huh?"

I nodded.

"Like my little Joey."

For sure, Jarmon was unlike any kid I had ever known. But did I know him, really? He'd never said how he got to Evanston or how his mother had died or where he'd been the years before that. At fifteen, he had a highly developed sense of right and wrong, sometimes finding both in a single matter and then struggling to determine where he stood in that murky moral mix. His deep and brooding concern, more evident every day, was for the world in general, but also for himself, for what was left of his family, and maybe for me. Was I of interest as one more example of society's failure? I was both rich and oppressed—two failures in one. Was I a case study he would, of necessity, have to abandon one day?

Sitting there by the lake with Jarmon, I realized just how small my own desires were—to be the young woman I believed myself to be and to be with someone I loved. Jarmon would make the world a better place. I would cook dinner.

He held the diagonal ends of the scarf and twirled it a couple of times, then leaned over and tied it around my neck. He ran the backs of his fingers along my cheek. His dimple deepened. "You okay?" he whispered.

I nodded and Jarmon undid the buttons of my shirt and pushed the collar open, exposing my bare neck and collar bones. I forced a smile, trying to picture myself as Jarmon saw me.

"You look pretty," he said.

Heat rose in my face. Overwhelmed, I turned to the horizon, where identical blues meshed, water and air indistinguishable. Jarmon took my chin and turned my face back to him. He leaned over and kissed me on the mouth. His lips were damp and warm, and their touch sent a tremor through me that I imagined could be felt in the shifting currents of the lake, all the way to the invisible horizon.

Excitement or terror, who knew?

7

THE COPPER BEECH

Soon, longer days proclaimed the arrival of spring in earnest. New leaves unfurled their delicate, veined faces. Daffodils and hyacinths scented Crown Park. But, as can happen in the Midwest, spring soon succumbed to an airless humidity, school ended, and I marveled that Jarmon and I had known each other for over nine months. My first love had arrived unbidden and yanked me along with it, a thrilling and alarming sensation I now feared doing without. What if something were to happen to Jarmon? Or what if he suddenly left Evanston, as he had any number of towns before, seeking a home where he hadn't yet overstayed his welcome? And there was always lurking along the edges and around the corners of our time together this mission of changing the world, which he could hardly accomplish here in little-noticed, suburban Evanston.

He took a summer job at a bicycle repair shop. I spent my days reading, tweezing a sprinkling of fuzz from my upper lip and experimenting with various hair and clothing styles, filling the time until I could meet Jarmon at four o'clock, when the bike shop closed. What a sloth I was then, with no interest or ambition or desire other than Jarmon. Perhaps, besides raging hormones, first loves are gripping because they divert us from the emotional perils of proceeding from child to adult, which Jarmon so effectively held at bay for me.

But Jarmon's discontent mushroomed that June. He accused his boss of being oblivious to his abilities, assigning him the lowest of tasks and never allowing him direct contact with customers. Was this routine for an entry level job at a bike shop? I had no idea. Would a handsome, willing white boy be denied access to customers? Did Jarmon's surliness come through and spoil his chances? Jarmon was increasingly convinced that the opportunity to prove himself would never come. I listened to his complaints and wondered how you change someone's view of the world, how you describe hope to somebody who has never known it.

Freed from the confines of school and encouraged by Jarmon's inexplicable approval, I became more radical in my presentation. On a particularly sweltering July 2, I wore pink shirttails over skintight Bermuda shorts, set off by skimpy sandals. Such garb seems innocuous enough now, but then? I would find the true me, I trusted, by letting myself be seen in all manner of guises and observing people's reactions, including my own. What self-concept do we have, after all, other than what we read in the eyes of our beholders? But my questions went beyond the insufferably superficial. What would I believe in, what important contribution would I make, and to what cause? I had no idea, though I suspected that the answers to these questions lay somewhere alongside Jarmon. Outsiders, we would conspire together to find our purpose.

We met that afternoon under the copper beech, whose leaves of ruby rust glowed golden in the afternoon sun. Even Jarmon seemed to shine that day. When I asked what all the good cheer was about, he simply said, "Get on," indicating his bicycle seat. "We'll miss it." I gripped his sides as he pedaled furiously in the direction of South Evanston and the lake. His t-shirt clung to his sweat-dampened back, his power, grace and undefined potential seemingly unlimited that day. After several blocks, he pulled up in front of a decrepit-looking bar. We dismounted and he leaned his bike against the side of the building.

"What's going on?" I asked him, glancing to several cases of empty liquor bottles and some abandoned beer kegs littering the ground.

Jarmon jumped on top of a rusted barrel, standing on end against the building, pulled himself atop the shed roof and turned to help me up. He cupped his hands to a window and peered inside. "What are we doing, Jar?" I whispered. His hand indicated that I should wait my turn. Finally, he stepped aside. I wiped away the cloud of moisture left by his breath and squinted through the glass. Twenty or thirty patrons, most of them men, all of them black, sat on stools and stood in small groups around the bar. "What?" I hissed, nervous about being discovered.

"The TV."

A jumpy screen showed President Johnson sitting at a desk, signing what looked like a graduation diploma. "The Civil Rights Act," Jarmon whispered, cupping his hands against the glass so we could both see. "History in the makin'."

A group of men in suits were arrayed behind the President and he handed each one a pen when he finished signing. One was Bobby Kennedy, my own personal hero. He looked incredibly sad, like Jarmon did that summer. Maybe he was thinking it should have been his brother signing that bill instead of

Johnson. Life was unfair, his look seemed to say. He was the first to turn away from the proceedings and angle his way out through the crowd.

Jarmon and I stood there, side by side, watching as the President acknowledged silent applause before the screen switched to some reporter for comment. A few men in the bar hugged and patted each other on the back. The bartender poured drinks.

Jarmon jumped down and I followed. He threw his leg over the bike's crossbar.

"Aren't we going in?" I asked him, gesturing toward the bar. Maybe one of the men in the bar was Jarmon's father. Who knew? Or at least a stand-in.

Jarmon laughed. "You're thirteen, Joey Maxima, and white as Hellmann's Mayonnaise. Hop on." He patted his bicycle seat.

"Fourteen soon enough," I said, wrapping my arms around Jarmon's middle. I wondered if he would still want to be with the likes of me now that he had his civil rights. We never discussed the fact of his brownness and my whiteness. Sometimes the most obvious things are the most difficult to address. I would have said it didn't make any difference, though of course it made every difference in the world and no doubt accounted, at least in part, for our attraction to each other, for our absolute isolation from other teenagers and for our eventual demise as a couple. Watching the signing of the Civil Rights Act together could conceivably have raised such a discussion, had we been more prepared to deal with our situation realistically. We might even have acknowledged what we both probably feared, that things couldn't last for us. That there was no way.

He rode us back to the park and leaned his bicycle against the copper beech. We sat against the tree's huge trunk. I preferred the lake, where we could be alone on the rocky shoreline and hold hands. "So, we're equals now, you and me," I said, stepping gingerly in the direction of that dreaded discussion.

"According to the law, anyways." Jarmon's joy on this momentous occasion for all black people faded, had been subdued to begin with. He didn't do happiness.

I pulled at the leather strap of my sandal, a deluge of undecipherable questions descending on me. Was Jarmon my boyfriend? Did that mean we were homosexuals? Nothing about Jarmon seemed homosexual, but how could you tell, anyway? And me? Whatever sexual category I fell into defied definition. I wanted to *be* a girl, not have sex with one. I was attracted to boys. Yet, it seemed I was neither a gay boy nor a straight girl. My problem was gender, not sex. Sex, itself, seemed like some mysterious hurdle that lay somewhere off in the future. Would Jarmon and I ever go there? What would that entail, exactly?

"It'll take a while to work out the kinks, I guess," Jarmon was saying. "Years, probably, if I know white folk."

So many worries Jarmon held inside. Takes one to know one, I thought. "But it's still cause to celebrate," I said, pulling an Almond Joy candy bar out of my pocket, Jarmon's favorite. I tore off the wrapper and handed him half.

He smiled, took a bite and scanned the park. The afternoon was unnaturally quiet, as if a bomb had been dropped, which, metaphorically speaking, I suppose it had, a thousand miles east in Washington, D.C. And that bomb, according to Jarmon, would send tremors through this country for years to come. I felt scared, for Jarmon, and I suppose for myself. His "otherness" was out there for everyone to see. My rejection of my gender was less obvious, an "otherness" I could possibly hide if I had to. And yet it seemed an anathema beyond any sort of acceptance, something even worse than being black. I removed a Lucite bangle of my mother's from my wrist and stuffed it into my pocket.

"There should be a parade, or something," I said, biting gingerly around the almond atop my Almond Joy, saving it for last.

"Two hundred years my people have been at the low point on the totem pole in this so-called land of the free, home of the brave. Isn't anybody braver than Dr. King. He's the one true American."

I felt as if I had learned more about my laconic boyfriend in the last half hour than in the entire nine months since we met. And everything I heard I liked, or at least respected. The truth is, it scared me to think that life as I'd always known it, with people knowing their place, might be on the way out. Imagine those dreaded playground girls with more rights! Still, I was happy for Jarmon. I even dared to think that if Jarmon could have his freedom, maybe it would follow that I could have mine, that people like me—there must be some somewhere—could be who they truly believed they were. I handed him the almond I'd saved. "We could make our own parade," I said.

"You can't have a parade with two people."

I eyed a line of office workers making their way along Main Street, heading to the bus stop or the parking lot and eventually to their homes. The workday was over, the holiday weekend was here. How ironic, I remember thinking, that the Civil Rights Act should be signed on the Fourth of July weekend, the anniversary of our Declaration of Independence. I hoped, for Jarmon's sake, it would have as long and successful a life.

"Two people and a bike," I said, jumping up.

"We need a flag or somethin'."

A rush of sadness rose in my throat, thinking about Dr. King and his people, all those marches that had dwelt, until now, on the edges of my awareness. All those dignified men and women in ties and jackets and dresses and hats silently proclaiming their right to be treated like anyone else—such a simple and reasonable demand—and risking their lives in the process. People like Jarmon. People like the three civil rights workers who had disappeared that spring in Philadelphia, Mississippi, probably the victims of the local sheriff and his posse of thugs.

I pulled my mother's paisley scarf out of my back pocket. Nearby, I found a five foot length of fallen branch and tied the scarf to it. I danced around the base of the copper beech, making a gigue of our parade, waving my makeshift flag back and forth, the scarf hanging limp and uninspiring.

Jarmon laughed and sprang to his feet. "You get points for tryin'," he said, glancing up into the copper beech. "What if we climb up with our flag? People'd have to look then."

I gazed up at the maze of silver branches that reached at least a hundred feet into the sky, the underside of their ruby-red leaves fluttering in the dim reaches of the tree's canopy. Of course Jarmon had to pick the tallest tree in all of Illinois. I shivered. The only heights I had ever experienced were emotional, with Jarmon. Yet I yearned to make him the celebration he deserved. We wouldn't have to climb that far up, I reasoned. We'd wave the flag, sing a couple of verses of "We Shall Overcome" and come back down with a vital memory etched into what I dared to hope would be our shared history of political demonstrations, fighting alongside each other against the injustices that afflicted us both. Climbing into the copper beech would be as much a demonstration of our love for each other as a celebration of this milestone of the civil rights movement.

Jarmon stepped onto his bicycle seat where it leaned against the massive trunk and reached for the lowest branch. He swung himself up like a circus performer. I handed him the flag and he reached his other hand down for me.

"I don't know," I said, suddenly weighted with misgivings. Couldn't we celebrate by sewing a real commemorative flag and running it up the park's flagpole? I was so much better with needle and thread.

"You can do it, Joey."

I looked around once more. Expanded groups of people made their way toward buses and parked cars. The sky had darkened, threatening rain. No one was going to see us, anyway. But here was Jarmon, smiling and reaching down to me. "Please," he said. What could I do but haul myself onto the bicycle's seat and reach shakily for his hand.

The climbing was easier than I expected, due to the great number of branches spiraling around the copper beech's trunk and Jarmon's hand on my butt, pushing me on. The trick was not to look down, or up for that matter, and not to think about what happened when we got high enough to please Jarmon, and not to think about making our way back down in the dark, and not to think about the sky opening up and soaking every branch.

Finally, he told me to stop climbing. I straddled the branch I had reached and gripped the trunk, which was no bigger around than my waist at this height. I kept my eyes ahead, looking out over the crowns of nearby trees, across the tops of buildings to the darkening vastness of Lake Michigan in the distance. My stomach flipped. I focused on the tree trunk, with its elegant maze of tiny black holes which I imagined to be the leafy penthouses of who knows what creepy arachnids.

Jarmon climbed past me and settled on the branch above, framed by a maze of branches criss-crossing a cloud-laden sky, barely visible through the leafy crown. Obviously a veteran tree-climber, he leaned his back casually against the trunk, not even holding on as he scanned the horizon and waved our colorful flag back and forth. He yelled down to passers-by. "Yo! Up here! Yo, check it out!

One man looked up, shook his head and moved on. A woman carrying a briefcase stared for a while, admonished us with her finger and walked away. Jarmon waved the flag at her and yelled, "All men are created equal. Women, too." I cringed.

I couldn't help thinking that, if our little celebration fizzled, we would make our way back down sooner rather than later. I'd make it up to Jarmon with a vanilla coke at the pharmacy before we split for the day. When I glanced up at him to suggest we start down, he was untying his shoes. "What are you doing?" I demanded, my voice quavering.

"Hold on better this way," he said, pulling off a now badly worn brown shoe that I had first spotted under the dumpster ten months ago. He tossed it out into the lacy extremity of the tree, where I watched it bounce off branches as it fell to a silent landing maybe thirty feet from the bicycle. I shuddered and tightened my grip on the trunk. Jarmon removed his other shoe and tossed it. Panic produced a metallic taste in my mouth. Sweat burst from pores I didn't know I possessed. Until I met Jarmon, I had avoided drawing attention to myself even more than I'd avoided heights, insects and sporting events. Jarmon was making a scene of being different, my long-term worst fear. And I was right there with him.

He stood and picked up the flag and started waving it back and forth in a jerking motion. He maintained his balance, one bare foot cupping a higher branch, as if he were leaning casually against a fence for a chat instead of mounting a demonstration from eight stories up in a tree. "Yo!" he yelled. "Up here!"

I glanced at my watch. It was long after six. A steady stream of people made their way through the park now. A clump of ten or twelve waited for a bus.

"Look here," Jarmon yelled. "It's a celebration. Do you even know what happened today?"

Gradually, people moved into the park. By six-thirty, a crowd of perhaps a hundred men and women and a few screaming children had gathered in a half-circle around the base of the copper beech. I gaped down at them for a few seconds at a time, hoping not to see any familiar faces, like my father's foremen at the plant or a teacher from school. An older woman yelled for us to climb down, but her message got lost in the mounting drone of voices around her. I turned my attention back to Jarmon whose bellowing had turned into a strange, meandering monologue having to do, at first, with the act signed that day, but then segueing into a variety of subjects—how hard it was to find a decent job if you were negro, being held back in school when he wasn't stupid, never knowing who his father was because steady work and a home weren't options for most blacks, losing his mother because she couldn't afford to see the right doctors, the general hopelessness of his negro life. The speech made sense as a wandering sort of autobiography of pain. Absurd and frightening as our situation was, a hundred feet up in a tree, I was touched and I could have cried if I hadn't been so scared. What had started out as a celebration had turned into some strange shrieking agony, all those arguments Jarmon had been forming and holding back for months, complaints against his dad for disappearing and his mom for dying, his boss for ignoring him, his teachers for giving up on him. I knew, as the crowd thickened below and a siren wailed in the distance, that we were in serious trouble now. But at that moment, all I felt was an overwhelming love and sympathy for Jarmon.

Soon a fire truck, lights whirling amid the deep blasts of its horn, slowed on Main Street and rocked across the curb into the park, pressing its way into the crowd. Its pulsating lights cast the facades of adjacent buildings into a ghoulish glare. Another blinding light panned the sky, searching the branches of the copper beech until it settled on the two of us. The whites of Jarmon's eyes gleamed madly in the garish glow. I turned away, gripping the tree. Jarmon continued his harangue. The fire truck's extension ladder was hoisted into position; a fireman climbed up to its top and began manipulating the controls there, maneuvering himself to a position perhaps twenty feet from Jarmon. He yelled to us through a megaphone. "We're going to take you boys down now."

"We want Cokes," Jarmon yelled back, cupping his hands to be heard over the din, standing strong and free, a figurehead on the bow of an ancient African vessel.

The fireman cupped his hand behind his ear.

"C-O-K-E-S. COKES!"

"We should go down, Jar."

"And make 'em cold!"

The fireman spoke into a walkie-talkie to someone on the ground.

"And gimme that thing."

The fireman looked back, questioningly.

Jarmon mimed the megaphone. "Toss it."

The man must have been advised to meet our demands because he tossed the megaphone gently to Jarmon, who reached out with one hand to catch it. But the orange cone flew two or three feet shy of Jarmon, who nearly lost his footing reaching for it. A collective gasp went up from the crowd below. The megaphone bounced from one branch to another until it disappeared into the dim haze below.

Jarmon steadied himself.

I contained an urge to throw up. Looking up at my boyfriend, I felt a mix of admiration and pity that was far more powerful than anything I have felt since. Adults who disdain puppy love don't remember their own. Yes, it's immature and frantic and crazy, but it's as intense a love as any there is. I fixed my eyes back on the tree trunk to steady myself. We will get through this, I whispered again and again like a mantra.

Refracted light gleamed off the windshield of a Lincoln Continental as it made its way into the park following a police cruiser, its lights flashing. The crowd parted again and the two cars pulled up alongside the fire engine. My mother and father emerged simultaneously, leaving their doors ajar, characters in a distant earth-bound drama. Someone must have recognized me and told the police. My father spoke to a fireman. My mother, her hands cupping her eyes, stared up into the tree, oblivious to the commotion around her. My first thought was that they didn't deserve this. They didn't deserve me. Second was the realization that the me I had held so much inside my whole life was suddenly exposed for my parents and everyone else to see. I felt peculiarly, momentarily free. Free from the humiliation, the shaming, the inward agony of my life. It was all out there now, where, surprisingly, none of it seemed to matter. Our safety was at issue—Jarmon and me—not who we were.

Camera bulbs flashed below.

"Yo!" Jarmon was shouting. "Power to the people!" He raised his fist in a power salute. "Everybody's created equal. Even Joey here. And me. Joey's my boyfriend, or my girlfriend. It don't matter which. It's our right!"

"Jarmon?"

He glanced down at me and winked. He had the attention he'd yearned for his whole life. "We got us our parade, didn't we baby? Look at this!" He grinned, spreading his arms to encompass the entire bizarre scene, looking a lot like a dark Jesus Christ on the cross.

A wet gust sent a chill through me. It had begun to rain. The drops, tiny shards of glass in our high circle of white light, pattered the rusty leaves of the copper beech and dampened Jarmon's shirt. "Please hold on, Jar," I yelled. "I'm scared."

He grabbed a branch with one hand. "Of course you're scared, my sweet Joey. You think I'm not? We're always scared, you and me. That's why we're here, baby. That's what we need to change." He stared at the crowd, shivered, and then steadied himself. Turning back to me, he said, "Promise me, your whole life, you'll never forget this day. We need this day, Joey. The only way we are ever gonna learn to love our difference is to make people see it, make 'em understand it. Make 'em see *us*, Joey. Yeah, sure, we're different but we're really like them, underneath. That's what they don't understand. We're all the same underneath." He gestured over the world of darkness beyond our perch. "All different, all the same."

Everything Jarmon said was right, of course, and yet his recklessness seemed to indicate how little he valued the life he wanted. He hated the hand he'd been dealt. Who wouldn't? Yet wasn't his very presence up in this tree expressing some sort of hope? In his eyes I could see a sudden astonishment at his own power and an inkling of the hope it might inspire. I could see, or wanted to see, a faith in our friendship. And I could see despair holding steadfast against hope, each somehow clarifying and enhancing the idea of the other, making them both great and small. I knew that whatever happened in the next few minutes was what would forever make him him, and me me.

"Anything you want to tell the people, Joey? Say it now, baby."

"They can't hear us, anyway," I said, feeling myself begin to separate from Jarmon, watching myself literally turn away. Jarmon had a right to be angry. I should be too. But all I wanted right then was for us to be down on the ground, apologizing to the authorities, taking whatever punishment was due us, accepting that status quo that Jarmon so vehemently opposed. As a result of our little performance, I could well be heading for boarding school in another month and Jarmon for a brief detention in some juvenile facility. None of that mattered. We'd be safe. I'd visit him, bring him Almond Joy candy bars. That glaring disparity in our imagined punishments, that simple avowal of all that was unfair, didn't even register with me then. Up in the copper beech on that day of Jarmon's people's emancipation, I simply wanted to save us. "Let's go down, Jar. Please."

The ladder arrived and groaned into position among the branches. My father stood behind the fireman, a leather harness linking him to the ladder. For the first time that I could remember, I wanted his arms around me. The fireman carried two soda cans.

"That's Pepsi," Jarmon shouted between his hands. "I ordered Cokes."

"Joey!" My father yelled into the dented megaphone. "I don't know what this is all about, but you can come down now. We can talk it over. This fireman is going to pick you up. You'll be safe."

I looked up at Jarmon who kept his eyes on the two men. "Go get us our Cokes," he shouted.

"Jar?"

He turned to me, a whole world of sorrow and misery contorting his face now, a lifetime of defeat. I could see in his eyes that he knew the cokes wouldn't come, that our celebration was over, that I was ready to leave, that defeat had won.

"I want to go down," I said.

He stared at me, in what? Anger, pity, disappointment, love? I turned away, cupped my hands and yelled to my father. "What about my friend?"

The fireman shouted back, "I'll come right back up for him. It won't take five minutes."

I watched resignation seep into Jarmon's eyes. He was shivering from fear or cold or acquiescence, who knew?

"We'll climb down ourselves," I yelled back. "Just give us a few more minutes."

The fireman turned and conferred with my father. They nodded. My dad raised the megaphone. "Joey," he yelled. "Your mother . . . Your mother and I . . . We love you."

The fireman spoke into his walkie-talkie again and then took the controls and maneuvered the ladder away from the tree and down.

The rain was picking up. I didn't know which was worse, being plucked out of the tree or making our way down on our own, but we would go down together. I braced myself. Jarmon had slumped against the tree trunk and gripped his knees to his chest. Tears streaked his cheeks. I stood, shakily, and climbed up to him. I squatted and wrapped one arm around his shoulder, holding fast to a branch with my other hand.

"You really know how to celebrate!" I told him. "You even upstaged President Johnson today. Everybody."

Jarmon opened his mouth to speak, but what came out was a moan, an unbearably agonizing sigh. I pulled his cheek to mine and held it there. "Let's go," I said, taking my arm away.

He blinked, his eyes vague and unfocused, as if they couldn't quite take in the abiding misery of their sudden inward turn. I touched his knee. "Jar?"

I would wonder, later, whether those eyes had spoken lasting defiance or simply the loss he had already embraced. Or had they been imploring me for some other resolution than the one awaiting us? I would wish, later, that I had kissed my first real friend and wiped away the tears from his gleaming cheeks. I would wish, later, that I had made him smile so I could see that tender dimple in his cheek one more time.

Instead, I lowered myself to the branch below, holding onto the trunk of the copper beech. It was then that I heard another gasp from the crowd, followed by a chilling silence. When I turned back, Jarmon was airborne, gliding straight out among rain-glistened branches, everything slowed to near stillness, floating for what seemed forever, kicking gently like a freestyler. At that moment it wouldn't have surprised me if he could fly. But no. His body turned, almost leisurely, and began its descent. Branches—or were they Jarmon's limbs?—cracked and shattered, the dry snaps seeming to echo like distant gunshots, raging fire. Jarmon's body bounced this way and that, like a lone soldier dodging through enemy lines, until it came to rest with a startling huff, folded over a branch just above the ground, Jarmon's arms reaching down for his shiny bicycle, leaning against the tree where we'd left it.

HANK AND JOEY

My friendship with Joey Maxima twisted up and down and around before it crashed and burned nearly a year ago. The second of only two close connections in my whole life—the first my friend, Ted, in Vietnam—and the second to end in disaster. Which meant I had to think a lot about what happened between us. What had I done wrong? What had I missed? Was there something wrong deep down inside me that meant I would never be close to anyone? This thought was no less disturbing for its familiarity.

I think about our friendship as having had three stages. In stage one, I was put off by Joey's effeminate nature, not something I'm proud of, but there it is. It's one thing to be gay, I told myself, something else to broadcast it. To each his own was my general view of things, plain and simple. I mean, who am I to judge anybody? But discretion seemed like a concept Joey Maxima had somehow missed all together, the way you might miss an appreciation for nature if you grew up in Manhattan, or for haute cuisine if your mom specialized in meatloaf, like mine did. If you ask me—gay, straight or otherwise—certain things are better off kept to yourself.

When he offered me this job shelving books, I almost didn't take it, as much as I needed the money and had enjoyed stopping here during my wandering first weeks in Manhattan. In my interview, Joey was all crossed legs and jewelry manipulations. A butch woman is one thing, I remember thinking. Trust me, we saw plenty of them overseas. It's funny how that's so much easier to take than a fem man, as if masculinity, whether it's in a man or a woman, is more valuable, which I don't necessarily agree with.

I'll say this for Joey, though—all that mincing wasn't for show. It was just him, whether he was talking on the telephone, yelling downstairs to the cashier or bending to pick up a paper clip off the floor. And that's what decided me to take the job in the end. Misfits had peppered my life for nineteen years, starting with my mom and running on through a series of high school rebels and army oddball loners. I'm not exactly a perfect fit in the world, myself, in case you haven't noticed.

Still, in that year of stage one, I pretty much steered clear of him, except when he handed me my paycheck, or at staff meetings. I have to say, I never saw anybody—even in the army, where authority is everything—lead a group of underlings better than Joey. Some people might assume there's not much to running a bookstore, but—trust me—they'd be wrong. Just keeping the ledger in black ink is a major challenge, say nothing of settling all the internal rivalries of a staff who would just as soon be writers or actors or artists as they would book schleppers.

Once a week, five or six of us sat around Joey's desk upstairs, while he went over profits and losses, goals and procedures. Some smoked, others picked at a hangnail or fiddled with a paper clip. But the meeting came alive when we turned to gripes and grievances. Not that we were unhappy. It was more as if group therapy had become a perk we all grew to depend on at the Strand. As our boss/therapist/parent, Joey listened, even when somebody strayed off the subject, which was routine. Things personal—family problems, love problems, landlord problems—slipped easily into the mix with overtime compensation, a preference for Scott paper products and the coffee break schedule. Joey was wise enough to know that his workers, not employed in the profession of their dreams, would benefit from voicing their life-grievances, and that, ultimately, this would make the Strand an all-around better place. When he could, he intervened with a suggestion or an accommodation, always gentle, fair and generous. Interpersonal relations came as naturally to him as his raised pinkies.

This sort of indulgence flew in the face of the general impression Joey gave of being in a hurry. But Joey's big rush, I figured out later on when I got to know him better, was an internal race against his own sense of lost time. It was as if Joey was catching up with his life, as if the struggle of his early years had robbed him of valuable time, and he could somehow compensate by capturing and savoring every minute of his galloping present. At twenty-whatever, he was in his prime, which only meant that there was more than ever to accomplish.

I guess what I'm saying is, everything I learned about Joey, that first year, made me question my prejudice about effeminate guys. Still, it took me a good while to get on board with the other staffers who had long since accepted his girlie ways as no big deal. I had always relied on some pretty solid boundaries to get by in what I always saw as a hazardous world—men and women, north and south, good guys and bad guys, and not a whole lot of in-between.

Was I threatened by Joey because I wasn't so downright convinced of my own manliness? Probably. I had only dated one girl for six weeks in tenth grade. You don't get to age nineteen with that paltry bit of romantic know-how and not wonder about yourself just a little. Far more significant was my time with my buddy in Vietnam, Ted. We ate and slept and marched and bored the hell out of ourselves, always together, every minute, for an entire year. Got so I was uneasy when he lingered too long behind a tree, taking a pee. I didn't think I was gay, but I also never gave the question a whole lot of thought.

Stage one ended when Joey asked me to help him crunch some numbers one night after work. It was mid-April, tax time. After a few hours of massaging income and expense figures, I leaned back and rubbed my neck. "You know," I said, "you could put all these numbers on punch cards and then use a computer to do everything we're doing here, only a whole lot faster."

Joey set down his pencil and looked across his desk at me. His eyes were red and spent as dish-water hands. I realized then that I hadn't been my usual uneasy self around him all evening, for several days in fact, weeks maybe. "Really," I said. "A buddy of mine at Fort Bragg, that was his whole job. Every number you punch makes a hole in a column on a card so the machine can read it. You take the cards to one of these computer places and they run the totals or averages or percentages or whatever you want. You can come up with all kinds of reports, get an idea of what really goes on here in the store. It's a whole lot easier in the long run, and more accurate than this thing." I pointed to Joey's adding machine with the sticky 9 key.

"What was it like in Vietnam?" he said. No smooth segues for Joey, something I liked about him, and yet this question threw me and I turned back to my column of miscellaneous expenses.

The truth was I didn't have an answer. Vietnam was something I tried every day to put behind me. I thought about it in the middle of the night, or while riding my bike along the Hudson River, or whenever it thundered and poured and steam rose off the hot Manhattan pavement like the Asian mist that shrouded that war. But there was nowhere for my thoughts to go. The war was over, lives lost, bodies and minds maimed. What would be the point of trying to explain that time to anybody? There was no sense to be made of it.

Joey said, "It must have been awful for you, watching people die and wondering if you were even doing the right thing by being there."

"What makes you think I wondered that?" I asked him, losing my place in the column of figures.

"It's just a sense I have of you, from watching you here at the store."

Later, at a burger place not far from the Strand, we talked some more. Not about Vietnam. He didn't push that. About store politics at first and then, after our burgers and a couple of beers—Joey drank Pinot Grigio—about ourselves.

"I don't have a whole lot of friends," he admitted, as a bunch of late-night revelers amassed around the bar and took the decibel level up a point or two. "People find me . . . different."

I crossed my knife and fork over my plate, adjusting them until they divided the sphere into perfect quadrants. "We're all different," I said.

"That's sweet of you, Henry, but I don't think your compulsions are quite on a par with my gender eccentricity."

I could feel the heat rise in my cheeks. "My what?"

He pointed to my immaculately cleaned and quartered plate, which could easily skip the dishwasher and slip unnoticed back onto the shelf. "I do have to say it's an asset when it comes to your work. You're by far the neatest shelfer we've ever had at the Strand."

I took in the crowd that continued to gather around the bar—guys and gals in their twenties, still in suits and dresses from their office jobs, briefcases nestled against their legs like pets. I wasn't like them. Neither was Joey.

"Now I've made you uncomfortable," Joey said. "I'm sorry."

"It's okay."

"My point is that people probably find you far less threatening than they do me."

I got his point, but this wasn't a debate I cared to join. Who could judge who had a harder time in life? We spent an awkward minute or two checking out the Yankees-Braves game on the TV over the bar, though the ruckus sent up by the crowd pretty much blocked out the sound. "So how are those Yankees doing this season?" Joey yelled to me.

"They're three and. . . ." I glanced back to his smirk. "You're putting me on, right?"

"A nasty habit of mine." He pushed back a cuticle with his fingernail. "I wonder if we could make a deal," he said.

"What?" I leaned over the table to hear him better.

"A deal," he repeated. "I'll try my damnedest not to make you squirm, if you'll try to get beyond my femininity." He pointed to his chest, as if that's where his true nature resided. "There's a somebody in here you might like if you would give her a chance."

Her. I winced inside. Still, I was pretty certain he was right, and the deal he offered seemed like a pretty good exchange, since trying to get beyond Joey's femininity was something I'd been working at from day one. "Why do you do it?" I asked him.

"Act like a girl?"

"Deliberately make people uncomfortable."

"My shrink says it's a defense. He says I take over the resistance."

"What resistance?"

"I offend people before they can offend me."

I took my knife and fork off my plate and set them on the paper mat, making sure they didn't line up right. "I saw a shrink once," I said.

"Really?"

"You're not the only kid who ever had a problem, you know?"

"Did you break the law or something?"

"Fat chance! I always did everything right. Maybe too right."

"What, then?"

Joey tucked his streaked hair behind his ear, and I thought that, without trying, I'd found somebody as odd as me, and somebody I could talk to the way I had talked with Ted, somebody who had known plenty of turmoil of his own. I knew I needed help now, just as I had then, in Vietnam, though I didn't have a clue what to ask for. I just knew that everything I did, everything I thought about, seemed distant, outside of me, like I didn't really inhabit myself or even my thoughts. That made no sense, but it was the closest I could come to describing what plagued me every day since Vietnam, and maybe before that. Maybe even my whole life.

"I believed I could fly, when I was a kid," I told Joey.

His eyebrows shot up. "Fly? As in leave the ground? Defying gravity?"

I nodded.

Joey studied my face for a long minute. "You're serious, aren't you?" Then he lit up like he'd just found the perfect pair of shoes on sale. "Hah! I knew we had a special connection!"

"You thought you could fly?"

"You're very literal, Henry. It's part of your charm. Don't you see? I've been defying gravity my whole life, the gravity of my gender. And trust me, it was heavy. Believing I was a girl was just about as outrageous as you believing you could fly, don't you think? What did your shrink say?"

"He diagnosed me delusional." I pushed my fourth beer away. "Guess I've had enough of that."

"I could have fit into that category, myself. Don't you love psychiatric diagnoses? Manic-depressives, paraphilias, paranoids, people who don't happen to fit into some arbitrary standard of behavior as defined by a very uptight and probably very mediocre group of doctors, whose specialty is generally considered the low end of the professional totem pole. Most of the shrinks I've met would fall into one or more of their own categories." Joey sipped his wine, set down his glass and perused the room. The television blared and the crowd roared as the Yankees scored two runs.

"Tell me about it," he said, turning back to me.

"What, flying?"

"Feeling different from everybody else."

Refolding my napkin, lining up the corners, I told Joey that it had been both scary and incredibly exciting, believing I had this special ability. I told him about standing on the window sill of my mother's house, in the middle of the night, preparing to take off. I told him about circling above the maple and birch and elm trees behind our house, about looking down at the sleepy darkness all around, about the amazing lightness, the floating, the soaring sensation. And then I told him how, when you hide something about yourself like that, you learn to hide other things too, and eventually hiding becomes who you are. The more you hold back, the less there is left of you that's real, until you're nothing but all you've held back, you're nobody anybody knows but you.

Then I stopped, suddenly embarrassed, suddenly amazed at things I'd never said before.

Joey stared at me, having blotted out the roar of the bar with his concentration. He blinked, swallowed hard. I had the strong sense, right then, of what he had been up against his whole life. Something similar to me but far more difficult, because he didn't have a prayer of hiding it. Now, after who knows how much torment, he was being the person he believed himself to be. What more can you ask of somebody than that?

Stage two lasted another year. Joey and I became pals. We went to movies. We went to dinner once a week. Sometimes we drank wine after hours from a bottle he kept hidden in his desk drawer. The taste of Pinot Grigio will always remind me of that dingy office, perched over the main floor of the Strand, and of the amazing lightness of having a real friend again. I talked and talked, just as I had walked and walked in Vietnam, and with a similar mindlessness as to where I was headed, surrendering to somebody else's direction, and to the notion that to keep going was to keep on living.

Joey listened. "So what was that like?" he'd ask, and I'd say, "What do you mean, what was it like?" and he'd say, "What did you feel?" and I'd look at him, stumped, like he'd suddenly switched to German or French. Joey believed that feelings were attached to all behavior, and that they actually mattered more than whatever happened. He was this startling mix of wisdom and common sense, insight and compassion, challenge and reassurance. He made sense of my ramblings, and I began to thrive on this diet of revelation and trust I had never known before, not even with Ted. I couldn't get enough.

During stage two, up there in his second floor office, Joey told me that he'd been adopted at birth. "I was never that interested in finding my birth mother," he claimed, "as some adopted kids are. My parents were old school. Not that old school, I suppose—they did tell me, after all. Most parents kept adoptions secret back then and sprung it on their unsuspecting offspring when they were adults, giving them something to stew about and resent for years to come." He fingered the rim of his wine glass, hooked his hair behind his ear. "It wasn't so much that I wasn't interested as that I knew my parents would have been hurt if I went off and found my birthmother and had this big reunion that led to some awkward two-family arrangement. My parents did a cool thing, though. They gave me the middle name, Allen, which had been my birthmother's last name."

"How did they know her name?" I asked, enjoying the rumble of our voices in the high reaches of the empty bookstore. "I thought that sort of information was kept secret."

"It was. Something bizarre happened though. I don't know all the details, but the girl—my birthmother—got hold of my parents' name and address somehow and contacted them after the adoption. I think my father gave her some money and that was the end of it. She went away."

"I thought they didn't tell you anything about her."

"My bedroom was over the kitchen. I made a point of overhearing things, particularly when they had to do with me. Years later, they were still talking about that girl. Made me wonder if she was bothering them, or at least staying in contact, and if I would meet her one day."

Joey poured us more wine, his pinky elevated over the bottle. "I always liked the sound of my name—Joseph Allen Maxima, a certain phonetic pleasure as it slipped off the tongue, a touch of class, you know? But mostly I appreciated that little connection to my birthmother, this reminder that there was someone else out there who cared about me, or had once, at least. It occurred to me, much later, that my parents had been wise. They'd given me just enough of my origins to satisfy my curiosity. I didn't need to go any further and disrupt everything."

"Seems like it would have made you, of all people, more nosy, having that little bit of information like that."

Joey smiled. Not for him, apparently.

Stories like that one put me in a kind of awe of Joey. He'd thought of things most people never got to. More than that, he caused you to think about your own life and all that might have influenced the kind of choices you struggled with, the person you turned out to be. He seemed to have taken the adversity he'd known as a kid and made something of it, which inspired me to think I might be able to do that one day, too.

This is my favorite memory of stage two. It was a sunny day in Central Park. Whatever that early spring smell is—trees greening, daffodils blooming, the earth itself surrendering some of its stored-up richness—it was out in force that day. We were watching a group of boys sail their toy boats on the reflecting pool, not far into the park from Fifth Avenue. Some of the boats were four feet long and rigged like the real thing. The boys and their dads carried long poles to redirect their crafts when they neared the molded concrete edge of the huge pool.

"I never had that," Joey said, half under his breath.

"A sailboat?"

"A dad who wanted to spend time with me."

I hadn't either, of course. Nor had I thought much about it. Dad-less was just who I was, like dark-haired and tall. Now, it felt like something important I had in common with Joey.

The sun angled through burdened clouds and flashed off the gleaming sails of the boats. The water glowed silver, highlighting the gentle rippling wakes as the boats traveled back and forth across the pool. One of the kids at the near end started crying because his father wanted to leave. "No doubt I was a challenge for any dad," Joey said. "Sailing wasn't my thing, or baseball or any other kind of ball. I played with dolls and took piano lessons. I never once remember my father sitting down and listening to me play."

"That seems like something he could have done," I said.

Joey nodded.

"I always wanted to take piano lessons."

"Really?"

"If you saw where I grew up, you'd know how crazy that idea was. It'd be like you going out for football."

"I'd like to see where you grew up sometime."

An old sense of embarrassment rose up in me at the thought of bringing anybody home, especially somebody who had grown up in a mansion on Lake Michigan. Of course, Joey would see beyond the mess, though he'd register its importance.

The man had convinced his son to leave by then, and we watched the two of them recede down the walkway toward Fifth Avenue, the man carrying the boat, the boy carrying the two steering rods.

"Listen to us, feeling sorry for ourselves on a beautiful day like this," Joey said.

I took in the glimmering trees lining the paths, but my mind went back to Joey's mention of piano lessons. "I had a buddy in grade school whose parents had an old upright in their basement. I used to make him take me down there to play it. He taught me the lower parts of "Chopsticks" and some other tunes I can't remember now. I was always thinking up excuses to go to his house and play that old upright."

Joey jumped up, took my hand and pulled me to my feet. "Follow me," he said. Then, just as suddenly, he dropped my fingers and walked on ahead, his empty hand angling as if it might have been pulled away before it was quite ready. At Fifth Avenue, he hailed a taxi. "West Fifty-Seventh," he told the driver, "across from Carnegie Hall."

Ten minutes later, we stood in front of Steinway Hall. The store's shiny, curved wall of glass made you feel like you were standing inside the showroom, where a dozen or more gleaming pianos were displayed on a plush green carpet like a bunch of gems in a jewelry case. Joey pushed open the heavy door and I followed him inside. The most striking thing about the showroom, after the hustle of Fifty-Seventh Street, was the complete lack of sound, a silence probably intended to showcase the instruments. The room smelled of polished wood and fresh flowers. Joey straightened his jacket and tucked his hair behind his ear. I looked down at my worn sneakers. With Joey, there was never any turning back, so I let that idea drift.

"Can I help you?" A saleswoman with blond, cotton candy hair, scary fingernails and daggers for heels appeared behind us. Joey took her in with a smolder of envy around his eyes that got extinguished by a douse of disdain you wouldn't notice unless you knew him as well as I did by then. "We're looking for a piano," he said as the saleswoman read us as nimbly as Joey had read her. "To purchase," Joey added, with a haughty extension of the syllables.

"I see," the woman said, shifting her weight from one skinny leg to the other, her ankles at right angles like the Donatello David I'd discovered in an art textbook at the store that week.

"It's for him," Joey added, pointing to me. "A major talent. Major!"

The woman glanced at me and smoothed her skirt across her stomach as if crumbs had dropped on it. "Follow me," she said, turning and working her hips across the room. She stopped at a baby grand and ran her fingers over the lid.

"Bigger," Joey said. "And ebony. How about that one over there?" He angled, as gracefully as the sales lady, around two more pianos, their lids propped at sharp angles, and sat at a big mother grand that had to be seven feet long. He raised his head, pausing the way a concert pianist might, his hands suspended over the keyboard. Finally, he dropped them and a dissonant run of random notes jarred the room.

"Sit, Henry," he said, sliding over and gesturing to the space beside him.

"We have audition rooms," the woman said.

"This will be fine. Sit down," he directed me again, patting the bench.

"Joey. . . ."

"You'll excuse us, won't you?" he said to the woman.

She hesitated and then retreated, glancing back at us as she crossed the room and disappeared behind a mahogany door.

"So. 'Chopsticks.' My intro, if you please."

I sat to his left on the bench, mumbling. "She's probably calling the manager."

"She can call anyone she likes. I'm ready for my intro, Mr. deMille."

I wiped my hands on my jeans and looked around once more. "Jesus, Joey!"

I started the base—ump bah bah, ump bah bah, dee bah bah, dee bah bah. Joey joined in with the melody. "Okay, quiet and slow at first," he said over the din. "Leave some power for the climax."

After "Chopsticks," we played "Heart and Soul," which Joey improvised into half a dozen variations. We played for maybe ten minutes before I convinced him we should quit while we were ahead. A security guard appeared with the woman just as we were sliding off the bench. "Major," Joey said, gesturing grandly to me as we made our way past the resting pianos to the front door. "Major talent."

Back out on Fifty-Seventh Street, he said, "I bet that's the first time they've ever heard such renditions of the classics."

"Major talent," I said, resting my elbow on Joey's shoulder. "Major!" He pointed toward Carnegie Hall, across Fifty-Seventh Street. "Practice, practice, practice," he yelled. He led us a block east to Wolff's delicatessen at the corner of Sixth Avenue, which he claimed made the best corned beef sandwich in Manhattan, aside, of course, from the Second Avenue Deli downtown. "You can't be shy in New York, Henry," he lectured as he hustled us down the wide sidewalk, twisting around stragglers. "Or anywhere else, for that matter. You only go around once, you know."

Was it too much to expect a relationship between a straight guy and a gay guy who thinks he's a woman to last? That year of stage two was the best time I ever had anywhere, with anybody. But then, abruptly, we stumbled into stage three, which lasted less than an hour.

One Friday night after work, Joey and I sat opposite each other at his desk upstairs at the Strand, drinking his Pinot Grigio. "I have something to say," he announced.

"Shoot," I said, figuring he was going to ask me to help with the books again.

"I'm not so sure I should. I value our friendship so much."

"So do I," I said, an uncomfortable surge rising in my chest, a feeble echo of the way it felt when I heard the snap of a twig in the Vietnamese jungle that could be an animal, a buddy or a gook.

"You must know I'm in love with you," Joey said, holding my eyes.

As much as I admired Joey, as much as he'd changed the way I thought about things, including myself, I wasn't attracted to him, not that way. I had enough orientation problems—a natural drift toward solitude, a general floundering when it came to any sort of a career, a tendency to obsess about things I couldn't change. But on the issue of sexual orientation, I was pretty clear. Or, truth be told, blank, empty. I didn't really think about it. Jerking off was pretty much limited to the need to produce a semen sample, and whatever fantasies might have surfaced were crowded out by the need to get across town for an on-time delivery. I'm ashamed to admit this, but, at twenty-one, I had put sex aside. I tried not to think about it, and for the most part, this worked. I was sexless, crossed the finish line before I had even joined the race.

Joey and I had spent nearly all our time together for a year, two loners latched on to each other with the grip of a plumber's pliers. I didn't know what to make of his thin, curvy, pale, hairless body, so I looked the other way. There were times, though—split seconds—when Joey sat in his desk chair or spoke into the telephone or swayed across a room, when I actually took him for the pretty woman he was becoming. And during those split seconds, I felt attracted. But then the feeling flitted away, appropriately enough, and I was left confused, embarrassed, scared. That year, I'd been chipping away at the dam which, my whole life, had held back every unpredictable or unmanageable feeling I'd ever had, and now they were all gushing forth, threatening to drown me in my own debris-laden tsunami.

I adjusted a pile of books at the edge of Joey's desk, lining up the bindings, wishing he would take back what he had just said. I knew right then that those words—you must know I'm in love with you—were going to mean the end of all that had gone on that year, including my burgeoning potential for a more authentic life.

"I'm not asking you to love me back, or make love to me," he was saying. "I'm not asking you for anything, really. It's just. . . . We've always been so honest with one another, Henry. I don't see how I can go on without at least telling you what I feel."

The truth was, I loved him too, in my own limited way. And yet, a stab of anger hit me as I downed the last of my wine. Suddenly I questioned Joey's formidable forthrightness. He himself had said once that honesty can be manipulative and that the truly honest person has to question his motives prior to making a revelation. I felt backed into a corner.

"You can't be entirely surprised, Henry."

I thought about Ted. Something I had missed all along had complicated that friendship too, and eventually killed it. Was I really so dim?

"Say something, Henry. You're not talking."

I tried and failed to look at Joey. I ran the toe of my boot along the bottom edge of his desk, back and forth, back and forth, taking in the huge silence of the empty store. Finally, I said, "A year ago, you promised not to make me squirm. Those were your exact words, Joey. And now I'm squirming."

"I'm sorry."

"If I could get beyond your feminine ways, you said. That was the deal, and I kept my part of the bargain."

"You did, and I'm grateful."

"How can I get beyond something that's just you? Sometimes I think. . . ."

"What, Henry?"

"Sometimes I almost forget. . . ."

"I'm sorry." Joey was suddenly on his feet. "I shouldn't have said anything. Let's pretend I never opened my big mouth." He re-corked the wine and set it back in the bottom drawer. He grabbed his coat off the rack behind his desk. "I should be getting home anyway," he said.

Pulling on my jacket, I never felt so heavy. I tried to think how we could possibly unscramble ourselves back to a friendship that seemed, now, to have been based on an unspoken agreement never to reveal what we had just revealed. We'd come smack up against the wall we'd been careening toward for over a year, whether we knew it or not, and there was no way over or around it now. In a situation like that, in Vietnam, you hit the ground, closed your eyes and crawled away as fast as your elbows and knees would take you.

Joey locked the Strand's front door behind us. We stood opposite each other at the corner of Broadway and East Twelfth Street. Drizzle dampened our shoulders. There were no words to save us. I wiped the back of my hand across my forehead. Fat eerie clouds drifted among the skyscrapers surrounding Union Square, absorbing the white light of the city into their vaporous mass, like a sheet drawn over your face. Suddenly, the Empire State Building broke through that drifting haze, its tip glowing blue and majestic.

"Look," Joey said, pointing to it.

"I know," I said. The proud silvery mass seemed to leap forward, before receding back into the scrim, as if it had winked at us. When I turned back to Joey, he was gone, and I tumbled headlong into stage four, in which the lonely pain of stage one seemed even more acute, with the sudden loss of potential, and of hope.

The next day, Joey apologized for stepping out of his role as my boss and asked me not to leave the Strand. I'm not one to give up, I told him, which he should have known. I stayed on. Feelings, I mused, were immutable, if pretty much indecipherable, facts. But that didn't mean you couldn't ignore them, or dodge around them, when you needed to. I'd done that my whole life. I was an expert.

In stage four, out of shyness or stubbornness or just a lack of resourcefulness, we avoided each other. One-time friends, cordial boss, responsible employee, we went on working together at the Strand, with distance our familiar, if heartless, companion.

9

HANK BEHIND THE SCENES

Karen Tuckwell drops by the store for the third time since she showed up at my apartment a week ago. With each visit, she sheds a little more of that tough New York exterior, like a sheep inching out of a wolf-skin coat. She arrives mid-morning and brings me two raisin Danish and a cup of coffee the way I like it, with one sugar and plenty of milk. The store isn't busy then and I take my break with her, sitting on the floor in Mathematics, where not that many people venture anyway. She does most of the talking, about the play she's in on Broadway, about Cher's divorce from Sonny, about the first-ever daytime Emmy awards coming up in May and people she knows who might be in the running. I listen, down the Danish and wonder what this dazzling woman wants with me.

"Have you seen *Towering Inferno*?" she asks me.

"I've heard about it."

"It's amazing. You won't believe how realistic the fire scenes are. It's like you're right there in the middle of all the carnage. We have to go."

"But you've already seen it."

She scoffs. "I've seen *The Godfather* seven times. The sequel comes out soon. I can't wait."

Every now and then, I glance to the window upstairs, expecting to see Joey staring down at us. But he's too cool for that. Or, at least, too clever to be caught. Store policy dictates that employees take their breaks in the snack area in the basement, but Karen Tuckwell is just not the stale-coffee-warming-on-a-hotplate type of woman. I should tell her we need to meet somewhere away from the store. I should tell her a lot of things, like that I feel intimidated by her, restless in a way I can't put words to, and sleepless at night with the possibility of her getting pregnant with my sperm. McAvery is going to be calling me in ten days or so for another delivery for Karen. It's just not right, our meeting like this. No doubt, it's weird for her, too. She never expected to meet her derelict donor, hitching a ride in the elevator. Of course you'd be curious. You might even feel romantic about the guy. But then, you'd have to consider your husband, right? Taking up with your donor when he's already insecure about the whole pregnancy thing?

But neither of us mentions Karen's husband, and sometimes I forget he even exists, especially when I imagine her sitting on the back seat of my bike, her hands clutching my waist, or when I picture her red hair draped over a pillow.

Should I tell Joey about Karen? He doesn't even know that I donate my sperm, one of the few things I held back during those months we were close. I had begun to suspect, with all the introspection Joey encouraged, that my motivation for donating was complicated, and I was afraid Joey would recognize one more thing that I hadn't figured out for myself. So the time passed and the donation business became a secret.

Joey would tell me to stop seeing her, of course. He'd point out how crazy it was. And he'd be right.

Karen is currently appearing in *Vanities* at the Chelsea West Side Theater on West Forty-Third Street. She plays one of the cheerleaders. As she goes on about the play, I can't help but wonder if one of those little squigglers in her last insemination, one of *my* squigglers, made it to pay dirt. How long will she continue to get thrown in the air on that stage if she finds out she's pregnant? None of my business, of course. She can do anything she wants. Anything she and her husband want.

"You haven't seen it yet, I hope," she says, handing me an envelope with her name scribbled on the back. Karen Grave.

"Grave?"

"That's my stage name."

"Couldn't you have picked something a little more cheerful?" I'm a little bolder with Karen these days.

She only shrugs.

Inside is an orchestra seat for tonight. "Wow, thanks," I say.

"Three cheerleaders tell their life stories. You'll like it."

"Karen. . . ."

Her big brown eyes are like a Collie pup's. "What? You look like you just spied a ghost in the mystery section." She chuckles, elbows me in the ribs.

"Meeting the way we did, I'm not sure this is such a good idea. I mean. . . ." I am so far out of my depth with this woman. Whatever I say sounds pathetic.

"Come backstage," she says. "We can get something to eat afterward." She brushes some crumbs off her slacks as if she's getting ready to leave. It wouldn't occur to her that I'm the schmuck who'll be sweeping them up later on.

"Won't you be tired by then?"

She jumps up. "I'm off."

That's probably true, I think as I pull myself to my feet. There's definitely something a little off about Karen Grave Tuckwell. But what do I know? My whole time in New York, I've occupied a reserved seat on the sidelines. "Okay," I say. "I'll see you tonight then." I drop our empty cups into the paper bag they came in and stand there crunching the whole thing into a ball as she disappears at the end of the aisle.

As soon as she's gone, Joey shows up. Mathematics is a busy aisle this morning. A stab of dread crosses my chest as I remember I'm supposed to have dinner with him tonight.

"Who's your friend?" he asks me, splayed fingers spread over jutting hip.

"Her name's Karen Grave, or Karen Tuckwell, depending on when you talk to her." I toss the crunched bag onto the lower shelf of my cart.

"No detritus on the carts, Henry."

"Sorry." I lean down to retrieve the bag.

"A little old for you, don't you think?"

"Joey, I. . . ."

"Before you know it, you'll be throwing a linen cloth over your cart and setting out candles."

"I need to reschedule our dinner."

"Tonight?"

"Yeah, I. . . ."

"You have a better offer." He fingers some stray strands behind his ear, hurt registering around the eyes, despite himself.

"She gave me a free ticket to her play. You know how I like plays."

"Right," he says.

"What about next week?"

"Sure. Next week. That will be fine."

"Thanks, Joey. Sorry about that. I'll do Philosophy next." I wheel my cart to the elevator and press B for the basement, feeling Joey's eyes on my back.

In the dim storage area downstairs, with its dry odor of concrete and boxed books, I park my cart next to a stack of cardboard containers lined up along the wall. I retrieve the razor knife from its perch on a hook by the door, return to the boxes and start slicing them open.

My mind jumps back to the mysterious and notably strange Karen Grave, to the wounded Joey, to my own confusion and excitement about these events. If I had it to do over again, maybe I'd tell Karen I needed to take a rain check. But. . . .

I jump back, a substantial nick sliced off the end of my thumb. I curse and drop the knife. A puddle of blood overflows into my palm. I suck at the wound, that familiar metallic taste of blood, and wrap it in my handkerchief.

I squeeze my thumb and sink to the bed of my empty cart.

A steamy, swamp-reeking blast smacked me in the face when I stepped off an air transport with 212 other grunts landing in Vietnam in 1969. The heat fried my nostrils and coated my teeth with a less than delectable scum. Flies dive-bombed my face. My eyes teared. My lips puckered. I squinted and tightened every orifice, right down to my butt hole. I heard myself whimper with the realization that, if I was lucky, I'd make it through this torturous year of conscription, a time that stretched out ahead like a corridor to Hell. Booby traps, Agent Orange, body bags, worry-weary madness—we'd heard all about it in basic. I knew what was coming and that the odds of surviving intact, physically or mentally, weren't all that good.

The flight from the staging area in Germany had been long and rough, two hundred plus neophyte warriors crammed into a rattling, cavernous plane. There'd been one line for puking, a second for shitting. Guys in a hurry used plastic bags for either or both and dropped them into a barrel along with anything else they'd finished with, including any hope they'd had of somehow staying out of this war. Flying over the North Pole, we wrapped ourselves in blankets. Uncle Sam must have gotten a good deal on the plane—probably some retired mail carrier adapted for human freight, teenagers mostly, trained to shoot and ask questions later.

I met Ted on that fourteen-hour flight and we hit it off like a couple of boy scouts on a camping trip in the middle of a hurricane. We were jittery with fear and this strange mix of excitement and dread, having known only the dehumanizing and weirdly comforting regimen of basic training, where you don't have to think or plan or decide anything. Now we had to think about being killed, or killing, which, despite having been taught how to shoot or stab or blow up another human being, I still couldn't get a hold on any better than I had in Vermont. We joked the way guys do when they're an extreme sort of nervous that they never knew existed. I packed and repacked my satchel. Ted's eyes took on a restless jump and his voice quavered as we approached the other side of the world.

In the cold florescence of that night, he told me about his girlfriend in western Pennsylvania, how their fathers had both been farmers, how he and Rosemary Becker had learned to drive tractors and clean milking machines when they were only ten years old. How they'd been inseparable from the time they were kids. Ted had hated farming, and it seemed that he had joined up in order to get himself out of a life he couldn't picture five years into the future, a life that demoralized him even worse than leaving Rosemary for a year. Hopeless and broke, he'd seen the army as a could-be-worse option, an opening up of the world to new possibilities, a plan he was already questioning as that tired jet groaned its way over the pole. It sounded like he was the sort of guy who could sidestep a tight spot, half out of common sense and half out of dumb luck, qualities I knew I lacked.

I told him about my mother, the would-be actress, about sleepless nights wishing Lick would leave and take his shoebox with him, about the one girlfriend I'd had for a total of six weeks in high school, about how I wanted to turn my whole life around someday but didn't have a clue how to go about it. Ted listened, nodding once in a while. If he'd commented, I probably couldn't have gone on the way I did. By the time we reached the other side of the world, I felt like I had a buddy.

In Vietnam, we walked, heads down, one foot in front of the other, twenty-five miles a day. My fatigues itched, my helmet stunk, my boots never dried out. My rucksack contained forty pounds of hoarded C-rations, bug repellent, a wrinkled photograph of my mom sitting on the front step of our house, packets of freeze-dried soup, Jell-O, Kool-Aid, chewing gum, clammy matches, a pair of semi-dry socks, band-aids, one dog-eared letter from a guy I'd worked with at the motel, a note to my mom in case of the worst. As PFC's, Ted and I carried M-16 rifles and up to twenty magazines of ammunition apiece. It was always hot and always wet. Our skin chafed. We scratched. A fear-reeking sweat infiltrated everything.

I kept my uniform and my pack as neat as if I was in some July 4th parade back home in Vermont. It was a losing battle, of course, but unpacking and cleaning and shining and replacing kept the edges of my fear from getting too sharp. Maintaining such a strict sense of order was, to me, like smoking weed or card-playing was to some of my fellow grunts, who eyed me suspiciously at first, before we all learned to forgive the most ridiculous behavior as understandable, given our situation.

When I dropped my gear at the end of a day's march, I felt as if I could float away with that sudden momentary lightness of my body, a feeling that felt vaguely familiar from when I used to stand on my windowsill looking out over our back yard, about to take off. Ted and I picked at blisters and body lice, smoked, dozed. We talked through endless periods of boredom between the sudden horrors of death and dismemberment and the mundane tasks of preparing and eating rations, cleaning up, walking, sleeping, sleep-walking. The potential for one of those dreaded Ds was everywhere, all the time—a bullet, a booby trap, a mine. That tension sent curtains crashing down in my brain, closing off terror and, with it, any other feelings, turning me even more inward and numb than usual.

Except with Ted. I couldn't tell you what we talked about, only that the reassuring murmur of our voices meant everything to me—that we were alive, that we'd gotten through one more day, that I wasn't alone. Fear opened us up to each other. And yet, I probably couldn't have told you a whole lot of facts about his life. Our closeness was probably as much physical as verbal, having to do with our constant proximity, the sound and warmth and smell of a body always within reach, the sharing of lives that had become meaningless wastes and yet were still somehow incredibly dear. I died inside over there—less to lose that way—except for this connection to Ted.

We patrolled villages, farms, jungle. I always walked behind Ted. The back of his helmet, his shoulders, his butt, his boots, became familiar and reassuring parts of the landscape. We shared a tent, demanding nothing but each other's presence. Ted wondered over and over if his Rosemary Becker would wait for him, if she would respect him more or less for fighting, if she would find him too changed when he got back. He didn't seem to get a whole lot of mail from her, or anybody else for that matter. But who was I to question? I had only my mother and she wasn't exactly a pen pal.

Looking back, I can see how much was going on between Ted and me, clinging together in order to survive, which was everything, of course, and nothing in a way. Deep in some wordless recess of my brain, I believed that if Ted made it through, I would. Ted was my talisman, my rabbit's foot, my lucky ace. And I was his. We talked about taking a trip to the Grand Canyon when we got back stateside, or Mount Hood or Los Angeles, places neither of us had ever seen before. Shared prospects took us into a future. If one of us didn't make it, he would be letting the other one down, which he would never do.

We both hated every minute of that war. But what choice did we have? We went along with needless killing and burning mostly because we were embarrassed not to. Next to staying alive, the most important thing about Vietnam, from President Johnson on down to lowly grunts like us, was not to lose face. Guys developed tics or stutters rather than acknowledge fear. Worse was showing remorse. A VC—teenager, woman, baby—was not a person. They were the disembodied focus of anger, frustration, terror. We killed our anger and burned our terror, leaving no traces. Shying away meant ostracism, if not obliteration. Nobody risked it.

And I killed, the one thing I said I couldn't do. Nothing I saw, up close I mean, no bloodied body, only the unmistakable sense that the bullet expelled by my trigger finger had found its way to a Vietcong's face or chest or leg or arm. I knew it somehow, it registered, though not with the horror I had expected. Horror was all we knew over there, and the dread I'd harbored all along, the dread of killing, got all muddled up with other revulsions and kind of disappeared. I guess it had to.

The thing I can't get out of my mind though, almost a year later, is something that happened between Ted and me. It was on a weekend furlough in Saigon, late in our tour. Ted knew I was a virgin—it was his ongoing joke about me—and he was determined to get me laid. After plenty of drinks one night, he brought me to this brothel. I hadn't expected the two girls he hired to be so young or so pretty. They looked like sisters. We took off our boots and drank strong tea. They sat on our laps, kissed our necks and giggled. Of course, we couldn't understand them or they us. The atmosphere in that shabby room, though, was jittery with this tension between Ted and me, not those girls. Everything felt forced. We weren't having fun. For some reason, I thought about Rosemary Becker. I wanted some girl like her to be my first, somebody I loved the way Ted loved her. Still, I went along in the oblivion I had resigned myself to months before.

Eventually we went to separate cubicles. The girl unbuttoned my shirt and unzipped my pants. I stopped her, shook my head no. Confused, she sat back on her ankles. I ran my hand over her long shiny hair and touched her shoulder. I had a hard-on, but a sadness heavier than any rucksack weighed on it. How had this pretty Vietnamese girl and I fallen on such desolation, and how would we ever move beyond it, how would we ever survive it? I had reached a low in which obscenity and evil had become routine. There was no meaning left in anything, except maybe not to violate this poor abandoned girl.

Beyond the paper-board partition, I could hear Ted and his girl thrashing around. After a while, the commotion stopped. I heard some footsteps and Ted pulled back the curtain of my cubicle. He was naked. His dick was wet, half-erect and glistening. "What's wrong?" he yelled at me. He was in a rage. "What the fuck is wrong, Hank?"

I just stared up at him, dumbstruck and foolish.

"Get undressed," he said.

We were almost eleven months into our mutual dependence on each other. I was far beyond any sort of ability to resist Ted. With him standing there suddenly, telling me what to do, I couldn't recall why the girl had seemed so important to me just a minute before. I stood and took off my shirt. I dropped my pants and shorts and stepped out of them.

"Fuck her, Hank," he said.

I stood there, not moving, paralyzed.

"Fuck her, God damn it!"

The girl sat on her haunches, looking away from us, probably hoping we'd have a fight and leave. Ted pushed her and she fell back onto the floor.

"Leave her alone, Ted."

"She could be a gook for all you know. Cut your throat if you turn your back. Get on her, goddamn it."

I lay down next to the girl. Her hair made a glossy mat on the rough plank floor. She closed her eyes and waited, as numb as me probably. With his foot in the small of my back, Ted pushed me against her. "Put it in her."

I raised her leg and managed to insert my dick a ways inside. Ted lay down behind her. He spat in his hand and rubbed it on her ass. He spat again and rubbed it on his dick. He moved against her and jolted himself inside her butt. Her eyes went wide and she bit her lower lip. Bile rose in me. Ted reached across her and took hold of my back, pulling me to him, making a sandwich of the girl. "Now fuck her," he said, and I did, feeling Ted's dick moving against mine with whatever thin membranes and muscles she had down there the only thing separating us.

Karen's play is great and so is Karen, who is somehow completely convincing as a cheerleader even though most cheerleaders are about twenty years younger than she is. She's one of the three leads, the outrageous one, the one with all the schemes, the one who gets the others in and out of trouble. I watch her move across the stage as I used to watch my mother back in Vermont, impressed with the ease of her delivery, the confidence, the bigger than life aspect. Truth is, I'm awed by Karen Grave and all my concerns about spending time with her, given how we met, disappear for a couple of hours. I just take in the amazing sight of somebody I know, somebody who wants to know me, on a Broadway stage in New York City.

When I knock on the stage door, she's waiting just inside. She's like a teenager, as if she's still that cheerleader and I'm some laconic football hero. She takes my hand and examines the bandaged thumb. "What happened?" she asks me.

"Cut myself at work," I say. "Nothing serious."

She switches to my good hand and leads me back to the dressing area. Everything about her seems exaggerated, and I feel a lot like the kid I was back in Vermont—mute, compliant, trying to read my mom's mood or desire of the moment. It wasn't until I was well into high school that I realized my mother was not a whole lot clearer about things than I was. She was just more outspoken, more irate. I'm pretty sure Karen is all soft inside too, just lacquered over with that shiny coat of bluster that seems to go with the profession.

I recognize some of the faces from the cast. They smile politely, but nobody stops to say hello. It's almost as if they're avoiding Karen. It occurs to me that I've never seen her *with* anybody—not her husband when she arrived at the clinic, not a friend when she stops by the Strand. Even here, among the other actors, it seems like she's alone.

She changes out of her cheerleader costume while I check out the backstage area which is smaller and dingier than I'd expected, with a narrow hallway serving cramped dressing rooms. Even the space behind the stage seems undersized and abandoned, like one of our campsites overseas after everybody's moved on. I venture onto the stage and stare into the dark house that stretches back and up as far as I can see, row after row of plush red seats with touches of gold leaf catching the dim red glow of the exit signs. I look down at the lengths of tape stuck to the stage floor, denoting prop locations, actor positions, and then at the empty orchestra pit with its chairs and music stands arranged hit-or-miss as if they'd been pushed aside by musicians in a hurry to get home. How does Karen Grave work up the nerve to stand here in front of a house full of people, all of them staring back at her and hanging on her every word and facial expression? How does she even get her voice to work?

Ted and I were five weeks from the end of our tour. It was the rainy season, not that they needed to set aside a time over there especially for rain. I never knew the stuff could come down like that. Hours, days at a time, weeks. Morning when we woke up, night when we zipped ourselves into our soggy tent. Rain dripped off our noses as we walked. Our boots rotted. The pads of our fingers and toes developed a permanent pucker. Fat droplets oozed off drenched leaves and splotched on our shoulders. Leeches dwelt in our crotches. Paddy algae, mold, jock itch. Matches, their sulfur tips fallen away, were discarded, a couple of lighters passed around to damp cigarettes. Stowed letters smelled of moss and fell apart.

In rain like that, you lose your sense of what's real. You forget whether the oxygen your exhausted body craves comes from air or water, whether you're swimming or walking. You forget the truth of who you are. The little of yourself you claimed and held onto all those months washes away like an eroding streambed. I heard voices at night. My mother calling me to supper. The motel manager telling me I needed to sweep out the linen storage area, where arid sheets and towels smelled of dry soap powder. I heard that guy with the shoebox, Lick, mumble a goodbye when I headed north from his place toward the Canadian border. I heard our dogs barking behind the house and wondered why I had never untied them. Why hadn't I set the poor suckers free?

Ted and I still shared a tent and I still followed him on marches, but after the incident at the brothel our conversation dwindled to a prickly silence. We never mentioned what happened. Maybe he felt some sort of remorse, which was a dangerous thing in Vietnam because there was no place for that feeling to end. We'd gotten close to something that day with the girls, something profound between us, and it had stumped the hell out of us both. I'd catch him staring at me sometimes, and he'd nod just a little bit before he looked away. It scared me to see our closeness dwindle because I was convinced that that's what had kept me going for a year, the idea that there was someone else in the world who cared about me enough to keep me in his sights. I think it scared Ted too.

He developed some kind of a stomach disorder. Acid, I guess, dripping inside him like the rain off those giant ferns. He ate cold noodles and broth out of a can. Nothing else. Then he'd grimace as he tried to hold it down. He shit constantly. I could tell by the way he walked and sat that his raw ass burned like pepper in a wound. He lost weight. But he was not quite bad enough to get himself flown out. Or probably he was, if he'd complained, which he wouldn't do. I wondered if it was the Vietnamese girl that was eating him up inside, the guilt of using an innocent person that way, though maybe that was just me. I wondered if Ted had been trying to love me that day, crazy as that sounds, through that poor girl. I loved him, too, of course. Not that we were gay. It had never been like that with us. Yet, the question was definitely there now, with that weird feeling of our cocks rubbing so close together inside the girl like that. And we weren't going anywhere near discussing it.

But the problem, of course, was much deeper than that one experience. The war had sapped our souls. In those last few weeks of our tour, Ted had been lost in a mire of revulsion, and I was right there with him. Maybe he had used that girl to try to save himself, to reach out and hold onto me before he slipped into the disheartened oblivion he'd been resisting. I wish I could have said these things to him, could have told him I understood how, with that girl, we had confirmed that every last bit of humanity in us was lost. But that we still had each other.

That possibility disappeared when Ted started picking on me. I don't even remember how it started, probably with something silly like the way I always cleaned my rifle so thoroughly and always folded our soggy tent so the corners lined up. The taunts became constant those last weeks, and eventually I started pushing back. Before I knew what was happening, one afternoon Ted was on top of me on the ground, jamming his fist into my ribs. I hit back and eventually managed to throw him off. With that fight, that desire to really hurt each other when our whole time together had been about helping each other, the ultimate damage had been done. From then on, I kept my distance.

My last day with Ted, the rain stopped in the early evening and some misty rays of sun angled through stalled clouds, raising my spirits unduly. Eleven days and I'd be headed back to headquarters and then to debriefing, and finally, home. There'd be no trips out west with Ted. I'd have only myself to think about, which was okay now. In our tent, after dark, I couldn't sleep with that excitement and weird sort of guardedness about taking anything for granted. There was still time for everything to change, one bullet, one booby trap. I knew Ted was awake too. Eleven days and I'd never see him again. After all we'd been through together, it didn't make any sense to end things this way. I decided to try one last time to talk to him. "Just eleven days, Ted." He didn't say anything. "We made it through."

"Don't say that. It's bad luck."

We listened to Ted's stomach growl its nightly upheaval. I was thinking that soon this would all be just the darkest, remotest part of my history. I'd make it that way. I'd force it out of my mind, all of it, the horror of killing, the disappointment of friendship. I'd go to New York where I'd always dreamed of going and Ted would go back to Pennsylvania to Rosemary Becker. He'd marry her and have a bunch of kids. I would do whatever I would do. We would bury this year deep in some black oblivion.

"You're the best friend I ever had, Ted. Whatever I did, I'm sorry."

"Goddamn it," he said, sitting up, his reduced bulk a silhouette in the dim light of the tent. "Just leave it."

Still, I reached up and rested my hand on his shoulder, my heart clomping around in my chest. However things were now, whatever had happened between us, I believed Ted had saved my life that year. I would have done anything for him, still, despite the craziness of the last weeks. The war made people nuts. We all knew that. I wanted us to forgive each other, and ourselves, for whatever we'd done.

He shoved my hand away, unzipped our tent and crawled out. I heard him step off toward the woods instead of heading to the latrine, where he went at least three times a night. Maybe he didn't want any more jokes about the explosive gush of his diarrhea. Funny how certain comportments die hard. We'd pulled leeches out of each other's crotches and he was shy about anybody hearing him take a shit. Proud was more like it, I suppose. This constant diarrhea was a weakness he couldn't accept.

There was an eerie quiet after his footsteps went out of range. I don't remember what I was thinking, beyond that absence of sound. Maybe recounting the days we had left, which I had done every night for weeks, like a mantra to get me to sleep. Maybe whether I should recommend to Ted that he take a med-evac, now, even though the time was so short. I'd thought of it before, but had procrastinated, afraid to suggest anything that Ted might misinterpret, and afraid to part with my good luck charm so late in the game. Superstition dies hard in war. And I knew Ted would have seen himself as giving in, which he would never do. Eleven more days. He wasn't about to quit now.

The explosion was muffled, probably by a foot or more of wet vegetation. But it shook the ground. My head seemed to explode with it. I put my palms to my ears, holding my skull together. Then I crawled outside and was on my feet, running and squealing like a wounded pig. I tripped, got up and ran some more. The cloud cover had continued to break up and a crescent moon shed a mottled white light, eerily still, over the ground, the trees, the tall grasses surrounding the camp. Where were the sentries? Where was the fucking medic? I ran. I shouted, "HELP! MEDIC! HELP!" And then there was blood everywhere, and glistening hunks of silvery flesh dripping from lush leaves. I didn't see Ted right away. Then I heard him moan. He was only a few feet away, in a dark spot under an uprooted bush. He had no legs and only one arm. Half his face was gone. Still, he moaned and burbled my name.

Karen finds me, kisses my cheek, and soon we're back out the stage door to the street. A freezing wind whips down Forty-Third Street, lifting a paper cup and a page of the *New York Post* along with it. Half a dozen people in puffy down parkas and knit hats ask for her autograph and she willingly obliges. They look at me like they're disappointed I'm not somebody important.

Karen talks nonstop as we make our way to Eighth Avenue, where we walk north, our shoulders hunched against the frigid wind. Wisps of powdery snow ride the gusts like in Vermont. I'm grateful that she has a lot to say as I ran out of words once I told her I had liked her performance. I'm not one of those people who critique a movie after the credits glide by. Usually I don't know what I think until much later. It's not that I'm unmoved, more that there is this yawning distance between my feelings and the words that might explain them. Karen's words are an easy reach for her, looping and disappearing like the snowflakes swirling around us.

"Then Eric misses his cue," she's saying. "Christ! I'm standing there, my next line meaningless without his, and. . . ." The wind swoops the rest away. The whole diatribe has an unreal quality about it, anyway, as if being irritated is just a role she's playing now, emanating from her own interior backstage, as dark and eerie as the one we just left.

"You could have fooled me," I say. "I didn't notice anything amiss."

She smiles and takes my arm. "You're sweet."

We turn onto Forty-Fourth. Karen's hair flails behind her. Her eyes tear in the wind. Suddenly, she stops in her tracks. "I'm freezing," she shouts, turning her back to a fresh gust. "Screw Sardi's. I'm not in the mood to be around theater people anyway. Let's go to my place." A taxi happens to be discharging a passenger fifty feet away and Karen runs to it, that quick little dancer's step from the first time I saw her at the clinic, three weeks ago.

I catch up to her. "What about your husband?" I yell into the gust.

She gives me an impatient look and I climb in behind her and slam the door. The cab's heater groans reassuringly. She gives the driver her address, 230 West Twenty-First Street, and we pull slowly east and then turn into downtown traffic.

"I thought you lived in SOHO," I say.

10

HANK SLOWS THINGS DOWN A LITTLE

Riding downtown to Karen's apartment, I mention the possibility that her hotshot, Wall Street husband might walk in on our cozy little midnight get-together. What happens then? I ask her.

"My husband is a very long story," she says, pulling off her gloves and blowing on her fingertips. "Please don't make me tell it now."

There was a message on my machine yesterday from Dr. McAvery, saying he would need a delivery at the end of next week. It's for Karen, of course, since that Friday is exactly four weeks since the day we met in the elevator, the day of her third insemination. My gut tightens as the wrongness of Karen and me being in this cab together takes up a position between us.

The driver swerves around Seventh Avenue's potholes like a slalom skier. "I'm pretty tired," I say. "Why don't I drop you and take the cab back up to Fifty-Seventh." I feel for my wallet in my back pocket, wondering if there is enough cash there to cover the fare.

She studies my face. "You're scared, Hank Preston."

I glance out the side window, where the wind makes frozen pathways across the roofs of parked cars. "Maybe," I say. "Aren't you?"

"Sometimes I think I've been scared so long, the feeling doesn't even register anymore." She reaches across the seat and takes my hand. "I don't have a husband," she says.

I turn back to her. "You what?"

"There is no husband."

"I don't get it."

"You're not alone."

"You're not married?"

"Lloyd was somebody I created for the clinic. You know McAvery never would have inseminated me if he knew I was single."

"You lied to the clinic?"

"I hired a guy to play the part of my husband during all those humiliating tests and interviews. He answered my ad in the *Village Voice* for somebody with a nonexistent sperm count. It's amazing what you can find in the *Voice*! I even coached him on how to play my husband. I thought of everything, and it all worked beautifully."

I stare out the window again. This is too weird. This is more than I can handle.

"Are you mad?" she asks me.

"Karen. . . ."

"You can't say I'm not determined."

"Jesus! You're not married? And you're trying to get pregnant?"

"Lloyd gets really big in my mind sometimes, but no, he doesn't really exist."

I try to make sense of what Karen is telling me. But there is no sense in it. She's lying to the clinic, to me, to herself, apparently.

"Don't be mad, okay?"

I squeeze her hand. "I'm not," I say. And mad really isn't it. Stunned, bewildered, scared. All of the above.

The taxi stops at a light. I wipe a dense layer of condensation from my side window, where gems of green and red light flicker. A couple waits at the corner to cross, their shoulders hunched, their heads pitched into the wind. My mind swirls. I let go of Karen's hand as the taxi pulls ahead.

"Forgive me?" she says. "I should have told you from the beginning. I'm sorry."

"Why didn't you?"

"I guess, once I told you my last name was Tuckwell, the name I gave the clinic, I took on that role. I didn't think I'd see you again. I didn't think I'd like you so much."

I brace my hand on the back of the seat in front of us, as if we're about to rear-end the double parked limo looming ahead to the right. The taxi swerves around it and turns onto Twenty-First Street.

"Do you find me attractive?"

"Of course I do. I think you're beautiful."

We pull to the curb in front of her building. "Why don't you come up?" she says. "We can talk some more."

I pay the driver and follow Karen Grave inside her cramped hallway. She sorts through some bills and drops them back onto the table. I have the urge to gather them into a neat little pile. Instead, I follow her up the creaking stairs. Despite myself, I imagine Karen naked—the long shapely legs, the muscular rear end, her small breasts resting against her skinny ribcage. Excitement and dread battle it out in my chest. What the hell am I doing? Is this woman crazy?

She flips on the overhead light in her entryway and closes the door behind us. She throws the deadbolt lock, glances at me and touches my arm the way she did a week ago at my apartment. Can a woman be vulnerable and sweet and calculating all at the same time? I shiver, wipe snowflakes from my shoulders.

The apartment smells steamy and closed in and has the cluttered look of a storage area. Three cardboard boxes line one wall, their lids jutting at odd angles, as if she had given up on finding drawer space for their contents. There's a pillow at one end of the sofa, left over from a nap or a house guest. Dirty dishes overflow the sink in the kitchenette across the room.

Karen pulls off her scarf and drops her parka on a chair. I pocket my gloves, shed my pea coat and look for a hanger. "Just drop it somewhere," she says. "Drink?"

"Do you have any tea?"

"How could I not have known that?"

"I drink alcohol sometimes. Just thought some herbal tea would taste good on a night like this, if you have any." I also need to keep my wits about me, I'm thinking. I rub my hands together. "If not, it's no big deal."

She runs water into a kettle and sets it on the stove. She strikes a match and watches a blue flame work its way slowly around the gas ring. Magazines cover the floor by a chair, old movie posters paper the walls—Hepburn and Tracy in *the Philadelphia Story*, Rock Hudson, James Dean and Elizabeth Taylor in *Giant*. I glance into a bedroom that might be pleasant during the day, with two windows overlooking a garden. A huge, painted cupboard takes up one wall and makes the room feel like a set for *Alice in Wonderland*.

"Tea is served," she says, setting two steaming mugs on the coffee table in front of the sofa. She moves the pillow out of the way and we sit, wrapping our hands around our mugs.

"How'd you ever get that cupboard up here?" I ask her, gesturing toward the bedroom.

"The armoire? Huge, isn't it? I hired some guys to take it apart. You want something bad enough, you find a way, right?" Karen extracts a cigarette from a pack on the coffee table and sticks it between her lips. I suppress an urge to straighten up the littered surface, which wouldn't make a dent in the onslaught this place needs.

"So, what do you do for fun?" she asks, setting a match to the end of the cigarette.

"Me? I like to read. And I like going to plays once in a while. It was great seeing you tonight. Amazing, really. I don't see how you do it." Karen inhales and expels a blue haze that rises toward the ceiling. Then she strikes another match and stares at the tiny flame as it burns almost to her fingertips. She tosses the remnant into the ashtray, where it smolders and dies. "You could burn yourself doing that," I say. She smiles and strikes the last match in the book. Together, we watch it burn down, again almost to her fingertips. Play with fire, you get burned, my mom used to say. "Probably my favorite pastime is looking at people. New York is one big parade and my bike's my private little viewing stand."

"Sounds like you do a lot of watching."

"I guess."

"Alone."

I nod. "Being here with you is like coming down out of the bleachers." I picture myself stepping onto Karen Grave's rowdy playing field, ducking, not knowing what's going to hit next.

She takes my tea from my hands and sets both our mugs on the table. She leans over and kisses me. Her lips are dry. I kiss her back. But then she slips her tongue into my mouth and leans in further. She wraps her arms around my shoulders as if she's not about to let me go. I taste cigarette smoke and the slightly soapy essence of lipstick, familiar from my six-week girlfriend in eleventh grade. Where is that cigarette she was smoking, anyway, I wonder.

My hands grip the cushions. Karen stops suddenly and sits back into the sofa. "Are you a virgin?" she asks me. She is still holding the cigarette. She takes a drag.

I blink into the kitchenette's overhead light. "Well, yeah, sort of."

"You either are or you aren't, my sweet Hank Preston. There's no 'sort of' about it." She laughs and pulls away. "I'm sorry. I'm just laughing at the situation. It's so ironic."

"Because you've already had my semen inside you?"

"Because I finally meet someone I like and he's asexual."

I pick up my tea. "I want it to mean something, that's all."

"A man saving himself in 1974. Am I missing something here? Did the sexual revolution not happen ten years ago?"

"You say you like me, but you haven't exactly been honest, you know? Give me a break!"

Karen picks up her mug. We sit out an awkward silence, sipping our tea. "I need a drink," she says, jumping up. In the kitchen, she pulls a bottle of Southern Comfort from a cupboard and pours herself a small glass, not bothering with ice. "Sure you won't join me?"

I shake my head. She leaves the bottle, uncorked, on the counter, crosses the room and sits back down next to me.

"In this fantasy you have of Lloyd," I ask her.

"I don't want to talk about Lloyd."

"Do you love him? I mean in the fantasy."

"Love? What's that?"

"You know."

She takes another sip of her drink. Has Karen Grave really rejected any concept of normal or is this all an act, too? There's something strangely appealing about her oddball behavior, especially since my whole life I've had both feet inextricably stuck in some muddied search for the truth about people, including myself. I always believed that at some point my real life would start—when I turned seventeen and got my own truck, when I finished high school, when I got back from Vietnam. But you know what? My real life isn't waiting for me around some corner. It's happening right now, right here in Karen Grave's apartment. It's been happening at the Strand for three years. It happens when I donate my semen or when I postpone my dinner with Joey.

"I guess I loved this guy in summer stock in New Hampshire, eight years ago," Karen is saying. "My God, it's hard to believe it's been that long. We spent every minute together. It wasn't as if he was perfect or anything. The truth is, he bored the hell out of me. But I got it in my mind that I was in love with him and I threw myself into that role, you know? I did everything I could think of to make him want me."

"And? What happened?"

"He was gay."

"That's a problem." Or is it? I wonder. If you watch the talk shows on TV, which my mother did, it seems like plenty of married couples don't have sex, and yet they love each other, or at least live together. I cross my boots under the coffee table, trying to relax. "Maybe the fact that he was gay made him more interesting to you in a way. More of a challenge. Holding off on sex, you really got to know each other enough to fall for the guy."

"Holding off? We weren't exactly delaying. He wasn't interested."

"But I think. . . . Hell, what do I know? I just think sex is a really big thing, whether people admit it or not. And if you're offhand about it, it has the potential to come around and bite you in the butt."

Karen Grave chuckles. "That would have been fine if he'd been into it. You have an awful lot of opinions, for a . . . for being so inexperienced."

"I just don't think it should be a big game, that's all. People get hurt in contact sports!"

"Are you really still a virgin? A cutie like you?"

"Pretty much."

"That's not a 'yes'."

"I messed around with a girl in high school. You know—petting, clothes half off, or half on, depending. . . ."

"But never intercourse?"

I pass my empty tea mug from one hand to the other before setting it back on the coffee table. "Once," I say.

"Aha!"

"In Vietnam."

"See?" She jabs me in the ribs with her finger. "An Oriental girl turned your head." She sets her drink down, stamps out her cigarette, and in one swift move pushes me back onto the sofa and climbs on top of me. She pulls my shirttails out of my jeans and grabs at the buttons. I run my fingers into her hair, something I've wanted to do since that first morning, in the elevator. Before long, our clothes are off and we slide to the floor, half under the coffee table.

And then Ted's face flashes on the backs of my eyelids, oversized as a drive-in movie villain. He grimaces as he yanks me against the Vietnamese girl. He spits out words, Fuck her, Goddamn it, Hank. His thick fingers dig into my shoulders. A drop of his spittle lands in the girl's shiny hair.

"Shall we go into the bedroom?" Karen asks me, getting up. Numb, confused, I follow her, reaching to pick up my boxers on the way. "You can leave that stuff there," she says.

She dives on top of unmade sheets, laughing. Her breasts bounce playfully. She turns to where I'm standing by the bed. "You are so damn hot," she says.

I look down at my hard on, which projects straight toward Karen, as if it's pointing the way to its own fulfillment. So that's where the term "selfish prick" comes from! "Do you have an appointment at the clinic next Friday?" I ask her.

"You're asking me that now?"

"I'm sorry. I just. . . ."

Karen turns over in her bed and starts screaming and pounding her pillow. For a minute, I think she's really mad, but then she's laughing. "Why?" she yells. "Why me? Why do I get the virgin with principles? Why? Why?"

I sit on the edge of her bed and run my hand down the back of her arm, which is damp with an exhilarating mist. She rolls onto her back. "Are you okay?" I ask her.

She smiles.

I rub her arm some more. "You know, tonight, I kept thinking about this buddy I had in Vietnam," I say. "Ted. He died over there."

"I'm sorry. Were you guys close?"

I nod. "Sometimes I think it was my fault."

"How so?"

"It's a long story. Remember I mentioned the girl I had sex with over there? Ted kind of forced me to do that."

Karen lifts her head and flips her hair across the pillow. "Why would he force you? What was it to him?"

"I wondered about that, too. I'm not sure." I stop, uncertain about confiding in Karen Grave. If you ask me, most revelations are only important to the guy having them, anyway. Still, I go on. "The more I think about Vietnam and Ted,"

I say, "the more blurred the truth gets about what actually happened over there. Everything was so messed up."

"As you know, I'm not the one to ask about the truth." She smiles up at me.

The light from her bedside lamp makes a lurid crown of her hair and casts elongated shadows under her eyes and lips, making her look her age, whatever that is. And yet, she seems more like a weary child, waiting to be tucked in. "There's such a thing as a lie, though," I say, finally. "My mom used to tell me that if you lie to somebody, you take responsibility for what happens. The other person isn't playing with a full deck from that point on, so it's your fault."

"Guilty as charged," Karen says. "I'm sorry."

I smooth out the sheet next to the beautiful curve of Karen's hip.

"So, you think you had something to do with your friend's death? Is that it?"

"Yeah, I do."

"But is that likely? Knowing you, I doubt it. So where's the truth in that feeling?"

"There was no reason for Ted to stray so far from camp that night. He knew how unsafe it was. Maybe he left because he hated me too much to spend one more night in our tent, side by side, close like that. Maybe he left because I was saying things he didn't want to hear."

"What sort of things?"

"We were a week or so away from discharge. I wanted him to know how important our friendship had been to me, despite what had happened with that girl."

Karen glances toward the armoire. "Do you think he had a thing for you?"

Something tightens in my chest. "No. I don't think so. Maybe. All I know is, he couldn't be my friend anymore after that night at the brothel. That's what I mean about sex. It's dangerous." I look around the messy room, underwear discarded over a chair, a pile of laundry waiting to be folded. "Maybe it wasn't my fault. I don't know."

"Which is my point about truth—who's to say, really? Maybe it's just our desperate need to create order out of life's natural chaos."

Karen stares into my eyes until I look away, suddenly aware of my nakedness, my flaccid dick, my long hairy legs. Karen runs her fingers down my chest. "You can stay if you want to. We can just sleep."

The idea of sleeping next to Karen Grave and not getting a hard-on strikes me as even more absurd than my constant ruminations.

"Sometimes you just have to dive in and pick up the pieces later on, you know?" She sighs and slips deeper into the bed.

"Want to go to Central Park on Saturday," I say. "We could have a picnic."

"It's winter, in case you haven't noticed, and colder than. . . . Well, you know."

"Maybe it'll warm up."

She takes my hand. "A picnic. What a lovely idea. Do you mind letting yourself out?"

I stand and pull the comforter up to her pretty white neck. I kiss her cheek.

In the living room, I step into my shorts and jeans. I pull on my coat and wrap my scarf around my neck. Before leaving, I stick my head into her bedroom. "You never said—do you have an appointment next Friday?"

She lifts herself onto one elbow and winks the way she did that first day. "We could save each other the trouble, if you like. Bypass the middleman!"

Outside, at ten after two in the morning, the wind has let up. I decide to walk to Fifty-Seventh Street. Feathery snowflakes accumulate on the windowsills of the dilapidated brick townhouses along Ninth Avenue. I tilt my head back, squint and let the gentle flakes land on my face, like when I was a kid in Vermont. Beyond the occasional lighted window, I think I can see a sleepless young mother, nursing her baby, and then an old lady who might be baking a cake for her grandson's birthday. Tomorrow, Karen will probably come to the Strand with a couple of raisin Danish. Maybe I'll walk her to the theater and drop her off for rehearsal. On Saturday, we'll go to Central Park. Next week she'll have her fourth insemination with my semen. I wonder, as I pass the back of the Port Authority building, where I arrived three years ago, if this is a moment I need to take stock of. This woman lied to the clinic. What kind of mother will she make? Single mother, not married. Snow swirls under the street lamp, a cab slows and stops at the light, a homeless guy wrapped in plastic wheels a cart full of his possessions.

There's no way to know what's in store for me now. Maybe that's a good thing.

11

KAREN IN SUMMER STOCK

On the subject of great, if somewhat ill-conceived performances, I should recount my summer of 1966 at the White Mountain Theater Festival in New Hampshire, my summer of Dan Bailey, my where-is-this-leading man. Not an episode I'm proud of, certainly, but a sort of dismal confirmation that I can't seem to make things work with men, no matter how I try.

My colleagues in summer stock liked to call me The Great Pretender. Whenever I arrived for rehearsal, rarely on time, they'd hum that song by The Platters, a quartet of black men in shiny sport jackets that got sidelined by the Beatles. Of course I can remember the lyrics to this day.

Oh yes, I'm the great pretender,
Pretending that I'm doing well,
My need is such, I pretend too much,
I'm lonely, but no one can tell.

What actor is not a pretender? When I took on a role, I *became* that character, which could easily extend to a late-night drink with the cast or waking up alone in my little dorm room the next morning, my real self someone I couldn't quite place, or perhaps face. When I thought about it, my character was real. Dan's was real. Didn't the audience believe we were madly in love?

Too real is this feeling of make believe,
Too real when I feel what my heart can't conceal.

The second verse went something like that. Was my pretending that obvious? Did I appear desperate?

I had recently turned thirty, a crisis for any actress. My skin was beginning to lose the tight glow a woman takes for granted in her twenties. And my eyes—well, let's not go there. Just that spring, I had replaced the hundred-watt bulb over my bathroom mirror with a sixty, and lined up some soft-white forties and twenty-fives in the cupboard like a supporting cast. I couldn't shake this vision of myself one day as a fifty-year-old career spinster, a she-was-quite-beautiful-in-her-day sort of actress. I know there's dignity in aging gracefully, but only if you've been married at least twice. How mortifying to have no out of date monograms, no silver-framed photos of disgruntled teenagers, no handsome divorce settlements. The thought sent shivers up my spine.

I'd had plenty of dates in Manhattan during the years after I stepped off the bus from upstate New York and settled down in a walk-up in Chelsea. Trust me, Chelsea was not "Chelsea" back then, but that's another story. I was eighteen. What did I know? But these romances tended to last only as long as the role I was playing at the time. After all, the guy had fallen for Stella Kowalski or Miss Pipperidge, not Karen Grave. Boasting to friends of my independence had begun to sound pathetic. In truth, I'd grown tired of my staunch individualism, my affairs that had become as boring as John Wayne reruns, John Wayne first-runs for that matter. My East Village singing coach, for one, eastern and mysterious, with a Zen-like calm that extended all the way to his penis. And a director friend, who liked to watch himself in the mirror when we made love. I had developed a tic in my neck, straining to make eye contact. The last straw had been leaving a party a little tipsy one night and having to wait, in more ways than one, for the doorman to get off. Things had gotten out of hand. I needed some stability.

That August in New Hampshire, my moon was in Jupiter with Venus rising, which meant romance was imminent, though my tarot cards were cautionary, something about the man in my future not being completely right for me. Who worried about completely right when completely wrong had become routine? I wanted a husband.

But not just any husband. I wanted Dan Bailey, who, twice that summer, had played my leading man. Dan was decent looking, but not so handsome as to steal glances away from me. He was younger, but so what? He possessed a modicum of talent, but more important, he made me laugh, that essential ingredient in any relationship. And Dan was single. The fact that he was gay seemed like an awkward line in an otherwise graceful dialogue, a line that might easily be edited out. I could make it work, just as I had rescued many a scene from some playwright's ineptitude. Besides, Dan wasn't like other gay men. He wore cheap sneakers and sometimes forgot to comb his hair. He didn't even call himself Daniel.

Late one evening, during the final week of performances, we sat together on the terrace of the granite mansion that functioned as a dormitory for members of the cast. The rear of the house overlooked a field that sloped gradually to a pond. An occasional restless star flashed along the horizon, its flaming tail reflected in the placid surface of the water. You couldn't ask for a more romantic setting.

"You were magnificent tonight, my lady," Dan said, bowing before me. Dan flattered, another excellent quality in a mate. "Hungry?" he asked, reaching for his backpack. To celebrate the end of the season, he'd brought sandwiches—provolone cheese and roasted peppers. Dan was vegetarian. Unconsciously, I had begun to eschew meat, as well. Whatever Dan did seemed right, somehow, from his Tai Chi workout in the woods at dawn to the casual way he pushed sunglasses back on his head when schmoozing a director. Adopting Dan's tastes felt natural, effortless. We were even drawn to the same men.

He withdrew a bottle of rosé from his backpack. Dan was like that, sensitive to my preferences, extravagant. He said, "The Beatles played their very last concert ever tonight, in San Francisco. Gosh, I wish I could have been there."

Dan was beyond avid when it came to the Beatles. "Tonight? Really?"

"I'm so bummed I never got to see them live. Now I never will."

Worse things had happened that summer, I remember thinking, like the sniper who killed thirteen people three weeks ago at the University of Texas, or the final episode of the *Dick Van Dyke Show* in June. I've always had a bit of a crush on Dick Van Dyke, and dreamed of landing a part on that show. So many possibilities extinguished every day, it's hard to get too excited about not seeing the Beatles.

"Only two more performances," Dan said as he poured the wine into plastic cups. "It's hard to believe we'll be going back to Manhattan on Sunday."

With the season ending, I was becoming more and more nervous about being apart from Dan. We both claimed to be loners, yet we had slid so easily into this relationship. Relationships! I remember musing about how few words there were to describe them, preferring to think it was words that disappointed me, not men. "I wish it wouldn't end," I said.

We had quarreled about silly things over the summer, the way lovers often do. I'd felt wounded at times, then flighty as a schoolgirl when he apologized. I'd never known a man who threw me off balance quite the way Dan did.

"I'll miss our chats," he said, unwrapping our sandwiches and setting out napkins.

Chats? Is that all they were? I'd never spent this much intimate time with a man without having sex.

"And Billy, of course."

I flinched at the mention of Billy, one of the chorus boys in *Good News,* the musical that was closing the season. Most young actors hid their homosexuality in 1966 on the off chance that one day they'd be called on to play a Hollywood action hero. But Billy, blond and bland, followed Dan around like a puppy. I could see that he was no more to Dan than a Godiva chocolate was to me, a whim one hopes to suppress but of no real consequence either way. What was a little fling compared to the closeness Dan and I shared that summer? Sex was hardly the most important aspect of a relationship. And besides, I was certain that somewhere deep down, Dan felt an attraction to me based on a devotion that transcended bodies. How different were they really, men's and women's bodies—a curve here, a swelling there? What did any of that matter?

Dan sipped his wine. He chuckled. "What's funny?" I asked.

"Oh, just something Billy said this afternoon." He took a hefty bite of his sandwich. "Nothing important."

"Is anything important to you, Dan?"

He set down his wine. "Whoa! Is something wrong, my sweet?"

"I don't know." I retreated. I was so afraid of losing him. My affairs with men had always possessed a natural sort of rhythm, determined by me, at least at first. But Dan had been in charge from day one. "Just end-of-the-season jitters, I guess. I hate endings."

"Maybe it's not an ending. Maybe it's a beginning."

"Of what, though?" I asked, feeling suddenly hopeful.

"I don't know." He poured himself more wine. "Something new, I guess."

By midnight, I was edgy with a sense of expectancy, like that hushed moment before the curtain goes up, when the house goes dark and no one moves or breathes. Would he hug me as he sometimes did and assure me that our evenings together would continue back in New York? Would that hug lead to something more, finally?

It struck me then, with a shiver, that I was quite unalterably in love with Dan Bailey.

I sipped my wine and tried to relax into the notion that the end of summer stock wasn't our final act but merely a scene-change. I knew that the notion that men were gay because they had never met the right woman was an odious cliché, yet I found myself believing I might just be that woman for Dan Bailey.

Back in New York, three weeks passed without a call from Dan. I began to wonder if something terrible had happened to him—an accident, appendicitis, a job waiting on tables. Finally, that third Friday, I dialed his number.

"Karen!" he said. "I've been meaning to. . . . What's up?"

"I was just on my way home and wondered if you'd like to have dinner?"

"It's five-thirty."

"I could wait."

"Give me a couple of hours, okay?"

I met him outside his apartment building on Christopher Street in the West Village. His tan had faded, but his eyes still possessed the intensity I had found so irresistible all summer. We walked together to Hudson Street. Yellow ginkgo leaves accumulated along the curb. Summer was definitely over.

At dinner, he asked about some of the actors we'd worked with in New Hampshire. "Billy says hi," he said.

"You're still seeing him?"

"We talk. He's on the road." Dan dipped a French fry in ketchup.

"You should be discreet. A lot of directors. . . . Well, I'm not telling you anything you don't already know."

Dan gave me a quizzical look before going on to mention parts he'd auditioned for.

"I've missed you," I said.

"Have you been out?"

"Out?"

"To auditions."

"Just one. A road-show revival of *Oklahoma*. It wasn't for me."

"That would be so cool! Chicago, LA. God, I'd love that."

"You wouldn't mind leaving New York?"

"Are you kidding? What's to keep me here?"

"Love?"

"Right!" He guffawed.

For several nights, I hardly slept. In fitful dreams, Dan and I were paired in all the classic films, replacing Gary Cooper and Deborah Kerr in *High Noon*, out-romancing Clark Gable and Vivien Leigh in *Gone with the Wind*. But always, at the climactic moment, Dan rode off with Gary or Clark and I jerked awake, clutching the bedspread.

That week, I started doing things I'd never done before. I joined a weight lifting club on Sixth Avenue that was nearly all men with huge chests and arms. I worked out for hours at a time. I supplemented my vegetarian diet with plenty of cheese and tofu. It wasn't long before my body took on a masculine kind of firmness. I even worked with my voice teacher—the Buddhist with the Zen penis—on developing my lower register. Soon I could speak quite naturally in tones nearly an octave lower than before. I stopped wearing makeup and cut my hair. Those thick auburn locks I had once considered essential to my career hit the salon floor like so much edited film footage. In the end, over the protests of my stylist, I insisted on a pixie cut that Audrey Hepburn had popularized a decade earlier, and a bleach job almost to white. I took to wearing tee shirts and jeans. I remember surveying the effect in the mirror, recalling how my mother had told me once that she would have named me Kevin if I'd been a boy. Turning sideways in my sleeveless tee, I flexed my new biceps. "Go for it, Kevin," I whispered.

Finally, in November, I called Dan again and he agreed to meet me at the Metropolitan Museum. We sat on a bench overlooking a hundred or more Greek and Roman statues, their musculature lustrous and alluring. "You look great, Karen," he said. "Pretty extreme—the hair! I like it."

"I've made a lot of changes," I said.

"Not me. Still doing auditions, voice lessons, same old boring bit. When do I get my break?" He rolled the museum map in his hands, recounting how nervous he was at call-backs, the pressure, the uncertainty of the business. "Wish me luck," he said, stuffing the map into his pocket.

"It's not luck." I told him, taking his hand. "You know that. It's hard work."

"I guess you're right." He grinned and let his hand be held.

"Maybe you need some help," I said. "Remember how I used to coach you last summer?"

"Gosh, Karen, would you? That would be so cool."

In the weeks leading up to Christmas that year, I spent hours devising exercises to enhance diction and focus emotions. It was intense and it paid off. Soon Dan got a role in an Off-Broadway production of *Summer and Smoke* and was up for a one-time appearance on *Star Trek*. Somewhere around that time, I met my friend, Diane, for lunch at One Fifth, just up from the arch at Washington Square.

She sat into our booth at the back, her glossy black hair styled like a 1940s movie star, her cashmere sweater clinging to her shapely figure. "You look fabulous," she said, whether she meant it or not. Diane's career had surged recently. Unlike me, she'd never let anything get in its way. She'd recently landed a role on *Dr. Kildare*, with Richard Chamberlain, that hunk with the dreamy lips. "That boy look is so . . . How did you ever get the nerve?"

"I've been ready for a little alteration."

"That's more than fine-tuning, my dear." She sipped her water. "Don't tell me, you're seeing someone. Am I right?"

"You could say that." I giggled and glanced out the window onto Fifth Avenue, where a group of young men in tight bell-bottoms stood talking.

"I knew it! No wonder I haven't seen you." Diane eyed the waiter as he handed us menus and disappeared. "The men in this place are to die for," she whispered. "Too bad they're all gay." She draped her napkin over her lap and opened her menu. "Why didn't you bring your boyfriend? I want to meet him."

"He's rehearsing."

"He's an actor? Good golly! How long have you been seeing him?"

"Since summer." It was true. I *had* seen Dan since the summer.

"You've been seeing someone for six months and you haven't told me? I cannot believe this!" Diane broke off a tiny crust of bread and nibbled some crumbs. "So who's the lucky guy?"

"Dan Bailey," I said, his name slipping off my tongue with the ease of a well-rehearsed line.

"Dan Bailey?" Her thin-plucked eyebrows darted together. "The actor?"

"We met in summer stock last season, in New Hampshire."

"Dan Bailey?"

"Yes, Dan Bailey." I glared across the table at her.

"Karen, Dan Bailey is. . . ." But she stopped, her hand darting to her nose—talk about alterations—and then to her ear, as if some part of her face were suddenly amiss.

"Is what?"

". . . so . . . cute."

The waiter arrived to take our orders while I savored the exhilaration of finally opening up about Dan. People might be surprised, like Diane, but eventually they'd come to accept us as a couple. "I'll have the cheese and fruit plate," I said, handing the waiter my menu, "with extra cheddar." I smiled across the table at my friend.

Dan called the next day. "Diane Downey loved your new look," he said.

"You saw Diane?"

"She called. She has this guy she wants me to meet."

"A guy? What guy?"

"She was all weird on the phone. Said she heard you and I were an item."

I snickered. "Diane said that? She does get confused. What guy does she want you to meet?"

"I think she said he was her cousin."

"Not the one who got arrested on morals charges, I hope."

"Keith Young?"

"That's him."

"Morals charges?"

"Boys, I think. Sounds like Diane's idea of a joke. She's such a goof!"

"Are you sure? She sounded so high on him."

"That's Diane. What are you doing for dinner?"

Dan landed two important roles that winter, including an appearance on the *Beverly Hillbillies*, but with each, ironically he became more insecure. "There's so much farther to fall now," he kept saying. We talked on the telephone every day and met most evenings for dinner. Then, in March, he met Alex, an architect who couldn't seem to get enough of him.

"I'm not sure he's good for you," I said during a break from voice exercises. A gray late-winter light angled across the unmade bed Alex had probably left that morning.

"What do you mean?"

"I don't know. He sounds so . . . self-involved."

"Self wha . . . ? Karen, I do believe you're jealous."

"Of Alex?" I felt wounded. After all I'd done to help Dan. "What a thing to say!"

"Well, it's been just you and me for months," Dan said, thumbing through the pages of a new script his agent had sent over. A sudden freezing rain gusted against the window like scattered rice at a bride and groom. "But now, there's Alex."

"What about me?" I asked, tucking a new tee into my jeans.

"What do you mean?"

I felt a chill. Clearly, Dan had not thought about me at all.

"We'll always be friends," he said. "I'd never let Alex come between us."

"He already has."

In April, I attended Diane's thirty-fifth birthday party at The New Yorker Hotel on West Thirty-Fourth Street. Diane certainly was doing well for herself, I thought, as I made my way through the lobby and climbed the stairs to the ballroom, though she should think twice about admitting to turning thirty-five. Kiss of death in our business. Yet, at the sight of the packed room and the press lined up outside, I panicked. I hadn't been to an audition in months. I looked like a damn boy. I'd given up everything for Dan Bailey and now I was getting dumped for some art major with a protractor and some number three pencils.

I managed to elbow my way to the bar and down a quick martini. The attractive crowd looked so young. There was a man wearing a bunch of gold chains around his neck, a woman with a belt of bullets—fake?—across her chest, Che Guevara style. How many people would come to my birthday, I wondered, signaling the bartender for another. There was some ruckus at the far end of the room and Richard Chamberlain entered with an entourage of young men, all of them breathtaking. I spotted Diane talking to a director I recognized, grabbed my glass and made my way there.

"Karen!" Diane shouted.

"Happy birthday." I hugged her and air-kissed the director.

"Karen Grave. I hardly recognized you," he said. "We were just talking about Dan Bailey. You worked with him last season in summer stock, didn't you?"

"What about him?"

"We're thinking of casting him as Biff in a revival of *Death of a Salesman*. For the road, hopefully bring it to Broadway. Dan's getting hot these days."

I sipped my martini, rage curdling remnants of my power shake lunch. Diane was busy waving to someone. "No, I don't think that would work," I said. "I can't see Dan as Biff, really."

She turned back, incredulous. "He'd be perfect. Dan would be great, Karen."

"He needs a woman to play off of, a contemporary, a love interest. It would never work. And there were some problems in New Hampshire. A bit heavy with the wine. No-shows, that sort of thing."

"You're kidding," the director said.

"Dan Bailey?" Diane was astounded. "Karen. . . ."

"Don't quote me on it," I said and excused myself.

I pushed my way through the crowd, dropped off my glass at the bar and fled down the stairs to the street. I hailed a taxi downtown. What had I said? How could I be so cruel? Well, Dan *was* a drinker, I suppose. Or at least some day he might be. Damn that Alex! By the time the taxi turned onto Christopher Street, I was in a frenzy. What had I done? I was a horrible person. I paid the driver and walked the remaining block to Dan's. I would own up to the whole thing, apologize, swear I would never do anything like this again. I rang his buzzer and checked my watch—11:30. I rang again.

Dan buzzed me in.

Upstairs, the apartment door stood ajar. I pushed it open. A dim lamplight from the street slatted onto rumpled sheets. Dan, wearing only sweat pants, stood by the bed. "Karen?"

I sensed right away that there'd been a problem with Alex, a fight maybe, that he had likely just left and Dan thought I was Alex returning to apologize.

"You turned in early," I said.

"I'm not feeling so great."

"Shall I make us some tea?" I unzipped my jacket and threw it over a chair. Clearly, this was not the time for confessions.

Dan climbed back into bed and pulled the covers to his chin. He looked like a boy who'd lost his dog. I sat on the edge. "Are you okay?" I asked him.

"Not really."

"Everything's going to be all right," I assured him, running my fingers through his wavy hair.

There are moments in life when an opportunity presents itself, a moment you would never have expected, could never have planned. This was my moment. Dan was even more needy than usual. I was here, shoving my guilt aside, ready to give him whatever assurance I could. And I dared to think that if I could get him to make love to me, he might forgive me when he heard from Diane, Maybe he could even forget about Alex. Maybe he would finally see how important I was, how he could never do without me.

I stood and walked to the other side of the bed, undressed down to my panties and climbed in next to him.

"What are you doing?"

"Everything's going to be all right," I said, stroking his hair again.

He lay there, tense as a piano string, as I caressed his neck and the baby-smooth skin of his shoulder. Frolicking men's voices rose from the street, along with the vague scent of cigarette smoke. After a while, he rolled away from me and not long after that, he was asleep. We were finally together the way I had always imagined we'd be. Dan needed me. Eventually, I fell asleep too.

He called the next afternoon, furious. "So I drink too much?" he said.

"Dan. . . ."

"No-shows?"

"I can explain."

"Explain how you blew my biggest chance yet? Maybe my whole fucking career?"

"It was a misunderstanding."

"I'm the one who misunderstood, Karen. I thought you were my friend."

"Dan, please. I can explain." But he'd hung up. I fell onto the bed, certain I would never hear from Dan Bailey again.

For weeks, I paced the streets of Chelsea. I stopped working out, couldn't eat. I lost muscle tone. I grew dark roots. I'd given up everything for this man. I didn't return calls other than to confirm my commitment to another season in New Hampshire. One night, late in May, distraught, I paced for nearly an hour outside Dan's building. I was out of control. I knew it, but there seemed to be no way to stop, no way to curb this need I had to get back at Dan, to hurt him the way he had hurt me, as if one could ever get even that way. Upstairs, his window was dark. The thought of what I was about to do appalled me, and yet I couldn't resist. I needed to eliminate Dan Bailey from my life. It was him or me, that simple. This was self-defense. As I crossed the street to his building, my legs were somebody else's legs, my arms, my thoughts, all belonging to somebody I didn't recognize or ever want to know. From under my jacket, I withdrew a quart container of lighter fluid. I doused the entryway, struck a match and threw it.

I ran the fourteen blocks to my apartment where I stripped and bathed. In the bathroom mirror, I could see my old self beginning to emerge for the first time in months. The tension was receding from my face. My eyes were clearing. I retrieved mascara from the back of my medicine cabinet and resolved to dye my hair back to auburn that very night. The boy look had been all wrong.

I decided to leave for New Hampshire right away. Rehearsals wouldn't start for two weeks, but I could use the time to relax. I packed a few things, thinking I would treat myself to a new summer wardrobe when I got there. By fall, my hair would reach below my ears.

The next morning, at LaGuardia, I was myself again. The person I had been the night before, the last nine months in fact, was gone. I had allowed myself to fall in love. That was growth. The affair had been difficult, but it was over now and I was ready to move on.

I picked up a copy of the *New York Post* at the news counter and sat with my coffee, waiting for my flight to be called. A small article in the local news section reported a two-alarm fire in the West Village. The ground floor tenant had escaped to the back garden with her three cats and then climbed the fire escape to rescue the third floor tenant, an actor, and an architect "friend" who was staying with him temporarily. Right! A witness reported seeing two young men with blond hair running from the scene. Two? How our perceptions fail us! There were no serious injuries, though the building was badly damaged.

I settled into my seat by the window. As the plane taxied to the runway, I stared out to the sunny tarmac, a dreamy smile soothing my face. My tarot cards had been favorable that morning. This summer I would get it right.

12

THE PARIS COMMUNE

The Paris Commune is a charming and relatively inexpensive French bistro—a rarity in the West Village in 1974—on Bleecker Street, across from a small cobblestone park with weathered benches. Twenty or so recently planted Chinese pear trees, gray and brave in the overhead street lamps, provide leg-lifting relief to neighborhood canines. The evening is warm for mid-March, and I, who after almost six years in New York City should be inured to delusion, sense the onset of spring in the faint breezes off the Hudson River.

Optimism looms, ethereal as mist.

I pause as I approach the restaurant's sign—a colorfully plumed rooster, strutting over block letters. It occurs to me that that rooster captures my prejudicial view of the male—awkward and somehow out of place, yet self-satisfied. But there's also a kind of dignity about the poor creature, alone up there, day after day, keeping watch over the bustling street. A dignity I fear I lack. I should be less critical, less defensive, particularly since I am about to have my rescheduled dinner with Henry Preston and I'd like it to go well, despite the fact that he threw me over for that brassy actress with the gray roots.

I was disappointed, of course, and hurt, an emotion I rarely allow myself. Like I needed a reminder that this dinner was more important to me than it was to him. As always, I give Henry the benefit of the doubt. He's so easily swayed, a stalwart sprig of seaweed in the stiff currents of Manhattan.

Henry Preston, New York's most delightfully oblivious and disarmingly sincere bachelor, who, despite having worked at the Strand for nearly three years, acts as if he just stepped off a bus at Port Authority. Henry Preston, who I fell in love with not long after we met, a feeling I haven't been able to shake, even after this last year of relative estrangement.

I can see from a glance into the tiny café that he hasn't arrived yet, and I cross the street to the park. There's nothing more pathetic than a (wo)man sitting alone in a restaurant, waiting. I take possession of a bench and arrange my cape over my knees as a quick frisson of excitement surges up my spine—the stunning sense of possibility that Henry and I could get back on track, despite the entrance, stage left, of this minor diversion, this aging actress who seems bent on introducing him to French pastries, New York theater and, I suspect, a whole lot more. I'm determined to stay out of it. Henry should sow his wild oats, tame as they are. Any woman who so shamelessly pursues him won't hold his attention for long. I know Henry. He needs to feel as if he's the one in charge, which means he does the pursuing, and at the pace of an aardvark.

I need to trust that happiness and right will prevail in the end. For now, I will focus on myself as I proceed rapidly down the road to becoming the true me, a full, complete woman. That is the picture I can see Henry fitting into quite comfortably—the smiling couple beside the wedding cake, walking hand-in-hand down Bleecker Street, clinking glasses over a table for two. Could I be more schmaltzy? Could Henry be more traditional? But really, what if I were to have what I long for? What if I were no longer yearning to be who I am? What then? I wonder.

I cross my legs under the cape. Modesty aside, I can honestly say that I'm a person of above average intelligence. I can also be amusing. I'm a good listener, a common trait among those whose own stories make people uneasy. I hope that someone seeing me might think I'm attractive, if they can get beyond the gender-bending aspect, which most people, alas, cannot. In short, I make an excellent dinner companion. Still, a romantic repast, even a quick lunch with a friend, is a rarity for me. I make people uncomfortable, my specialty it seems. Or my femininity does, which makes it sound as if that were a separate part of me, when it feels absolutely immutably to *be* me.

I'm tall—five feet eight inches—and a bit lanky, though I've learned to walk with some grace. I have a gentle cleavage, hormonally induced. But hey, aren't they all? Increasingly, there are times when I pass as a woman. Blissful, fleeting moments when I'm taken for who I really am—not an effeminate man, not a carnival act, not some pathetic ambiguity. A woman. I have a long face, full lips and, some might say, enviable cheekbones. My eyes are shielded under an even brow that suggests fairness. I can be alluring. Were I living anywhere between the coasts of this magnificent country, I probably wouldn't get to the grocery store without being heaped with abuse. But here in the West Village, where every misfit-oddball-eccentric with an ounce of guts has landed, I'm an enhancement of sorts to the infinitely varied landscape.

It's been a long haul, this process of going from an effeminate man to a woman. I won't bore you with the details, but it started as long ago as I can remember, with the perfecting of mannerisms—my walk, my speech, the way I sat or smiled or carried a book. Then, as soon as I turned eighteen, I began years of hormone treatments and electrolysis. Then there was psychotherapy and the eventual certification by a professional that I wasn't just indulging some passing fancy. This affirmative nod from my therapist some months ago has qualified me, at last, for surgery, surgery that is scheduled, very soon as a matter of fact, in Baltimore of all places. Not an easy road, but one that has been well worth it to me and one I do not complain about, though there have been moments, solitary moments of enormous despair and self-pity. Why me? I would ask, a question for which there is no answer.

The long and short of it is, I bring a lot of baggage to a relationship. But trust me, it's Louis Vuitton from handbag to trunk.

There he is now, that handsome rogue! Of course, he's not a rogue at all, but he is attractive if, as I do, you prefer natural-looking men who don't spend an inordinate amount of time primping, men who buy their clothes at the Gap and don't pump their bodies into grotesque shapes at some gymnasium. At six foot two, Henry is tall enough for me. He always appears deep in thought, like now, as he passes the restaurant's door, stops and turns back. I try to read his thoughts from his bearing, but Henry is a bit inscrutable, which of course, is part of his charm. A woman doesn't need a man who broadcasts his feelings, particularly when she has plenty of her own to go around. No doubt he's as nervous as I am about rekindling our friendship, and possibly even guilty about this woman he's been seeing. He's likely more troubled about her than I am. Henry has a tendency toward darkness, which I could help him with if he would only let me. I've memorized enough sonnets to keep us both enthralled for the duration. This actress cannot compete, except in one way, of course. She's a woman.

I have known Henry almost three years and, at times, I have felt as if I knew him quite well. But now, watching him, I wonder if, as much as we think we know someone, we ever really get them right. We see them at work, we see them at dinner, we watch them with friends. We file away mental note after mental note as to who they are, but inevitably our assessments have more to do with us than with them—our histories, our fears, our dreams. We fool ourselves, skew our perceptions into one-sided slants. Isn't the belief that we're right about someone simply a vain attempt to assuage the realization that we are, after much scrupulous contemplation, nearly always wrong?

As I had done, he glances into the café's window and determines that I have yet to arrive. Hands stuffed into the pockets of his pea coat, he leans against the wall by the door. If this were the 1940s—the classiest period in Manhattan's illustrious history—he'd remove a silver case from his breast pocket, tamp a cigarette against it and light up. Of course, he'd be wearing a suit and a felt hat.

I wave. He brightens when he sees me and dodges a taxi as he crosses the street. One would think he was eager. "Sorry I'm late," he says, puffing lightly. His voice is a rumble of swallowed exuberance. He rubs his hands together and then stuffs them back into his pockets, an endearing gesture. Henry is almost never late. Ambivalence has slowed him, I suspect. My heart flutters. "Not a problem," I say. "Have a seat. It's a lovely evening."

"What about our reservation?"

Ever the responsible one. Henry's time cards at work have a military precision about them—in exactly at eight, out precisely at five. "I know the owner," I say.

He sits beside me, feet flat on the cobblestones, hands on knees, the good boy that he is. "Don't you love to watch people in this town?" he says, after a while.

"The Village has always been a haven for eccentrics."

Henry glances at me and smiles. He's showered and put on a fresh shirt, the collar barely visible beneath his plain wool scarf. His hair, which he's taken the time to slick back—for me?—is still damp and emits a faint soapy fragrance. "You look like Gary Cooper with your hair that way," I say, reaching up and smoothing it. "Biggest dick in Hollywood."

Henry leans away. "Speaking figuratively, I assume."

"That was the only thing all those Hollywood nymphettes could agree on," I pick a piece of lint off my cape, ball it between my fingers and drop it onto the cobblestones. I've embarrassed him already. Some people go mute when they're nervous. I spout off. "Hungry?"

"Are you kidding? I'm always hungry."

"Then let's go," I say, getting up. "And order anything you want. The evening's on me."

The Paris Commune consists of a single room of perhaps a dozen tables. A gas fire smolders on one wall and lends warmth to a time-darkened mural of fields bordered by hedgerows, a mas and a bewigged gentleman holding a horse, some art student's idea of Paris in the seventeenth century. Probably not far off. A mirror behind the bar relieves the room of feeling cramped. Half a dozen people sit on stools, rearranged to accommodate their brisk conversation. Sam, the owner, greets me and I introduce Henry. We're shown to a table next to the fireplace. I take the "woman's seat," facing into the crowded room. "Red wine?" I ask. Henry nods. "My usual," I tell Sam, who smiles obsequiously and leaves.

I fix my hair behind my ear. "The atmosphere is sort of old world, don't you think? Like me."

Henry adjusts his placemat so it lines up with the edge of the table. "I wouldn't exactly call you 'old world,'" he says.

"In spirit, I mean. I'm convinced I had a previous life as a madam in one of New York's finer nineteenth-century brothels."

Henry chuckles.

"I'm quite serious. A profession esteemed by the most powerful men in New York society. Her underlings performed an essential function, since so many wives back then thought they shouldn't enjoy sex, at least not with their husbands." I grin, pleased to have found a benign level of provocation. "Madams were articulate, well-dressed, and often quite wealthy."

"But they sold themselves, right?"

I unfold my napkin and place it in my lap. "You think those guys down on Wall Street don't sell themselves? Or their pretty little wives up in Greenwich? We all sell ourselves, Henry. Even you." We've hardly sat down and I'm preaching some tired homily. Henry looks put in his place, not exactly what I had hoped to accomplish this evening.

"What's good here?" he asks, glancing at the menu.

"The soups are always yummy. And the ragout. I like the duck, myself."

The Pinot Noir arrives. I wave away the tasting and Sam pours two glasses. He sets the bottle on the table between us. "You two want to sit a minute, or shall I send the waitress over?"

I flutter my lashes at Sam.

He chuckles and disappears.

"Speaking of selling yourself," Henry says, "did you hear about that Japanese soldier from World War II?"

I shake my head.

"His name is Hiroo something-or-other. Walks out of the woods somewhere in the Philippines, yesterday, and surrenders his rusty old sword. Can you believe that, almost thirty years later? Talk about commitment. Talk about selling yourself."

"Makes you wonder, about loyalty. It's got to be love, don't you think?"

"Love?"

"Of Emperor, in this case. But it happens all the time with spouses, too. They remain loyal, no matter what, long after the partner has died or taken up with somebody else. Some primal coupling instinct, no doubt, like geese."

"If you ask me, the human couple instinct is to uncouple."

"You're too young to be cynical."

"And you're too worldly to be naïve."

Who's putting whom in her place? Perhaps he's right. I take in the room which happens be filled with couples, mostly men and women, one table of gay men. At twenty-three, I've yet to be one of a pair, unless you consider nine months in eighth grade with Jarmon. Could I ever be paired with Henry Preston, a man of integrity and responsibility who goes quietly about his business? What do people require in a partner? Admiration, attraction, one or two common interests? It seems so simple in the abstract.

We study our menus. "Look, can we get right to the point?" I ask, closing mine and setting it on the edge of the table. My tone is harsher than I intended.

Henry flashes me a look of tolerance tinged with amusement. "I thought the point was to enjoy dinner."

"You know how I hate it when something's hanging in the air that needs to be addressed. I want to enjoy the evening."

"Shoot, then."

What is this need I have to destroy any real potential in my life? I'm a child smashing his favorite toy. "I'm very happy to see you, Henry. It's been, well, a very long time."

Henry starts to say something, but I raise my hand to silence him. I have rehearsed this little oration over the past few days, unwittingly, and it sounds it. I should stop, but I can't. "Nothing has changed as far as my feelings are concerned. And I don't think I can hide them any better now than I could a year ago. Why should I be required to?" I pause, feeling aggressive and foolish now, yet unable to curb this compulsion to make myself understood—or miserable. I hold his eyes a few seconds longer, and then give up.

Sam arrives and tops off our glasses.

"I just think you're swell, that's all," I say, after Sam departs. "Don't you love that expression? Very forties!"

Henry sets down his menu. "I'm real happy to see you, too, Joey. I've missed you. But I'm straight, and. . . ."

"Of course you're straight. How could I love you if you were gay?"

"Straight men don't go out with other men. We've been through this. Let's not. . . ."

"But I'm not really a man. You know that." I pull myself up in my chair and then finger my emerald ring into position. Glass or the real thing? Only I know for sure. There's nothing left to do now but complete the job of wrecking our evening. It hurts less when I do it myself. "I may have a dick, but there's no way I'm a man."

Henry raises his glass. "To women," he says, grinning, making light. Bless him.

A waitress appears to take our orders, but I wave her away. I stare into the fire, not quite able to let the issue drop. I have always believed that if two people can really and truly understand one another, down deep, really empathize, then they can love each other. They almost have to. I tell myself that Henry Preston is a man who is not going to hurt me, though that thought seems as paradoxical as me in a Brooks Brothers suit. "Can I tell you a story?" I ask him.

He nods and takes a long haul on his wine.

"For as long as I can remember, I was a girl—little weenie between my legs or no. Behind my parents' house, I had a playhouse. We're not talking a fort or service station or anything like that. I made curtains. I had little cups for tea and little plates and spoons for cake. I used to go around the neighborhood, knocking on doors and asking women for their discarded dresses. I had a whole eclectic wardrobe that I altered with my own needle and thread. I had an old mink stole that was a full length coat on me. I was a *girl*, Henry. Thank god, my mother didn't try to change me, or at least she gave up pretty fast. She used to yell out the back door, "Yoo-hoo, Joey, Take your dress off, honey. Your daddy's home."

"Sounds like you had a good mom," Henry says.

"My dad used to go for days without speaking to me. Of course, you can't blame him. I wasn't exactly what he had in mind for a son."

"No, I think you can blame him."

"Thanks for saying that. Anyway, I disappeared into this whole hidden world of my playhouse. I used to steal stuff from stores—cheap perfume, fancy soaps, hairpins—little things I could have bought with my allowance, but how could I walk up to the counter at Woolworths with a lipstick and a can of Endust?"

Henry straightens his napkin. He's heard a lot of this before. Still, I persevere. "I wallpapered the rooms and braided rugs for the floors. Are you getting the picture? I was as girlie a g-i-r-l as you'll ever see."

"Busy every minute, even then."

"In school, I wore khakis and button-down shirts and penny loafers, though it didn't make a whole lot of difference. Boys still didn't see me as one of them just as the girls didn't when I slipped on a bracelet or a rhinestone ring." The waitress arrives. I raise my hand again and she retreats. "I'm sorry, Henry. I know I'm way too intense."

He sets down his wine. "You look really good, Joey. I mean. . . ." He straightens his knife and fork, lining them up perfectly with the edge of the placemat. "You get prettier all the time. You really do. And you seem happy. I'm glad for you."

"It's true—I've never been happier. I'm entering the home stretch of this journey of mine. I'm looking more and more the woman I will be. I'm nearly there." I grin and run my hand over my chest. Henry glances away. "I'm coming to the end of electrolysis, too," I say, touching my fingers to my cheek. Christ, you have no idea how painful that plucking is."

"It's working, Joey. You look great."

Is he serious or just trying to end my tirade? No, Henry is nothing if not honest. "That's sweet of you to say. I've been seeing this doctor at the Gender Dysphoria Clinic at Johns Hopkins in Baltimore. Dr. John Money—good name because it costs a damn fortune just to talk to him. He's a Harvard-educated psychologist who's devoted his professional career to working with transsexuals. He's like this god, approving people for surgery—'you will be woman, you will be man.' I have no doubt whatsoever I am the real thing, and he seems to agree."

"Would you really, like. . . ."

I gesture lifting and cutting, and nod.

Henry looks suddenly queasy. "Shouldn't we order?" he says.

"Don't you want to hear about the procedure?"

"Not if we're going to eat."

"Big strong man like you, all green about the gills over a little blood. I love it!"

Henry picks up his menu.

"So, what about us?" I persist, pulling his menu out of my line of vision.

"I told you, I'm straight."

"And I told you, I'm a woman, or soon to be."

"Look, Joey. . . ."

"I know. I'm sorry." I can see the tension rising in Henry's shoulders. This is the point when he gets up, drops his napkin on the table and walks out, and I finish the wine on my own.

He says, "You're not the only person who ever felt at odds with the world, you know?"

I hold my tongue, hoping he'll go on like the old days when we talked for hours, say whatever he wants, even if it's not what I want to hear. Maybe say something about his time in Vietnam, which I know still bothers him a lot. But he doesn't. Instead, he signals the waitress, who doesn't notice. "You're right," I say. "I'm a self-centered fool."

Henry flashes that disarmingly earnest grin of his. "You know I like you, Joey. We have a great time together. Isn't that enough? Remember, you've thought of yourself as a girl your whole life, but for me the idea is still new. Give me some time."

I'm feeling at once grateful for Henry's attempt to see me for who I really am and annoyed that that recognition is so difficult for people.

"It's an adjustment," he says. "I'm working on it."

The gas fire sputters and glows yellow, then blue again. What more can I ask of him? I savor this first real suggestion of hope. He's trying. I bite the inside of my cheek to keep from saying anything to spoil it.

"I admire this whole thing you're doing for yourself," he says. "I really do."

I hook my hair behind my ear and pick up my menu. "You're sweet," I say. And he is. But can a simple guy from Vermont ever be comfortable with someone like me? I feel a shiver. "We should order," I say, smiling across the table.

13

THE ALBANY AREA ADOPTION AGENCY

On Monday, I find Henry crouched on the floor in Chemistry, a clutch of his dark locks inching over his forehead like the slow cresting of a wave. His portable radio, set on the lower shelf of his cart, plays a song by James Taylor, the title of which I do not recall. The volume is set so low it sounds far away, as if Taylor were rehearsing next door. Don't I wish.

Since our dinner at the Paris Commune, a week ago last Friday, I am more relaxed. I don't deny that I'd kiss this sleeping toad, given the chance, and shack up happily ever after with the prince I know him to be. And I don't deny feeling jealous of this woman who's been sniffing around here like a bitch in heat the last couple of weeks. But I will bide my time for a change, look the other way and settle for an occasional dinner or a movie, a knowing sidelong glance, those moments when I sense that our old intimacy has returned and might eventually settle in.

Meanwhile, I shop for clothes—women's clothes. No holds barred now. Not that there was much inhibition to begin with, but since last Friday, this burning need to be a woman is fanned by the potential for true love. Call me a dreamer, but I swear I saw the old affection in his eyes, but enhanced by a jittery agitation that could only mean something more, something just beyond Henry's own awareness. This reading of Henry augments my sense of lost time. I'm not sure what I mean, exactly, other than a more acute awareness of how quickly youth fades and time passes and opportunities are lost. Having watched my parents all those years, I know something about complacency, a suit of clothes you try on willy-nilly and then discover you can't shed no matter how you try. I know I sound like a forty-year-old spinster. I do dread that possibility. I want to be the woman that Henry Preston can no longer resist.

All week I have repeated and repeated his encouraging words at the restaurant last Friday—how good I looked, how he saw me as a real woman sometimes, how he just needed more time.

When he senses my presence, he looks up and grins. "You know something, Joey?" he says, getting to his feet. "You are one foxy-looking lady today."

See? It's working. I smooth the soft cashmere of my tunic, which extends to my thighs over wool slacks and a white turtleneck. Standing in front of my gaping closet this morning, I had wondered whether Henry would prefer the beige or the black, the blouse or the sweater. And yet, despite myself, I look away now, feeling self-conscious. We can't always accommodate the sort of attention we crave.

"If I saw you on the street," he says, "there'd be no doubt whatsoever in my mind."

"You're sweet," I say. Henry's compliment is double edged—saying that I look like a woman confirms that I'm not one—yet I know he means well. Still, I look forward to the day when the last vestiges of my manhood are removed. Yes, that day is coming, the day after tomorrow, in fact.

"I speak the truth, that's all."

I reach up and plant a friendly peck on his cheek, just as that new woman of his enters the aisle at the far end of Chemistry. "I hope I'm not interrupting," her voice rings out. She's taller and better looking than I had registered from my office window. She's dressed in a black leather jacket, bell-bottoms and platforms; her brown hair with the store-bought chestnut highlights is held back with a tortoise-shell clip. She's striking in a devil-may-care sort of way, the natural sort of woman I so long to be. I try not to hate her for it.

Henry swallows hard and moves away from me, a boy caught stealing a cookie. But no, I can see it's more than that. He doesn't make eye contact with her and his cordiality is forced. It's almost as if he's afraid of her. "This is my boss, Joey Maxima," he says. "Joey, this is Karen Grave."

I extend my hand. "It's Josephine, really, but who could live with a name like that? You can call me Joey, the way everyone around here does." Henry's jaw drops, then adjusts and recovers its imperturbable squareness. We're united, collaborating in my womanhood. A gush of affection warms my chest. "I've seen you here before, haven't I?" I say.

"I come here once or twice a year, looking for first editions of plays."

I can see her sizing me up. She's still unhappy about the kiss. "You're even prettier up close," I tell her. "I see you have your usual treats in tow."

Karen glances at the brown paper bag she's carrying. Her initial shocked expression softens a bit with the warmth of my greeting, though I can see she considers me competition. A frisson of excitement creeps up my spine. She's taken me for a woman.

"Sorry about the food," Henry says. "We'll take it downstairs." He seems eager to whisk Karen away. Is he uncomfortable having the two "women" in his life arrayed side by side? Does this mean I'm in the running?

"Don't be silly," I say. "Let's all go to my desk upstairs. I'll grab a coffee and we can have a little visit. What do you say, Karen?"

She glances to Henry who shrugs. "There's enough raisin Danish to go around," she says.

"Why not, then?" I say, turning and leading the way to the stairs. "So many possibilities are eliminated unnecessarily, don't you think? Life is too short to hold back." I give a little extra swing to my hips. "Do you find these first editions irresistible," I ask, turning to Karen on the landing, "or is it our star shelfer, Henry Preston?"

I sense a good deal of glancing and shrugging between them as we clear the landing and take the remaining flight to my office. Taking seats around my cluttered desk and settling into our pastries, we exchange the usual pleasantries. Actually, Karen and I do. Henry seems to have lost his tongue. She tells me she's become bored with playing a cheerleader. I don't recall any cheerleaders in their late thirties at my high school, but I don't tell her this. She asks me how I came to run such a fine bookstore and I make up a story about tending to the owner in his final days and vowing at the bedside to keep the store going. This I do as much to enjoy Henry's worried expression as to show him that this Karen Grave is not the only one with a flair for the dramatic. We even discuss our hair stylists and the best discount houses for designer clothing. It's all very simpatico, and, heedlessly perhaps, I imagine her becoming my friend. I know almost nothing about her and she's been stealing the attention of the man whose focus I'd most like to keep on me. Still, something draws me to her. Maybe it's the decadent classiness, the unabashed sort of self-involvement, that I cannot help but admire, or at least recognize. And, best of all, she has taken me for a woman—up close, even—a very heady experience, to understate it by half.

As we're finishing up, she mentions to Henry that she's been able to arrange a rental car for tomorrow.

"Are you taking tomorrow off?" I ask him. This is news to me.

"Well, not exactly." Henry seems startled, as if he'd been a thousand miles away the last ten minutes, scratching at who knows what hidden emotional itch.

"You agreed, if I could get a car," Karen asserts. I read annoyance in her tone, a girlish whine, though she hides it with a smile.

"I said I would try, and I will."

Henry's pace with Karen is obviously more dawdling than hers with him. "What sort of trip did you have planned?" I ask.

He studies his sneakers. "We didn't really. . . ."

"Oh Hank, we did, remember?" I know women—I've been studying them for years, after all—and this one is wrong for Henry. This is only an instinct, I admit, and I also admit to a certain vested interest. But I can feel it. She's needy and whiny and controlling. All wrong.

The discreet thing for me to do at this point would be to gather up our refuse and allow them a graceful exit, some time to straighten out their agenda. But I'm far too curious and I feel a little protective of Henry. He's in over his head with this Karen Grave. Of course, he wouldn't want protection, or at least wouldn't think he wants it, or most especially have Karen Tuckwell think he wants it. The truth is, I'm intrigued by this woman, and something tells me the more friendly I am toward her, the better, at least for now. To break the tension, I say, "I do adore this time of year, don't you? Spring in the offing. All this new life bursting forth. Nice season for a ride, that's for sure."

Karen is suddenly brimming with tears. Henry crouches by her chair. I stare, fascinated. I'm thinking, here is the female's ultimate weapon, as disarming (and subtle) as a Sherman tank. I have seen very little of this tactic. My mother was not a crier. I probably won't be either, though its power is impressive.

How often does a woman—me, in this case—get to see the man she loves interact intimately with another woman? If you can get beyond the jealousy, there's an opportunity to obtain crucial information. What's he like, really, when push comes to shove? So far, Henry is behaving just as I would want him to—solicitous, contrite, kind as he could be.

"Don't cry, Karen," he says, resting his hand on her arm.

She snivels into the handkerchief Henry has produced, another amenity I had somehow missed all these years, wipes her nose and turns to me. "Men can be so insensitive," she says.

I nod agreement. This whole scene is so delightfully bizarre. "What's the problem, Henry?" I ask, barely able to keep a straight face. "Can I help?"

"She wants to. . . ."

"As a woman, you can surely understand," Karen butts in. She's either upset about something more than this excursion they've planned or she's a very fine actress, most likely the latter.

"Karen. . . ." Henry stands to make his case.

"Don't interrupt," I tell Henry, my eyes glued to Karen's performance.

"Last night, Hank agreed to drive upstate to where I grew up." She wipes her nose before going on. "I had a baby, once, and I gave it up for adoption. For weeks now, I've had this urge to find him. Well, at least find out what happened to him. I don't know. It was all a very long time ago. Hank said he would help me. Since we've been trying to get pregnant, we've become closer, and he agreed."

"Joey. . . ."

I raise my hand again to silence Henry, a painful pang invading my chest. Pregnant? We? How long has this been going on?

"But there's this part of me that just thinks I can't have this baby until I find out what happened to my first one, you know?"

I straighten my tunic, finger my cuffs. Bizarre is hardly the word. Fantastic! Weird! As if it weren't unfair enough that Karen Grave bore a child without so much as a thought to the consequences, that plenty of women get pregnant every day without an ounce of appreciation for the miracle that has occurred, that Karen Grave can have sex with Henry before she even gets to know him or love him. Does she have any concept of how fortunate that makes her?

I glance to Henry long enough to see him shake his head slowly back and forth, his mouth a straight line. To Karen, I say, "You and Henry are. . . ."

"I can explain," Henry says.

"There's no need," I say, not looking at him. I don't want my anger to show. I don't want to care as much as I do.

"Maybe you would come," Karen says to me.

"Me?"

"Instead."

"I. . . ." I glance to Henry, who has moved behind Karen. He mouths a no and I turn back to Karen. "Of course I would," I tell her. "This is clearly a task for women. What do men know about babies?" How dare Henry not tell me he's . . . whatever he's doing with this . . . this. . . . "It's a date then," I tell her. "Tomorrow."

"Oh Josephine, would you, really?"

"It's Joey. Of course I will."

I'm already warming to the idea of driving upstate with Karen. A dozen or so reasons spring to mind—get to know the competition, learn the real story of whatever is going on here, prevent Henry from turning into her hero by finding her long-lost son, get even with him for . . . well, for not wanting me instead. And then, I suppose, somewhere deep within me, there is a long-simmering sympathy for the idea that a mother still longs for the child she gave up and has never entirely forgotten. I suppose I had always imagined that was the case with my own birthmother, and now, here is that sentiment, laid out for me to appreciate and somehow savor, vicariously. How can I not help Karen Grave?

"Where are we headed, by the way?" I ask her as she stuffs Henry's handkerchief into her pants pocket which is so tight I'm surprised it can accommodate even a hundred-times-washed hankie.

"Schenectady, New York. It's just above Albany, about a three hour drive."

It could be halfway to Niagara Falls for all I care. We're taking a trip, Henry's new girlfriend and me. "We'll make a day of it," I say. "Just us girls. And with a little luck, we'll find out what happened to that baby of yours."

Henry moves from behind Karen's chair and stands with his hands stuffed into his pockets, looking as uncomfortable as I've ever seen him. Good!

"Don't you have Physics to do?" I say. "I'll see Karen out."

That afternoon, Henry appears in front of my desk, a contrite schoolboy come to see the principal. I notice, for the first time, that he's wearing a new shirt. A present from Karen? Tan is not a particularly flattering color on him.

"Can I help you?"

"You know why I'm here."

"I believe you were supposed to complete Physics and Mathematics this afternoon. We're supposed to be done with the sciences by the end of the week."

I turn my attention to the open file on my desk, though peripherally I can see him run the back of his hand across his forehead, as if the strain of re-shelving all those theories and formulae was suddenly too much. "I'll be done with more than that, when you get through," he says.

"I beg your pardon," I say, still not looking up.

"Karen and I aren't . . . involved. Not that way."

"There's only one way I know to get pregnant." And the best way for you to zero in on my ultimate vulnerability as a would-be woman, I'm thinking. Is it deliberate or inadvertent, this uncanny ability of Henry's to throw me off my guard?

"It's a long story."

"Isn't it always?"

"I've listened to yours."

"So you have." I sit back in my chair and give him my full attention. There's no way I can stay angry with Henry for long. My heart melts when he is sad or confused or whatever he is right now, and anything but love evaporates like cactus tears.

"I donate my semen at the New York Hospital Fertility Clinic, uptown. Karen's a patient there. We met by accident, and since then she's been coming around."

"Sounds like you're the one who's been coming around."

Henry turns away, grins.

"How long has this been going on? These donations?"

He shrugs. Something tells me he's been playing the stand-in dad for a long time, probably since he arrived in Manhattan.

"I've gone out with her a few times" he says, now. "She's an unusual person. She just told me recently about this baby she gave up. She was so sad, I offered to help her find out what happened to him. I thought maybe that would satisfy her, and she'd give up on trying to get pregnant now. She seems a little unstable. I feel sorry for her, but she doesn't seem like somebody who should be having a baby."

"My, you *have* been busy!"

Henry turns away again. He's clearly worried. What right do I have to be angry? He's the most decent person I know, even if his judgment is a little flawed at times. He has every right to shop around. We have no commitment to one another other than to be fair which, at the moment, I'm finding a challenge. "She must be married then, if she's a client of this fertility clinic?"

"I don't think so."

"Not married?"

"That's what she says."

"Wake up, Henry. You're having an affair with a married woman."

"I'm not having any affair. If she gets pregnant, it's by the New York Hospital Fertility Clinic, not me."

"She said Grave was her stage name. What's her married name?"

"Tuckwell. I told you, she's not. . . ."

"Indeed! Henry, this is all a little hard to. . . ."

"For you of all people?"

After a seething stare, I say, "That's rude."

"It's just that I'd expect you to understand something that's a little out of the ordinary."

My annoyance, a bitter-coated pill consigned under the tongue, dissolves once again. Henry is clearly overwhelmed, this simple guy who, as far as I know, hasn't ever really been with a woman. "Look, I'll find out what I can about her, okay? It all strikes me as strange, though, I have to say. You need to be more careful about who you get involved with." I pick up the file from my desk, letting Henry know I'd just as soon end this conversation.

"You, too," he says, with another irresistible grin. "And I told you, Karen and I are not involved."

I thumb through the file. "I'll need you to cover for me tomorrow."

Henry ambles out of the office, his ample shoulders slumped, his gait even slower than usual. Such an uncomplicated man. And he seems to have happened into a hall of mirrors. Or is it the lioness's den? I'll find out.

On Tuesday morning, I set my shoulder bag on the seat next to me and adjust the rental car's rearview mirror. I slide the seat up, then back, then settle for a spot mid-distance, where my sensible patent leather pumps can comfortably depress the pedals. Karen rented the car, a Ford Fairlane, metallic blue, in need of a powerful vacuum and some Windex. Thank God! Imagine the clerk's reaction to my driver's license, with the four-year-old mug shot of an effeminate man with bushy eyebrows and remnants of a five o'clock shadow. I make a mental note to burn all my old photo ID's and pose for new ones, which will require several new outfits and who knows how many trips to the salon.

Actually, I wonder just how obvious the difference is between me now and me at some "then" point. As a teenager, I imagined a line I would skip over one day, from the strain of armpit hair and tie clasps to the joy of skirts, heels and face creams. But that wasn't how it happened. The transition has lasted for as long as I can remember really, with little setbacks here and there along the way, followed by thrilling freefall plunges deeper into the sweet-scented warmth of young womanhood. It's as if I left some frozen tundra and trudged across an occasionally stormy but generally more temperate no-man's-land to reach a lush garden, the long-dreamed-of oasis. And I'm right there on the edge now, that oasis a mere step away. My surgery—scheduled for this week, which no one but my assistant knows—will simply be the culmination of a process, an end to a long beginning so to speak. Will I miss Joey? I don't think so. Deep inside, I'm still that precocious child of the Maximas of Evanston, Illinois, the first love of Jarmon of the south side, and then the effeminate little runaway who made his way to New York City, harboring desires and ambitions not so different from anyone else's. Just one thing dreadfully wrong all along, and now, finally, nearly righted.

Karen opens the passenger door and slides onto the seat next to me. She's wearing a long, knitted vest over a black turtleneck, those favorite bellbottoms of hers, this time with high-heeled boots, and wrap-around sunglasses, ala Jackie-O. She lights a Salem, stares at the flame, watching it burn down, and then throws the spent match out the window. Why wouldn't she be caught up in her thoughts, considering our mission? I open the ashtray, letting her know I'd prefer she use that rather than the street. I haven't driven a car in two years, not since my parents died in an automobile accident and I spent several weeks in Michigan, seeing to their affairs. That was a sad and strange time. I felt suddenly even more alone than I'd been all along. And I was rich. My parents' attorney prevailed upon me to draw up a will of my own right away, which had taken time. You find out who and what is important to you in that process. I came back to New York, my values clarified, and determined not to let being wealthy change the way I lived my life. And so far, I haven't, though the money has made certain things easier, like therapy sessions and my impending elective surgery.

Karen said it was more like five years since she'd been behind the wheel, so I'm the designated driver. She spreads a map of New York State across her slacks and brushes ash from her blouse. She's thrown her mink coat into the back seat. Apparently Mr. Tuckwell, who Henry denies even exists, does all right for himself.

I negotiate the uptown traffic and turn left off of Amsterdam Avenue onto Seventy-Ninth Street, where I pick up the West Side Highway heading north. Karen smokes and usurps the rearview mirror to check her lipstick. We cross the George Washington Bridge, an adventure in itself since we miss the exit for the Palisades Parkway and have to back up into oncoming, horn-blaring traffic. Clearly Karen's forte is not navigation, except perhaps among men. I wonder if, besides acting, she excels at getting people to do things for her. In any case, by default, and due to my own insatiable curiosity, I wind up in a familiar spot, the driver's seat.

Soon, we're speeding blithely north on the New York State Thruway, gossiping like girlfriends, complete with their fundamental competitive edge. I catch her eyeing my pumps and I imagine myself in her mink. I can see how Henry would be drawn to this woman, once you adjust to the unmistakable sense that there's an explosion inside her awaiting ignition. I can't help feeling that cringe that accompanies a splendor of fireworks, just before the final boom. She's lively and funny, with plenty of stories about her years in the New York theater scene. Despite her apparent age, there's a girlishness about her, a blustery sort of innocence mixed with the world-weariness of an aged monarch. She gives the impression of having been around without ever having grown up, a permanent sort of vulnerability that probably inspires the caring instinct in a lot of men. And then there's this explosion waiting to happen.

She asks little about me, which suits me fine, since baring my soul is not exactly a priority for me with this woman. She doesn't register disappointment that the dear and gullible Mr. Preston isn't the one driving her to Schenectady. I get the impression that anyone would do, that it's company she wants, to assuage a dreadful loneliness underneath.

About an hour south of Albany, she seems to have exhausted her repertoire of entertaining stories, including the mention of Mr. Lloyd Tuckwell, a Managing Director at a downtown investment firm. I make a point of asking for specifics, in part to set Henry Preston straight. Salomon Brothers, she says, as if she were picking the name out of a telephone directory. But perhaps Henry has made me overly suspicious. Succumbing, once more, to my relentless curiosity, I say, "I'm dying to know about this baby you gave up for adoption. How it all happened, if you don't mind telling, that is."

"It's a painful story."

"Childhood stories always are, don't you think? I mean, if you really try to understand what we were like as kids, what we thought about, what we felt, it's so weird and complicated, and so difficult to put together with who we are now, or who we like to think we are, anyway. Are all childhoods tortured, do you suppose?" I turn on the wipers as protruding bellies of clouds release a half-hearted spatter. "We've got nothing, if not time," I say, smiling across the seat.

Karen stares out her side window, where barely budded trees, rock outcroppings and brave, late-March grass shoots pass in a burnished blur, glazed by the rain. We've had our share of actors working day jobs at the Strand. In fact, I became rather close with one talented young woman who went on to become quite the star. She once told me that her daily experiences fueled her acting, that her real-life feelings fed the well of emotion she drew upon when she portrayed sadness or anger or love on the stage, where feelings—it seemed—really mattered. This made me feel used in a way, unimportant at least, and generally wary of her. I'm ready to take whatever Karen tells me with a healthy grain of salt. Still, I'm intrigued.

Karen Grave, or Tuckwell, or whatever her name is, speaks in a dreamy tone, as if the hilly terrain and the Catskill Mountains in the distance to our left are taking her right back to that time when she lived in upstate New York. It strikes me that she might be the sort of person who feels things acutely only when they're thrust in front of her, an emotional out of sight-out of mind sort of person. It makes sense, I suppose, that contemplating having a baby now would bring up thoughts of having given one up long ago. But why had she not asked her husband to accompany her on this trip? Perhaps he doesn't know anything about this long-ago pregnancy. I wonder if anyone gets a full picture of Karen Grave Tuckwell.

She turns away from the window now and clears her voice. I half expect the lights to dim for this monologue, but I'm being unfair.

"I grew up in a blue-collar area of Schenectady. My father taught English at a junior college and my mother was a legal secretary, so they were a little different from the neighboring factory workers and their wives who tended to stay at home with the kids. We pretty much kept to ourselves. I hated the numbing monotony of our life. I used to pretend I was a figure skating champion or that I had a best friend who visited from New York City or a boyfriend who sent me notes at school. I'd mention them sometimes, at dinner or while watching television. Lies! my mother would yell, slamming her palms against her forehead. My poor mother. She didn't like my father much either."

"My home life wasn't so different," I say, by way of encouraging Karen to go on. And yet, it's true. I made up all sorts of scenarios to make childhood bearable.

She continues as if she hasn't heard me. "I'd always been the sort of girl no one noticed, awkward and plain. Invisible, really."

But at least you *were* a girl, I'm thinking. But then, the more charitable part of me recognizes what a challenge any child's world can be, even if she's lucky enough to be born the right gender.

"That fall of ninth grade, though, everything changed. I had filled out in all the right places. All of a sudden, these obsessed adolescent boys were whistling at me and following me around. It was all pretty overwhelming, and yet lots of fun in a way."

I look across the seat at Karen, feeling an incipient bond over our shared unhappiness as adolescents. And yet, I can't help feeling that I would have changed places with her in a heartbeat. She was a girl.

She lights another cigarette, rolls down her window and throws the match out. "I'd always taken refuge with my dad. Not that we talked much. We used to pick up muffins on Sunday mornings or drop my mother off at the hairdresser on Saturdays. Our whole relationship transpired, mostly in silence, with him in the front seat of his Chevrolet and me in the back."

"Waiting for your life to begin," I say. "God, I can relate to that."

Karen inhales and expels a blue line of smoke that gets whipped out the window. "But then, when I started showing signs of becoming a woman, he suddenly withdrew. That was the end of our rides to the muffin place."

"Parents are so weird."

"John Riley changed everything for me," she says. "When he arrived that September of sophomore year and took the desk next to mine, I thought he was the most beautiful boy I'd ever seen. He had this fair complexion, chartreuse eyes and dark curly hair that sent me into orbit. I made rude comments about the teacher just to make him laugh. I guess that was my first realization that I could make guys like me, that I did, actually, possess the power with them that had taken up my fantasies for so long.

"When he walked me home from school that first day, he told me his goal was to leave town as soon as possible. He couldn't have known, of course, that I'd been dreaming the same dream forever. But that clinched it for me—we were destined for each other. He ignited a fire in me that had been smoldering for fourteen years. From that afternoon, John Riley was all I cared about."

"I had a boyfriend when I was that age," I tell Karen. "People can say what they want about puppy love, but I don't think I have felt anything that powerful since."

"Maybe that's why I need to find out what happened to my son. That whole time was so intense." She takes a final drag and flicks the butt out the window. "What happened to your boyfriend?"

"Jarmon? He died, I'm afraid."

"Oh, I'm sorry. Gosh, he was so young."

"I know. I sometimes wonder what might have happened if he'd lived."

"I often think that too. I mean, if I had kept my son." Karen reads the road signs overhead and then checks the map. "The next exit is ours," she says.

I turn onto Route 2 which Karen says will lead us right into Schenectady. "Unfortunately, Jarmon and I never got very far with sex," I say. "We kissed a lot, but that was about it. I sometimes wish we had gone further, you know? That I had those sorts of memories, too. He was black, which put us in a pretty impossible situation then. There was probably no way we could have been together, even if he had lived."

And the fact that I was a boy would have presented an even more insurmountable obstacle, I'm thinking. The question of how much to reveal about my past is as new to me as the possibility of making a friend, however strange she might be, and whatever her designs on Henry are. No doubt I am particularly drawn to this possibility of friendship because Karen Grave is my demarcation person, the first to know me only as a woman. With Karen Grave, I cross over—life before Karen Grave, and life after. Who would have thought Henry's girlfriend would play such a pivotal role in my life? And not even know it.

"I think first loves are always impossible," Karen says. "That's what makes them so heartbreaking."

"And compelling. It wasn't so long ago that people got married as teenagers and had kids right away. Life ended when they were in their thirties. Now, there's a lot more time to find just the wrong person!"

Karen laughs. "You got that right."

"So tell me," I say, eager to know what actually happened with Karen and John, and, in a more general way, to learn more about a teenage girl's adolescence, having been deprived of mine. "What happened? How did you . . . you know?"

Karen plays with the corner of the map, and I wonder, again, about the veracity of her stories. Maybe it's the total lack of emotion, or maybe it's this sense that she's devising rather than recalling an incident. I could be wrong, of course. In any case, it's an odd feeling. Henry's right, she's a strange one and definitely not the mothering type.

"It was pretty simple, really," she says. "Oh, it hurt the first time, and I guess I worried for a while what would happen if we got found out. And then, one day, we did. I hadn't heard the door open and close in the kitchen and suddenly my father was standing there in the doorway to my room."

"Oh my God. What did you do?"

"I should have been freaked out, right? But by then, like I said, nothing really mattered but John. When my dad turned away and left, I motioned to John to get off me. We fixed our clothes and I saw him out the front door. I went directly to my dad's office at the end of the hallway."

"Seems like boldness is your strong suit."

Karen gave me a look I couldn't read.

"That's a compliment."

"Like I said, I believed John and I were destined for each other. My father sat in his chair, staring out the window into our backyard. 'I'm sorry, Daddy,' I said, but he just continued to look out the window. I wanted to smooth his hair down in back like I used to when I was a little girl, but I was afraid of being pulled back into the misery that had always surrounded us. Then he asked me the strangest question. Do you think we have a choice about things or is everything all laid out for us in advance?"

"A philosopher, your father. Even in a pinch."

"Of course there was no answer to the question, which was probably the point. No answer meant no end to contemplation, and contemplation meant never having to take a stand, to do anything. The real issue being that, like him, I was lost, and there was nothing either of us could do to help each other."

She's a smart woman, I'm thinking, this Karen Grave Tuckwell, and I'm loving this woman-to-woman talk. "So were you pregnant, already?" I ask her.

She nods. "My mother went berserk, of course, when I told her. I withdrew from school. John was attentive for a while, before he disappeared. Thank God my parents didn't force a marriage on us. I got a couple of postcards from him, then nothing. I had the baby. The nurse handed it to my mother and that was the end of it. We never spoke of that baby again, or any baby, for that matter, as if the lovely innocence of a newborn encountered at the market or at the hardware store prompted the ugly image of my own impurity. We avoided babies altogether."

"Wow! That's so sad."

Karen points out a turn, and I take it. "So what do you want to find out, today?" I ask her.

She glances at the houses lined up beyond wide sidewalks, three-story Victorians, once grand no doubt, now divided into shabby apartments. Three or four cars huddle in gravel driveways. "I guess I just want to spend some time with my son."

"But that's not very likely, right?"

"I need some sort of closure."

"So you can have this baby by Henry?"

"I know it sounds silly. I wanted my first baby so much—John's baby. This one I'm trying to have now. . . . I'm not so sure. I'm not making a whole lot of sense, am I?"

"You can't replace a baby."

"I know." Karen fiddles with the glove box, opens it and closes it a few times.

"Don't you think you should figure all this out before getting pregnant?"

"Please don't chastise me. I'm so confused right now."

"Got it."

We pass through a blue-collar neighborhood like the one Karen had described growing up in. On Main Street, she has me turn left at a light. She says she wants to drive down her old street. A couple of turns later, she points out a simple Cape with pale blue shutters and a bright yellow door. "That's where I lived."

"What a sweet little house!"

"It wasn't that house, actually. Our house burned my senior year. But that's the lot. It all looks so much smaller now."

"Childhood is always smaller than we remember it," I say, feeling slightly awkward with all this information entrusted to me so fast. Be careful what you probe for.

Karen misses a turn back to Main Street, and we have trouble finding the adoption agency. No doubt her home town has changed a lot. Finally, we spot a nondescript brick building with a discreet sign that reads Albany Area Adoption Agency, four A's overlapping in the logo, like alpine peaks. I park next to a Cadillac with glorious fins and shut off the car's engine. Karen turns to me and says, "I've really enjoyed getting to know you, Joey."

"Me, too," I say, though there's been so little about me in our exchange I'm not sure what it is she has enjoyed getting to know.

She takes my hand and squeezes it. "Will you come in with me?"

"Are you sure you want me to?"

She nods.

"Then of course I will."

Inside, the agency shows its age. The tile floor has a pattern of intertwined, black and white rectangles that reminds me of the entrance to my father's factory and the chrome-based chairs of the waiting room are similar to those that stood outside his office. There's a dusty Plexiglas partition between the waiting area and the receptionist, the sort you'd find protecting a bank teller. The place has a bureaucratic papery odor. Karen looks around doubtfully. I take her arm and we approach the receptionist's window together.

"What can I do for you?" the woman with a blond-gray bun and teardrop glasses asks. She looks as if her employment could possibly date back to Karen's time.

"I was a client here twenty-three years ago," Karen says.

So she's thirty-eight, I calculate.

"Yes?" the woman says.

"I wonder if I could get some information."

"We don't give out the whereabouts of the adoptee, if that's what you're after. That was all explained to you, years ago."

"I'm not sure I remember much of what was explained to me," Karen says, her voice quavering a little.

"I'm just telling you our policy, that's all."

I intervene, hoping to defuse the situation. "We've driven all the way from New York City," I say. "Do you think you could at least confirm for us that my friend was a client here? You would have a record, correct?"

"That was before my time, but yes, our records go back to the very beginning. We've been in this business for forty-two years. One of the first. Made a lot of people happy in all that time."

"I'm sure you did." I flash the woman a smile that would melt steel. "I think my friend would feel better if she could at least see a copy of her old record." My intention here is twofold—to help Karen out and to confirm for myself that her story is legitimate. I hate doubting her. It's possible that my own lack of experience with friendship is at fault. Still. . . .

"I can't let you see the record, of course," she tells Karen, "since it contains the disposition."

"Maybe the intake form," I say, smiling again. "Anything would help."

The woman raises her eyebrows.

Karen and I nod in unison, eager for any tidbit of information.

"I'll need your name and the date of the birth."

"Karen Grave," Karen says. "Oops, that's my stage name. I'm an actress. Karen Allen. And the date was—let's see—July 19, 1950."

I turn to Karen. "Allen?" I say.

She nods.

The receptionist rises from her chair and disappears behind a door.

"Karen Allen?" I ask her, again. "1950?"

"Yes," Karen says. "Is something wrong?"

"Allen was my birthmother's name. I was adopted."

"You're kidding! What an amazing coincidence!" Karen stares at me a moment with another look I find impossible to read. "But my baby was a boy."

"Wait here," I say, "I need to go to the ladies room."

I push open a wooden door labeled with the silhouette of a woman and brace myself against the sink. I take in the closed-in smell of disinfectant. I stare into the mirror. Beads of perspiration accumulate on my upper lip. Karen Grave or Tuckwell or Allen, the woman Henry has been seeing, the woman who might possibly be carrying his child—my mother?

I open a stall, sit and pee. What did I expect, a lady knitting socks and rocking a cat in her lap? But surely Karen Grave is not right. Back at the sink, I search my face for evidence of her features, but find little to go on. I recall the story she told me on the way here in the car, that her baby's green-eyed father took off when things got complicated. That much I can believe. He'd probably had enough of Karen Allen. But there they are in the mirror, staring back at me—the green eyes.

When I get back to the waiting area, Karen is talking to the woman behind the desk. She's clearly upset. "But I know this was the place. I remember this office."

"What seems to be the problem?" I ask.

"This woman says there's no record of me ever having been here, and that's impossible."

"No record?" I say to the receptionist, feeling strangely relieved.

"We keep very complete files. We have to. We are accountable to the State. Trust me, if we don't have a record, this woman was never a client of Albany Area Adoption Agency."

I turn to Karen and shrug, but she's already halfway to the door, her coat flailing.

14

HANK FINDS JO(S)EY

On Wednesday morning, the day after Joey's trip upstate with Karen, I wake up early, sweating into a corkscrew of sheets and blankets. In the dream that wakes me, I am back in Vietnam with Ted. It's nighttime and pitch black. There's an awful stench of burned and rotting flesh. I'm starving, tearing at a bone, pulling off the rancid meat. Then I realize it's Ted's leg I'm gnawing at. But that doesn't stop me. I keep at it, horrified, yet unable to stop. This dream stays with me as I shower, and I look forward to the distraction of work.

Last night, after thinking all day about Joey and Karen and their trip upstate, I took myself to see the new movie, *Chinatown*, where Jack Nicholson gets his nose sliced and Faye Dunaway gets shot in the back while driving away in that beautiful 1948 Packard convertible. Nicholson plays the detective who's trying to help this beautiful woman who's covering up the real story of what's really going on with Los Angeles' water supply. This may sound strange, but Faye Dunaway reminded me some of Joey. This realization probably didn't do much for my dreams. I wish I identified with the detective, who doesn't mind confronting the nastiest, most intimidating men in search of the truth. But even he can't save Ms. Dunaway, and that was what disturbed me most. This uneasy feeling follows me as I ride my bike down Ninth Avenue to downtown, punch in at the Strand and stow my bike in the dim, parchment-smelling basement.

By eleven o'clock, Joey still hasn't shown up. In three years, I've never known him to miss a single day, much less two in a row. I spoke to Karen last night, so I know they got back okay. She said she let Joey off at Penn Station when they got back to the city late in the afternoon. She was all high on Joey, what an attractive woman she was, how lucky I was to have a friend like her. Who knows what she really thinks? I just don't trust her after that little performance in Joey's office on Monday. And all that talk about truth being neither here nor there. I don't buy it.

But why Penn Station, I wondered last night, after I'd hung up with Karen. That's not the best subway line for Joey to get back to Brooklyn. Of course, it was convenient for Karen. I ask around the office, but nobody seems to know his whereabouts, or they're not saying, which is the impression I get from Joey's assistant, Celeste. I go through the motions of pushing my book cart down the Travel aisle, waiting for her to go on her coffee break. When I see her descend the stairs and take the elevator to the basement, I head up to the office.

Feeling sheepish, I sneak behind Joey's desk, taking in the chaos crowding its surface, the vague lingering essence of his perfume. Of course, I have the urge to straighten things up, which would send him into orbit. Then I get this tightening sensation in my chest. Could Joey possibly have slipped out of town to have the surgery he alluded to that night at the Paris Commune? The only occasions I've ever known him to take time off were for his pre-op sessions at that gender clinic in Baltimore. Would he really go through with it? And alone? My balls rise a couple of centimeters just thinking about it.

I push stacks of books and papers aside to reveal his calendar, the old-fashioned blotter type, spread across his desk. It's blank. Joey's routine never varies. A calendar is as superfluous to him as his dick.

Reflexively, my eye travels to the square for this Friday, the day I'm scheduled to make a fourth delivery to the clinic for Karen Tuckwell. There's no way this woman is cut out for mothering, particularly if it's a solo performance. But can I just quit supplying at the last minute, with no explanation to McAvery? Is it any of my business what the clinic does with the semen I sell them? I bite my lip, thinking about all the times in my life I didn't take a stand—to run from the draft, to refuse to penetrate that Vietnamese girl. Do I let things slide again, now, and maybe bring a child into the world who will have a rough time of it at best?

But I see now that Joey's calendar isn't completely blank after all. There's an entry, four faint letters scribbled in pencil in the margin next to today's date— JHMC. JHMC? Johns Hopkins Medical Center. Jesus! He *is* going through with the surgery. Why am I surprised? Joey decided months ago, years ago, and probably only went along with the counseling sessions because they were required. I picture him in a hospital bed, his hair needing a wash, which would bug the hell out of him, a thick bandage around his middle.

I dial information and get the number for the medical center. I call, half suspecting that Joey has some sort of long-distance block on the office phone. But the call goes through. "I'd like to speak to a patient named Joey Maxima," I tell the operator. I spell out the last name.

She puts me on hold. When she comes back, she says, "I have a Miss Josey Maxima going to 5H, Surgical."

"Christ!"

"I beg your pardon?"

"Can you connect me?"

"The patient is in recovery. No calls there, I'm afraid. She should be up to the floor by this afternoon."

She. "Can you. . . . Do you know how he's doing?"

"The condition is listed as Fair. That's all I can tell you."

"Fair?"

"That's the standard listing after major surgery. She's probably fine. If there were a problem, they'd list her as Serious or Critical."

Her. "Thank you," I say. "That was 5H, right?"

"That's right. Surgical, 5H."

I hang up, staring at the letters—JHMC on Joey's calendar. Would he have told me, or maybe even asked me to go with him, if I hadn't taken up with Karen Grave these last weeks? Probably not. This is a process he had conducted entirely on his own, for years. He'd be unlikely to depart from that approach now, at the end. Still, I know it hurt him when Karen said she was trying to get pregnant, and I'm not sure my explanation made much difference. He left here angry after work on Monday, swallowing whatever impulse he might have had to let me know where he'd be today.

I sink into Joey's chair. Truth is, I hated the distance that pushed itself between Joey and me after we broke things off a year ago. As the months passed, I didn't stop missing him as I thought I would. All my reasons for keeping the distance—and there were some pretty good ones to latch onto— didn't change the fact that I was pretty miserable without him. The alone I felt was different from the alone I'd felt all my life. I'd known something else, a not-alone life, and its absence left me with an ache in my gut, an emptiness you could park a blimp in.

Enter Karen Grave. I can see now that half the excitement of meeting her was that she took away that ache. She was a distraction, the romantic notion guys carry around from seeing too many movies or TV soaps. I told myself that feeling out of whack the way I do around her is what being with a beautiful woman is supposed to feel like. Wrong! Now I can see that it wasn't Karen that I had fallen for so much as the idea that I *could* fall for somebody, that it was possible for me like it seemed to be for everybody else. I was too dense to notice that real caring had entered through the side door a long time ago, taking me by surprise, appearing when I least expected it, by a person who became a complete woman—today.

For the rest of the day, I'm worthless, and Wednesday night I hardly sleep at all, unable to rid myself of this picture of Joey lying under a sheet with a giant blood stain where his dick used to be. But, surprisingly enough, it's not the surgery I can't reconcile. It's his being down there in Baltimore all by himself. Joey, who would help anybody through a difficult time, no matter what it cost him.

Thursday morning, I leave a message on the office machine that I'm not feeling great and won't be in. At twenty after ten, I'm on a train to Baltimore with my nose buried in a copy of *Sports Illustrated* to calm my nerves. The train lumbers through the Lincoln Tunnel under the Hudson River. I confront my reflection in the window to my right, a guy whose life went from zero to sixty in the last four weeks, hanging out with a fantasy-obsessed actress and letting his true feelings for his best friend catch up to him in the process.

And now that best friend had his dick lopped off!

I ask myself if I'd be taking this train to see Karen if she were recovering from surgery? Would I want to be at her bedside when her baby is born? Then, for some reason, I think about that Vietnamese girl sandwiched between Ted and me, and I have an old familiar urge to find her and apologize, make it up to her somehow, give her money, as if she'd even remember one more faceless thug who raped her.

The train pulls out of the tunnel into blinding sunlight and accelerates across the wetlands of northern New Jersey. Birds flit in tall grasses. The still waters meander with hardly a current to direct them. I imagine myself in the middle of it all, flexing the casting rod I had as a kid. I even picture Joey at my side, though as far as I know, the only thing Joey ever fished for was a compliment.

New passengers board the train in Newark and one heavyset, middle-aged woman, winded from toting her luggage, sets her briefcase on the empty seat next to me. I help her stow her travel bag in the overhead rack. She sits, fingers strands of hair behind her ear in a gesture that reminds me of Joey, and pulls a sandwich from her briefcase. She offers me half, which, out of courtesy, I decline.

"Don't be silly," she says. "Young men are always hungry. I should know, I have two sons. Or had. They're away at college now. One's a senior, the other's a freshman. Imagine my checking account! But that's life."

I thank her for the sandwich—turkey, lettuce and tomato on a roll, with plenty of mayo—and take a bite, trying to remember when I ate last. Beyond Newark, we pass the industrial ruins of New Jersey. Power plants with flaming smokestacks stretch into the dreary distance. Tiny steel staircases encircle storage tanks, like garlands on birthday cakes. A nasty chemical stench seeps into the car.

"I'm taking a deposition in Philadelphia," the woman says. "I'm an attorney who hates taking depositions. There are certain things you just have to put up with in life, don't you think? Mine is depositions." She takes a bite of her half of the sandwich. "How about you?"

"Baltimore."

"Baltimore, the neglected city. It has a beautiful old section most people don't know about. What are you going to do down there?"

I consider making up some story, but decide on the truth. "I'm visiting a friend in the hospital," I say, wolfing the last bite of my sandwich.

"Nothing serious, I hope."

"Not sure," I say. What could be more serious than changing who you are?

"Oh dear. What's his condition?"

"Would you excuse me?" I say, getting up. "I need to go to the bathroom."

I squeeze by the woman and make my way down the car's swaying aisle to the toilet, where I close the door behind me and sit on the seat without raising the lid. Damn you, Joey! Leave it to you to choose the most unmentionable medical issue. What am I doing visiting you anyway, when you didn't even bother to tell me what you're up to? This is just like you, making light of the most outrageous action, doing everything on your own, never asking for help. But then I realize that Joey did ask. He had asked directly for what he wanted, more than once—me. Joey had been honest all along. I'm the one who couldn't admit the feelings we had for each other.

My balls do that tightening thing again as I picture the scalpel slicing into Joey's scrotum. I stand, raise the lid and hold onto the walls to steady myself against the rocking train. The half sandwich has balled up somewhere in my throat, not coming up, not going down. I take a leak, zip up and leave.

Back at my seat, the woman finishes eating and crumples up the paper wrapping. She smiles as I step over her thick legs again. I pick up my magazine, leaf through it, set it aside. Fuck it! Maybe I should be more like you, Joey. Maybe I should just tell the whole unlikely truth, let people deal. "It's a sex change," I say to the woman. "My friend's surgery."

Her eyes dart to me, then back to her yellow pad where she's made some notes. But for the glance, I'd think she hadn't heard me. She erases a word and replaces it with another one. "As I said, there are certain things in life you just have to accept," she says, finally. "And it seems to me your sex is one of them."

"Gender."

"What?"

"It's his gender that's the issue, not his sex life," I say. What's gotten into me? Why does this woman's every comment irritate the hell out of me? I watch her add a sentence to her notes. Her handwriting is cramped. No smiley face dotted i's for her. Letting this discussion fizzle seems like being untrue to Joey, so I push on. "Don't you think it's weird that just the mention of sex makes people uncomfortable? Not that I'm any different. I was nineteen before I could force the word out of my mouth and even then it made me blush. How stupid is that? Something that's supposed to be so natural. It probably has something to do with my mother and her boyfriend, Lick, going at it all the time in the next room. Can you believe a name like that? Lick? Do you think it had anything to do with his technique?"

The woman looks around to see who might be overhearing our conversation or maybe to look for an empty seat she can move to.

"But, like I said, Joey's surgery isn't so much about sex as it is about who he is as a person. He just believes, deep down, he's a woman."

"But he's not," she says, not bothering to look up.

"Well, he believes he is. It's more common than you think, or there wouldn't be hospitals like Johns Hopkins who do the sexual reassignment surgery. Who would know better than Joey and his doctor whether he's a man or a woman?"

The rugged Joe Namath stares off the cover of my *Sports Illustrated*, kneeling on one knee, holding a football against his thigh. If that's what a man is supposed to look like, then no wonder Joey doesn't measure up. How many men would? But Joey doesn't care to measure up, unless it's to some model on the cover of *Vogue*.

"He's actually my boss," I tell the woman, despite her obvious discomfort with the whole discussion. I'm surprised at how good it feels to say what I think, no matter how it sounds or who gets offended. I'm not doing it for Joey anymore. I'm doing it for me. "He runs the bookstore where I work in New York. He's smart as hell and he has a great sense of humor. And he's kind to people. Of course he can be a big pain in the butt too."

"He doesn't sound very appealing," the woman says.

"Oh, but he is. He's just. . . . Imagine, waking up every morning to the enemy world of your own body."

The woman slips her pad into her briefcase, closes the lid and rests her head against the seatback. She sighs, looking more defeated than mad. I wonder if she's thinking about some problem in her own family. Maybe one of her sons is sleeping with his roommate. Maybe she hasn't had sex with her husband in sixteen years. It's possible, of course, that she's just trying to end this conversation. "I believe that God made us the way he intended us to be," she says, with a sigh. She stares at the combination lock of her briefcase, lining up the four numbers—all nines, all eights, all sevens—then spins them back to random.

"Then he sure messed up with Joey," I say.

"God doesn't mess up."

"Just us people, you think? Which makes life pretty remarkable, you have to admit." She looks at me like I'm crazy, which is actually what I'm thinking too. "Well, I guess you don't really have to admit it if you don't want to," I say.

We both turn to the suburban New Jersey landscape whipping past our window. Rows of cookie-cutter houses, cars in paved driveways, plastic jungle gyms in fenced yards. I'm thinking that every mom and dad and kid inside those walls is trying to stay the way God made them. I picture them never leaving those houses God intended for them, growing old with their same God-intended neighbors, getting a new God-intended car every other year at the same God-intended dealership, dying of the same God-intended boredom. Of course, it isn't God really. It's people who come up with all the restrictions. I say, "The world is such a rigid place, don't you think? If we were all a little looser about things, maybe Joey wouldn't have had to have this surgery. He'd have been fine just as he was, somewhere in between male and female. American Indians looked up to effeminate men. They believed these girlie guys had two spirits, male and female, and that they had special powers. They were called berdache. Joey knows all kinds of stuff like that."

"I'm sure," the woman says.

We ride along in silence for a while. I'm thinking how Joey, lying in 5H of the surgical unit at Johns Hopkins, is a woman now. I'm thinking I should probably start calling him Josey, like the hospital operator did—I mean *her*, calling *her* Josey.

"This is a big adjustment for me, too," I say. "I mean it's not going to be easy, but the more I think about it, the more I know it's all going to work out better this way."

The woman twists her engagement ring until the prominent stone is centered on top. Whether it's the dreaded deposition in Philadelphia or hearing about Joey—she asked, after all—or thinking about her own life, she looks sad now. I wonder if she's contemplating some big change, herself, but I guess that's just my imagination taking over. Maybe she's running off to Philadelphia to meet her lover, or to break up with him, or maybe her lover is some wonderful big lesbian who cooks stews and does macramé and smells of Irish Spring soap.

"You really like this guy, don't you?" she says after a while.

"Gal," I say. "And yeah, I do." Very much, I'm thinking, very, very much. I have for nearly three years. There's nobody I've ever admired or respected as much as I do Joey—Josey.

The conductor walks through the car, calling out the approach to Center City, Philadelphia. "This is my stop," the woman says, tightening her scarf. She stands and pulls on her coat. She picks up her briefcase. I retrieve her suitcase from the overhead rack and set it in the aisle.

"I think a bunch of violets makes a nice presentation," she says. "I've never been a fan of roses, and carnations seem so funeral."

"Good idea," I say, reaching out my hand. We shake on it.

She makes her way down the aisle, dragging her bag and banging her briefcase into a seatback.

It's nearly three in the afternoon when I pay the taxi driver and step out onto the parking lot in front of the Johns Hopkins Medical Center, a dreary stand of red brick buildings probably dating to the last century. A brick heat stack spews lazy drifts of smoke into a gray sky. Two interns, in short white coats, stethoscopes flopping from side pockets, make their way down the stone steps from the main entrance. A man in an overcoat makes his way up. The air is brisk and eerily quiet. I find the surgical building and obtain a pass for Josey Maxima's room. The elevator, filled with a jostle of visitors carrying smiley balloons and fat teddy bears, lumbers aloft, slowing and stopping at every floor along the way.

Damn, I meant to buy those violets!

I get off on the fifth floor and find 5H, where I stand outside Joey's door, trying to pull myself together. I'm a jumble of nerves. Part of me wants to scold Joey for not telling me he was here. The other part wants to tell him my sleepless thoughts since four o'clock this morning, my retarded realizations, my pent up feelings. I could tell him about my conversation with the woman on the train, how I took a stand for him, me who never argued for anything in my whole life. I could also tell him how, these past weeks, I was always comparing what I felt when I was with Karen to what I feel when I'm with him, how times with Karen didn't measure up, not even close. I could tell him how much I've missed him since Monday, and the year before that, how sorry I am about that whole thing with Karen, how much I've worried since yesterday, how sorry I am for every way I've ever hurt him.

But what Joey needs most right now is just plain comfort and support. My revelations are going to have to wait for another time, urgent as they feel right now.

I push open the door.

Joey has a private room, which I might have guessed, given his unusual "condition." A window overlooks nearby buildings, drab in the flat light, with a view of the city beyond. An empty television stand hangs off the wall. A vinyl chair has been pushed into a corner next to the door to the toilet. A strong smell of disinfectant vies for prominence with an adamant, gray silence.

Joey—I decide to let him tell me to call him Josey, if that's what he wants—stares away from me, out the window. He's hooked up to an IV whose clear liquid drips steadily into a tube inserted into his bruised arm, a woman's arm, a woman's fair smooth skin, no doubt about it. He hasn't heard me or sensed my presence. A ticking monitor by his bed draws a meaningful jerky line across an endless, slow-moving graph. Its red light looks as if it could spring into a pulsating ruckus if upset in any way. The windowsill lacks balloons or flowers and it occurs to me that I'm probably the only person in the world, other than the surgical staff, who knows Joey is here. Something flips over in my midsection and I want to pick up that lifeless white hand and hold onto it until he's ready to go home.

Moving closer, I realize Joey is asleep. His lower lip flutters a little when he exhales. Gray patches underscore his eyes. A crisp sheet angles over his shoulders, chest and his normally sharp hip bones, dulled now with wrapping. There's something about watching somebody sleep, something illicit, secretive. My poor Joey, I'm thinking. My poor pal. What awful pain must have driven you to do this to yourself?

Tears brim in my eyes. I can't help it. It's too much, Joey's wounded body, the whole last year hardly speaking, that year in Vietnam with Ted, his guts spread on the ferns. It all comes on me in a rush now, the aloneness, the anguish—Joey's, Ted's, my own. I swallow hard and steady myself against the rail of Joey's bed. The IV drips, the monitor hums its vigil. I walk to the window and stare out at the forlorn spread of Baltimore, so much lower in scale than Manhattan. A random ray of sun breaches a hole in grazing clouds that threaten snow. Strangely, I miss my old house in Vermont, my room overlooking the woods, the dogs, my distracted mom who probably has a new man by now. You can miss a place, even when you weren't happy there.

Turning back into the room, I see that Joey's eyes are open now. He smiles, weakly, and runs his tongue over his lip. His eyelids dip and rise again. "You look like shit," he says.

I laugh. "And yourself?"

"I'm sure I'm a mess." He starts to raise a hand to his hair, but even that seems too much for him and he lets it fall back onto the sheet. "Why don't you take a seat," he says.

"I think I'll stand. Been sitting all day."

"You probably should have checked with me before leaving them shorthanded at the store. How did things go yesterday?"

"I might ask you the same thing. Do you ever think of anything besides that damn store?"

"Obviously," he says, gesturing vaguely toward his lower torso.

"How are you doing, really? I've been worried as hell."

"I'm okay. How'd you know where I was?"

"I had a suspicion, confirmed by your desk calendar."

"Quite the sleuth."

"Jesus, Joey. How could you do this?"

"How could I not?" He wets his lips again, accomplishes another weary blink. "I am quite aware of the enormity of it all."

"Do you always have to go whole-hog? Have you ever heard of compromise, restraint?"

"Whole-hog. What an unfortunate descriptor."

"You know what I mean."

He turns to me. "I'm me now, Henry." He almost seems to fade off, but then whispers again, "I'm me."

I hear myself and I hear Joey, and I like the sound of him better. "You might have told me," I say, refusing to yield completely to his invincible will, his superior insight, his greater courage.

"You've been otherwise occupied lately."

I decide not to let that one go. "You, too. How was your trip to the orphanage?"

"Adoption center." Joey shakes his head as if that says it all. "How long are you staying?" he asks me.

"I thought I'd take the late train back tonight so I can make it to the Strand before opening tomorrow." What I don't say is that I'm due at eight o'clock tomorrow morning at the New York Hospital Fertility Clinic with another semen delivery for Karen Grave.

"Sit down, Henry. You're making me nervous standing there, rubbing your neck like that."

I take the chair from in front of the bathroom door, set it by the window and sit. We're quiet as I glance outside, looking for some sea change in the landscape, a storm maybe, something akin to what's roiling inside me.

"I did a little research after my trip upstate with your friend," Joey says. "A quick telephone call to Salomon Brothers. You know, that esteemed investment firm downtown?"

"So now who's the sleuth?" I knew all along that Joey's trip upstate with Karen was a mistake, but of course I didn't try to stop it.

"There is no Lloyd Tuckwell at Salomon Brothers, Henry." He grins, and then grimaces from the discomfort, confirming that smugness comes from somewhere deep.

"I know," I say.

"What do you mean, you know? Karen Tuckwell, or whatever her real name is, made quite a point of telling me about her illustrious husband, the investment banker with the graying hair and the deep pockets."

"You just happened to inquire into her personal life?"

"I think it's pretty basic when you're getting acquainted to ask a woman about her husband."

I have the sense there's more Joey learned from Karen than he's telling me. Not that Karen's nonexistent husband isn't enough to spark a healthy skepticism. I just know Joey. He has a way of extracting information and relinquishing it only after he's digested it fully himself. He's been suspicious of Karen since day one, with reason, and whatever he found out, it's bugging him more than he's letting on.

"If that husband exists, that is," he says now, "which he doesn't."

"Are those pillows okay?" I ask him, getting up. Joey leans forward. He smells of dried blood and disinfectant. The pillows feel hot. I fluff them and he leans back, closing his eyes. He coughs and grimaces.

"I repeat, they've never heard of a Lloyd Tuckwell at Salomon Brothers," he says, after the coughing subsides.

"I know. She told me."

"She told you she's not married? When?"

"A couple of weeks ago."

"And you . . . ? I think this woman may be crazy. And you, too."

"She definitely has an active fantasy life. Probably why she's such a good actress. It goes with the territory."

"You seem awfully casual about this, Henry." Joey's hands form fists on the crisp sheet. "Jesus Christ, she's lying. A lie that got her into a fertility clinic and possibly pregnant. By you. There is no father for this child. And no nanny or SoHo loft or trust fund for college."

"I know, Joey. You're right." A kid should have a father, and a mother who's a little more grounded than Karen Grave. No doubt about that. "She isn't pregnant, though, I don't think. Not yet, anyway."

"You don't *think*?" Joey's lower lip tenses and relaxes, like his fists. "She already abandoned one child, twenty-three years ago. I would think you might. . . ."

"What, Joey? Not see her anymore? Disappear on her? You know I can't do that. What if she does get pregnant? What about that kid?"

"You were the one who told me you had nothing to do with this potential offspring. Now, there's no husband and you're talking about this progeny as if it's the latest in a long line of Prestons."

I get up and stand at the foot of Joey's bed. "You need to stay calm, Joey."

"Obviously, before she met you, she was planning to raise the kid on her own. What makes you think she needs you now, or any father?"

"She's not a strong person."

"That much is clear." Joey turns away, taking in the blank green walls of the room, the empty TV stand. "There was no record of Karen at the adoption agency," he says.

"So she said."

"You talked to her?"

"She called, night before last, after you two got back."

Joey turns away. "Come on! There's no way to know what's real with this woman."

"Why would she make up giving a baby away?"

Joey is getting more and more exasperated. He doesn't understand my complacency. Neither do I, I guess. This conversation is not going the way I had anticipated. I'm not saying any of the things I'd wanted to tell Joey.

"Maybe to get you to feel sorry for her, or to justify this crazy scheme to have a kid now. How should I know? It's all too weird. And what if it's all lies?"

"Karen doesn't really think that way."

"What way?"

"About lies or truth. It's all kind of vague for her."

"How convenient!"

"You should rest, Joey. We can talk about this later."

"What upsets me most is that none of this seems to upset you. I always admired your honesty."

"It does upset me, and I am being honest, I just. . . ."

"But she's not. She must be damn good in bed."

"Watch your manners."

"I'll be as rude as I have to to get you to react. What the hell is going on inside that rock-hard head of yours? You never say. Do you have any idea how frustrating that is? Take a stand, Henry. Wake up!"

"You're right," I say. "There's a lot I need to tell you that I haven't said."

Joey waits.

There have been times—when my girlfriend stopped talking to me in eleventh grade, or when I left my mother sitting in my pickup at the side of a dirt road in Vermont, or when I put my hand to what was left of Ted's face the night he died—when all there was to say had stopped up in my throat like a clogged drain. And it just sat there. The words wouldn't have come close to describing what I felt, anyway, and wouldn't have made a whole lot of difference in the end. Whatever was going to happen was going to happen. Words didn't matter. Now, I can see that that was a cop out. Words do matter. They're just hard to get right.

If Joey had been born the girl he always believed he was, I'm pretty sure we'd be married by now and parents of our own offspring. But then, if he'd been born that girl, everything would have been different. We'd likely never have met. Life is just one long string of chances. It's about time I stood up and took mine. I step around the end of Joey's bed.

He's turned toward the window now and appears to be sorting through his own thoughts. Letting his head fall back onto the pillows, he says, "You still don't see me as a woman."

"Is that what you're mad about?"

"I am a woman, Henry, and I'm smarter and more attractive than that . . . fabricator."

"Joey, I. . . ."

"God damn it, look at me. How much more do I have to do?"

"I am looking at you. And you didn't do this for me. I would never have. . . ."

I have the urge to leave, but more than anything right now, I need to stay. And I need to say something.

"You're right," he says. "That was unfair. I'm sorry." He fingers a strand of hair behind his ear, a gesture that is so familiar it makes me want to cry. He's a woman. And yet, he's the same person he always was. And the reality here, that elusive truth Joey demands and I've always claimed to prize though was never quite able to articulate, is that I love him. I love Joey Maxima.

"Maybe you could run out and get me a milk shake," he says, brightening, perhaps realizing he's said as much as he can and the rest is up to a force beyond his control—me. "I've been lying here all day, dying for a vanilla malt. I think I even dreamed about one just before you came in."

"I could do that, I guess, but I just want. . . ."

"There's one other thing, Henry." He moistens his lips.

"What's that?"

The snow I sensed on the horizon earlier swirls in thin blustering gusts against the glass. We both turn to it, then back to each other. "Would you touch me?" he asks.

Once again, I swallow hard.

"I know it sounds ridiculous, but it's been so long since anyone's touched me—except with a knife, of course. That and the vanilla malt and you can go back to New York assured that you satisfied my every need."

He smiles and the warmth in my chest usurps the tiresome trepidation there. I move closer to the bed. He rests his head on the pillow and I let my fingers fall onto his hair, stroking it and smoothing it down the side of his face. I touch his cheek with the backs of my fingers the way you'd touch a kid's cheek to let him know you're there, that he's safe, that everything's going to be okay. His skin is warm and dry, smooth and unflinching. I touch his eyelids, his earlobes, that delicate spot where his hairline reaches the stark whiteness of his neck, a woman's neck. I keep going. I touch his narrow shoulder, lingering there a while, half massage, half caress, and the same on his arm, ending up with his hand, which I squeeze once, and then again.

My heart thumps away in my chest as if it's always been out ahead of the rest of me and tired of waiting for me to catch up.

"It means a lot to me, your coming here," Joey says.

"Joey, I. . . ."

He looks up at me. "Are those tears, Henry?"

"I don't know."

"Are you okay?"

"I love you, Joey." I try with all my might not to turn away. "Don't say anything, okay?"

He nods.

"It's taken me a long time, I know, too long, and I'm sorry. But I love you, Joey. I do. I love you more than I ever loved anybody my whole life."

He stares at me a while, then nods again, and smiles this time.

"I'll go get that malt now," I say. I step to the door, then turn back. "I hear you're Josey Maxima now."

"What do you think?"

"I like it. It suits you."

"Really?"

I nod and pull open the door. "I'll be right back, Josey. Don't go away." I pause in the doorway. "What would I do if you ever went away?"

Josey smiles at me, as if I'm being absurd, which of course, I am. But the truth is, the idea scares the bejesus out of me, all of a sudden. "I don't know what I'd do if anything ever happened to you."

"I'm not going anywhere, Henry."

"Me neither."

"Except for the malt."

"Right. Right away. The malt."

I pull the door closed behind me, aware that I have opened another door, a wide open entrance to a new life I can hardly wait to begin.

15

KAREN TRIES IT THE OLD FASHIONED WAY

On Friday, I stare at my TV screen, watching security camera photos of Patty Hearst, holding a rifle during a San Francisco bank robbery. One way or another, it seems, the Symbionese Liberation Army, now referred to familiarly as the SLA, is going to get it's money for poor people's snacks. I have to say, I envy that little heiress, suddenly too busy to attend benefit functions. A whole new thrilling life that would never have been possible had she not been kidnapped. Another unanticipated drama appearing out of nowhere. At some point, in the middle of the whole adventure, she unmasked catastrophe and stumbled on possibility.

I flip off the TV. Speaking of possibilities, I need to get to the clinic.

At five minutes to eight, I step out of a cab in front of New York Hospital, where I'm due for my fourth insemination with Hank Preston's semen. The standard procedure is to inseminate during each ovulation until you miss a period and you're on your way, so to speak. But McAvery, the clinic director, thinks my uterus is as battered as an old doll, and my ova equally lackluster. I'm just praying today's slothful egg has enough life in her to snag one of Hank's strapping freestylers and show him a good time. We need to get this show on the road.

But on the road to where? That's the question. To single parenthood? Lloyd Tuckwell is so elusive. It's not his fault, of course. And Hank Preston? All indications are that he prefers a distant sort of fatherhood, one in which he comes and goes, so to speak. Men!

I yawn, run my fingers through my hair and heave open the building's bronze door. I'm wearing my usual black leather jacket and boots today, having turned in the $35-a-week mink after my trip upstate on Tuesday with Joey

Maxima. I never even liked the look. And who am I trying to impress at this point? Certainly not Dr. McAvery.

Joey, my long lost son. He's good, I have to admit. I should be such an actress, switching genders like a costume change. Now I have to adjust to having a daughter. Sons are so much more fun. Not that we were close, though I've observed him from a distance at the Strand since I discovered him working there three years ago. I'd been a customer for years, but then, all of a sudden, they had a new manager with an unusual name.

And there he was, descending the stairs one day from his perch above the store. Perhaps I should have introduced myself. Perhaps we could have become friends, who knows? My son, presenting himself in New York City, all grown up and ready to enjoy. But Joey was no longer the *boy* I'd delivered to the world. At twenty-one, he was obviously on his way to becoming a woman, and that discouraged me. His rejection of his maleness felt personal, as if the life I had given him hadn't been good enough. Yet it was difficult not to read some cosmic significance into his sudden return to me after all those years. Had he come back, finally, seeking the love of his real mother? He wasn't my *boy*, though. He was some inter-gendered misfit I feared I might not be able to love. Would I reject him a second time? I just couldn't see going shopping for dresses or sitting in adjacent chairs at the salon. How could I have a son who was prettier than me?

I decided to keep my distance.

I was never the same after I let them take my baby from me. But what could I have done? I was barely fifteen, with no one to help me. My mother certainly wasn't about to become a stand-in parent. There was nothing I could do. I never forgot my baby, though. Never!

Of course there was no record at the Albany Area Adoption Agency when Joey and I went there on Tuesday. I stole it on the night of my senior prom. While my friends were jitterbugging at the gym, I was nose-down in a file drawer, searching under Allen, pulling my record and stuffing it under my sweatshirt before climbing back out the window and slamming it shut behind me. Back then, security wasn't what it is now.

Then why the trip to Albany, you might wonder? I'll get to that.

From there, I circled around to my high school, where I snuck in and watched the dance from the top of the bleachers, fingering the rolled file. You'd think I'd have been sniveling into sodden tissues, taking in the girls in their frilly pastel dresses, the boys in their ill-fitting tuxedos, all dreamy and hanging on each other. But all I felt was the huge distance I'd always sensed between myself and them, only now I was higher up, above it all, and done with that town. I was headed for New York City and a career on the stage. Stealing that file had been my way of making a fresh start. Later that night, I set a match to the only record of my adolescent blunder and watched its glowing embers drift off and die beside my parents' barbecue.

Of course, I had taken down the address of the Maximas, first, my baby's caretakers. And they hadn't been hard to find, six years later, never having moved from the address they had given the agency. I was making decent money by then, waiting on tables while studying acting at HB Studio on Perry Street. I'd even landed a couple of minor roles off Broadway. The trip to Evanston, Illinois had been my first vacation. I observed Joey—though I didn't know his name then, only the Maxima part—grocery shopping with Mrs. Maxima, playing behind his fancy house, and in the lovely stone Episcopal church on Sunday before my flight back to New York. He had seemed, from a distance, like the sweetest little, no-trouble six-year-old. And why not? He'd lucked out. The Maximas were rich and doting. I was satisfied that I'd done the right thing by letting them hold onto him for a while.

So why did I arrange the whole trip upstate with Joey? To have some time alone with my child, of course. Perhaps I'd been too precipitous, four years ago, rejecting him because he had rejected his gender. When Hank Preston introduced us, I liked Joey right off. He was smart and spunky, like his mom. Not to mention pretty! Here was a chance to get to know Joey without revealing who I was. What could be more opportune? And I have to admit, the absurd irony of being introduced by the man who would father my next child appealed to me, too.

Yes, our attraction to the same man might pose a problem, eventually. Joey's love for Hank was obvious. But we'll cross that bridge when we come to it.

At first, as the Manhattan skyline receded behind us and the Palisades Parkway opened up ahead, I felt silly treating Joey as a woman. But then, as the day went on, it seemed increasingly right. Not only was she clever and determined, she was also sly and quite the maverick, as any child of mine should be. Ultimately, I decided to reveal the truth, or at least reveal enough for Joey to suspect. That was mean, maybe, but isn't it my turn for a little satisfaction, after twenty-six years?

As I enter the New York Hospital lobby now, I half expect—hope—to see Hank Preston waiting at the elevator door, just as he was a month ago, a vial of semen nestled in his shirt pocket. But he's not here and a stab of longing darkens the already dim entryway. Men. If there's any possibility at all, they will disappoint you. Like Dan Bailey. I've told myself so many times over the years that the fire at his building had been an accident. And it's true, I hadn't intended to hurt him, not really. He disappeared after the fire, his career going up in smoke, so to speak. Had I been rash? Unfair? These thoughts plagued me, afterward. But there was nothing I could do about it by then.

At the elevator, I press five, wondering if Hank has been and gone upstairs, or if, by chance, he's at the back of McAvery's office right now, delivering his potent little parcel. As the elevator lifts off, I recall Hank standing behind me a month ago—it seems so much longer than that—his bike resting on his shoulder, his disheveled look so endearing.

The elevator swoops me to five and I enter the clinic's waiting area. I sit and thumb through a copy of *People* magazine, with that new sensation, Mia Farrow, on the cover. Inside is a photo of Chris Evert who is expected to win at Wimbledon, and Mikhail Baryshnikov the latest dancer to defect from the Soviet Union. Where did I go wrong? With one break, I could have been a star.

At twenty minutes after eight, Dr. McAvery appears and asks me to follow him inside. But instead of directing me to the insemination room, he shows me into his office and offers me a chair, taking his own behind his massive mahogany desk.

"I have to apologize," he says, adjusting his long white coat, "but I don't have your insemination. The donor didn't show up, I'm afraid."

"Didn't show? How could that be?"

"He's one of our most reliable. This has never happened before. I'm quite at a loss."

"I don't understand." My heart does a tango in my chest.

"I know how difficult this is, the emotional preparation involved and all. Is your husband picking you up?"

"My husband? No, I'm here alone. I just. . . ."

"I do apologize. I'll try to reach your donor and see if we can get a delivery for later today, or tomorrow. If not, I'm afraid we're going to have to skip this ovulation and shoot for next month." Despite himself, the good doctor stifles a chuckle.

I try to think what's behind Hank's decision not to show. My little performance in Joey's office on Monday? He was obviously not pleased. I get up to leave.

"This is a very rare occurrence," McAvery says. "We pride ourselves on our efficiency here at the clinic."

"I can see myself out," I say, not bothering to mask the irritation in my voice.

"We'll call you about this afternoon, or tomorrow."

A chill threads up my spine and into my shoulders as the elevator descends to the first floor. Hank is nothing if not boringly reliable. I cross the lobby. Has he decided not to continue with our inseminations? I'll kill him. Maybe it's Joey's influence. Maybe, after our trip upstate together, she convinced Hank I wasn't right for him so she can have him for herself.

I check my watch. Hank might not have left for work yet. I hail a taxi and give the driver his address across town.

As the taxi lumbers down Second Avenue and turns west on Fifty-Seventh

Street, I review the weeks since I arrived, unannounced, at Hank Preston's apartment. He'd been shocked at my obvious interest in him, my boldness in being there at all. And then my morning visits to the Strand, toting coffee and raisin Danish. I probably blew his mind, all that attention from a Broadway actress. And then I tore his clothes off the first night he came to my apartment. Restraint was never my long suit. Still, we told one another things, private things. I liked him and he was beginning to like me. What happened?

"Put the pedal to the metal," I yell to the driver. "I haven't got all day."

My shrink has been pushing me to go back on meds. But they make me fat and sad.

At 501 West Fifty-Seventh Street, I pay the fare, step out of the taxi and glance up to Hank's fifth floor window. No sign of life. I've probably missed him. The door to his building stands ajar, as always, and I press on, taking the stairs two at a time to the top floor. I knock on his door and wait, tapping the toe of my boot on the worn linoleum. I knock again. Finally, I hear his bare feet scuffing the floor inside. He's here.

Hank appears behind the few inches allowed by the chain. "Karen! What time is it?" he asks me, all drowsy.

"Where the hell were you?"

"Jesus," he says, suddenly more awake. "I overslept. Damn!"

I gesture toward the chain.

"Sorry," he says, unlocking the door and stepping back to allow me in.

"I wondered if you'd gotten cold feet," I say, glancing at his crotch. I've got a dowager egg descending that needs an escort and behind those boxers he's got a million or so stalwarts just dying for the job.

"I had to go to Baltimore, yesterday," he says, apropos of what, I'm not sure.

"Baltimore?"

"I didn't get back until three in the morning." I glance around the room. Hank scratches and stares "Christ, I've never missed a clinic appointment. McAvery must be pissed."

"What about me?"

"Sorry, you want some coffee? I suppose I can be a little late to work."

I've always expected perfection in my leading man, a sexuality at once aggressive and tender, attentive and generous, innovative, romantic, loving. But it's never going to happen. This morning, I'm prepared to settle for efficient. I brush a wisp of hair from my face, trying to think of how to get things started with Hank, not a new thought. Should I kiss him, profess love? I don't have time to wait for him to make a move.

When he turns back from setting the kettle on the stove, I say, "Do you think, unconsciously, you might have missed the appointment on purpose? Maybe you'd rather do it the old-fashioned way." I chuckle, making light. I'm tempted to mention a daughter he could take to the park, a fabulous new apartment we could find for three, the candle-lit snacks we could all have together, whatever it takes to stir him.

He looks sheepish. "Karen, I. . . . We should talk."

I knew it. Something's up.

Hank moves to his baggage cart bed, where he reaches for his jeans hung on the handle. "A lot's happened in the last twenty-four hours, and. . . ."

I fly at him. He gasps as he falls back onto the bed. The iron wheels creak and slam to a stop against the wall of books. My mouth touches down on his. My hands are all over him, pulling down his shorts. He utters something, but I can't make it out. Is he reciprocating or struggling to free himself? Who knows? Who cares? I press his wrists to the bed. Suddenly he's too strong for me. He rolls me over, shoves me off and in one deft leap is on his feet. He stands with one leg still caught in his jeans, his shorts around his shins. His eyes are wide, his jaw hanging amiss. I grab his erect dick and thrust it into my mouth. Trust me, nothing kills ambivalence like fellatio. For a minute, he seems to relent. Then I hear him gasp and he's cupping my face, trying to push me away. I pull back and look up at him. Can this possibly not feel good? Hank's whole body seems to contract. He moans and jolts forward. Together we watch a trajectory of semen spurt over my shoulder, a second land on my chest, and a third dribble down the shaft of his shuddering dick.

My first impulse is to gather up his semen and somehow insert it into myself, then to run. Hank grabs the band of his shorts and pulls them up. He rubs the back of his hand across his forehead. "Jesus," he says. He turns toward the window, then back to me. "Christ, Karen, I. . . ."

I bite my lip and try to breathe. I straighten my blouse.

"What I was trying to tell you was. . . ."

"I'm really not interested," I say, standing, my feet still clad in their spike-heeled boots. "Guess we shouldn't fire McAvery quite yet," I say. I grab my jacket off the bed and head for the door. "Pathetic!"

"Don't go. We need to talk."

I step into the hallway and slam the door behind me.

16

HANK IN LOVE

I follow Karen into the hallway, lean over the railing and yell to her to come back. The only response is the slap of her soles on the last flight of stairs. I hear the front door swing open and shut on its rusty hinges. Standing there in my shorts, shaking my head, I picture us half on and half off my futon, my thirty-dollar semen splatting inconsequentially on Karen's shoulder. I have to laugh.

I strip and step into the shower. It makes a weird sort of sense, I suppose, that my relationship with Karen would come to such a tactless and downright embarrassing conclusion. Is it a conclusion? I suspect it is. She's angry and frustrated, and I can't really blame her. I don't see Karen as the sort to stick around and try to pull a warm friendship out of the ashes of a smoldering and hapless love affair. It was all wrong from that morning I stepped into the elevator at the clinic and she rushed in behind me. Forbidden from the start. Still, I feel like a loser for not knowing my own mind, that old becalmed vessel, the SS Hank Preston, seeking a current. Pathetic, as Karen said, and rightly so.

Hot soapy water—a much-appreciated luxury this morning—splashes off my chest and swirls around my dick. What is your problem? I ask it, as if my dick is a guy I hardly know but have been teamed up with for special matches, with precious few wins so far. Do you really think this donor business is going to be enough for us? Would it kill you to be a little more social? Of course, my dick just hangs there, looking put upon. I rinse, shut off the water and grab a towel.

I love Josey Maxima, my mantra since yesterday. I've loved her for months, though she had to become an actual woman for me to realize it, or maybe to admit it. Okay, so I lack imagination. Call me old fashioned, but I know now that I could never make love to anybody else but Josey, feeling the way I do.

I should give my dick a break. Maybe it knew what was up—so to speak—long before I did.

I caught the eleven-ten train out of Baltimore last night, arriving in Manhattan about three in the morning. Back at my apartment, I lay awake, worrying about Josey. I have a habit of rolling my cart-bed around the room when I can't sleep, my bare foot jutting from under the blankets and pushing along the floor. Last night, I followed a moon beam that angled through the window and made its way across the floorboards, like some meandering ghost. My mom used to say it made you crazy to lie in moon beams, but I find it calming. What if Josey had some kind of relapse, I worried, whatever that would be? Nobody at Johns Hopkins would even know to call me. Josey would face whatever happened on her own, which she certainly can do if anybody can. But no one should have to be that alone.

Of course, it's not just Josey I'm worried about. It's me. Yes, I love her. I know that now for sure. But does this mean I can actually *be* with her, as in marriage, sex, adopted kids? As in forever? So she's an anatomical woman now. Everything works as it should, supposedly. But in my mind, Josey is still a lot of Joey. She's still the person I've known and admired for three years. Can I make the leap to lover. If I know Josey, she'll give me all the time I need. But still. . . .

I wish I'd had the chance to tell Karen that I finally stumbled on the truth, whether she believes in it or not. Whatever the complications, I want to spend my life with Josey Maxima. She's welcome to be our friend if she likes. She said she was fond of Joey. Maybe that could all work out.

Drying off, my dick goes on the offensive. "So, you found love? Congratulations! But guess what, it's still me you're afraid of. Christ, if you can't be honest with me, who can you be honest with? You were thinking about that Vietnamese girl this morning, weren't you? I mean when Karen jumped you. Am I right? Of course I am. The same old questions whenever sex is in the picture. You came inside that girl. Did she have your little Amer-Asian baby? How do you ever expect you and me to work together if you think about that girl and her baby every time I pop up?"

I wrap the towel around my waist, drowning out the rest of this familiar tirade. I do still cringe when I think of that Vietnamese girl and what Ted and I did to her. My dick is a smug know-it-all, which I suppose is pretty standard.

I make coffee and take it with me as I search for fresh underwear and jeans. The hit-or-miss pile of clean clothes spilling off my trunk reminds me of Karen's place. Whatever happened to the upbeat, anything-goes attitude Karen had when I met her? A pinprick to the balloon and all that bluster hissed out with an odor of trapped emptiness.

I drop my towel and my dick has the last word before the muffling slap of my boxers against my stomach. "Be careful of that woman, that Karen Grave

Tuckwell. She has too many names, for one thing. Christ, there are flashing red lights all around her. She's trouble."

I pull on my jeans, pick up the phone by my bed and dial Dr. McAvery.

"What happened to you?" he asks, a football coach dressing down a fumbling quarterback.

"I overslept."

"I had to send the recipient home."

"I know. I'm sorry."

"You know?"

"I mean I assumed that's what happened."

"And do you know how emotionally upsetting this whole process is for our clients?"

Had Karen been driven by some primal mothering instinct when she jumped me this morning? The question, like so many others, splutters in a square of sunlit, rumpled bed sheets. "I don't think I can do this anymore," I say.

There's a lengthy silence on the other end of the line, then, "No reason to overreact, Hank."

"I'm sorry, but I think I need to stop."

I hear the click of McAvery's pipe against his teeth. "It's up to you, of course, but take some time. Think about it. This is important work, you know."

"I appreciate you saying that, Doc." In fact, this is the sort of reassurance I'd sought a month ago when I ran into Karen in the elevator and started waking up to the significance of this donation business. Now, it's too late. McAvery, with my input, so to speak, was messing with people's lives in a major way. There might be reasons that some couples are infertile, good reasons we mortals don't have access to. For jerking off, I got grocery money and the chance to play God, or at least his assistant, the acolyte of fertility. But what about the bigger picture? What about the people whose lives I change with a few strokes of my palm and a sigh?

I picture Karen's messy apartment, her late nights at the theater, her fantasy husband not showing up for dinner. What would have become of *that* little clinic success? It might have been any woman I met in the elevator that day, but it was a flakey actress with no husband, a short fuse and a tentative grip on reality.

"Give me a call if you change your mind," McAvery says, and we hang up.

I finish dressing, set my empty cup in the sink and lock my apartment door behind me. I shoulder my bike and take the four flights to the street. Outside, the March morning is unseasonably warm. All vestiges of February snow and ice have melted away, leaving a layer of grit in the gutters of Fifty-Seventh Street. Riding downtown, timing traffic lights, swerving to avoid a taxi taking on a fare, my mood lightens. The sun clears the east side skyline—the Chrysler

Building, the Citicorp Building—and bounces off storefront windows along the west side of Fifth Avenue. I ponder how dense and convoluted New York City is, as intricate as the workings of people's minds, with thousands of pedestrians and cars like thousands of thoughts and feelings, crowding in all directions. Hundreds of thousands of people of all ages are making their way to work or play right now, each one with a problem he needs to solve or a person he needs to see or a desire he needs to fulfill. All the intrigue and joy I've spent my whole life avoiding. But I can see now just how wrong that approach has been. I can't help grinning as I pull up to the corner of Broadway and East Twelfth Street and greet the owner of the hardware store up the block. I shoulder my bike and pull open the Strand's front door.

My morning with Karen Grave probably worked out exactly like it was supposed to.

Upstairs, Joey's assistant watches as I clock in. "Where were you, yesterday?" she asks me.

I glance at Joey's desk—Josey's—wishing she'd return to work so things can get back to normal, though they're not going to be normal ever again. At least not the kind of normal they've always been. Everything's changed. "I told you, I wasn't feeling so great. Any word from the boss?"

Celeste pages through a stack of bills. "He called, said he wouldn't be in until a week from Monday."

That seems really fast. Guess it doesn't take that long to change your whole life. "Was he okay?"

She drops the bills and looks up at me. "Have you figured out where he is?"

"Yeah, have you?"

"He told me before he left. I guess he wanted somebody to know, just in case."

"In case what?"

"I don't know. What does anybody know? He's been planning this for a long time. I think he's the bravest person I ever knew."

I nod. "I went to see him."

"You what?"

"That's where I was yesterday, in Baltimore, at the hospital."

"Oh my God!" She pushes the stack of bills aside. "You two. . . ." She tilts her head again, like a bird interrupted in the middle of its song. "He was just checking in, making sure we're all on the job. He said everything went fine."

"She."

"What?"

"She said everything went fine."

"That's so weird. I mean it is and it isn't, you know? The thing is, I'm not sure whether Joey wants us to tell the rest of the staff or not. Do you think we should?"

"Josey."

"Josey?"

I nod.

Celeste grins.

After my philosophical moment biking downtown, Josey's public relations issue regarding her sex change seems like just one more ripple making its way ashore on the great lake of happenstance, where it will make an imperceptible landing, break over on itself and disappear. I head toward the stairs. "I don't know," I say, "about telling the staff." Telling, not telling, it all comes out in the end, anyway, though I suppose just how it comes out does make a difference. I consider telling Celeste about Joey and me, but decide Josey should do those honors. "Don't you think she would have told them if she wanted them to know?"

"So he. . . ."

"She."

"So she's just going to show up a woman?"

"Surprise a minute with her," I say. "If you think about it, she's been a woman for quite a while."

Celeste considers this and nods in agreement.

"Let's play it by ear," I say. "If somebody asks, we'll tell them."

I take the stairs two at a time to the cellar, where I greet the other two staffers by the coffee dispenser. Even the cheerless subterranean atmosphere can't stifle my mood. I feel as if I managed to avoid a scrape that could have ended with a baby for one fragile actress and, for one lowly shelfer of books, a sense of responsibility for the wrong woman. I slice open a carton of books and load up. Back upstairs, I push my cart off the elevator and down the long aisle into Fiction. Then, ten minutes into shelving, I have an idea that can't wait and I take the stairs two at a time back up to the office.

Celeste looks up from her ledger and runs her eraser over her lower lip, waiting for me to state my business. I glance at Josey's desk and the mounting bedlam of files and mail there. I turn back to Celeste. "What if we had a party for Joey?" I ask her.

"Josey."

"Right. A welcome back party, with balloons and a cake and plenty of good hot coffee." I pick up Celeste's empty cup and drop it into the wastebasket by her desk. "Throw out the old crap and get some fresh Columbian. Start things off right."

Celeste smiles for the first time in days.

"You know," I say, emboldened, "you have a great smile."

She blushes and looks away.

"I'm serious."

She fingers her bangs, and I wonder if, during her long tenure at the Strand,

Celeste has fallen a little in love with Joey, which might account for her glum mood lately, watching him pick up the pace toward womanhood. "I really like the idea," she says now, "a tribute to Josey's accomplishment. Make this all completely positive."

"Exactly."

"We could fix up this place, too. Throw out all this stuff, renovate, make it all new."

"Great idea!"

A week goes by during which I talk with Josey every night, first at the hospital, then at her apartment in Brooklyn. She doesn't let me visit her there, says she wants to wait until she's steady on her feet and can walk up to me in a pair of heels and throw her arms around my neck and kiss me. On Friday morning, I arrive at work early, climb the stairs and say to Celeste, "Let's get on it."

"On what?"

"The renovation we talked about. Josey's coming back on Monday."

She looks around the office as if daunted by the idea that had so much appeal ten days ago. Then, she brightens, flips off her typewriter and stands up. "I always hated this office. Go get the others."

Back on the main floor, I tell the cashier and today's other shelfer that Celeste wants to see them upstairs. I run up the block to the hardware store, aware of the potential in every minute. What is Josey Maxima, after all, if not the personification of possibility, a living testament to change and hope? I buy a cardboard sign that reads CLOSED FOR RENOVATION which I hang in the window back at the Strand. I usher out the single browser and lock the door.

Upstairs, Celeste and the others have pushed the three metal desks into the center of the room. I lend a hand with the filing cabinets, unearthing a mouse skeleton, a plastic bangle, half a pack of Tareytons and a month's supply of paper clips and pencil stubs. We pile chairs and lamps and typewriter stands on top and cover the whole island with some mildewed sheets unearthed in the basement. We each chip in twenty bucks and return to the hardware store to buy spackle, paint, rollers and brushes.

It turns out that Josey's sex change surgery is no surprise to the others, this final step having been anticipated by everybody for months. The discussion, as we sweep and wash, prime and paint, focuses on how Josey's new status as an anatomically correct female should be reflected in the décor of the office. (Anyone referring to her as Joey is assessed a dollar which Celeste puts into the renovation kitty.) Drapes are suggested as are soft colors, a throw rug and a love seat, subject to funding. Celeste, as Josey's assistant, takes charge. She directs and advises, and we, less invested in the outcome since we spend little time upstairs, give her free rein.

I half expect Karen to show up at the store and knock on the glass, maybe even offer an apology, but she doesn't. At six o'clock that evening, I dial her number, thinking she might have cooled down during the week that has passed, but there's no answer. I leave a message to call so we can talk.

On Sunday morning, the staff meets at the Flea Market on Sixth Avenue at Twenty-Sixth Street. A rainy late-March wind rattles the vendors' stalls. Celeste selects an area rug, two lamps, yards of heavy maroon velvet, a slightly dilapidated settee and two end tables, for a total of ninety-four dollars. Somehow, we maneuver it all to East Twelfth Street and up the listing stairs to the office.

By four o'clock, everything is in place for Josey's triumphal return at eight the next morning. We all sit, exhausted, savoring our success. Josey's desk commands a corner of the room, sporting an antique leather desk set and an electric clock with glowing numbers that click into place like tiny flash cards. The Victorian settee is placed, like a peacock, against a wall of velvet curtains that suggests a hidden view of lower Manhattan. The new lamps cast a soft pink simmer onto the fresh cream-colored walls, where prints of the Duomo in Florence and the Roman Forum hang in chipped, gilded frames. This is clearly a woman's office, a woman much loved and admired by her staff. Celeste ordered the cake for delivery in the morning. We're ready.

No word from Karen.

"I need a shower," I say, getting up and sliding Josey's chair carefully back under her desk. "We should all be here by seven-forty-five, the latest. You know Josey. She'll be on time."

Celeste and I hug goodbye and I descend the cramped stairway, feeling content in a way I haven't felt for weeks. Crossing the landing, I realize that this is my real home now, the Strand Bookstore at Broadway and East Twelfth Street, and Josey is at the center of it, where she should be.

As I take the remaining steps to the first floor, I hear somebody close the front door and mumble something under her breath. I watch her back as she yanks the renovation sign out of the window and sticks it under her arm. Her hair spills over the back of her camelhair coat. Her shoulders are a little stooped, and she walks gingerly, carrying her briefcase. Whether Josey's scowl reflects her physical discomfort or outrage at the sign in the window is anybody's guess. As she walks, her coat spreads open, revealing jeans and a white blouse, her usual weekend work clothes. She's lost at least ten pounds, which gives her face even more prominent cheek bones and an even sharper chin.

When she emerges from aisle six and notices me standing on the stairs, a momentary smile flickers across her face, like a rare burst of warmth from one of the Strand's unreliable radiators. "What are you doing here?" she asks me.

"I could ask you the same thing. We were expecting you back tomorrow."

"I've got a ton of work to catch up on. I can just picture my desk."

"I doubt it."

"What's the meaning of this?" she asks, raising the sign for me to read.

"I'm ready for that hug you promised."

Josey smiles, softens a bit and reaches her arms around me. Gently, I embrace the frail body that has been through so much. We hold each other. "I've missed you," I say.

"Me too."

"Come see your office." I offer my hand and she accepts it.

As we reach the landing, where she needs to rest a minute, I sense someone at the window at the front of the store, hands pressed to the glass. When I lean over for a better look, whoever it is moves quickly away. In that blur of black leather, I think I see Karen.

"What's the matter?" Josey says.

"I thought I saw somebody. It's nothing, I guess."

"Are you all right, Henry? You seem nervous or something."

"I'm just glad you're back," I say, as I watch her climb the remaining flight. Still on the landing, I glance once more to the sidewalk in front of the store. Karen, if she had been there at all, is gone.

17

HANK AND JOSEY AT THE CENTURY

At five-thirty on a May evening, Josey and I step out of a taxi in front of The Century, an art deco apartment building on Central Park West. Holding the door for her, I scan the sidewalk and the street. It's been two months since Karen Grave left my apartment in a huff. Since then, I've seen her at least twice, once outside the store where I buy my groceries and once pulling away from my apartment building in a taxi. That is, I'm pretty sure it was her. Each time, she'd been moving away from me and I wondered if my mind was playing tricks. But I don't think so.

I close the cab's door behind Josey and together we climb the steps to the Century. Taking in the bronze lanterns on each side of the entryway, I wonder what ace Josey has up her sleeve now. She's more enigmatic since she's become this foxy lady. The doorman smiles and nods as Josey leads us into the dimly lit lobby that resembles the interiors of the great mid-century luxury liners I've seen in picture books at the Strand. "Just follow me," she says, knowing full well that I will because I pretty much gladly do these days. Josey has the upper hand with us now, which is fine with me. I remember my mother telling me once that that was a woman's place, in charge, whether men like to admit it or not. Men were lost without a woman to tell them what to do, she claimed. Now that I think about it, Karen Tuckwell would probably agree, and probably Josey, if you pushed her on the subject. So where does that leave us men? Calling on whatever reserves of trust we built up over the years for our moms? Bottom line is, if I'm going to trust a woman, let it be Josey Maxima.

In the two months since her surgery, Josey has exploded into womanhood, leaving behind any semblance of her former manliness, however feeble it may have been. An amazingly difficult process, when you think about it, changing your gender. Of course, Josey wouldn't have thought of it as a change, rather putting things right, finally, the end of a process that began when she first noticed the differences between boys and girls and realized the group with the trucks and guns felt all wrong. Slipping into the group with the Barbies and the high heels was a struggle that would take up the next twenty years of her life, a struggle she never retreated from, never questioned. All those years of electrolysis and feminizing hormones have melded now with her resolve, and then her final ordeal under the knife two months ago, from which she's made a spectacular recovery. Josey Maxima is finally the woman she knew all along she should be, and a fabulous woman she is.

Her makeup softens the former assertive edge of her cheekbones; her hair has taken on the sheen of the Breck Shampoo girl. Even her breasts, no longer the primary proclamation of her femininity, have been allowed to relax into natural arcs against her chest. Today, she's wearing a loose-fitting blouse over bell-bottom pants, a couple of gold bangles and a heart on a gold chain. The femininity that seemed forced in the body of an effeminate man has evolved into a grace that didn't really surprise any of us at the Strand. Josey's transition had been going on for as long as any of us knew her. Still, we're all impressed at what seems the innate rightness of her now, our memories of an edgy, frustrated Joey faded, almost gone.

Our own transition from friends to lovers has been a little more tentative, like sailing into calm waters when we're still rigged for storms. Some adjustments still need to be made. We kiss and we hold each other, but for now that's as far as things go, physically. For different reasons, we both steered clear of sex our whole lives. But that's going to change now, in time. We're not in a rush. When we do get there, I know it'll be right. Meanwhile, we talk every night on the telephone. We spend weekends together at her place, trusting that the specifics will work themselves out as we go along. Josey and I will be together; that much is certain.

I continue to follow along now in the narrow wake of her perfume, taking in the lobby's bronze mirrors, the over-stuffed settees and deco-patterned rugs. The insertion of a prominent "s" in Joey's name served to soften its overall effect at the Strand, while doing nothing to diminish its authority. Josey still runs the store as a firm yet benevolent feudal lady, demanding strict adherence to her rules of propriety and responsibility, while always ready with a twenty when she senses one of her "family" in need. With this subtle yet remarkable change in her being, she might easily have made a clean break with the store. She could have moved on to some hefty management position in a law firm downtown or at a Madison Avenue advertising agency, leaving her friends behind, turning her back on Joey once and for all. But Josey stayed put.

At the elevator, she presses seventeen. "I have another story to tell you," she says. "I hope you don't mind."

"I love your stories."

"I think they've become a little pedestrian lately."

"You mean compared to before?"

Josey grins, one-sided. "So you agree?"

"No, I don't agree. I just learned some time ago not to argue with you."

She smiles and steps into the elevator, and I have the fleeting image of Karen Grave stepping into the elevator at New York Hospital that wintry morning back in February. It's hard to believe how much has happened in the three months since then. "Should I be nervous? About this latest story?" I ask Josey.

"Do I make you nervous?"

"Sometimes."

"Good. A woman should have that power with her man. Anyway, this is the last of my stories. I promise."

"Yeah, right," I say, knowing Josey can't resist a good story, no matter what.

The elevator door slides open and she leads the way to the end of the pale-carpeted hallway, past cream-colored doorways with bronze handles, key slots and peep holes. She retrieves a key from her purse and slips it into the lock of 17A. Before opening the door, she turns to me, studies my face a minute and grins. I'm wondering, by now, of course, if 17A belongs to her. She kisses my cheek. "Don't look so worried," she says, as she opens the door.

Inside, she flips a switch and a single bulb, hanging from a pair of wires, casts a harsh glow onto the parquet floor of the entryway. The apartment is bare, with an abandoned kitchen at the far end of the hall, its cupboard doors gaping at odd angles. Josey takes my hand and leads me along a cast iron railing wrought with art deco bolts of lightning flashing across small ovals of sky. She descends two steps into a sunken living room which she crosses, leading me to a set of French doors. A breeze flares her blouse, causing it to cling momentarily as she pulls open the doors and steps onto the terrace.

I follow her outside and stand there with my hands thrust deep into my pockets, stunned by the panorama of Manhattan stretching out before us. Below are the green treetops of Central Park, their spare new leaves shimmering in the glow of a million city lights. At a right angle to the terrace, Central Park South stretches east along a line of apartment houses and hotels—the Essex House, the Saint Moritz, the Park Lane—extending all the way to the Plaza. Straight across the park, shoulder to shoulder, stand the imposing apartment buildings of Fifth Avenue, looking a lot like the bastions of the super rich they've always been. Tiny squares of windows glow in their darkening facades and I think about all the complicated lives going on inside, the worries and pleasures of the wealthy probably not so different from those of us ordinary folks.

"All those people out there," I say.

"I know. It's amazing, isn't it?"

"So this place is yours?" I ask, turning to her.

She nods, a finger grazing her chin, coyly. "I told you. It's a long story."

I put my arm around her shoulder and we stare out over the sparkling city. "I knew it. This is too much, Josey! So shoot, tell me. I'm all ears."

"No you're not!" She takes hold of one and squeezes it. "You have very cute *little* ears."

I laugh and step away, suddenly self-conscious. I thrust my hands back into my pockets. Bastions of the rich . . . is that what Josey is now, rich? How many more changes does she have up her elegant sleeve? Does it matter? A sudden gust lifts and drops her hair like a sigh. The chill I feel is the realization of just how happy I am to be with Miss Josey Maxima, on Central Park West, or in Brooklyn, or at the Strand, it doesn't matter where. I glance back at the park, which grows darker by the minute, with constellations of streetlamps flashing to light along its walkways. I close my eyes against an old euphoric feeling from when I was a kid, when I used to imagine flying over the hills behind my mother's house in Vermont. Closing my eyes now, I picture myself soaring off this terrace with Josey in my arms. I picture us rising over the park and staring down at the Sheep's Meadow, the Bethesda Fountain, the Boathouse, like Clark Kent and Lois Lane. But I'm no Superman, just an ordinary guy who finally allowed a beautiful woman—formerly his best friend—to fill his unsuspecting life with wonder.

"Remember I told you how I thought I could fly?" I ask her. "When I was a kid?"

"I remember."

"I was having that feeling just now, like I could take off from this balcony and soar out over the park."

"Please don't."

"I could take you with me."

"You're scaring me, Henry."

"Sorry." I glance into Josey's storm-green eyes which, themselves, feel like spaces I could fly into. "Seeing the trees from above like this reminds me of that time. I still get that weightless feeling when I'm as happy as I am right now." Josey smiles, tolerating my weirdness as I've learned to tolerate her surprises.

"A lot of kids make things up in order to get by in a world they don't feel a part of," Josey says. "I didn't just think I was a girl, I was convinced, whatever the anatomy or whatever some people might say were the facts. I still believe it. I will always believe it."

"So, does that make it true, then?"

"Actually, yes. That's the only truth that ever held up for me, my feelings. Everything else was debatable."

"You might have a hard time selling that idea to the people out there." I gesture toward the skyline.

"I wonder. It seems to me people try so hard to squeeze their feelings into some authority's arbitrary definition of reality, and it almost never works."

I turn back to the park. Josey steps beside me and, shoulder to shoulder, we lean against the parapet, seventeen floors above the street. "Flying seemed to come to me as naturally as running did to other kids. I remember the first time. I had just turned eleven years old. I lay in my bed for the longest time, watching my model airplanes ride the gentle air currents from my open window and make restless moon shadows on the wall next to my bed. It was a warm spring night, like this one, and that same breeze flustered the birches out back. I felt the kind of edginess a kid feels working a loose tooth that needs to be yanked. Eventually I got out of bed and stepped to my window. Our two dogs, staked out back, pricked up their ears at me. Leaning out, this strange feeling came over me, a lightness like I was as flimsy as a kite, like I might just float into the moonbeams stretching between the trees."

Josey slides her arm under mine.

"All of a sudden, the birches stopped swaying and their leaves went all limp. That rich, earthy scent you get this time of year in Vermont rose up at me. The dogs sat back and relaxed on their haunches. It was so quiet you would have thought the world had just taken a breather from its rotations. I climbed onto the window sill and stood, holding on to the frame. The air felt all dense and magical, as if I could easily step into it."

She squeezes my arm. "And did you?"

"I wasn't scared. It never occurred to me that I would do anything but soar upwards into that heavy scented air. I could feel my pajamas against my skin, the goose bumps as big as marbles." I turn to Josey. "I guess I got carried away—literally."

"Getting carried away is not exactly your most prominent quality, my sweet."

"I was such an average kid. I had no particular academic or athletic abilities. All of a sudden there was something extraordinary about me. I could fly. I believed it. I had no doubt."

"I think you're quite extraordinary," Josey says, smiling up at me.

An audience of clouds saunters above the apartment buildings across the park. "Thanks," I say.

Josey cups my chin in her palm. "My flying knight in shining armor. It sounds as if flight was your way of feeling good?"

"I started thinking I should guard against any sort of happiness, especially when I was around other people, like I might just take off if I got too excited, you know?"

"You were quite the master at avoiding pleasure when you first came to the Strand," Josey says. She lets go of my chin and brushes my hair off my forehead. I lean over and we kiss.

"This is the ultimate New York fantasy," I say.

"This apartment?"

"You and me. If I die tomorrow, I can say I felt it all—love, the spell of New York, the whole thing."

"Well, please don't die just yet," Josey says, kissing my cheek. "And come away from that wall!"

She steps through the French doors into the living room just as the buzzer rings out at the apartment door. She takes off to answer it, her heels clacking the parquet. I hear a brief exchange and then the door closing again. Turning for one last glimpse of the view, my eyes travel from the distant Fifth Avenue buildings, with their caps of clouds and tiny spots of yellow light, to the closer tree tops and finally to the sidewalk across Central Park West, directly below. There's a woman leaning against the granite wall that separates the sidewalk from the park. She's dressed all in black; her auburn hair drifts lazily across her face. She's thinner than two months ago, yet I'm certain, even from seventeen floors up, that it's Karen Grave. She stares up at the building, at this terrace it seems. I yell to Josey, who is crossing the empty living room, carrying a large paper bag. "Dinner," she says, grinning. "General Zhou's Chicken, sesame noodles, broccoli and string beans in oyster sauce."

I take the bag from her and set it down. "Come here," I say, grabbing her hand. "Look down there." I point to the sidewalk.

"Where, Henry? What is it?"

"Across the street."

But Karen is gone. The sidewalk is empty except for a man in a sport coat, walking two dogs.

I let go of Josey's elbow. "Never mind. It's nothing, I guess."

"What did you see?"

"Nothing," I say.

"Was it Karen Grave?"

"Why?" I ask, taken aback.

"Tell me, Henry. I want to know."

"I thought I saw her across the street. But it's seventeen floors down. I must be wrong."

"I think not. I've seen her, too."

"Really?"

"Outside the Strand, once, and outside my building in Brooklyn. She looked different, though, haggard, unkempt."

"Why didn't you tell me?"

"The same reason you didn't want to tell me just now, I suppose. It's eerie, and a little scary. I keep thinking she'll give up and go away."

"Jesus, Josey." I turn away from the street.

"She's probably harmless enough," Josey says, unconvincingly. "Let's go inside." She picks up the bag of Chinese food and steps back into the living room.

"I'm not so sure," I say, following her inside.

"What do you mean?"

"I think she's angry with me for rejecting her. And probably jealous of you. And we both know she's capable of weird stuff, like lying to the clinic to get pregnant."

In the kitchen, Josey sets the bag on the dusty counter and starts removing fragrant white cartons with little metal handles. She pulls a bottle of wine out of a cupboard and two glasses she must have stashed there earlier. She hands me the corkscrew. "I get the impression Karen was angry with everybody, for years," she says. "Not just you."

"What do you mean?"

"You always think things are your fault, when they're not. Like Ted, in Vietnam."

"Do you ever forget anything?" I undo the foil wrapper and go to work on the cork. Josey sets out chopsticks and opens the steaming cartons.

"Like an elephant," she says, pointing to her head. "And that Vietnamese prostitute. You told me you have thoughts of making things right with her somehow, when that wasn't your fault, either. You wouldn't have touched her, but for Ted."

The cork surrenders with a satisfying pop. I pour two glasses.

Josey says, "Let's change the subject, okay? Here, take these." She hands me paper plates and two sets of chopsticks. "Go find us a spot for a picnic, anywhere but the terrace."

The living room is larger than I had realized, maybe thirty feet in length, with a high, beamed ceiling. I calm myself by assessing its condition, which appears to be excellent, though it could use a coat of paint and some floor polish. But Josey probably has that all arranged.

She arrives with a folded sheet. "Can you spread this somewhere?"

"So how did you get this place?"

"In a minute," Josey says.

I set down the paper plates and take the sheet from Josey. I search for a spot, resisting the impulse to check the sidewalk one more time. Instead, I close the terrace doors and peek into a bedroom, where the only light source is the refracted flicker of park lanterns through the newly leafed trees. Turning back, I decide on the center of the living room for our picnic, where we can look out over the Park but not down to the street. I open the cloth, flip it and let it billow onto the floor like a flag of surrender. I set out the plates.

Josey appears with the cartons balanced against her chest and a handful of napkins and soy sauce packets. "Would you grab the rest?"

In the kitchen, I gather up the bottle of Beaujolais and glasses. I set the wine down next to Josey who has arranged herself demurely on the sheet. "So, do we eat," I ask her, sitting down, "or do you tell me what this apartment is all about, first?"

Josey picks up her chopsticks and starts coaxing clumps of rice onto plates. "Let's do both," she says. Light from the entryway bulb pierces the glasses and casts red prisms onto the sheet.

"To you," I say.

"To us," Josey says. She sips her wine and sets the glass down. "You eat," she says, passing me a full plate. "I'll talk. I'm not very hungry, anyway."

I unwrap my chopsticks and wait, not sure I want to dig in alone.

"It's not such a long story," she says, running a polished fingernail along the rim of her glass. "I told you a long time ago that I was adopted and that I grew up in the Midwest, outside Chicago. Being adopted had always made me feel kind of special as a kid. That was an idea my parents had promoted— sweet of them—and it worked. I felt wanted, at least at first. Later, when their disappointment became obvious, I told myself that they had brought me on themselves. I was their fault, not mine. But of course, since I was adopted, they could reason that I wasn't really their fault. And I liked that idea too. I wasn't anyone's fault. Or the person whose fault I was wasn't around to blame. She floated in some unreal world, where she watched out for me from afar. I believed she was the one who got me through all those hideous times at school. With a flick of her sparkling wand, she made the pain go away, or some of it. Her presence out there gave me hope. I vowed that one day I would find her, and thank her for playing a role she never even knew she played for me."

Josey, who had kept her eyes on her wine as she talked, looks toward the terrace now and grows silent.

"What are you thinking?" I ask her.

She turns to me and produces a particular sort of grin I have long-since learned is a cover for whatever she is feeling. "I was thinking about Karen," she says.

I nod, not knowing what to say.

"Did she tell you everything about our trip upstate in March?"

I picture the veiled figure of the woman across the street, seventeen floors down. "I don't know. What's everything?'"

"She told the woman at the agency that her last name had been Allen, my birthmother's last name."

Fear jabs me in the ribs, steals my breath. "Karen?"

"I'm not sure I believe her, Henry, but it's possible. There was no record at the adoption agency. My parents are dead. I don't know where to look for verification."

I shake my head and then take a long pull on my wine.

"Probably none of it is true," Josey says. Once again, her tone is not very convincing.

"But how could she have come up with that name?"

"I know. That's what I keep wondering. When Karen first started visiting you at the store, she looked familiar to me. I couldn't place her, but since then, I remember that she used to come to the store several times a year, often enough for me to recognize her. She always looked glamorous, but a little distracted, like she wasn't that interested in the books. She would browse for half an hour or so, and then she'd leave. As far as I know, she never bought anything."

I start to pour myself more wine and realize my glass is still nearly full. I set the bottle back on the cloth.

"Of course, a lot of people just browse at the Strand. But they focus on the books."

"You mean she might have been coming to see you? Watching you from a ways off?"

Josey fingers the rim of her glass. I sip mine. "Finish your story," I say, "about the apartment."

"My parents were rich. My father owned. . . . Well, that doesn't matter. When I left college after one year, they were furious. Any parents would be, I suppose. But college just wasn't for me. I used to wander the campus alone after dark, wondering if I would ever belong anywhere. And I felt so much older than my peers, always have. The only real friendship I ever had was with a black kid when I was thirteen. I was a hopeless misfit. If I couldn't find someplace that felt right, well, I couldn't see going on. Anyway, after I quit college and came here, I didn't speak to my parents for about a year. Then one day I called and we reestablished contact. They never visited me here in New York. I went out there occasionally—holidays mostly. We maintained a kind of distant affection based on the years we'd shared the same house. A year ago, during that time you and I were hardly speaking, they up and got themselves killed on the icy intersection of Routes 58 and 83 near O'Hare Airport."

I wonder if this casual attitude about her parents' deaths is Josey's way of coping with the loss, or if she really had, during all the years she felt like such a disappointment, grown not to care much about them. Or is she just distracted now by the possibility that Karen Allen Grave Tuckwell is her birthmother. This is the biggest surprise yet, and the most disturbing by far. What if Karen really is Josey's birthmother? What happens then? What does that mean, for us?

Suddenly, the smell of Chinese takeout makes my stomach turn over.

"So, that's it. End of story. I'm a wealthy woman." Josey gestures to the empty living room as if to confirm her financial status, and to divert us from further discussion of Karen Grave. "The curious thing is that, while I was Joey, I never touched the money they left me. I guess I was still proving I didn't need them. And, as an effeminate man, probably I didn't feel entitled to it. I don't know. But now I feel as if I earned every penny."

We both look around the room, taking in its empty splendor. Her eyes stop at the terrace doors, and then glance away. "And besides," she says, "a woman can't live in squalor the way a man can. At least not my kind of woman! This place suits me, don't you think? Or it will when we're finished with it."

I nod, then guffaw. "Jesus Christ, Josey, look at this place!"

She rests a hand on my shoulder and gestures to the Chinese food. "Do you want this stuff?"

"Not really."

"Let's go out then. Someplace fabulous!"

We gather up the plates and cartons and take them to the kitchen, where we shove them back into the paper sack they came in. I cork the wine and set it back in the cupboard, empty the glasses into the sink and follow Josey into the hallway. She locks the door behind us while I find the trash chute for the refuse.

At the elevator, I reach out and tuck some stray strands of hair behind her ear. She blurts out the words we avoided for so long and now can't say often enough. "I love you so much, Henry," she says.

"I love you, too, my little heiress," I say.

The elevator arrives. I put my arm around her shoulder and we bump hips, laughing as we climb aboard.

After seeing Josey into a taxi in front of Café des Artists, a few minutes after midnight, I make my way south on Broadway and then west on Fifty-Seventh Street. I realize I'm still smiling, as I had all through dinner. We could have returned to her apartment at the Century, I suppose, and maybe even made love on that sheet we left on the living room floor. I imagine that, and my smile broadens (and my impatient dick stiffens). Someday soon, it will happen.

I've crossed Ninth Avenue and walked halfway down the block before I notice the fire trucks lined up at the corner of Fifty-Seventh and Tenth. Smoke billows from the roof of my building. I run to where a tape extends into the avenue, slowing traffic to two lanes and holding back a crowd of onlookers. An extension ladder reaches to the roof, where a fireman swings an ax directly over 5S. My window is a black gaping hole framed by shards of dirty glass. Smoke funnels from one corner and curls into a black sky.

18

KAREN MOVES INTO THE LOFT

Help me!
You want to know what it's like?
That's what it's like.
Help!
Help!
But nobody answers. Nobody's there. Everybody's out for himself. That's just the way it is.
Help!
Two weeks ago, I found myself on the station platform at White Plains, New York, with no idea why I'd come or any memory of buying a ticket, boarding the train, taking a seat. As I stood there on the platform, strangers bustled past me to the stairway, each with somewhere to go, a car to unlock and drive away, a spouse to meet, something. Others rushed to board the train, heading north. I shook all over. I knew no one. Nobody to ask where to go, what time the next train was back to Manhattan. Sweat broke out on my forehead. I was afraid to reach into my jacket pocket and find it empty of cash. I looked around. I might have been anywhere. In Syracuse or Rome or Utica, New York. Don't you love those names? So ancient, so grand. Time. What did it matter? What did anything matter?

It had begun to rain, fat drops splashing around my feet, clad in sneakers, the laces flopping. The crowd quickly thinned. I stood alone in the throbbing grey light. Please, I whispered.

I lift a six-pack of Coke from my kitchen counter now, carry it to the bedroom and drop it in front of the armoire. Yes, I made it back to Manhattan from White Plains. Don't ask me how. I bummed the money, that's it. Made up a story that I'd forgotten my wallet, which was not exactly made up. I'd forgotten more than that. But not enough. I can't forget the stuff that really hurts.

The six-pack bounces and turns upside down. Now it's going to be all fizzy. I hate it when it's fizzy. I pop one and just as I thought, it explodes and brown fizz roils over the top and down the sides like some dumb movie monster, the Coke Blob, determined to annihilate all other cola blobs, especially the Pepsi Blob. I lick the ooze off my fingers and watch it pool on the floor. I should get a cloth and wipe it up, but then, there's a lot I should do that I don't feel like doing. So shoot me.

The TV drones. David Brinkley catches my eye. Now there's one boring man, boring voice, boring looks, that Nixon hair, plastered back. And damn if he didn't land an anchor spot on the most popular news show on TV. He and Huntley who looks like he had a real acne problem once. Irresistible, both of them. That's the best the networks can do? And where are the women anchors?

Brinkley announces that the Los Angeles Police Department has raided the hideout of the Symbionese Liberation Army, killing six of their members, while rescuing Patty Hearst. So, she's freed, or recaptured, depending on how you look at it. The film footage shows the relieved parents in a crush of reporters, making their way to the police station to see their daughter. She'll get off, of course, though it's clear to me she crossed over from heiress to rebel. Who wouldn't? Another urban drama you never could have predicted, with lives altered and prospects transformed. Six people dead. Happens every day.

My mistake was thinking Hank Preston was different. My mother was right. Men are unreliable, pathetic jerks, all of them. Of course, she was right. She was always right, one of her more irritating qualities, which meant that somebody else—usually me—had to be wrong. Don't parents know that being right doesn't matter in the end? As if choices are rational, as if there is a right and wrong when it comes to what you feel.

I remove the remaining Coke cans from the six-pack and set them on the floor inside the armoire. For years, I berated myself for buying a piece of furniture this huge. Cost me a damn fortune to get four men to carry it up the stairs and put it together again. Now it makes a nice, roomy entryway. I gather up several empty cans, along with some candy wrappers, popcorn bags and a greasy pizza box, take it all back to the kitchen and pile it on the overflowing trash under the sink. Never was much of a housekeeper. So arrest me.

Sweet, innocent Hank Preston. Right! In the months since our first sexual fiasco, under the coffee table, I've finally seen the light. Hank Preston is just one more man who set about to confuse me, to get me to let down my guard, to get me to fall for him. All of which I did, of course. And how does he reward me? By taking up with my long lost son, cleverly disguised as a vogue model.

Pitiful is all I can say, those two. Neither of them is worth the time I spend thinking about them. Trust me, I'll have the last word. You watch.

I load up with a loaf of bread, jars of peanut butter and grape jelly, and head back to the bedroom, where I set them down beside the Coke cans. They make quite a little still life together, the glass jars and the cellophane wrapper catching the light, the cans like columns, framing the scene. If I were a painter, I'd. . . . I'd make some money and get some respect. Call the painting "American Wonder" But that's not going to happen.

Nobody ever understood. All they saw was the bright lights and curtain calls and autographs. They saw pretty hair, manicured nails, big smile. They missed the maze of confusion inside, turning this way and that way, wondering if I was getting anywhere, where I'd come out, if it even mattered. And all because of men. Hank Preston was mean to me. He took advantage. Now he makes love to my son with the wounded genitalia.

What difference does any of it make? Even if somebody had seen inside, he'd have turned away. Nobody wants what's real. They may say they do, but they don't. Not really. They want fantasy. They want their dream. So that's what I gave them, from the stage, or up close. Of course dreams are short-lived, and a lot of them are nightmares you wouldn't want to last anyway. So where are you in the end? Nowhere.

I should never have cheated on Lloyd. Lloyd was devoted, the sort of man no woman in her right mind would do wrong. There was no reason he ever had to know about Hank Preston. It only hurt him. Revelations of infidelity do more damage than any protective lie ever could. Better the truth rot on the end of your tongue than cloud a partner's charmed illusions. Thirty-eight years on this earth and that's the wisdom I have to impart. Not that what I think matters. Not that I've had any success with people. Except onstage, where everything turns out the way it's supposed to.

I would never have strayed from Lloyd if it hadn't been for meeting that sexual malfunction lurking in the elevator that day at the clinic. Or is it dysfunction? Nonfunction? Hank Preston was determined to humiliate me, probably to get even with all the preoccupied, self-involved women in his past life, starting, no doubt, with his mother. That's what men do. They find a woman who's willing to take their retribution. Men have no scruples, except for Lloyd, who never gave me one ounce of trouble, and who now, after all the heartache I caused him, has forgiven me.

I sweep up inside the armoire and take the last of the detritus back to the kitchen. That sperm donor baby idea was such a farce—the expense, the degrading procedures, the whole fluorescent sexless atmosphere. All organized, of course, by a man. That first day should have been enough to finish me. After Lloyd and I filled out questionnaires and submitted to those dreadful physical exams, McAvery sat us down in his office. Well, I can see why you've been having trouble getting pregnant, he said to me, a grin spreading those thin lips of his. He went on to tell Lloyd how low his sperm count was. Well, wasn't that why we were there? Wasn't that a given? Then he turns to me with the grin and the tobacco breath, and he says, The picture with you, Karen, is a bit more complicated. Complicated? Women have been getting pregnant for centuries without counting days or recording temperatures or submitting to embarrassing pelvic exams. How complicated can it be?

Back at the armoire, I take another pull on my Coke and set about dismantling the still life. The bread goes into the back corner, the jars next to it. The Cokes stay up front, for easy access.

So he asks me if I ever had an abortion. Says there's significant scar tissue around my cervix and in the uterus, as if there'd been an infection from a rather primitive attempt to end a pregnancy. Rather primitive, those were his words. Botched up. Ruined. By a fucking knitting needle or a fork or a spatula for all I know. His point was—it was unlikely that I could get pregnant again, ever, no matter how many fertility clinics I tried, no matter whose sperm.

I remember smoothing my slacks over my knees, knowing I had a story in my head that would answer McAvery's question about the abortion, but unsure whether it was just a scene I had played once, years ago, or if it had happened, for real. My memory gets blurred sometimes. I tell myself it doesn't matter one way or the other, that truth is only the most plausible of a whole bunch of possible explanations, and sometimes not even that. But I'm not sure if I even believe that anymore. What *do* I believe? That life is some cruel joke and I've been the brunt of it for thirty-eight years? Yes, that, for starters.

And all for nothing, the whole crazy debacle at McAvery's. The mortification, the expense that dwindled my savings, the dashed hopes. It never fails—those that want can't have, and those who never even try get blessed with riches.

I remove a couple of slices of bread from the plastic wrap. I unscrew the peanut butter jar, dig out a wad and press it onto the bread, which tears like a gash. I push the whole mess aside.

Mark was handsome in a Charlton Heston sort of way. I was only nineteen and I fell for him like a stack of Playbills off a balcony rail. He was much older, and a doctor! Do you believe that? The sort of guy you could take home to your mom and dad. Except for one thing, he was married—unhappily, of course. It seemed there was an epidemic that year of unhappily married men who didn't want to leave their wives. Things were more secretive in 1955. Sexiness was confined to a Rita Hayworth poster. Nineteen-year-old girls, even those living on their own, were expected to hold off until they were married. Hell, I knew, deep down, that the all-American approach—the virginal wife with two kids and a station wagon—was never going to work for me, wasn't even an option, for that matter. What I didn't know was that I was as fertile as a cat in heat.

Help me, Mark, I should have said. Marry me. But he wouldn't have, and then I would have begged and it might have gotten ugly.

I pull a wrinkled pack of Salems out of my pocket, light one and drop the spent match on the floor. I exhale a line of blue smoke and watch it spread into a lazy cirrus film along the ceiling. I feel sleepy. Why wouldn't I? I lost track of night. It's all pretty much the same in here, with the curtains all drawn. And when I do sleep, it's not long before some dream startles me awake. Or is it a dream?

I don't know what I thought was going to happen to me back then, pregnant, alone, nineteen. Maybe I hoped my condition would just go away like a bad cold or something. Then, one day, Mark shows up at the coffee shop where I work and hands me a wad of twenties. Inside was a note with a name and address on it.

I take another drag of my Salem and watch the ember glow, cozy as a campfire. I let the ash fall on the floor.

I found the man. He was older, gray stubble. He took the money, jammed something up inside me. The pain was unbelievable. He gave me a diaper for the blood and sent me home. I took a bus back down Ninth Avenue, feeling a warm wetness accumulate between my legs. Two days later, I was in Bellevue with a major infection. I nearly died, not that it mattered to anybody.

Here's a secret nobody knows. Two weeks later, I was admitted to Bellevue again. This time to the psych ward. I got fired from my job because of all the sick time. I was hearing voices, and not very pleasant ones either. I was scared. So fucking scared, I . . . well . . . I lost it, that's all.

I grind my cigarette on the floor.

I had two babies, one for the Maximas of Evanston, Illinois, and one for the rubbish heap the Sanitation Department barges down the Hudson River and out to sea. I used to think about my baby, lying somewhere in all that refuse at the bottom of the sea. At Bellevue, I learned not to think about such things, and not to talk about them. That's where I really learned acting, the psych ward at Bellevue Hospital, New York City, where I played a recovered young woman, healthy and able after her ordeal.

But now, miracle of miracles, I *am* pregnant. And even better, it's not by one of Hank Preston's rambunctious little sperms at the clinic. I'm going to have Lloyd Tuckwell's baby.

What an astounding end to this whole baby saga! And there's not going to be anybody around to bother us, no doctors, no men, except for Lloyd, who is not at all like other men.

From inside the armoire, I can see right into the kitchen of the loft I share with Lloyd. The brushed aluminum appliances gleam in a yellow light from a wall of windows. Lloyd is home from work, his tie loosened, his collar undone. He's making a drink. Water splashes onto the counter. He reaches for the sponge at the sink. How dear he is! He's forgiven me for my indiscretion with Hank Preston. He's forgiven me for Doctor Mark when I was nineteen and for John Riley in tenth grade. He understands and he forgives me.

I step into the armoire, sit, and close the door behind me.

19

HANK FINDS ROSEMARY BECKER

Except for my trip to Baltimore to visit Josey, I haven't been out of Manhattan since I stepped off the bus at Port Authority three years ago. Where would I have gone beyond the bridges and tunnels that link this twenty-four square mile island to the rest of the country? If it is linked, which I sometimes wonder. Viewed from the air or the ground, it's a place all its own—paved and spined, hectic and impenetrable and yet somehow vulnerable amid the currents of the Hudson and Harlem and East Rivers, the eddies of New York Harbor. Vermont and my preoccupied mom didn't exactly beckon me back there when I got back from Vietnam, and everything I had ever dreamed about seeing or doing in my life was a few blocks uptown or downtown or just across Central Park. And then, enter my sweet Josey. If anybody had told me, three years ago, that I'd be in love with my boss some day, I'd have told him to guess again. But here I am, over the edge as any teenager, ready to say "I do" and settle in for the duration.

The fire was a major bump in the road, I have to admit. That fifth floor studio hadn't been much other than a place to stow my stuff and the heavy parcel of numbness I had dragged back with me from the Far East. But with time, it became my neat little home, the only place that ever felt like it was really mine. The acrid smell of my charred bike, my railroad cart bed, my soaked wall of books, prompted memories of those split second napalm conflagrations on the other side of the world, families watching their thatched huts reduced to a powdery ash, the smell of charred bodies, the hopelessness of a scorched Vietnamese landscape. And Ted, of course. In the three years since he died, he's never been far out of my thoughts—died in turmoil, never finding the sort of happiness I have with Josey now. I keep wishing there was some way I could take back that night he wandered off to what he must have known was the end, something I might have said or done differently to hold him back.

The blaze at my apartment took another sort of toll, too. I was pretty certain that the enemy this time had been somebody I knew, a friend once, the potential mother of my offspring, Josey's mother maybe. What had I done to hurt her so badly?

But it's over now, and there's nothing I can do about it. Or what I might do, find Karen and have it out with her, I don't want to do. She's a messed up woman. Better to leave her alone and out of my life for good.

Instead, I look at the bright side, which is Josey. A guy can lose himself just as easily among the skyscrapers and subways and libraries and museums of Manhattan as he can in the rice paddies of Southeast Asia or the snow-covered hills of Vermont. Josey rescued me from that long stupor. I owe her my life and, amazingly enough, she wants to be a part of it now. The loss of my little studio above Tenth Avenue can't offset such a miracle as that. I like to think that Josey put a period at the end of my run-on sentence of aimless longing.

The day after the fire, she bought me an air mattress and sheets, a saucepan and some plates and set me up temporarily in 17A at The Century. To let me know this was to be my new home for as long as I needed it, she had the lock changed and gave me the keys. She made it mine, sensing that I needed time on my own to come to terms with the fire and that old feeling of menace I'd thought I was rid of. And I suspect she stayed away because she didn't want us to start our life together in the wake of the fire. She stayed at her own place until moving in together could be the joyous occasion we both wanted it to be.

Mornings and evenings, from my seventeenth floor perch above Central Park, I take in the carefree scent of grass and new leaves mixed with the sweet smolder of hot dog and peanut carts, of popcorn and coffee dispensers, all rising from the greenery below. Taxis honk and brake reassuringly on Central Park West, proclaiming New York's relentless indomitable life, crowding out memories and worries. I walk back and forth to the Strand every day, a five or six mile roundtrip, and along the park's meandering paths at sunset, when the buildings that edge the darkening green flicker on like carnival rides, with thousands of tiny yellow lights jeering at nobody in particular. Back at Josey's, I sleep on my raft, adrift in the sea of her living room, becalmed, momentarily, amid the buffeting currents of my restless mind.

I have the urge to hunker down here with Josey, but then I worry that Karen isn't finished with me yet, and I'd be putting Josey in danger just having her near me. To return the favor of letting me stay here, I plaster and paint, re-grout tiles and wax floors, all in anticipation of the day when we live here together and have breakfast on the terrace before heading to work, not a care between us.

Fortunately, nobody died in the fire at 501 West Fifty-Seventh Street. The building was waiting for the wrecking ball, anyway, and several apartments had been vacated over the years. The tenant below me smelled the fire right away, grabbed his wife and baby and alerted the few other tenants on his way down the stairs. The investigator from the NYFD confirmed that the fire had been set. He also learned that drug dealers and prostitutes and pretty much anybody with time on his hands came and went from the unlocked building. A fire, it seemed, had been long overdue.

But why on the top floor? I asked him. Why would an arsonist climb four flights to set a fire? The investigator held my eyes as if I knew the answer better than he did. I didn't tell him that I'm pretty sure Karen Grave had been stalking me, and that she always seemed to have a soft spot for matches. Why? I feel like I'm the one who pushed her over the edge. I should never have taken the elevator instead of the stairs that morning back in February, no matter how cold or wet or rushed I was. I guess maybe I led her on after that. There's no doubt I enjoyed the attention of a pretty Broadway actress. She threw the match, but I'm responsible too. So, right or wrong, I protect her now.

Naturally, Josey suspects Karen too, but we don't talk about this, probably because we both know that that discussion can only lead to what neither of us is prepared to do—turn her in. Josey has her own reason, of course. Karen could be her mother. I try to imagine what it must be like for Josey, wondering if this crazy woman is really the one who gave her life, the woman she'd thought about for years as a benevolent fairy who looked after her, the only person who, somewhere out there, understood her.

So Josey and I, in a silent conspiracy of avoidance, try to put Karen Grave out of our minds.

Lying on the floor of Josey's apartment, I tell myself that Karen has to be satisfied now. I tell myself she's not crazy enough to try anything else, that she'll forget about Josey and me. But I know that's probably just wishful thinking. If Josey is, indeed, her child, she'll never leave her alone.

Then, somehow, Ted gets all mixed up in my thoughts. Maybe it's that sense of dislocation that overtook me after the fire, or the sense of menace that stalks me now, all familiar from Vietnam. As much as I resist it, the old numbness that Ted and I had employed to get through that year is crowding out the shaky zest for life I had allowed myself to feel with Josey. And, holed up in her apartment with nothing but my thoughts, that old guilt takes hold that I came back and Ted didn't.

Some nights, I can almost feel him lying next to me the way he did over there. I can almost feel him reach out and squeeze my shoulder or muss my hair the way he had early on in our tour, for comfort, for reassurance. That touch was never sexual, but the fear that it might have contained that hidden component had troubled me as I'm pretty sure it did him. As time passed, the touching stopped, keeping at bay the comfort we might have afforded each other toward the end of our duty over there.

So what if it *had* felt sexual? Would that have been worse than what did happen? Easy to say now, but would it? And was it that particular fear that drove Ted to make me have sex with the Vietnamese girl and then, a week later, to get himself blown up?

These thoughts take over as I lie on the floor of 17A, listening to the late-night traffic on Central Park West, seventeen floors below, the occasional rowdy voice from within the park, a siren in the distance to the north. Ted's gone, I tell myself. What's the sense of questioning? Let him rest. And then, as if to counter that line of reason, I wonder if Rosemary Becker, Ted's old girlfriend, is married now, whether she's happy, whether she still feels Ted's presence the way I do.

And whether she has any light to shed on my relentless questions about Ted, or any wisdom to help me let him go.

When I first got to New York after debriefing, a hundred bucks in my pocket and a bunch of disturbing memories, I tried any number of times to get myself to take a bus down to western Pennsylvania. Ted and I had made a pact the year before on that flight over the pole—if anything happened to me, he would go see my mother in Vermont, and if anything happened to him, I would go see Rosemary Becker. Those first months back, I kept putting it off. What would I say to her? How much would I reveal about the Ted I knew? Where would I start to tell her what it had been like over there? The more time passed, the harder it became to imagine visiting her. At some point, I realized I had created this imaginary Rosemary, this sweet, chaste and abandoned waif of a young woman, still alone, still like me mourning the loss of Ted. I even fantasized that she and I would bond over our loss and that something might come of it. I imagined the comfort of lying next to her at night the way I had with Ted.

These thoughts only bumped up my guilt back then. How could I go see my dead buddy's girlfriend when I'd already half fallen for her?

Staring at the ceiling now, unable to go any further with these thoughts and unable to be rid of them, like some song playing over and over in my head, I decide I need to do what I've been putting off all this time. I need to fulfill my promise to Ted and go see Rosemary Becker. But now, it's for me that I go, to put the ghost of Ted Bratcher to rest, once and for all.

I say Rosemary's name out loud in the empty apartment the way I used to repeat names during the worst times in Vietnam, mantras to keep me alive. Anybody's name—my mother's, Ted's girlfriend's, the names of the Beatles or the names of particular models of cars—Malibu, Caprice, Bonneville, Cutlass

Supreme. A whimper, a giggle, any sound I could keep going in my head because that simple repetition meant I was still thinking and breathing and forming words on my tongue.

The evening of the next day, after everybody else has left the Strand, I climb the stairs to Josey's office. She's typing a letter and doesn't notice me standing in the doorway. Her profile is the sort you'd see on a Roman coin, framed by hair that gathers at her shoulders like a curtain overflowing onto a temple floor. I try to picture my old friend, Joey, but I fail. He's gone and yet he's still there somewhere in a calmer and gentler and more beautiful version of his loveable old self.

"Josey?" I say.

She looks up, startled, and then smiles. "I didn't know you were still here."

"I never leave without saying goodbye."

"That's true, you don't. I'm so distracted these days. It helps to bury myself in work."

Before the fire, Josey and I always knew where the other one was. We always had a plan for the evening. We assumed we'd get dinner together and talk until I dropped her at the subway and made my way back to Fifty-Seventh Street. Each day, since the fire, we seem a little more separate, which I hate. We shouldn't let Karen or my thoughts about Ted or anything else do this to us. And yet, neither of us seems to know how to stop it. I'd like to take her in my arms right now and kiss her and invite her to our favorite Mexican restaurant on MacDougal Street. But I know that as soon as we got there I'd sink into these ruminations about Ted, leaving Josey to play with her food and think about Karen, the two of us unable to reach across the table and help each other.

I recall how we used to talk right here at her desk when we were first getting to know each other, the atmosphere hushed, a circle of light spilling around us from her desk lamp. I'd do things differently, if I could be back there now. But not so different, I guess, only faster. But these are silly thoughts, as if any of us knows how things are supposed to work out. "I need to take some time off," I say.

A flash of alarm tenses Josey's face.

"Just tomorrow and Friday. I need to take a little trip."

"Alone?"

I glance down at my feet.

"Forget I said that. Of course alone, feeling the way you do." Josey closes the file she was typing from. "I hate seeing you so sad. I just wish there were something I could do."

"It helps a lot to see you every day, to have you close by." I sit in my old chair by her desk, hearing how weak that sounds, how watered down. Why don't I just tell her we're moving to California, starting a new life away from everything. We could do that. There's nothing stopping us. Does Josey think I'm cooling toward her? Sometimes I think I don't deserve the way I feel with her. And I think that's where Ted comes in. I think that's why I need to go to Pennsylvania. "I just need to figure some things out," I say.

"I know, and I really hope you can. Where are you going?"

"To Pennsylvania. That unfinished Vietnam business with Ted."

Josey grimaces. "Haven't you got enough going on here?"

"Sometimes I think I hurt anybody who gets close to me."

"You haven't hurt me."

"And I don't want to, either. That's the point." Too restless to sit any longer, I get up and walk to the window that overlooks the main floor.

"Don't you think people have a hand in it?" Josey says. "I mean when we get hurt, aren't we responsible too? From what you told me about Ted, he was messed up a long time before he met you."

"How so?"

"He always sounded so angry to me. You said yourself that he was always getting into fights. And then, that whole episode with the girl in the brothel."

I turn to Josey. "How do you know about that?"

"Karen told me, when we drove upstate."

"Why didn't you tell me before?"

"I figured you should bring it up if you wanted to talk to me about it. Are you angry with me?"

"I don't know who to be angry with. I wish I never met Karen Grave."

"That's all behind us now."

"I wonder. I still worry about her, and I know you do, too."

Below, the aisles of books that have occupied me for three years are dim and empty. The Strand always seems eerie to me after hours. The stale smell of dusty, aged paper, is how I imagine a tomb would smell. I turn back to Josey, who's probably waiting for me to say what's bothering me so much. I've gotten to the point, over the last week, where I can deal with losing my things in the apartment. I can even accept that Karen Grave needed to hurt me. It's Ted I can't get beyond. Ted, always Ted, for three years now.

"I killed Ted Bratcher, Josey. I might just as well have put my M-16 to his head and pulled the trigger."

"That's ridiculous, Henry. You wouldn't kill a fly."

"We fought all the time toward the end. He couldn't take the sight of me anymore."

"I don't care. . . ."

"I mean really fought. I broke two of his ribs. He did this." I point to a scar by my left eye. "We hated each other. I couldn't wait to get away from him."

"Don't you think it's understandable? Look what you'd been through together. Look at all you'd witnessed. Where was all that fear and hate to go? All you had was each other."

"Being over there together, it's supposed to make you close."

"Who says?"

"Nobody walks away from camp in the middle of the night. That's suicide."

"So he killed *himself.*"

"When we're coming home? He couldn't take ten more days?"

"Maybe he couldn't take coming home."

"What do you mean?"

Josey shrugs and turns back to her desk.

"Now you're angry," I say.

She turns back to me. "I think we should leave New York, Henry. I've been thinking a lot about it these past days. Get a fresh start somewhere completely new. It'll never be the same for us here now, with Karen, whoever she really is, with what she did to you. Somewhere quieter. I was just reading about all the development going on in Phoenix."

I grin, picturing Josey and me pulling up to our condo in our convertible, two sets of golf clubs hanging out the back. "It's funny," I say. "I was just thinking the very same thing, only California."

"Really?"

"Really."

Josey smiles for the first time in days.

"But I need to do this thing, first. I promised Ted I would go see his girlfriend if anything happened to him. I'll probably be back on Saturday, Sunday, the latest."

Josey hooks her hair behind her ear. "I'll miss you," she says.

I go to her and kiss her cheek, taking in her lemony fragrance. "I'll be thinking about you every minute."

She opens the file she was working on before, but I can feel her watching me as I walk to the stairs, can almost feel her frustration and concern vying for prominence like gears that won't mesh.

"Josey?" I say, turning back. She smiles, probably pleased that I'm having a hard time leaving. "Will you marry me?"

She guffaws.

"I'm serious."

"Henry. . . ."

"I'm not leaving until you say yes or no."

She laughs and flicks her hair off her shoulders. She waves me away. "I have to finish this letter, first."

Buckhorn, Pennsylvania sits off Route 80, about a three hour bus ride west of New York City, a remote town in every sense, not far from the Susquehanna

River. After a scenic drive through the rolling hills of northern New Jersey, the ground flattens out. Industrial complexes litter the landscape, their smoke stacks piercing the gray sky like a bunch of tarnished football trophies. Not long before my stop, Route 80 crosses the Susquehanna and I stare down from my window to where a blinding badge of sunlight glimmers off its still surface. I imagine the rich scent of the river's edge, where scrub oaks dapple the muddy bank. Spring is my favorite time of year, probably because it was always so long in coming to Vermont and rarely lasted more than a few hopeful weeks before the gemstone days of summer took over.

It hadn't been hard finding Rosemary. Her parents were one of two Beckers listed in Buckhorn, and her father gave me Rosemary's married name and her telephone number. When I called, she said she'd be willing to meet me at the bus terminal as long as I was okay with not being invited to her house. She'd put a lot of that behind her, she said, meaning Ted. A lot, I remember thinking, not all. I heard a guy yell something in the background. Maybe her husband had known Ted and preferred not to have him intruding, even from the grave, on the life he'd taken over from him. That was probably unfair, yet it was what I thought.

As the bus pulls into the terminal parking lot, I think, What if Rosemary Becker and I have some big catharsis and it makes no difference at all? What if I keep on wondering why, exactly, Ted died, why he had made me have sex with that Vietnamese girl, why we fought nonstop after that? What then?

I recognize Rosemary right off. She leans against the door of a well-used pickup, a lanky woman in tight blue jeans and frayed sneakers with light hair pulled back into a ponytail. It's easy to picture her with Ted—both tall, fair-skinned, milk-fed. She tosses a cigarette butt into the weeds at the end of the macadam. Her son plays nearby, running away from her and then back as if to reassure himself she isn't taking off someplace without him, a behavior I recognize, having grown up with my own version of a distracted mom.

She recognizes me, too, because she looks away when our eyes meet. Maybe she's wondering if she should have let me come to Pennsylvania, which for starters, is something we have in common. When I reach her, she shakes my hand and manages an uncertain smile, as pretty as Ted said she was, a plain sort of beauty that shines despite a lack of attention to it. Her eyes are her most intense feature, pale and resolved, the sort of eyes that could draw you in and then just as abruptly blink you away.

"Let me be straight with you right off, Hank," she says, letting go of my hand and pinning me with those eyes. "I have about an hour." Her accent—the long, flat vowels and clipped consonants—startles me. It's exactly the way Ted spoke. "I have to pick up the little one by two, then. . . . Well, you don't need all the details. You're probably thinking I could make more time if I really wanted to and you're probably right. The fact is, I've pretty much forgot about Ted Bratcher. The only reason I'm here is because he obviously meant a lot to you or you wouldn't have come all this way after all this time." She glances to where her son runs his toy truck around and around and eventually into a puddle at the edge of the asphalt lot. "Out of there, Travis," she says, and then, eyes still on the boy, "Ted had a way of getting under people's skin. For better or worse."

"I appreciate you taking the time to talk to me," I say, thinking Rosemary Becker is not at all the demure woman of my old fantasies.

"There's no way you can know what went on," she says.

"You either, I guess."

Her eyes flit from her son back to me, and then away. Everything about this woman seems quick, from her gestures and glances to her afternoon schedule. "We could get some coffee," she says, nodding toward the bus terminal. "You probably didn't have any lunch."

"I could eat something."

"There's a counter inside." She starts toward the drab cinderblock building with double-hung windows in need of a power wash. What better place not to be seen in a small town than the bus station? She probably hasn't told her husband or anybody else she's meeting me. I glance to a passing car on the highway. No doubt everybody knows everybody else's business in Buckhorn.

She reaches out and catches her son as he runs past. "Travis, say hello to Mr. Preston."

The boy stops and takes in the length of me. "You don't got a suitcase," he says.

"You're right. I'm not planning to stay. But even if I was, all I'd need is a toothbrush." I produce said item from my jacket pocket. He glances to it, isn't impressed.

"Manners, Travis. . . ."

"Pleased to meet you, Sir," the boy says, extending his hand.

I drop the toothbrush back into my pocket and take hold of that warm dusty flesh, smooth as a baby's, and something painful grips my chest. Something to do with the boy's staggering innocence, which will disappear before he even recognizes or appreciates it. And then the thought of my own lost boyhood, and Ted's. And finally, the thought that this boy will not likely ever hear about the man his mother had loved before she married his father. So many stories are left untold to kids, stories that might make their own lives easier some day. We all think we invented regret, that our shame is original.

There's a play area inside the terminal and Rosemary drops Travis there. The two of us settle into a booth not far away where she has a direct line of vision to her son. She orders coffee. I order a hamburger, fries and a coke with plenty of ice.

"How old is Travis?" I ask her.

Her eyes flash again. "He's not Ted's, if that's the question."

My uneasiness cranks up a notch. I don't feel up to this woman. I'm not sure why I came. "Cute kid," I say. I unwrap the flatware and place the wrinkled napkin in my lap.

"I don't know you from Adam, Hank, but you came all this way looking for something and we don't have a whole lot of time. I'm going to tell you a story because I promised myself, after your call yesterday, that I would. Most people around here know the story, though they pretend they don't. Maybe it'll help you, maybe it won't. But it's about all I've got to offer."

About all. This woman has a way with qualifiers that makes you think there's more she'll give if you hit the right notes with her, happen on the right key. Her tone suggests impatience at having to return to a story she'd long since put behind her. She runs her finger over a nick in the Formica tabletop while I continue to try to meld Ted's description with the Rosemary Becker sitting across the table. "Ted and I grew up together," she says. "My dad had a dairy farm outside of Danville, about ten miles from here. Ted's parents lived on the place. I suppose his dad worked for my dad, though it never seemed that way. They were like brothers. We all ate around our big table—my parents, my two sisters and me, Ted's parents and him. We drove to church together on Sundays, had Christmas together, the whole bit.

"The farm went under a few years ago. It's a subdivision now, but that's another story." She fiddles with the mottled salt and pepper shakers, then couples them together and abandons them near the napkin dispenser. "Ted and I were inseparable. I was a year older than him, but he was big for his age. And he was an operator even when he was ten years old, always out ahead, always an angle."

The waitress arrives with Rosemary's coffee and my burger and coke. "Excuse me," Rosemary says, as she slides out of the booth and goes to talk to Travis. Another boy about his age—four, I would guess—has joined him, and things are getting a little out of hand. I take a whiff of my burger and wonder why I ordered it. My stomach's a mess.

When she slides back into her seat, Rosemary pours milk into her coffee and dumps in sugar, everything rushed. Then, she stirs long enough for me to wonder whether she's going to go on about Ted or not.

"When our chores were done, we used to run down to the river that coursed through the back acreage."

"I saw it on the way in," I say, shaking ketchup onto the fries.

"Not the Susquehanna. A small river that dried up most summers. It ran along a grove of overgrown apple trees that still produced, but the fruit was runty. Ted's mother made sauce from it."

Rosemary's forearms are freckled from the sun, sinewy, the arms of a woman who hangs laundry, shovels snow, balances a baby on her hip. And I can see already why Ted might have loved her—at age twelve a force behind barn chores, playground antics and his first wet dreams. I picture him watching Rosemary burgeoning into womanhood and wondering if he can keep up in the manhood department. She pours coffee that had overflowed back into her cup.

"One afternoon. . . . It was late May, a day that was a lot like this one actually." She glances through the speckled window by our booth as if to confirm she's accurate in her recollection. "I remember how sickeningly sweet the apple blossoms smelled. Summer wasn't far off. That would mean more chores, but our parents didn't grind us the way a lot of parents do their kids. Particularly farmers. Ted and I always had afternoons to swim in the river or collect stuff from its banks, lie around and mutter nonsense to each other, whatever kids do."

I wonder what it might have been like if I'd had a friend in Vermont like Rosemary Becker. Would I have fallen in love with her, like Ted did? Would I have gotten over the inhibition I've always felt around women? Or never developed it in the first place?

"All of a sudden, Ted stops and stares up into the branches of one of those old apple trees," Rosemary continues. "His mom's hanging there, her body turning to one side in the breeze, only four or five feet off the ground, one shoe missing, face the color of a plum."

"Jesus!"

"I put my hands over Ted's eyes and held them there while I turned him back to me. I was still a little taller than him then and I think he might have rested his head on my shoulder a while, like eighth graders at a school dance. Holding himself up, more likely. Maybe I made that part up, the holding part. I've recalled that day so many times over the years, who knows what exactly happened anymore? But I'd like to believe that happened. I do remember thinking that nothing would ever be the same again. And I was right, of course. Eventually, I led him back to his house, where we sat alone until his father came home. I told him what we'd found. It was a long while—months—before Ted spoke about anything, and never again about his mother."

Rosemary pauses and takes a sip of her coffee. "Not hungry?" she asks, looking directly at me for the first time since the parking lot, when she'd seemed to be using that look to keep me back.

I pick up a French fry, chew it and swallow. Ted never mentioned his mother.

"Something clicked in him after that," she goes on. "Of course, how could it not? But what locked into place was not some understandable grief, some appalling outrage. No. What took hold was a ruthless attachment to me. He had to be with me every minute after that. He became wildly jealous of my friends. Our fathers tried to reason with him, but none of it did any good. He made his own little world and I was the center of it. It got completely out of hand. By high school, I wasn't even speaking to him. My father had moved us off the farm, but Ted still stalked me at basketball games and dances or lurking outside the A&P where I worked or some house where I babysat. It happened in spurts, not for months, and then steady for weeks at a time. I knew he would never hurt me, but still, it was freaky. Maybe it would have been better if I'd gone to the police or told someone who could have gotten Ted some help. I don't know. Lord knows it's easy to think of things you might have done."

True enough, I think as she glances over at Travis who is alone now, running his truck up and down a slide. My burger dries on my plate. I recall how obsessed Ted had been with Rosemary at first, how he said they'd been steady right up to the day he joined up. Had he believed it, himself? I take a sip of my coke which catches all fizzy in my throat, and I launch into a coughing fit. My eyes water. I dry them with my napkin, feeling stupid.

"You okay?"

I nod.

Probably determined to get the story over with, Rosemary pushes on. "When I heard Ted joined the army, I thought maybe he'd finally given up on me. I even told myself that if he went away for a while he might meet some nice girl and we could all be friends when he got back. We'll never know now, will we?"

That never would have happened, I'm thinking, as I shove my plate away. Ted was so angry. "I feel as if it was my fault that he died."

Rosemary stares at me a while, then says, "Ted had a way of making everything somebody else's fault."

"We fought a lot toward the end. I mean real fights, fists and all. Things got real nasty. I tried to make it up, but I couldn't reach him at all, no matter what I said or did. And then one night, days to the end of our tour, he just walked out of camp into the jungle. Gooks followed us around like coyotes waiting to pounce. Nobody would ever leave camp alone unless they wanted to die."

Rosemary stirs her coffee which she hasn't even tasted. She drops the spoon with a clatter onto the table. "Look, Hank," she says. "I don't know what happened over there, but I do know that when I heard Ted had died, I thought—well, he finally got his way. That was my first thought. I think I read somewhere that kids of suicides are at higher risk, themselves. Maybe he found a way to get to us, finally, all of us—you, me, his mother. Ted had no future here in Buckhorn, or anywhere else as far as I could see. He was stuck back there ten years ago and there wasn't anything going to move him forward, nothing. I'm telling you, I know. If you ask me, he stopped living a long time before he walked into that jungle."

Travis appears at the side of our booth. He doesn't say anything, just runs his truck along the edge of the table. I've noticed that kids are like pets. They're sensitive to tension, vigilant, knowing just the right closeness or distance to keep until it passes. Maybe, if Travis hadn't joined us just then, I'd have told Rosemary more about our time over there, how we believed that each other's presence kept us alive, how brave Ted had been in the face of the danger we encountered every day, how the other guys seemed to look up to him and hate him at the same time, how he'd fumed at the end, how he fell apart inside, how life—literally—drained out of him before he took himself off into the jungle.

But what good would saying all that do?

"Did you ever write to Ted?" I ask her. I've wondered, at times, if Ted might have gotten a Dear John letter and that's why he'd been so angry our last weeks, but of course, that doesn't coincide with Rosemary's story.

"I hadn't spoken to Ted in a couple of years. Did he say I wrote to him?"

"I just wondered."

"Ted was crazy, Hank. He was arrested a couple of times for beating guys up. He stole stuff he had no use for. He drank way too much. The local sheriff gave him a choice, the army or jail."

I nod and stare at Rosemary, wondering if there's anything more she wants to tell me. She turns away.

I pay the check while she and Travis take a tour of the parking lot outside, stopping at each car or truck Travis points to, probably identifying its make, as I used to do when I was his age. Leaving the terminal, I make use of the handrail by the steps, feeling more off balance now than when I left New York this morning. Another bus pulls in from the other direction, the greyhound on its side suspended in mid-stride, always running yet going nowhere.

I realize then that I came all the way to Buckhorn, Pennsylvania to confirm that Ted is really, actually, and affirmably dead. Sure, I watched my fellow grunts pick his guts off the bent grass. I heard the heavy zip of the body bag. But in my mind, I continued to be afraid of Ted. I never knew anybody to hate me the way he seemed to at the end. More than anything, I had wanted things between us to be back the way they once were. Ted had been my first real friend. I wanted that friend back.

But, and here's the truth. Even more than wanting my friend back, I had wanted to live. And that's what I did. I got through that year. I came home. I made a life. I lived. And Ted didn't.

Rosemary says maybe he didn't want to, or couldn't any longer, and that makes sense. Maybe he'd even gone all the way to Vietnam to put himself in the way of the death he claimed to fear so much on the flight over to war. Maybe he feared it because he planned to walk head on right into it and let it take him. I'll never know.

A sudden angle of sun hits the pavement and sends up that oily aroma of fresh asphalt. In this vacant landscape where he grew up, I can finally feel Ted's permanent absence. He's gone from the only place where he ever really lived; he's dead. Would it have made any difference if Ted had told me the truth, if he could have described that fleeting image of his mother swinging in a flowery spring breeze, or Rosemary's frustration and eventual rejection way back then? Might we have remained buddies in that case? Would he have accepted the fact that we were leaving Vietnam, that our improbably intense time together was over, that I was leaving him like everybody else he'd ever cared about?

When they reach the pickup, Rosemary opens the passenger door for Travis. He climbs in and she closes the door behind him. I watch him run his toy truck along the dashboard, absorbed in his own little world like any kid is, only Ted couldn't climb out of his. His mother had slammed the door on it, leaving him trapped inside.

Rosemary turns to me. "I'm glad Ted knew you over there," she says.

I nod again and manage a weak grin.

She walks around the front of her truck, then stops and turns back to me. "Do you want to see his grave?" she asks. "It's not that far from here."

I shake my head, picturing one of those little veteran markers with just the name and dates carved into the smoothed granite and a little American flag stuck in a spigot that says USA on it. I don't need to see that. I'm ready to leave Buckhorn, Pennsylvania. I'm ready to have the Ted I've carried around in my mind move over a little now to accommodate Rosemary's version. How much, I don't know. Her story is only a different rendering of Ted, no more accurate necessarily than mine. But the two versions fit together in some essential ways, and the whole picture, at least at this moment, seems a little clearer, maybe a little lighter to carry around.

People board the bus that pulled in a few minutes ago and I have the sudden urge to be on it, to be out of this town as soon as possible. "This one looks as if it's headed east," I say. "I think I'll catch it."

Rosemary nods. She raises her hand and waves as I back away toward the bus. "You take care, Hank," she says.

I take an empty seat halfway back. I don't look out as the bus accelerates and pulls onto the highway. In fact, I don't look until we're well out of Pennsylvania, careening east on Route 80 back to New York. It's only then that my mind drifts back to that afternoon in the brothel in Saigon, when Ted had been in such a rage. Maybe it had all come together for him right then and crashed down on him, crushed him, like the collapse of some tired coal mine outside Buckhorn—his fury at his mother for dying that way, at Rosemary for not caring enough, at himself for not letting go of them, at me for not understanding the story he'd never told me. Lulled by the steady hum of the bus's diesel engine, I can feel Ted pulling my shoulders to him, the Vietnamese girl sandwiched between us. Had he already decided he wasn't going back home? Had he been trying to get me to surrender to the potential that he'd given up on, himself?

The rolling hills darken in the distance. A shelf of dirty clouds floats above a muddy strip of sky. The thing about the death of someone you care about in some confused way is that it eliminates forever the possibility of coming to terms with all that happened while they lived. I will never know for sure what Ted wanted that day at the brothel. I will never know if our friendship might have outlived those few terrible moments and made them just a sad memory, just one installment in a whole series of crazy episodes that add up to a life lived alongside one another. I do know that I loved Ted. And I know that Ted loved me, as he might have loved himself if he'd been able to go ahead and try living a life he didn't want, a life without the women who'd left him. Ted died, finally, not because he was angry with me but because he was so damn furious with himself. He died because his tour in Vietnam was about to end and he couldn't return to Pennsylvania and the truth about Rosemary Becker, the truth about himself. In that brothel in Saigon, strangely enough, he was pushing me toward some sort of hope—making me sexual, making me live—hope that he didn't have for himself. He was desperate for me to see it.

Maybe now, I can.

20

JOSEY THE SLEUTH

The moment I hear Henry's steps descending the stairs, I dial the New York City Fire Department Investigations Unit and ask for the inspector assigned to the arson at 501 West Fifty-Seventh Street on the night of May 26. Of course I'm put on hold. I pace from my desk to the stairs, the telephone cord stretching behind me like the lead of an agitated poodle. Typically, I can't just sit and wait for the NYFD to resolve the question of who set the fire. I've always blamed my gender dysphoria for my impatience. But perhaps it was genetic. Perhaps I'm just the urgent, seeking offspring of an urgent seeking mother. This is, in fact, what I believe. It's all too coincidental. It fits together too well.

I continue to pace. Waiting is not my thing, despite having spent much of my life at it.

I take in the bold redecoration of my office. Curiously, Celeste and Henry and the others misread my taste completely—the heavy red curtains, the garish Victorian sofa, the brass embellishments. And yet I couldn't be more pleased. What finer tribute could anyone receive? What more heartfelt acceptance of Miss Josey Maxima?

I return to my desk and sit. Pressing the receiver to my ear, I play with a paper clip, bending it into sculptural forms—a stretching dancer, a reclining woman. Karen Grave is the only real suspect. I understand wanting to start a fire in Henry Preston, but arson was never my style. It was obvious to both of us, though, that it might be Karen's. I remember how she was always striking matches and watching them burn down nearly to her fingers. And that near hysterical teetering on the edge of violence, masked by alternating joviality and tears, so amply displayed right here at my desk back in March, before our drive upstate together. I can't help but wonder now if that whole trip had been some elaborate ruse to reveal to me that she was my birthmother. But no file, no definitive proof.

As far as I'm concerned, the worst loss in the fire was Henry's incipient optimism. It had been a huge source of satisfaction to me that a sense of well-being had blossomed in him lately. He told me once—something his mother had told him—that the only unpardonable sin is to deliberately hurt somebody. It's hard to interpret the fire in any other way, and it's thrown him for a loop. And, as if that weren't enough, it seems to have brought up this old issue with his friend who died in Vietnam. I imagine ways to reach Henry now, to comfort him, but then I hold back, fearing I'll disturb whatever internal process he might employ to move himself beyond all this. I simply want us to be together. And that day is not far off if I'm patient which, alas, has never been my forte.

There's a hopeful crackling on the line and I straighten in my chair, as if deportment might convince the inspector to make Henry's case a priority, and perhaps even to share any information he might have with me. I tell myself it's for Henry's sake that we need the conclusive truth about the fire, once and for all. But it's for me, too. How else can I put Karen Grave into whatever spot she should occupy in my life, or out of my mind forever if that's what seems best? Surely not through speculation and supposition. How many times since we drove upstate together have I tried to decipher the truth of that woman? And now, after the fire, it's all the more urgent. Was meeting Karen Grave just some bizarre coincidence, a cruel manipulation, or some sort of retribution? I have to know.

The inspector comes on the line. I identify myself as Henry's concerned employer. "He's a bit reclusive," I say. "Not many friends. If the fire was directed at him, there aren't a whole lot of suspects."

"You sound like you got somebody particular in mind." There's lethargy in the inspector's voice, as if arson investigation hadn't been his first choice of assignments, or perhaps he's seen one too many set fires. I picture him wearing a trench coat and a shoulder holster, but that's the wrong profession, the wrong late-night TV movie.

"Arson is a serious crime, Miss Maxima. It's sheer luck we had no casualties in that fire."

"It's not as if he wants to press charges," I say. I'm stalling, seeking a way to implicate Karen while not compromising her too badly. I'm protecting her, I realize, along with Henry and myself. If she did, indeed, set this fire, who knows what she's capable of? And whatever it is, it's only a matter of time until she hurts herself. "In fact, he doesn't know I'm calling. I'm just concerned about his safety."

"As any employer might be," the inspector says, dripping irony. "If your suspect set that fire there'll be charges, trust me."

I have a last minute case of the jitters and consider hanging up. But then I remind myself that we really must know. If we're wrong about Karen, then we'll make it up to her somehow."

"Name?"

"Pardon me?"

"The name of this person you think might have it in for your Henry Preston."

"Grave," I say. "Karen Grave."

"The actress?"

"You know her?"

"I've heard of her. I'm a bit of a theater buff, you might say. Address?"

"Manhattan. Somewhere in Chelsea, I think."

"I'll get back to you."

I hang up and step to the window overlooking the main floor. It's quiet down there, two or three customers, one a familiar elderly gentleman who seems to view the Strand as his local branch of the New York Public Library. I miss Henry already. This is his first trip out of the city since he came to see me in Baltimore, that lovely day when I realized, finally, that he did care about me in a way that surpassed friendship—all those quick glances and nervous shifts of position at my bedside, the tender affection, his beginning to see me as a real woman.

This old girlfriend of his pal who died in Vietnam—what does he really hope to gain by talking with her? Like me, Henry always needs to know, figuring things out as a way to master a situation. How many times, as Jarmon acted increasingly strange that summer he died, did I imagine finding his aunts and asking them about the boy we both loved? I never did it, of course. Afraid, no doubt, and not wanting any rational—or racial—interference with that beautiful first love. All I would have come away with was another version of Jarmon, which probably would not have fit with my own. We seek affirmation in others, not contradictions. And in the end, all that really matters is our own perceptions, our own feelings.

I just hope Henry's trip to Pennsylvania is worthwhile, that he learns whatever he needs to know in order to put this fellow Ted to rest after all this time. And that the process isn't too painful. He's been through enough these last weeks.

Back at my desk, I attempt to focus on a list of delinquent accounts, which seems to grow by the month. What if something were to happen to Henry, or what if he left suddenly to go live in Pennsylvania or Vermont or wherever he felt a need to be? Lord knows he could find a simpler life, with a simpler woman. A chill zigzags up my spine. The man asked me to marry him. He'd been on his way out the door, of course, but still, Henry wouldn't kid about something like that. He loves me. And yet he must have reservations. Certainly, I'm not the woman of his dreams.

After Jarmon died, my parents took me on a trip to New York City, hoping a change of scenery would pull me out of my frozen remove. They were concerned and well motivated, yet ineffectual. We stayed at the Roosevelt Hotel near Grand Central Station and took a limousine each day to the World's Fair in Flushing Meadows Park in Queens, probably not that far from where Kitty Genovese screamed her last. I remember silent lunches and dinners in air-conditioned restaurants. I remember my mother's worried expression and my father's ubiquitous tension, except at the Fair where he was in his element.

Though the theme was Peace Through Understanding, most of the exhibits were created to glorify American corporations—the Space Age, the shrinking globe, the expanding universe, all symbolized by a giant Unisphere in the center of the park. That twelve-story globe reminded me of the weight Jarmon had always carried around with him. Like me, he'd wanted to break away from the tyranny of his body, the dark skin in which no one took him seriously. It was his misfortune, in a way, to have found a cause more crucial even than his own life in that brown body, and he abandoned himself to it, shedding his own weight with that leap from the copper beech tree. The shiny silver sphere at the fair had revealed itself, up close, to be as hollow as the promises of Johnson's Great Society would prove to be, like all the promises that had failed Jarmon. His nobility had been to refuse to be taken in, refuse to participate, refuse to hide his rage under a mask of contentment.

My father's obvious pleasure in the fair's depiction of a rational world, where hard work produced results and a sure sense of satisfaction, must have exacerbated his sense of futility in regard to me. Intentionally or not, I had betrayed him, and for a moment he had lost his equilibrium. He had faltered, with this defective son, and everyone he knew in our hometown had seen it. With this family deficiency revealed, he'd been suddenly at a loss. Imperfection threatened to burst his dream and he had no choice, I suppose, but to turn his back on it. My father gave up on me that summer. I guess we all did. In the Italian Pavilion, I remember staring mute at Michelangelo's Pieta and seeing Jarmon once again, held by his dead mother, and then by me, and finally myself being comforted. But by whom?

That September, I returned to Evanston High School, my femininity—now indelibly associated in my mind with death—firmly in check. I made those penny loafers and baggy khakis work, clinging to them for some elusive sense of protection that no one—not my parents, not Jarmon anymore—could provide. I used to wonder if Jarmon knew the effect his taking wing that day would have on me. Had he thought that, without him, I might alter my ways, conform to expectations, make an easier if not happier life for myself? Had he known that there was no future for us and little hope for me if I continued to act like a girl? Very likely he hadn't thought about me at all. He probably dived from that tree because he saw no hope for himself.

The truth is, surviving that experience, at such a young age, had a peculiar fortifying effect on me which remains to this day. After Jarmon died, I believed there was little I couldn't endure. My mettle had been tested and found to be surprisingly resilient. Sitting at my desk at the Strand twelve years later, I wonder if Henry's experience in Vietnam might have affected him in a similar way. Do we share a knack for survival? I hope so.

Fifteen minutes to closing, the inspector calls. "Your Karen Grave has an interesting history," he says, by way of a greeting. "I don't usually say much, I mean about what I find out, particularly to anybody who might be involved in the case. But. . . ."

He stops, and I say nothing, waiting for him to go on.

"Seems she was a suspect in a fire in '69. An actor's place—male. Friend of hers. But an eye witness saw two teen-aged boys messing around in the hallway just before the blaze. The case against Karen Grave fell apart."

That shiver runs up my back again. "Anything else?"

"Looks like she's high-tailed it. A no-show at this play she's in on Broadway. I sent somebody around to her domicile. Bunch of bills and circulars collecting dust downstairs. What's your relationship to this Miss Grave, anyway?"

This new information presses on my chest, making breathing, and any sort of disclosure, a strain. "I've met her," I say.

"And what about her and Preston?"

"I think they were seeing each other for a while."

Now it's the inspector's turn to hold back. I imagine him writing our three names on his pad and connecting them into a triangle. "You let us know if you do run into her, okay?" he says.

"I will."

"And Miss Maxima. . . . This Grave woman could be dangerous. Where's Preston living now?"

I pause yet again, not wanting to reveal Henry's new "domicile" and have it be traced back to me. "A place she wouldn't know of," I say, which I immediately realize is not true. She was standing outside the Century the night of the fire, I'm quite sure. She could be stalking Henry still.

"Don't be too sure." I hear him take a sip of coffee. "Is there anything else you want to tell me?"

I shake my head.

"Miss Maxima?"

"No, there's nothing else."

"We'll be in touch, then," he says and rings off.

I return to my window overlooking the main floor. How I wish I could go find Henry down there and talk to him. Celeste cashes out at the register downstairs. The older gentleman slips a small volume under his coat and heads to the front door. Everyone steals something, I muse, and that book seems miniscule compared to the sense of well-being Karen has stolen from Henry and me.

I decide to find her.

The telephone directory yields one Karen Grave, along with three K. Graves, one on West Twenty-First Street, the only one in Chelsea. If she's fled, perhaps the neighbor looking after her plants or taking care of her cat will know where she's gone off to. As I expected, there is no answer at that number, but the voice on the answering machine is definitely hers. Half an hour later, I'm stepping out of a taxi in front of 230 West Twenty-First Street. A brilliant splash of marigolds, all wrong for the occasion, encircles a struggling Gingko tree in front of Karen's building, the surrounding soil redolent with dog pee.

Such a mix of feelings I have about this woman. At first, I'd been jealous at the easy way she wielded power over men, over Henry, possessing a natural, appealing womanhood she took for granted. Then, after our trip upstate, amid all the confusion, there'd been this sudden yearning one might feel for a long lost mother, powerful, and yet bizarre, given the circumstances. Of course, I'm furious with her now for what she's done to Henry. But how quickly that anger softens to concern for a woman who obviously needs help. And finally, she scares me. I should stay out of it and let things resolve themselves as they will, with the inspector in charge. But, for better or worse, that has never been my way.

Karen's building is one of hundreds of once elegant Chelsea townhouses that were converted to apartment buildings in the nineteen fifties and sixties. The stoop has been removed, the current entrance now the old service entrance a few steps down from the street. The outer door opens into a vestibule, where a scarred wooden table is lit by an overhead light fixture from Woolworths. As the inspector had said, bills addressed to Karen, along with copies of *After Dark* and *Time* magazines, have accumulated there. I gather them up and ring the buzzer, not really expecting a response. Still, I wait and then ring again. The only sounds are the passing of a taxi on the street and the static hum of the intercom.

As I'm about to set Karen's mail back on the table, a middle-aged man in an expensive-looking suede jacket descends the steps from the sidewalk and pulls open the outer door. I smile a greeting, imagining how Henry would look in that jacket. The corners of his mouth slacken, the extent of his cordiality. He glances at the table and then slips his key into the inner door's lock. He holds the door for me. I follow him inside.

"I'm picking up Karen Grave's mail for her," I say, stepping past him, "and watering the plants."

"Lucky you," he says, checking out my skirt and boots. He's either interested or in the fashion business. Either way, the attention is half-hearted.

Leading the way up the stairs, I glance through the mail again, hoping to catch an apartment number on one of the envelopes. An AT&T bill obliges me . . . 3A. The man in the suede coat inserts a key in the lock of 2A. I climb to the third floor and knock, then wait.

Of course, there's no answer. I peer over the railing to be certain the man has entered his apartment below. Stepping back to Karen's doorway, I talk into the crack between the door and its bruised frame.

"Karen, it's me, Joey." I hate using my old name, but that's how Karen knows me. "I'm just checking to see if you're okay. Karen?"

I wait, then try again, knocking and talking into the empty silence. She could well have left town, yet something tells me she's inside, cringing in a frightened muddle. I've always assumed that women, or men for that matter, with a veneer as durable and shiny as Karen's, are quaking underneath. Otherwise, why the rock hard defense? I set her mail on the floor and tear off a piece of an advertising brochure from the Gap, find a pen in my purse and write her a note.

Dear Karen,

I came by to see if you were all right. I'll come back again tomorrow (Friday) about this time (5:45 pm). You can reach me at the store if you want.

Joey

Leaving Karen's building, I turn left and walk to Eighth Avenue. I pass a phone booth and have the urge to call Henry, but he hasn't allowed me to have a telephone installed at the Century. And he's not due back from Pennsylvania yet, anyway. I consider getting dinner and just as quickly dismiss the idea. Dining alone when you're in a good mood is one thing. . . .

If Karen set the fire at Henry's place, which I have little doubt she did, might she set another at some point? At the Strand? At the Century? At her own place? Can I help her, or am I the last person in the world she would want to see right now?

The next morning, to my surprise and great pleasure, Henry shows up at work. The tetchiness that had dominated my mood all of yesterday drains miraculously away. When he comes upstairs to punch in, I run to him and we hug. He kisses me. I try to appear jovial, though tears brim. I've missed him so.

I've been so worried about . . . everything.

"Are you okay?" he asks, pulling back to look me in the eye.

"I'm just so happy to see you." The truth is I had an entirely sleepless night in Brooklyn and have been here at my desk since five-thirty, unable to think of anything other than Karen Grave and what to do about her. "What are you doing back so soon? I didn't expect to see you until the weekend."

Still holding me, Henry says, "I finished quicker than I expected. And I missed you something awful." We kiss again and I rest my forehead on his chin, taking in the reassuring bulk of him, the comforting man scent. He seems much calmer than when he left here yesterday. He lets go of me, takes his card from the rack and slips it into the time clock.

I sit back at my desk, tussling with the question of whether to tell Henry I've spoken with the inspector. No doubt he'll learn soon enough from the man himself. I'm not ready yet to tell him I've been to Karen's building and that I suspect she's holed up inside her apartment, though that is only a woman's intuition. I don't want Henry insisting that he accompany me there later today for another look, which is my intent. To me, sleuthing is a solo operation. Forget Nick and Nora Charles, Perry Mason and Della Street, Clark Kent and Lois Lane. Please! A bunch of romantic hoopla. I prefer to present Henry with a fait accompli, my gift to him, the settling of the last obstacle in our path to happiness. An explanation of Karen Grave and whatever it is, exactly, that she's done.

"I hope it went well," I say. "Your trip."

"Pretty well, I think," Henry says, even brighter now. He moves toward the stairs.

"Where are you going? I want to hear."

"You will, but first, I need to get to work."

"What about dinner tonight?" I ask him. I can't possibly wait for Henry to initiate our get-togethers. He operates at such a slow pace, I could develop age spots.

My game plan is as follows. After one more very likely fruitless visit to Karen's building, I'll divulge to Henry that I want to help her. She is my mother, after all, even if there is no record of her at the Albany Area Adoption Agency, even if she's been lying about having a husband and who knows what else, even if she's an arsonist. She's my mother. I have to help her.

Henry turns back to me and I can see that the worry lines between his brows have receded some. His trip was a success. "Sure," he says, "I'd love to have dinner—if I can treat."

"I have some business in Chelsea," I say. "What if we meet at American, that new bistro at the corner of Seventh Avenue and Twentieth Street? Say seven?"

"Seven it is," he says, disappearing into the stairwell.

Henry's much lighter step on the stairs stops before he reaches the landing.

I hear him turn and come back up. He leans into the doorway. "You never gave me an answer," he says, grinning.

I give him a quizzical look.

"I asked you to marry me. Don't you remember?" He feigns offence.

"And I said I have to finish this letter first." I gesture to my typewriter, which I haven't touched since the day before yesterday.

"Taking your time," he says. "How should I interpret that?"

"You shouldn't."

He smiles and starts back down the stairs.

Feeling at once delighted and suddenly frightened, I watch him disappear at the landing. Should I run after him—say yes, yes, of course I'll marry you—and suggest we leave New York this very instant?

At a little before six, I'm back at Karen's building, ringing her buzzer. When there's no answer, I ring the bottom button, which in buildings like this one, usually gets you the superintendent. A few minutes pass and I decide this approach is getting me nowhere. I might as well go to the restaurant, have a glass of wine and wait for Henry to arrive. As I pull open the door to leave, a voice behind me says, "Can I help you?"

Clearly I have interrupted this man's dinner, a portion of which clings to the left corner of his mouth. He's wearing wool pants and a denim shirt. His glasses appear to reside routinely halfway down his nose. His skin is pale, his fair hair thinning. Not a smile in sight.

"Are you the super?" I ask him.

He nods.

"I'm Karen Grave's niece," I say, marveling at the continued readiness of my lies. "I'm supposed to be staying with her this weekend and she doesn't answer her buzzer." I adopt a Little Red Riding Hood demeanor, complete with batting eyes, hoping he won't notice that this damsel in distress travels without weekend luggage.

He takes in the full length of me, as if the veracity of my story were revealed in the cut of my jacket.

"I wonder if you could let me in upstairs," I say. "I've been waiting all afternoon."

"She's expecting you, then?" The super has more than a remnant of a cockney accent.

I nod.

His eyes linger on me again. "Wait here."

A few minutes pass during which I add one more advantage of womanhood to my lifelong mental list. Men believe you, or perhaps they only want to please you, or they've been schooled not to deny your pleas for help, however lame.

This super would never let a man into Karen's apartment. He returns now, chewing another bite of dinner, holding a handful of keys.

I spew pleasantries as we climb to the third floor. He knocks on Karen's door, leans into it and listens, knocks again. Finally, he tries a number of different keys. The fourth one works. He steps inside, glances around the dark living room and holds the door for me. My note to Karen, shoved under the door last evening, is nowhere to be seen. Nor is the mail I left outside her door. "I'll be downstairs if you need anything," he says as he steps back into the hallway.

The door closes behind him and throws the apartment into utter darkness which sends my heart ricocheting around my rib cage like a squash ball.

21

FOR MOTHER

I feel for a light switch but find none. Waving one hand back and forth in front of me, the other out to one side as if to stave off an attack, I make my way into the room. I imagine Karen lurking in a nearby corner, taking in my every move. The blackness of the room, the fire inspector's warning, the fusty closed-in odor, have turned her into a ghoul in my mind, as much as I resist the notion. I want to believe she is only misguided, misunderstood, lost. I tell myself I can rescue her, obtain the help she needs, turn her life around from the lonely woman I suspect she's always been. Poor Karen. Everything changed back in March when she uttered the name—Allen. I could no longer see her as competition. I couldn't dislike her. This powerful yearning took hold of me, to reach out, to embrace. It was as if I was ten years old again and she was the good-fairy-birthmother. I wanted to comfort her as she had once comforted me, at least in my dreams.

And then there was the fire, and my mind has been a muddle ever since.

For as long as I can remember I've been terrified of the dark. My mother left a small lamp burning atop my bureau when I was a youngster. In Brooklyn, I sleep with the TV casting jumpy gyrations onto the wall. I can hardly catch my breath now as I feel my way along the arm of a chair and bump into the back of a sofa. I creep sideways to an end table with a lamp. The click of the switch produces no light. Spent bulb, unpaid electric bill, who knows? I'm Audrey Hepburn in *Wait Until Dark.*

Have I finally gone too far? How long can stupid luck intervene? I am one of those people who, despite a lifetime of feeling wronged by my body, believed that someone was looking out for me. Ironically, it was the person I most fear now, the pretty, ageless birthmother of my overwrought childhood imagination, in blond tresses and sparkling white gown. I felt her presence that day in the copper beech tree with Jarmon. I felt it—altered by a vision of Karen Grave in black leather and died locks—in Baltimore when they wheeled me into surgery. My whole body quivers now. Karen, my protector, my betrayer, who are you?

Where are you?

And what?

My eyes adjust to a slit of street light filtering around a drawn shade. I make my way slowly to the kitchen alcove, where a switch lights an overhead bulb. Trash and dirty dishes clutter every surface. The faucet drips a steady plink, plink, plink into a bowl. Curiously, the bowl is not yet overflowing. That faucet could not have been dripping for more than an hour. I clench my hands into fists to stop the trembling and shove them into my jacket pockets. I turn back to the living room, where open cardboard boxes spill their contents onto the floor—pieces of clothing, playbills, magazines, a shoe with a broken heel.

A loud bang, like a hammer slamming against steel, grips my heart—the radiator clanking to life.

"Karen?" I whisper.

I notice a dim light reaching from under what must be the bedroom door. Had it been there all the time? Why had I not noticed it? As I approach, the light curls onto the toes of my shoes like a tiny sinister creature. The biting odor I can't quite identify is stronger here. "Karen?" I lean my ear against the door. No sound, only the metallic odor. "Karen? Are you all right?"

I glance back to the apartment's entryway. I need only go there, open the door and leave this horrible place, wait for Henry at American and promise him I'll never do anything so foolish again. I imagine him irritated with me momentarily and then relieved that I'm safe. I imagine the two of us, exhausted by the tension of these last two weeks, leaning close over our wine glasses and devising an exit plan. California would be my choice.

Leave Karen to her fate. As she once left me to mine.

But I can't.

I reach for the knob and rest my hand there a moment. This odor is familiar, though I can't quite place it. Cleaning fluid? Has she taken her own life with some substance? But what about the half full bowl in the sink? What am I to encounter if I open this door? My history of risks flashes before me, every day walking into school as a kid, every dark evening on the subway to Brooklyn, walking to the grocery, my favorite cape billowing behind me. Then there was the troubled Jarmon, and finally the decision to go all the way to being me. But this feels different, some sort of potential for pain beyond any I've known, pain I could avoid if I would only leave here, now.

But I turn the knob and the catch releases.

The lamp on the bedside table sheds a tent of dim light onto a bed piled high with dresses and blouses and jackets and pairs of slacks, arms flayed, legs twisted. Did Henry share this bed with Karen? Was he my mother's lover? Jesus! This is not the time for that question.

I lean into the bed's footboard, suddenly more exhausted than I've ever been in my life. Straight ahead of me, against the wall, looms an oversized armoire intricately painted with colorful vines and flowers that reach toward an ornate sky-blue cornice, almost as if the huge cupboard were an elaborate garden gate. How ironic, I'm thinking. A garden. It makes perfect sense to me that Karen would have such a cupboard for her things, a woman who sought some sort of domestic peace her whole life—a man, a child—and never found it.

Light leaks from under the armoire doors. An extension cord is stretched taught from an outlet to a crack in the piece's side. I reach for the wooden latch, quite certain now of what awaits me inside. I pause again, and then release it.

Karen sits at the bottom of the armoire, among candy wrappers, empty coke cans, wilted magazines. Her hair is uncombed, her skin pasty in the light from the bulb which she's stuck upright in a shoe. Her eyes are sunken yet wide, with a blank bemused stare. She registers no surprise, almost as if she's been expecting me. "Joey!" she says, offering her hand. "How nice of you to stop by."

The pungent, metallic odor I'd been unable to identify, is of gasoline, emanating from four full containers. Astounded, terrified and senseless, I take Karen's hand. I feel as if I have been reaching for that hand my whole life. And now, here it is, the real thing, cool, dry, limp.

"Won't you come in?" she asks me.

Karen occupies the right side and indicates that I should take the left. At either extremity of the wide space sit two wreaking metal containers, tightly capped except for one, where the rainbow surface brims to overflowing with gasoline. A puddled stain rings its base. Panic rising, I review my limited knowledge of the physical properties of gasoline—highly flammable, explosive when contained (as in capped cans). So, I conclude, one highly flammable can, three highly explosive. Are the fumes themselves volatile? Is that why they make you turn off your engine when fueling your car? What do I know? Gasoline, oil, kerosene—these were such boy things.

"Let me take you out of here, Karen."

She adjusts her legs to accommodate me. "You'll have to excuse the mess," she says. "Lloyd's been away and I fired the maid. I hate having hired help around, even in a loft this size." She gestures to the back wall of the armoire. "He's due back on Friday. What day is this, anyway?"

"It's Friday, actually."

"Then I better get hustling. Lloyd doesn't appreciate a mess. But sit a minute. We had such a fun drive upstate, didn't we?" She releases my hand, picks up some empty wrappers and crunches them into a ball which she casts onto the floor near my feet. I glance around the bedroom as someone boarding an ill-fated ship might look back at the shores of the beloved country she's about to leave behind. I start to remove my shoes. "Oh, don't worry about those," Karen says. "You can't hurt this floor."

Ducking, I step gingerly through the left door of the armoire.

Why? What am I thinking? I know this woman's history. I know that she has very likely set two fires, if not more. Didn't she say her parents' house had burned the year Karen graduated high school? Now, she has dwelt, for who knows how long, in the bottom of an armoire filled with gasoline, its tiny molecules of oblivion permeating the air like the chill of a mausoleum.

Probably no one, except a suicide, has a clear sense of how her life will end or what part she will play in her own demise. Will she die alone? If not, with whom, and what will happen during the last moments? Will she sit in the front of the doomed airplane next to the heavyset gentleman or over the wing with the young mother and her baby? Will she refuse treatment in consultation with her cancer doctor, or later on, alone at home, throw her prescriptions down the toilet? Will she lie down in peace, every dream accomplished or laid to rest, or face a finish full of regret for missed opportunities?

Lose the philosophical questions, I tell myself. Not the time. Focus on what you're doing. Focus!

I manage to settle in, facing Karen. I seem to have inherited this woman's astonishing determination and maybe her enduring sense of injustice, surely her curiosity. My need to know is fixed in my genes—her genes—as is my need to act and worry the consequences later. Just as Karen was driven to replace her lost son, I needed to become the woman I am. We were equally driven, equally desperate, equally certain.

For some reason, I picture my adoptive parents, an image so stark it takes my breath. They're young and happy. My mother has her arms outstretched to me, my dad smiles, the sun flashing off his round lenses. After they died, I felt painfully alone in a way I hadn't expected. Though I'd been on my own for three years, I missed them, or at least I missed knowing they were there if I needed them, that I could call or visit if I wanted. It was only after they were gone, and I felt so completely and utterly alone, that I began to wonder more about the woman who had borne me, and to think that I did, in fact, want to find her, something I had always denied. I did nothing about it, though. Henry had entered my life. We became friends, relieving a lot of that sudden loneliness, and presenting prospects I had never believed possible. I was also, abruptly wealthy, with a host of decisions to make about that. Time passed. I let the issue of my birthmother drop. Then, as if on cue, Karen Grave—Karen Allen—presented herself in the oddest of coincidences.

So, the choice to leave her now seems like not a choice at all, at least not one I can make. I enter her demented world, seeking this strange enigmatic woman, hoping to rescue her, hoping to make her a part of my life again after twenty-six years.

"Excellent," she says, reaching up and latching the door behind me, then pulling her own door closed, throwing us into the pallid light of the single bulb. "Isn't this lovely? I'm so glad you came."

I pull my knees to my chest, not knowing where exactly to put my feet. The ruthless odor dries my throat. "How long have you been here?" I ask her.

"We moved in a year ago," Karen says, gesturing again to the back wall of the armoire. "Lloyd loves this loft. It was a present to me, actually. I've never been able to tell him I would prefer to live uptown." She picks up a beer can, pulls the top and flings it in no particular direction. "My whole life I felt like I was on the outside looking in, my nose pressed to the glass, watching people who hardly even noticed they were happy and not alone."

"Me, too. But I'm here, Karen. You're not alone now."

"But why?"

"I want to help you."

"Yeah, sure." Karen tips the beer to her mouth. A rivulet spills down her chin. She wipes it away with her palm. "You'd have drained me, if I'd kept you. You'd have taken up all my potential and used it on yourself. That's what kids do. They make your life their own and then discard it like so much trash."

I stare at Karen. This is it, then, at last, our reunion. Not exactly as I had once imagined it.

She examines the beer can as if she's never seen one before, turning it this way and that, reading the label. Finally, she says, "You were one beautiful baby. Angelic, that's the word. When you think how ugly most newborns are. And yet I gave you up. I handed you over." She reaches behind her back and produces a manila envelope, decorated with stick-on balloons. She hands it to me. "Open it," she says.

I glance at the latch to my right, rehearse its release in my mind, the dash to the front door. I take the envelope and set it in my lap. I turn back the flap. Inside is a page of old snapshots pressed under cellophane—pictures taken from a considerable distance. One is blurred as if the photographer had been rushed. A bead of sweat trickles down my spine. The pictures are of me, one with my mother pushing a grocery cart, another on the playground behind my school. I glance back at Karen.

She says, "My theory is that parents have children so they can get love back some day. Like some petty bargain. Like buying stock."

"How did you get these? How did you. . . ."

"But not for my mom, back in Schenectady. Love was way beyond what she could deliver. Even though it was the 1950s when families were all perfect little units of love and affection. At least on TV. But that was pure bullshit. Ever see a mother on the subway, her two or three kids hanging on her, too exhausted or distracted to love them? What will those kids have to give back? Nothing. No love to give back."

"But you were an only child," I say, turning back to the pictures of me from years ago, still incredulous. "Like me."

"And did your parents love you? I mean really love you no matter what?"

I'm stunned. This woman followed me to Evanston. More than once. She followed me my whole life.

"Right," she says. "You didn't measure up. The perfect little baby didn't become the perfect big boy, did he? Sorry, no love for you."

I adjust my position and my back brushes against a gasoline drum. "I felt something really powerful that day we met at my office," I say. "I couldn't account for it, such a strong feeling."

Karen grins. She takes another sip of her beer. "I was trying to steal your man away."

"It wasn't that."

"The handsome Hank Preston."

"I know it's silly," I say, "but driving upstate the next day, I felt as if I loved you."

Karen sets her beer down next to her.

"And then, when you said your name was Allen, well, that was. . . ."

"Margaret Maxima, wife of Duncan P. Maxima of Evanston, Illinois. Joseph Maxima, son of Margaret and Duncan."

"Yes, and she was a good mother."

"Then you lucked out, didn't you?"

"I guess I did."

"You were better off with her than you would have been with me."

I pause. This is not a time to offend. "I suppose I loved her more than I realized," I say. My eyes brim with tears. Here. Now. All this feeling for the mother who raised me, for both my mothers. "But they're gone," I say, "and here we are, Karen, you and I. I want to help you. I'd like us to leave here together, right now."

"Then what?"

"I promise, I won't leave you."

"I've never needed anyone's help."

"I believed that about myself for a long time."

"If you're so damned capable, why couldn't you make it as the beautiful boy you were?"

I pause again, thinking that the right words, if I can only come up with them, can save us, words that Karen can take in, words that express the undeniable truth. "That was the hardest thing I ever tried to do, and I failed. You're right. I just couldn't do it."

"You gave you up just the way I gave you up."

"Me?"

"You abandoned my boy."

Strangely, what occurs to me is that the whole long saga of my gender is irrelevant now, finally. I've reached that point which I never imagined would exist for me. It simply doesn't matter. The truth of life is in its clichés. Love is what matters. Only love. The love of daughters for their mothers, mothers for their sons, sons for their dads. My love for Henry, too. Finding love where you can. That's what matters. Staying alive for it. That matters, too.

I try to resettle myself, but there's no way for me to adjust my legs. We're like sisters sharing a bathtub, Karen and me, with the awful stench of gasoline replacing the steamy fragrance of shampoo, and dread replacing glee. I want to lead us out of here to somewhere safe, but, since I have vowed to talk truth here, where would that safe place be for Karen? Jail? A mental hospital? In fact, there is no safe place for her. I picture Jarmon in our perch high up in the copper beech. There had been no safe place on the ground for him, either.

I glance at my watch—six forty.

"Are you expected somewhere?" Karen asks me.

"Actually, I'm meeting a friend for dinner."

"A special friend, no doubt, by the name of Hank Preston."

Karen's smile terrifies me. She's completely bonkers. "Yes, I am meeting Henry. You should come. We could all have dinner." So much for truth!

"Oh, I doubt that. No, I don't think so. You're just saying that."

"Please, Karen. Come with us."

"Hank Preston destroyed my chances. Everything was going to be so lovely."

We sit in silence a moment. Then I say, "I want to help you, Karen. My other parents are dead now."

"Aren't I awful, I didn't even offer you a drink."

"A drink would be lovely," I say, thinking we'd at least have to get to the kitchen for ice.

But Karen reaches behind her and withdraws another beer. She pulls the top, wipes away the foam and licks her fingers. Her eyes brighten like a four-year-old's. "Yummy," she says. She hands me the beer. I take a sip. "Good, isn't it?"

I nod and force a smile across the short space between us.

"I can see your panties," Karen says with harrowing innocence. I try to adjust my skirt over my knees. "It's okay. They're pretty. Very womanly."

As I sit across from Karen, smiling back at her, the feeling that I have done all that I can here crowds out my thoughts of helping her. This talking is getting nowhere. I have no sense of reaching her. The thought that I could save her seems futile now, even arrogant, grandiose. I can only save myself. I can only save my life with Henry that is so dear to me. I glance at the latch again, then back to Karen, then to the gas cans huddled behind her. I want to be out of here. Now! I want my life. I want Henry. Please, God, give me that life. I notice the smell of Karen's days-old sweat mixed with the odor of the gasoline. I see the blond fuzz along her upper lip. I see her broken thumb nail and the dirt underneath. My poor mother. I cannot help you. I am going to leave you now.

I guess that Karen has matches, perhaps even in that shirt pocket that gapes at her chest. Would she use them? She has before, though this time it would be suicide. Is she that despondent, that crazed? It's not for me to know. All I can do is heave myself against the armoire door, hope that it gives way, and scramble for the living room and the stairs.

"You can have all the dinners with Hank Preston you can eat," Karen says, "but you'll never give him what he really wants."

Despite myself, I bite. "And what is that?"

"Offspring, of course. Why do you think he donates his semen all the time? He wants children. Everybody wants children. Is that not obvious?"

"Karen, I don't think. . . ."

"No, you don't, do you? I have to do all the thinking. For everybody. Are you prepared to deprive Hank Preston of what he wants most in the world?"

I hold my tongue. Another argument I don't need to win.

"I'm pregnant," Karen says.

I let go of my knees and lean away, preparing to throw my shoulder into the door.

"Isn't it amazing? I can't wait to tell Lloyd."

"But. . . ."

"I don't think you're going to make your dinner date," Karen says, glancing at her watch. She reaches behind her back and withdraws a pack of matches. "We're having too much fun."

I heave myself against the armoire door. Karen strikes a match. Miraculously, it doesn't light. Maybe it's damp from her back pocket. Who knows? The latch gives and I fall headfirst onto the wood floor. I clamber to my knees as she breaks off a second match. In what seems the slow motion of a nightmare, I start to run for the bedroom door before I even have my feet under me. My heel collapses and I fall headlong into the brass footboard. I feel my right cheekbone shatter, a tooth crumble. I spit blood and roll onto my back in time to see Karen pull yet another match from the book. I drag myself away in a backstroke of arms and legs, reaching for the door to the living room.

With the deafening flap of an enormous yellow cape, flames engulf Karen and the gas cans. Her hair fizzes and disappears. Grotesque layers of skin melt from her face. As I push open the bedroom door, the cans explode, and I am aloft on a whirling bed of heat. In the searing white light, I see Jarmon's rain-glistened body spring from the copper beech, pause and hold there, grinning, waiting for me.

22

HANK REMEMBERS

I wake up early and step out onto the terrace at the Century. Constellations of lanterns flick off, one by one, in the park. The traffic along the Drive there picks up. The giant apartment buildings of Fifth Avenue in the distance are still mostly dark. I imagine their residents yawning awake behind drawn shades and white noise machines that drown out a cab's blaring horn or the whine of a hungry garbage truck, the rude intrusions I've grown to love about Manhattan. As I stand here, taking it all in, I realize why I'm awake so early. Today is the third anniversary of the fire at Karen Grave's apartment.

Karen Grave. I like to believe that she was Josey's mother because it lends their dying together a weird sort of resolution. No doubt Josey believed it, which I suppose is all that matters. She would have liked the idea of a birthmother as ballsy and pretty as Karen, somebody so different from the parents who had raised her, somebody she could point to as the genetic source of her own extraordinary determination. Who knows? After the fire, I spent a lot of time gathering up such fragments and trying to weave them into some sort of construction that made sense, that gave the whole episode meaning, rationalizing, I suppose, where there wasn't rationality. I don't do that anymore.

Maybe what we witness every day is disintegration, not integration. Maybe that's the simple truth of it all.

An hour later, my bike shouldered, I step off the utility elevator and take the Century's side door onto Sixty-Third Street. The sun clears the skyscrapers that bracket the park to the east and pulsates shades of its own mighty blaze. Chinese pear trees lean over the sidewalk in a late spring dampness laced with the city's ubiquitous whiffs of moist pavement, exhaust and the morning garbage bags that line the curb.

I set the bike down, pull my handkerchief from my back pocket and wipe the handlebars, the crossbar and the seat. I grin, remembering Josey that night we had burgers at a bar near the Strand—she was still Joey then—pointing out how I always lined up my knife and fork perfectly with my plate, saying my obsessive nature wasn't much of a match for her gender weirdness when it came to challenges in life. Of course, she was right about that.

Re-pocketing the handkerchief, I throw my leg over the crossbar, stand and pedal to Central Park West where I ride north along the edge of the huge green space. It's out of my way, but I want to take in the hopeful scent of grass, leaves, new life. And I'm not disappointed. The sidewalk is littered with crushed cherry blossoms, the last of them, their pink faded and brown at the edges, giving off a pleasant earthy odor. There's even the faint scent of new greenery coming from inside the park, hard to describe other than a clean sort of freshness vying with the subdued smoky odors of a sleeping metropolis soon to be overflowing with people and cars.

Satisfied, I turn west onto Sixty-Eighth Street and then ease into southbound traffic along Broadway, where I pick up the pace, keeping abreast of a taxi as we both turn onto Ninth Avenue in front of Lincoln Center. The fountain is still lighted from last night and splashes gaily to an empty plaza.

I've been living at the Century for almost three years now. Josey left me the apartment and enough cash to cover the maintenance for five years. She had added this codicil to her will the day she bought the place, a month or so before her surgery. She saw to everything, Josey did. If she survived the surgery, of which there was little doubt, she'd have this wonderful new home to go to. If anything unforeseen happened, she would take care of me. It warms my heart to think she cared that much, even back then, before I woke up to my own true feelings about her. The rest of her estate went to form The Maxima Foundation for Transgendered People, where I serve on the Board of Directors, and where Celeste, Josey's assistant at the Strand, does her competent thing to hold the operation on track.

I work at Barnes & Noble, having moved up from lowly shelfer to an office job, ordering books and overseeing their travel department. The job is pretty low key and I like the people there, most of them anyway. Two years from now, I'll have to decide whether to sell the co-op or get the type of job that can support it. What would Josey want me to do? I ask myself. But the answer is simple—she'd have me do whatever I wanted, knowing that that's always the hardest thing for me to figure out.

After she died, I felt pressured to come up with a meaningful career goal, but my thoughts always seemed directed backward rather than toward some hazy future I couldn't make out. Then the foundation work presented itself and took up a good deal of time, particularly at the beginning. And that had seemed right. I have the feeling that what I do now is not forever, though I don't know what that even means, exactly. Celeste says I'm not allowing myself to trust anything or anybody, after what happened. And I suppose she's right about that.

Riding down Ninth Avenue now, the misty morning air leaves filaments of moisture in the hairs of my arms and along the sleeves of my jacket. A line of buses inches its way down the overhead ramp at Port Authority. Cars cue up at the entrance to the Lincoln Tunnel. A taxi cuts me off as it pulls to the curb to pick up a fare. I raise my fist to the driver, and he raises his back at me. Thirty or more mail trucks, all in a line, load up at the Post Office at Thirty-Third Street. You gotta love this city!

I slow my pace and turn onto West Twenty-First Street, where I pull up in front of number 230. Karen's old townhouse is gone now, of course. A new building of the same configuration—three stories, side entry a few steps down from the street—tries unsuccessfully to blend with the line of older houses. The brick is new, the cornice half-hearted, the double-hung window sashes shiny aluminum.

The night Karen's building burned, I got to American, the bistro on Seventh Avenue and Twentieth Street, at seven, right when Josey had said to meet her. I'm not the type to order a drink and wait at the bar, so I walked back outside. It was a warm evening even for late May. From where I stood on the steps to the restaurant, I watched people come and go along Seventh Avenue. Some carried briefcases, some backpacks. A woman carried a kitten. A couple of guys laughed and poked each other. A bag lady pushed a grocery cart heavy with street treasure. A boy carried a boom box. It was your standard New York evening.

By twenty after, I was starting to worry. It wasn't like Josey to be that late. She wasn't compulsive about time, like me, but she was naturally prompt. We were both on edge after the fire at my apartment. I wanted to marry Josey, not only because I had realized how much I loved her, but because I wanted to protect her, wrap myself around her and not let anything happen to her. When she was late getting to American that evening, I fretted the way I had since the fire at my apartment, whenever Josey headed home to Brooklyn by herself or met with a client looking to sell a book collection or went to her hairdresser in the West Village. In other words, whenever she was out of my sight. I decided, standing there on the steps, that we should get married right away and leave Manhattan like she had suggested when I left for Pennsylvania to see Rosemary Becker. We would face life's considerable hazards somewhere else, watching each other's backs.

I remember wincing at the blast, resounding like a bomb, despite the muffle of a block and a half of brick buildings running interference. A passing woman locked eyes with me. We both turned and stared over the tops of brownstones, lined up like useless centurions along the avenue. A plume of gray smoke rose into the darkening sky.

This may sound like hindsight, but I knew right then that it was Karen's house that was on fire. She was probably on my mind anyway, since she lived close by. But, for whatever reason, I knew. My knees went weak and I sank to the steps of the restaurant. I let my head fall into my hands. I knew.

Still, I waited for Josey.

It seemed like barely two minutes had passed when a line of fire engines, their sirens blaring over the throaty blasts of their horns, made their way down Seventh Avenue and turned onto Twenty-First Street. People hastened in the direction of the smoke. I stayed put. I knew. Not the specifics, of course, only that horrendous damage had been done and I was implicated somehow. Minutes passed, a curious silence alongside the bedlam nearby. Finally, I had to go. If Josey showed up at American and saw that I wasn't there, she'd come to where all the commotion was—I know Josey—and find me there.

I darted across Seventh Avenue, ran north and then west on Twenty-First Street.

Being certain it was Karen's place hadn't made me any less dumbfounded when I got to her blazing building. Shattered window casings smoldered in the street, the buckled roof hung down at a steep angle and the chimney stack listed badly, like it could be toppled with the pressure of one hand. The wall of Karen's kitchen stood to one side, the sink hanging upside down by its drain pipe. Her sofa lay upended on the sidewalk, a smoldering piece of rubble. A blouse blazed in the branch of a Gingko tree like some festive torch at a luau. Flames darted out of a first floor window, engulfed the flimsy table in the entryway and worked their way up the listing stairs.

I joined a gathering crowd across the street, feeling the warmth of the fire on my face. Fire is nothing but superheated air, I remember telling myself. Insubstantial, almost nothing at all, different only by degree in its ability to heat, to light, to consume. All relative, warmth or devastation a simple function of the width of West Twenty-First Street. None of that made much sense, either, but the mind will do strange things when there's something you don't want to consider.

Red, whirling lights darted off the fronts of adjacent buildings. Firefighters rushed to connect hoses, raise ladders, peer into the roaring wreckage. Water hissed and turned to steam. Noxious billows of smoke—the flaming contents of Karen's chaotic life—plumed into rippling air in a darkening sky. A fireman climbed a ladder and directed a hose down into the space that had once been her living room. Medics treated members of a family that had escaped from the ground floor. Rumors circulated that the second floor tenant hadn't been at home. No word of the third floor tenant. I scanned the crowd for her, supposing that if she had set the fire in some crazy scheme to rid herself of her past, she might stay around to watch. But as time passed, that seemed less likely.

And still no sign of Josey.

It took the firemen over an hour to reduce the blaze to a smoldering heap of charred debris. The air reeked of doused insulation, soaked mattresses, rugs, clothing. Filthy water littered the sidewalk with ash before draining into the gutter. Parked cars were scorched, dented and drenched in a pitiful innocence.

Gradually, the crowd dispersed. I waited, mesmerized. What, exactly, had Karen wanted to obliterate in this ruin? If she had wanted to start her life over again, wasn't there an easier way? And where might she go now? Would this final act satisfy her?

And where the hell was Josey?

I started up the street toward American as a black Ford pulled up and the investigator assigned to the fire at my apartment, the one I had met with the morning after that blaze, three weeks ago, stepped out and joined a group of firemen. I watched them confer as he made entries in a small book. When he saw me, he excused himself and stepped over sprawling hoses to where I stood.

"You like watching fires, Mr. Preston?" he asked me.

I shook my head.

"You just happen to be outside the ruined house of the prime suspect in your case?"

"How did you find her?"

"I'll ask the questions, if you don't mind. Maybe you can explain to me how you happen to be here when Karen Grave's building explodes."

"I was meeting a friend of mine at American, the restaurant over on Seventh. We were going to have dinner. And I wasn't here when it exploded."

"A Miss Josey Maxima, maybe?"

"Well, actually, yes. Josey Maxima. But how. . . ."

"This is all very interesting," he says.

One of the firemen yelled to him. He waved and yelled back. "Rope it off, guys. We're going to need to look inside. Tonight."

It would all be over now. Karen would be taken out of circulation, and out of danger, to us and to herself, and I would meet up with Josey in half an hour to acknowledge, however sadly, the end of this whole odyssey and the beginning of our new life together.

My whereabouts earlier that evening were corroborated by the bartender at American, who remembered me standing on the front step of the restaurant when he heard the explosion. I was eliminated as a suspect. All night and much of the next day, I watched the inspector's men sift through the debris left by the fire. Josey never showed, of course, and I was beginning to fear what the firemen eventually found, the dental remains of two separate bodies—Karen's and Josey's.

Now, three years later, I stand astride my bike, staring up at the new townhouse. A man raises a window shade on the third floor. I turn away. A young woman, leaving an adjacent building, glances at me and determines that I'm harmless, apparently. She drops a plastic bag of trash into a can set at the curb and heads toward Eighth Avenue. Some workers begin unloading scaffolding in front of a building down the block, preparing it for a long-overdue facelift. A woman sweeps her stoop.

Three years is a long time. I've come here several times since the fire and my feeling has been the same each time. I stand like a zombie and stare at this ugly new building, feeling numb. I don't know how to pray or even what that would mean exactly. I don't think of Josey's soul waiting to enter some white-paved city of contentment atop some roiling clouds. She would hate a place like that, anyway. I don't think of her as being anywhere other than the place she occupies in me, and in Celeste, and a few other people who knew her. I suppose remembering our time together is a prayer of sorts, and so that's what I do, I remember.

As I said, I serve on the Board of the Maxima Foundation. Celeste and I have dinner or go to a movie once or twice a week now. We've moved from talking about the foundation and about Josey and all that happened, to talking about ourselves and our dreams, hers more than mine. I hope some of her enthusiasm and optimism is rubbing off on me, a little at a time. We'll see where it takes me, or us.

But this morning, on the anniversary of the fire, I try to focus on Josey, though sadly, the effort seems contrived. There's nothing for me on this street anymore. Will I eventually forget about Josey altogether? She isn't here. She isn't anywhere. I will hold onto my memories, but is that a good thing? Will I use them to keep me from really living, which is what Josey would have wanted me to do? From making a life with Celeste, which seems possible?

I stand and pedal down Twenty-First Street, stopping at the corner of Eighth Avenue, where I wait for the light to change. To my right, I see a woman approaching with a boy I guess to be five years old. They cross in front of me. He carries a school bag and a miniature first-baseman's mitt. They're talking, as they pass, about some issue the boy has with his teacher. I can't take my eyes off him. His lazy stride I recognize as my own, and the slouch to the shoulders. He has wavy brown hair and an earnest expression that also seems familiar. Could he be my offspring?

I pull onto Eighth Avenue and follow the two of them beyond a line of parked cars. His mom carries her coffee in one hand and rests her free hand on the boy's shoulder. I imagine them walking to his school like this every morning and having the talk that sets each of them up for their day apart. How oblivious they seem to their pleasure in each other, their remarkable good fortune! Probably his dad walks him some mornings and that's fine too. I imagine this boy having a good life, not scared, thriving, so much happier than either Josey or I was growing up. I want to tap his mom on the shoulder and tell her this. I want to remind her how lucky she is, but also what an awesome responsibility she has to see her son through, to not get in his way, to love him no matter what.

Reluctantly, I pedal away, continuing north and then east until I hit First Avenue, where I pull up in front of the familiar gothic towers of New York Hospital. Sunlight gleams off their white brick facades. I check my watch—seven forty. I'm early. On the sidewalk across from the clinic entrance, I lean against the crossbar of my bike and recheck the vial in my pocket. It's upright and securely capped, safe and warm.

Dr. McAvery calls me three or four times a year, when he has the need for a specific eye color or hair color or whatever combination of traits he's matching for that day and can't satisfy among his usual donors. The thirty dollar fee goes into the coffers of the Foundation, where I imagine it elbowing its way among much more substantial bequests, like a little anthropomorphised Josey. In my mind, these donations—the semen, not the money—are a way that I honor Josey's remarkable unconventionality. She never wavered from the belief that her idea of herself was more valid than anyone else's. Embracing her difference had ultimately left her with little to prove, less at stake. She'd freed herself of fear, finally, of that sense of inadequacy foisted on her so early, something people rarely do.

I shoulder my bike, cross the street and push open the heavy bronze door. I avoid looking at the elevator as I head for the stairs. I'll never know any of these offspring, of course, and they'll never know me. Yet, if I can give some couple the fulfillment of parenthood, and their child some of the fervor for life that Josey lent me and that has miraculously asserted itself into my feisty little sperm, then I'm doing the right thing.

BIOGRAPHICAL NOTE

Michael Quadland grew up in Williamstown, Massachusetts. He graduated from Dartmouth College and received a Masters of Public Health degree from Yale University and a PhD in psychology from New York University. In addition to his private psychotherapy practice, he taught human sexuality at Mt. Sinai School of Medicine in New York City, supervised a sex information hotline in Manhattan and consulted with many organizations about AIDS prevention and the emotional-psychological aspects of the disease. He has published many articles in professional journals about AIDS and sexuality. *The Los Angeles Times* published his nonfiction article, "A Red X", about the death of a friend.

Quadland left AIDS work in 1995, reduced the size of his psychotherapy practice and restored an eighteenth century farmhouse in Connecticut, doing much of the work himself. He also turned to writing fiction. His first novel, *That Was Then*, published in 2007, was a finalist for a Lambda Literary Award. He now divides his time between New York City and northwest Connecticut.